HER
SECRET

HER
SECRET

KELLY FLORENTIA

Urbane
PUBLICATIONS

urbanepublications.com

First published in Great Britain in 2018
by Urbane Publications Ltd
Suite 3, Brown Europe House, 33/34 Gleaming Wood Drive,
Chatham, Kent ME5 8RZ
Copyright © Kelly Florentia, 2018

A CIP catalogue record for this book is available
from the British Library.

ISBN 978-1-911583-68-4
MOBI 978-1-911583-69-1

Design and Typeset by Michelle Morgan

Cover by Michelle Morgan

Printed and bound by 4edge Limited, UK

URBANE

urbanepublications.com

To my mum Valentina,
with all my love.

CHAPTER 1

IF YOU COULD TURN BACK TIME, WHAT WOULD YOU DO DIFFERENTLY?

I stare at the swirly white writing set against the backdrop of a sunset in wry amusement. It's just the type of thing you'd expect from Vicky, right up her street. I heart my sister-in-law's Instagram post, just to show my support, notching up her *likes* to thirty-six. She'll love that. I don't bother adding a comment to the twenty-four already listed. I'm not into dwelling on the past, not anymore. I've let go – moved on. I'm a new woman now with a new name. I slide my thumb up lazily, a picture of a fluffy cat fills the screen followed by a bouquet of flowers, then a photo of my gorgeous nephews with George, my brother, looking awful, eyes half closed, mouth ajar. George will have a fit when he sees it. I laugh as I pinch the screen to zoom in, but as I gaze at their familiar faces on my iPhone, curiosity burns in my chest like a hot rod. I flick back to Vicky's meme and click on 'View all 24 comments.' A quick peek at what her followers think won't hurt, will it?

Comment 1: *I'd stay on at school* – Did that and came away with two A levels, not a great help in my job as a junior web designer but nice to have all the same.

Comment 2: *I would have had my kids later in life* – of no interest. I slide my thumb up the screen.

Comment 3 (from someone called xx_timetraveller_x99): *I'd travel more* – I'm not that keen on flying, to be honest. The furthest

I've travelled is the four and a half hour flight to Cyprus, and that was only to visit my parents, because, much too my protest, they retired there earlier this year. But no sooner had I waved them off at Heathrow Airport blubbing hysterically like a five-year-old child abandoned by her parents, than I was sipping a vodka and tonic on a British Airways flight to Larnaca. Pathetic, I know, for a grown, married woman. What can I say? I miss them terribly.

Comment 4: *I'd have started using anti-wrinkle cream as soon as I could read!* – I snort at that one. I suppose we'd all like to turn the clock back where youth is concerned. Although, thanks to my mum's genes, I'm often told I look much younger than my forty-two years. I certainly feel it.

I read the next few comments with a smile on my face. Vicky's got some amusing friends, no wonder she spends so much time on social media, despite my brother's protests. But it's the eighth comment that catches my attention. That makes me sit bolt upright in my seat.

Comment 8: *I wouldn't have rushed into marriage.*

The writing becomes a blur and I have to blink a few times, then as I glance up at the road I cry out in horror. "Watch out!" My mobile phone almost hits the dashboard as Fearne presses hard on the brakes bringing us to a screeching halt at the traffic lights on Archway Road. "Flipping hell, Fearne," I gasp, wishing that I'd joined that long bus queue on Oxford Street instead of accepting a lift home from my Formula 1 wannabe driver colleague. "You're going to get us killed!"

"It's that bloody bell-end behind us," she complains, glaring into her rear view mirror, thin lips twisted in anger. "He's been right up our arse since sodding Camden. I mean, what's the effing hurry? We're in rush hour traffic, for crying out loud." She blows a loose strand of wiry ash blonde hair off her sweaty forehead. Road rage.

I've never succumbed to it but Daniel, my husband, is plagued with it. In fact, I fear for my life each time I sit in the passenger seat of his brand new white Audi Q7.

Twisting in my seat, I duck my head for a better view of the bell-end, seat belt digging into my shoulder. Fearne does have a point. That black four-by-four tank of a car with its elusive dark tinted windows is uncomfortably close to us. "Oh, don't let him get to you, Fearne, he's an arsehole," I say, returning to Instagram. "Just let him overtake us, that's what I always do with impatient drivers."

Fearne ignores me and puts her foot down the moment the lights turn amber, hands gripping the steering wheel tightly, brows furrowed. The four-by-four keeps its distance for a while then suddenly overtakes us, swerves past the two cars in front, then disappears in a cloud of smoke, leaving an orchestra of car horns from irate drivers behind him. I shake my head. "He can add dangerous driving to his list. Where's the police when you need them?"

"Bloody idiot," Fearne yells, shaking her fist, as if the driver can see her. I smile as I sink back into my seat, and we travel the rest of the journey in companionable silence. I, pondering on comment eight, and she happily humming the tune of my ten-year-old nephew's favourite song by *Little Mix*.

"Where's your yard, Audrey?" Fearne asks ten minutes later, slowing down over a road bump. Fearne likes to keep up with the street lingo. She thinks it's cool, but doesn't realise that it doesn't sound so hip coming from a middle aged woman driving a Fiat 500.

Putting my phone into standby, I shove it into the pocket of my beige mackintosh. "Just over here on the right please, Fearne."

Crunching the car into second gear, she pulls up outside my flat on Dukes Avenue.

"Nice pad," she says, pressing her chest against the steering wheel and eyeing-up the three-storey building. "I've always wanted to live in Muswell Hill, but it's bit too expensive for me," she sniffs, dabbing her nose. Fearne always seems to have a constant cold, which she blames on a host of allergies. "I think I'll be living in my pokey two-bedroom flat in Edmonton forever," she groans, "You're lucky to have a husband in the trade."

I unzip my black leather Birkin. "I bought the flat long before I married Daniel," I say, fishing for my door keys in the abyss of my handbag, which Daniel refers to as the Bermuda Triangle. But all women's bags are cluttered, aren't they? It's a girl thing.

Fearne looks at me, mouth agape. "Oh, gosh, Audrey. I'm so sorry. Did you….I mean… was it…were you with, you know...?" She waves the tatty tissue in the air and I instinctively jerk my head back. I've got a thing about germs. I think it stems from mum wearing a mask whenever she had a cold when George and I were little. "Whatshisname?" Fearne says. I can virtually feel the heat radiating from her red face; her dry hair looks as if it's almost standing on end. "When you bought the flat, I mean?"

"It's okay, you can say his name, you know." I fold my arms over my leather bag and it hisses. We stare at each other in silence for a few moments, and then, "Nick and I were together when I bought it, yes," I say finally, and a little whimpering sound tumbles from her thin lips. "But I bought the flat on my own. It's all mine."

I wish people would stop treading on eggshells whenever my ex is mentioned. Yes, he was the love of my life, and yes, I did want to run away and marry him. Although God only knows why. He's the most unreliable, selfish man on the planet. But that's all in the past now. I'm a big girl. I won't crack if I hear his name, for goodness' sake.

Louise, my childhood friend who's hated Nick for as long as I can remember, refers to him as *It*. Jess, her nineteen-year-old daughter, calls him by the C word, with Daniel it's always *Him*, and to my family he's known as *That Twat*. All plausible metaphors given that he left me days before our wedding last summer and then did a runner when I was mad enough to give him a second chance just before Christmas. I think Tina, probably the easiest going friend I've ever had, is the only person who actually calls him by his name, but that might have something to do with them being in-laws. Well, sort of. She's dating his cousin Ronan, second time around. They've got history.

"I'm so sorry." Fearne's voice again. "I didn't think. I just assumed that Daniel had some stake in it, what with him being in the business. Oh, God, Audrey. Soz." She covers her face with her hands.

"It's all right, Fearne," I reach out for her forearm. Her blue eyes look big and wild between the gaps in her fingers. "Nick and I are history. Over. We've both moved on now. He's somewhere on the globe finding himself and I'm happily married, remember?" I hold up my hand and wriggle my fingers at her.

"Oh, phew." She hiccups then presses a hand on her heaving chest. "Daniel moved in here with you then?" she asks rhetorically, hiccupping again. "You'll be like an old married couple before you know it." Hiccup.

"What do you mean?" I unfasten my seatbelt and it flies across my body.

"Oh, n..n..no.. what I meant was we tend to fall into complacency once we're married, don't we?" Another hiccup accompanied by an expression that makes her look as if she urgently needs the loo. Now, usually I'd brush something like this off but given what happened this morning, because of what I heard Daniel say,

 HER SECRET

my face is deadpan. "Do you know what I mean?" Fearne says, desperate for reassurance. `

"Yes, yes, of course," I say, reason kicking in. Poor Fearne. It's only a bit of banter. It's not her fault that I'm in a shitty mood. A thunderous sound filters through the car window and I look round. My new neighbour is wheeling her bin onto the street, reminding me that it's collection day. Daniel's in charge of bin duties these days, which is just as well because I did have a bit of a reputation for being the midnight wheelie bin taker-outer when I was single, often disturbing the neighbourhood in my dressing gown and fluffy slippers at ungodly hours. Although miserable as sin, this new neighbour puts us all to shame. She's like an alarm, a wheelie-bin sergeant major, which we all secretly appreciate, especially during the festive months when we've no idea what day it is, let alone collection day.

"The Greeks had thirty different definitions of love," Fearne says randomly, gazing up at the grey clouds hanging ominously above us. "Shame my husband couldn't find it in his heart to remotely feel one of them for me. Mind you, serves me right for marrying him in haste. My mother did warn me." Fearne's husband walked out on her recently, leaving her to bring up Kylie, his fifteen-year-old daughter. Alone.

"How long were you together before you got married?" I ask, comment number eight flashing in my mind.

"Oh, about six, seven months," Fearne says absently to the ruckus of wheels rolling against the pavement. "Stupid, I know."

Lining up her bins in military fashion, my new neighbour darts a glance at us, as if we have no right to look at her, and then, with one final glare, she turns on her heel and scurries down the path, black ponytail swinging from side to side like a bladed pendulum.

 HER SECRET

"And he'd been married four times before," Fearne points out to the thump of misery-guts-neighbour's front door. "Bloody lothario. I should've read the road signs, really. He had form." Nodding, I pull a bottle of water out of my bag and offer her a sip; she shakes her head without pausing, "Apart from his first wife, who passed away, bless her, the other three couldn't have all been at fault, could they?" she reasons. I shake my head in agreement, mouth full of water. "Anyway, what about you? I know you had a bit of a whirlwind romance before you got hitched, but how long have you actually known Daniel for? Years, isn't it?" She watches me as I take another glug of water. I'm so thirsty – must be that pastrami baguette Raymond, our boss, treated us to at lunchtime. Fearne waits out my water binge, her chest rising and falling quickly with a silent hiccup. I hold up seven fingers, swallowing. "Seven years." Fearne nods approvingly, blowing her nose into a fresh tissue. "Good girl. He's an old family friend, isn't he? Yes, I remember you saying now. I wish I was as wise as you."

"Months." I screw the cap back on firmly, licking my lips. "My parents only met him in Cyprus last September. And I'm wife number three."

"OMG!" Fearne swallows hard, eyes glistening. "Audrey, I don't know what to say. I keep putting my foot in it today. It's this frigging menopause." Hmm…Fearne blames a lot on her menopause, but I didn't realise that putting one's foot in it was one of the symptoms. Then suddenly her voice speeds up, this always happens when she's nervous. "Oh, please just ignore me. It's just that when you said your parents introduced you, I assumed you and Daniel went way back. I mean, I know you were with…with…." She licks her dry lips. I think she's hyperventilating.

"N..i..c..k," I say slowly as if I'm teaching a toddler a new word.

"Yes, yes, of course, with Nick. For years." She drums her pink varnished fingernails against the steering wheel nervously. No wonder they're all chipped. "But I genuinely thought that you and Daniel were childhood sweethearts or something. It's just, I dunno, the way you talk about him, I suppose. My cousin only knew her husband for six weeks before they got married," she prattles. "They met in Italy. A holiday romance in Rimini. He's a native." She stares dreamily at shy Bob from number 32 chucking a loaded bin bag into his wheelie, head down, long, thinning, dark blonde hair falling onto his face. "They'll be celebrating their silver anniversary this year. They've hired a place in - "

"Fearne." I lay a hand on her arm to silence her. "It really is fine. Don't worry." The poor woman looks exhausted. I bet this is the last time she'll offer me a lift home from work when there's a tube strike on. "Look, why don't you come in for a drink?" It's the least I can do, and you're allowed one drink, aren't you? "I'll show you around." I collect my M&S shopping bags from between my feet and open the passenger door. "Or stay for dinner. Daniel will be home soon, you can meet him."

The idea of my dinner invitation seems to fill her with dread. "Thanks, but I'd better get off, Audrey." She turns the ignition on quickly. "I've got to get home and cook for a hormonal teenager whose only interest these days is *Little Mix* and Snapchat." Ah, that explains the *Little Mix* rendition earlier then. "And remember, we've got an early start tomorrow."

I nod. Raymond's organised a board meeting for 8 a.m. to discuss the particulars for a new client – Sam Knight, the famous author and body language expert. Fearne and I are working on his website together. It's an exciting new project, and it'll give me a chance to show Raymond what I've learnt on the web design course he sent me on recently. I can't wait to get stuck in and I don't want to let him down.

I watch as Fearne's little red Fiat becomes a red blob in the distance before stepping onto the black and white chequered tiles of my porch where I find Mr Gingernut, Alan and Margaret's one-eyed rescue cat from upstairs, whining at the door, sniffing at something in the corner of my doorway. I hope he hasn't brought them another gift in the form of a dead bird or rat. I bend down and stroke his back, and he purrs and pushes his head under my palm.

"What are you up to, Mr Gingernut?" He meows and turns full circle as I get to my feet, and that's when I spot them, nestled behind my pot plant. I shake my head, smiling to myself half-heartedly as I read the note attached – *Whatever I've done. I'm sorry. X*

I fill my lungs with the cold evening air, exhaling loudly to the swish of a pedal bike and a woman's voice yelling, 'Zach.' Flowers on my doorstep? Daniel must be gutted. He usually buys me shoes – it's our thing, how we met.

Mr Gingernut meows and winds around my legs as I get to my feet, tulips secured under my arm, then as I push the key into the lock guilt darts along my spine like a stone skimming in water and I shudder. Perhaps I was a bit harsh with Daniel this morning. I mean, leaping out of bed and locking myself in the bathroom does seem a bit childish now. I should've just come clean and told him why I was upset instead of screaming 'NOTHING!' when he rapped on the bathroom door and asked what was wrong. Because I'm sure even Daniel knows that when a woman says *nothing* she really means *something*, and it's usually a mega something, isn't it? But what did he expect after what he said as we lay naked in bed, limbs wrapped around each other?

Still, at least he's sorry, and the flowers are beautiful. That's a start. But he's still got a lot of explaining to do, because it's going to take a lot more than a bunch of my favourite flowers to forgive him for calling out his ex-wife's name while we were making love this morning.

CHAPTER 2

"WHAT A DAY," Daniel says, an hour later, shuffling into the lounge. "What's for dinner? Smells great."

I dart a glance at him as I drizzle olive oil over the salad. He looks whacked. His eyes are puffy and his usually smooth face is shadowed with a dark stubble, which actually quite suits him. "Only M&S food heated up, I'm afraid." It's what we usually have but I always feel compelled to give him an excuse for my lack of culinary skills. I'm not the best cook in the world but I am trying. "Didn't' have time for anything else, work was manic today, and the traffic was heaving. Bloody tube strike."

Mumbling a reply, he dumps his briefcase on the sofa, frowning at some paperwork. I hate it when he does this and he knows it – that briefcase has been on all sorts of surfaces today; it's full of germs. But now is not a good time to remind him, not when he's clearly got a grump on, and not when I've got more pressing things on my mind.

I feel his hand on the small of my back as I pour the wine. "Ah, Malbec, my favourite. What would I do without you?" He goes to kiss me, but, still irritated by this morning, I turn away, pretending to be distracted by a cat that's just leapt over the garden fence, and the moment is gone. He knows I'm annoyed with him, anyway; he wouldn't have sent me the flowers if he thought I hadn't noticed his slip up. He's the most perceptive man I know. I decide very quickly that there's no point in beating around the bush.

"Daniel, about this morning," I begin, wiping my hands on a tea towel.

"This morning?" Pulling a chair out, he settles down at the table and throws his red silk tie over his shoulder, tucking a napkin in to the collar of his white shirt.

"Yes, this morning," I reply crisply, pulling out a chair opposite him. "We need to talk about it, clear the air." A tiny fly hovers in front of my face and I bat it away with my hand.

"Er…the last time I looked at my C.V. it said Property Developer not Psychic."

I close my eyes for a moment, breathing in the aroma of garlic bread, as he fiddles around with his cutlery. He's doing this on purpose but I'm really not in the mood for his sarcasm. This isn't going to go away. I can't stop thinking about it. "Come on, Daniel, you know what I mean." I exhale loudly through my nose. "What happened in bed this morning – what you said."

He raises an eyebrow suggestively, a wicked grin on his lips. "It was great, wasn't it? I love morning sex." He looks at me beneath dark lashes, his blue eyes as deep and seductive as the evening sea. "You're such a minx."

Okay, any other time I'd lap up all this flirty talk, but his evasiveness is starting to irritate me now. "About what you said this morning while you were…you know." I rotate my hand in the air. "While we were…"

"While we were?" He eyes me over his wine glass. "Mmm…this wine is fantastic, Waitrose?"

"No, I bought it from Tesco, actually. Look," I tut, "stop trying to change the subject. This is important. You called out Sophie while we were having sex." My cheeks burn when I say it.

Taking another sip of wine, he stares at his food, hand loosely clenched on the table, wedding band gleaming. "I know and I'm

 HER SECRET

sorry." He pauses, looks at the tulips on the sideboard. "I thought that's what upset you this morning." Avoiding eye contact, he reaches for the gold rimmed Royal Albert salad bowl decorated with red and yellow roses. A wedding gift from my friend Louise. "It won't happen again," he says, as if calling out another woman's name while having sex is nothing more than a minor blip.

I look at him incredulously. "And is that it?"

He shrugs his shoulders and gives me one of his looks, as if I'm being unreasonable. "Well, what else do you want me to say?" He piles salad onto my plate before serving himself.

I spear a cherry tomato. "Well, an explanation would be nice."

Exhaling loudly, he rubs his lips, elbow on table, all the while regarding me. "Okay, look, don't take this the wrong way." Fuck. I hate sentences that start off like this, because I almost always take it the wrong way. "Well, I was dreaming about Sophie before you rolled on top of me, and it just came out. I'm sorry," he says, then picks up his cutlery and continues eating. His words are like a low blow and I struggle to hide the shock that cuts through me.

"What sort of dream was it? A sex dream?"

"No," he says sharply, "most definitely NOT. In fact, I haven't dreamt of her in years. It's all this business with Connie that's dragged it all up." Connie, Daniel's grownup daughter, recently found out that Daniel's second wife, Aliki, isn't her birth mother. Naturally, she wants to find her biological family; find out where she came from. I must admit, it has been a struggle, because, hard as they try, all they seem to do is hit a brick wall. It's as if the Coopers have been zapped off the face of the universe. "I'm sorry if I upset you, darling." He tears a piece off the garlic baguette. A few crumbs drop onto the wooden table. I'm a tidy freak and don't like seeing things out of place, especially when I'm stressed. "It really was an unconscious thing," he says matter-of-factly.

I'm actually a bit lost for words. I didn't expect him to be so stark. I cut hard into a piece of lasagne. The table, which has a piece of paper under one of the dodgy legs, shakes and the crumbs bounce. "Well, I hope not. Talk about a passion killer." I'm not a vain person and I've never thought of myself as beautiful, but this has never happened to me before, and, if I'm completely honest, it has knocked my confidence a bit.

We eat in silence for a few moments, cutlery tapping against china; and then he points his knife at me, grinning, "You're not jealous, are you?" he asks, and I almost choke on a mouthful of food.

"What? Of a corpse?" Sophie's been dead for twenty-eight years. "It just felt weird, that's all. As if….I dunno, you weren't with me… mentally, I mean."

He laughs, a hiss through his nose. "Don't be silly, Cinderella. You're the love of my life. I'm crazy about you, you know that. Oh, come on, Audrey, don't look at me like that. You're overreacting," he says, shaking his head. "That'll teach you for jumping on me while I'm still asleep."

"Hmm…" I murmur, twisting my lips. He was in a deep sleep, I suppose, and I did wake him. Maybe I am overreacting. Besides, I dream about Nick sometimes – not having sex with him or anything. Just random, weirdy dreams. Actually, they're more like nightmares, because I have woken up in a sweat once or twice. But then it is still all a bit raw for me, given that I was planning on eloping with him four months ago. "Okay," I sigh, "Let's just forget it."

"Already have," he smiles, chewing. I stare at a spot of lasagne sauce on his chin and cringe. "Actually." He lifts the napkin and

 HER SECRET

pats his mouth. Phew. "I've got a little surprise for you. I was going to save it for the weekend but....well, I think you could do with a bit of cheering up now."

Another surprise? My eyes widen. "Oh," I say, feeling a flutter of excitement. I knew the flowers couldn't be it. I wonder if he's booked us a romantic weekend away somewhere. I saw him searching for city breaks on his MacBook the other day. Or maybe it's those *Prada* shoes I was eyeing in a shop window on Hampstead High Street last week when I met him for lunch. "What is it?" I ask, unable to curb the slight hysteria in my voice.

Glancing over my shoulder, he chews on his food, grinning. I twist in my seat, following his gaze, as if I have some kind of super vision that can see around corners and into the hallway. I bet he's hidden them behind the coat stand. "Well, come on then, the suspense is killing me."

"I've bought us a house," he says, gesticulating towards the sofa with his head, "Paperwork is on the table."

"What, a house to let?" I smile. Daniel is building a portfolio for us, says it's to secure our future.

"No, for us to live in. We move in in six weeks."

Ten minutes later we're in the kitchen still arguing about the house purchase. How could he have gone ahead and bought a house, even paid a deposit, without consulting me first? Without even discussing it with me?

"But you said you'd like somewhere bigger one day."

"Yes, Daniel, one day," I explain, loading a plate into the dishwasher. "Next year, maybe, or the year after that. Not now. And when the time comes I'd like us to choose a home together."

Leaning against the worktop, he nods, says he understands, admits he got it wrong this time. "I messed up. I'm sorry."

I stop loading and straighten up. "And I'm sorry too. For shouting," I say in a little voice, because somehow I now feel like a complete ungrateful cow. "It's just that you took me by surprise, that's all. This is a big decision. But I know you meant well."

"Oh, come here." He pulls me into his arms and I breathe in his musky scent. "What're we like, eh?"

Guilt finds its way into my stomach and twists. Daniel was there for me when Nick left me. And, despite everything, despite choosing Nick over him when I was faced with a choice, he still stood by me, gave me a second chance. That's true love, isn't it? I know I have some panicky, wobbly moments sometimes, and question whether marrying him after only a couple of months of dating was a bit rushed, like the author of comment 8 on Vicky's meme. But deep down I know, without a doubt, that marrying Daniel is the best decision I ever made. I've really landed on my feet with him. He's given me stability, love, security. I want for nothing. And now I've caused our first fight by lashing out on him for trying to improve our lives. But in my defence, I did spend eight years with a man who used to call me from Tesco's to ask what type of salad bag to buy. I'm not used to a man holding the reins, and, if I'm honest, I'm not sure I like it. Clearly, this is something we'll have to iron out.

I pull away from him, switch the dishwasher on, then pad into the living room. "It's just that I love living here," I complain sulkily. "I'm a Muswell HillBilly." I bought my flat at a rock-bottom price because it needed work. I enjoyed every moment of the renovations. In fact, if I wasn't a web designer I think I'd have chosen interior design. "It's my home."

"Exactly," he says, emptying the last dregs of the wine between two glasses. "Your home, not ours. I mean, this place is great." He waves his arm around the room, the wine sloshes in his glass.

"But I want us to have a family home together. Our home. A fresh start…away from…" he falters.

Away from memories of my past, that's what he was going to say. But I can't erase the history from my life with a few clicks of a mouse. I didn't come with a squeaky clean past, I'm afraid. But he does have a point. I wouldn't like it if we lived in Aliki's house. I feel myself mellow – red wine always does this to me, before giving me a stinking headache, that is.

"I'm not selling it," I say indignantly, running a hand along the oak fireplace.

"You don't have to," he says quickly, pleased that I'm coming round to the idea of moving. "This flat is yours. You can rent it out if you like, that'll pay the mortgage for you. You can even stop working."

"No way," I stop and look up at him sharply. "I love my job." The security that Daniel has given me is incredible, but I won't be a kept woman.

"Yes, I know you do, but I'm just saying you could if you wanted, that'll all. It's an option." He sits on the armrest of the sofa and grabs the A4 folder off the coffee table. "Look, it's a lovely house, Audrey." He starts flicking through the paperwork. "You won't believe how much I got the vendor to drop in price." Daniel's speciality – buy low, sell high. "He's selling it for his old man, their moving him into a flat. You know, the ones with a warden."

"Where you wear one of those alarm thingies around your neck?"

He nods and my heart sinks, poor thing. I'd never let my parents live in assisted care. I'd sooner move them in with me. Maybe a house isn't such a bad idea. I have got an extended family now. Connie and her six-year-old daughter, Lily, have to share a bed whenever they stay over. And my parents aren't getting any younger. Perhaps Daniel's right; this flat was great when I was single, but now…

I clear my throat. "Where is it, then?"

"Highgate," he says, giving me one of his signature lopsided grins.

"I love it there," I say, peering at the paper over his shoulder, lips jutted.

"I know. I do listen to you, you know."

Leaning forward, I rest my arm on his shoulder and tuck my hair behind my ear, "Is it close to the village?" I squint at the paper in his hand, feeling the warmth of his face close to mine, but all I can see is a blur. I must get myself some contact lenses, Daniel says they're brilliant.

"Just around the corner," he grins and my eyes light up. "You'll love it, Audrey." I already am. I wonder if it's near all the shops and restaurants. "It's got four double bedrooms," he enthuses. "Lots of room for when your parents visit from Cyprus, or when the kids stay over. A huge kitchen diner that leads onto a conservatory, and a beautiful hundred-and-fifty foot garden. Imagine the fun your nephews and Lily will have playing in the summer." Nathan and Josh are only toddlers, but ten-year-old Florian would love a big garden to kick a ball about, given that they live in a small flat above a fish and chip shop in Archway. But a garden isn't really a major attraction for me. I'm only good with house plants, and preferably ones that don't mind being ignored.

"I'm not into gardening, Daniel, you know that." I watch as he licks his index finger and noisily leafs through paper after paper, then he jabs his thumb in the direction of the patio doors, his eyes not leaving the sheet in his hand, "You've done all right with this one."

 HER SECRET

Getting to my feet, I stretch my back, "I didn't do it. It was…" I falter, rubbing my neck as I slowly walk towards the patio doors. The garden is small and mostly decked, with a bit of green in the middle and plants on both sides, and an apple tree right at the back. Nick did all the gardening for me. He's got green fingers, but I don't think now is the good time to bring up it up. I don't want to ruin the moment. Daniel gets tetchy when I mention ex-boyfriends.

"I had a landscaper in when I first bought it," I lie, and suddenly I picture Nick standing on the lawn in his wellies digging and weeding and anger burns in my chest. I close my eyes, batting the image away. "It's south facing, so gets lots of sunshine," I say cheerily as I cross the room and pick up the empties. "All I ever do is water the plants." Whenever I remember, that is, which is hardly ever.

Daniel nods at the tulips on the sideboard, smiling. "They're gorgeous, by the way, beautiful colour."

"Yes," I say, realising that I haven't even bothered to thank him for them. "They're…"

"Did you buy them from that florist on Fortis Green?" he cuts in. He gets to his feet and starts rolling up the sleeve of his brilliant white shirt. "They do great bouquets there, don't they? Although I hardly ever buy you flowers." He scrunches his nose, making a start on the other sleeve. "I ought to really as you like them so much, but I much prefer to buy you shoes," he grins, pinching my noise. "My Cinderella. Just think, if you'd not lost your shoe at the restaurant in Larnaca, our paths may never have crossed." He makes it sound like a fairy-tale, but I actually got pissed and fell onto his lap trying to do the Zorba, during which I lost my shoe. He found it after I'd gone home and handed it in. "Audrey? You okay, darling? You look as if you've seen a ghost."

"Yes," I manage, feeling my blood run cold, "I'm sorry. It's the wine. I think it's gone to my head. You know what I'm like with red." I force a smile as my heart bounces around in my chest. If Daniel didn't buy me the flowers, it can only mean one thing.

"What after a couple of glasses? Not like you." Grabbing the bottle by the neck, he holds it at arm's length and frowns at the label. "Ah, 14%, strong stuff. Look, I'll wash these up," Daniel offers, taking the crystal glasses from my hands. "Your Soaps should be starting soon. Why don't you just put your feet up?"

He pads into the kitchen humming under his breath, and I sigh with relief, glad to be alone with my thoughts. I glance at the tulips as if they're poisoning the air, then as I switch on the T.V. and I notice that my hand is trembling. Shit. SHIT! I need to calm down and stop jumping to conclusions. "Corrie's about to finish," I yell with a shaky voice, "I'll watch it on catch-up but EastEnders will be starting soon. I can....." Then as I take a step back towards the sofa, I feel Daniel's arms around my waist and I jump.

"Never mind East bloody Enders. Fancy a shower?" he whispers, kissing my neck. His breath is warm and soft against my skin. "What's wrong with you, hmm? You're in knots," he says, massaging my shoulders. "You're not still upset about the house move, are you? Because I can..."

"No, it's not that," I cut in. "I've had a crap day...I'm..."

"Dr Taylor has something that can magically cure crap day syndrome," he groans. "Did you know that?" His tongue flicks against my earlobe and I feel myself stir.

But the moment my eyes close, the card attached to the tulips flashes in my mind – *Whatever I've done. I'm sorry. X.* Shit, they could be from anyone. I'm overreacting. I stroke Daniels thigh, desperate for diversion. He tugs at my cream blouse, planting hot kisses on the back of my neck. One hand unzips my skirt, the other makes its way up my torso. Maybe they were delivered by mistake. "You're so sexy when you're angry," he murmurs. "It's those dark, sultry eyes of yours." They might be for Margaret upstairs, or sour faced bin sergeant next door, although who in their right mind would buy her flowers? "Are you sure you haven't got a bit of Spanish in you?"

"No," I reply "How many times are you going to ask me that question? I'm English through and through." George and I have taken after my mum's side of the family. They've all got a Mediterranean look about them. "I'm beginning to think you're obsessed with Spanish women," I say softly. He unbuttons my blouse slowly and I close my eyes, TulipGate fading, fading, fading away. "Daniel," I whisper, opening my eyes briefly. "I've still…" and just then I catch sight of a black four-by-four crawling outside my flat through the bay window. Daniel's grip tightens as I try to wriggle free. "Who the –" But before I can finish, he spins me around and silences me with a long, hard kiss. Then all I can hear is the theme tune to EastEnders and the loud growl of a car zooming off into the distance.

CHAPTER 3

"OH MY GODDDDDDDD!! You're moving to Highgate?" Tina squeals while doing a little jumpy dance on Louise's grey slate kitchen tiles. "Congratulations!"

"Well, Daniel's arranged a viewing for tomorrow. But yes, all being well, we'll be moving to Highgate!"

"A surprise house. How romantic," she croons. "I'm SO excited for you – a new start as Mr and Mrs Taylor. Oh, come here." She gives me a rib crushing hug and her long, curly hair tickles my cheek.

I knew Tina would react like this to my news. She's very - how can I put this mildly? -amorous. Her life revolves around, well, men. A particular Irish ginger haired man by the name of Ronan, at the moment, a love lost and found. Over her shoulder, Louise is firing up her laptop at the square, chunky, solid oak kitchen table. Her 'pièce de résistance' as she likes to call it. I helped her pick it out from Camden Market a few years ago. Her kitchen is her life.

I watch her tap, tap away at the keyboard with slight trepidation to the buzz of the washing machine and the faint hum of music drifting from the radio on the wooden worktop. As a rule, Louise is more cynical than Tina. I expect she's going to have a bit of a go at me for letting Daniel take full control of our living arrangements. But then she does like him. Mostly because she dislikes Nick. Sadly, the feeling isn't mutual. Daniel thinks Louise is gobby and opinionated, especially when she's got a drink inside her. But that's

 HER SECRET

just her way. She doesn't mean anything by it. Louise just says it as she sees it, you've got to get to know her.

"That's really good news, Audrey. What's the address?" Louise asks, glancing up at me briefly. See what I mean? She's been Danielfied.

Tina and I hover over her. "Montenotte Road," I say with glee, swept in by Tina's excitement and Louise's reassurance. Perhaps, I was a bit harsh with Daniel. A surprise house move is romantic, I suppose. I twirl the Tiffany's horseshoe necklace, Daniel's wedding gift, between my thumb and index finger, feeling the edges of the encrusted diamonds. "I spoke to Vicky this morning too," I enthuse, "I've offered them my flat. Mates rates and everything. She was completely blown away." I pause as their praise fills the garlicky warm air - I'm such a brilliant sister. They're lucky to have me. But I'm the lucky one, I tell them, George and Vicky are always there for me. George and I are close siblings. I'm not sure if it's because there's only a year between us, or because it's just the two of us, but it works. "Daniel said it's close to the village," I go on, curling a lose strand of hair behind my ear. "We can walk to *The Flask* when you come over."

"No way," Tina's voice goes up a pitch, nearing hysteria. Louise cringes. Louise can't bear loud sounds, like chewing or sniffing, or even breathing. Apparently, it's a condition - misphonia, or sound-rage.

I nod fervently. "He said it needs quite a bit of work but..."

"Crouch End," Louise cuts in, and the smile dies on my lips. She's got it wrong, obviously. She must've typed in the wrong postcode.

"No, Highgate Village," I correct, frowning at her computer.

"Not according to movehousenow.com. Look." Shoving a few recipe books out of the way, she pushes the laptop back a little, giving us a better view of the screen then starts reading. "Montenotte Road, Crouch End. Location - north of Shepherds Hill, seven minute walk to Highgate Station. A short stroll away from the desirable amenities of CROUCH END with its bustling restaurants, shops and great atmosphere." She glances at me with a big grin. "I thought it sounded familiar. It's only a few streets from here. We'll be practically neighbours. How awesome is that?" That can't be right. Daniel said it was just around the corner from Highgate Village.

I push my sliding glasses up the bridge of my nose and lean forward, hand on her back. "Click on the map icon, Loulou." A street map springs onto the screen.

"Look, here it is," Louise moves the cursor over the map and we all tilt our heads like confused dogs. "And this is my house." She turns around and beams at me, face inches from mine. Phew, that elderflower infusion we had with our lunch is quite potent – it almost smells like booze.

"Oooh, that's handy, isn't it?" Tina says, helping herself to a fistful of dry roasted nuts from the bowl on the table. I focus on Louise's oil-stained notepad, bursting with her own recipes, my mind ticking away like a time bomb. "A bonus," Tina says, munching. "What's up, Aud, you look a bit miffed."

"He said it was close to the village," I complain, twisting my lips thoughtfully.

"Well, it's not far from Highgate station," Louise offers, her tone depicting, *why are you being so picky.* "And…"

"Enlarge that map, Louise." I squat and my knees creak. Tina grabs another fistful of nuts.

"Where do you put it?" Louise ducks her head and eyes Tina under my arm. "We've only just had lunch." Louise made us a gorgeous spaghetti lobster. A recipe she plans on using at the new restaurant she works at in Soho. She was headhunted for her culinary skills several weeks ago. Having a best friend who's a chef definitely has its plusses. We keep telling her she should go on MasterChef, but she won't listen. One day I'm going to download the application form and fill it in for her myself.

"I can't help it. The excitement has given me the munchies." Tina drains her tumbler of elderflower water then squeezes between us, licking her lips, face so close to mine that I can smell her peanuty breath. "What're we looking for, Aud?"

Louise gives Tina a long, sideward glance, annoyed. "Do you have to munch in my ear? You're getting on my nerves."

"Well, how am I supposed to chew? Silently? Because if –"

"Shhhhh…you two. I can't concentrate." The room falls silent. "I knew it!" I say finally, straightening up.

"Knew what?" They say in unison.

"Montenotte Road. I knew I'd heard of that street name before. Look." I lean in between them and snatch the mouse from Louise's limp grasp. "It runs almost parallel to Aliki's house."

"You mean Aliki as in ex-wife Aliki?" Louise frowns at me.

"How many Aliki's do you think she knows, Louise?"

"Exactly." I get to my feet, straightening my blue V-neck dress.

"Well, that's not so bad, is it?" Louise says, standing up too. "You like her, don't you?" Our empty tumblers clank as she secures them between the fingers of one hand. "And it's not as if you'll be living next door to her or anything." I watch as she crosses the kitchen, deposits the tumblers in the sink, then yanks open the door of her red Smeg, all the while keeping up a monologue of how lucky I am to have found such a great bloke, they don't grow on trees, you know, Crouch End is lovely, she'd never live anywhere else. She returns moments later with a bottle of Chablis and three wine glasses almost the size of fish bowls.

"None for me." Tina slides along the long bench, raising a palm. "I'm driving. But I'll have another glass of that posh water of yours, if you don't mind."

Louise tells her to help herself from the jug on the worktop as we settle down at the table. "The point is, I thought it was in Highgate village…and…" I hold my head in my hands. Did Daniel really try to mislead me just to get me to agree to the house purchase? I mean, obviously, he knows I'll find out where it is. I know I'm not the best street navigator in the world and, admittedly, still have to use my SatNav whenever I drive to Connie's in Bayswater, but I'm not that daft.

"You okay, Audrey?" Louise takes a sip from her wine glass. I glance up at her, wanting to ask her the same question. Her lips are pale and cracked at the sides, face pasty, eyes puffy and dark. She's lost quite a bit of weight, too. It must be the stress of the new job. The restaurant hasn't been open long and Manuel, the owner, is pressing her for new creations. Maybe it's all getting a bit too much for her, or maybe it's because of Gerry.

Louise and Gerry were the perfect couple, until Louise decided she wanted to have a baby, that is. The disappointment month after month became almost as unbearable for us as it was for them. Things took a turn for the worse when they discovered that Gerry's sperm count was virtually nil.

Louise went into meltdown almost overnight. Her dreams of having her perfect family were shattered. But life goes on, doesn't it? We all thought she was coping, getting on with things; but we were wrong, because behind closed doors she was fighting a different battle – a quest to secretly adopt Gerry's twin sister's baby. A baby we all thought Nick had fathered at the time (during one of our breaks. He's an arse and I hate him, but he was never unfaithful to me.) Of course, you can't keep a baby a secret, can

 HER SECRET

you? When the truth was out all hell broke loose. I think that was the final straw for Gerry – he'd had enough. "All I ever wanted was a quiet life with the family we already had," Gerry told me a few days before he walked out on her. "Her obsession to have a baby has broken us."

I'm not going to lie, it did effect our friendship, too. I felt betrayed, lied to. Louise and I didn't speak for weeks after that, but in time I came to realise that we all do strange things when we're under pressure, or when we're desperate. Louise and I had been through a lot together. I didn't want this one thing to destroy our friendship. I didn't want bitterness to seal itself inside me, or anger to twist into the fibres of my mind and make me hate her. Life is short, and to quote one of Vicky's memes, *'Time is a thief and a powerful spell, and regrets hang around like a bad ugly smell. Forgive more, resent less.'*

"I mean, there's nothing else troubling you is there?" Louise says, scratching her face. Louise has always had the ability to read my mind – scary. Either that or she's a witch. I focus on her white collars protruding from her pale blue sweater. I wonder if I should tell my friends about the flowers I found on my doorstep yesterday evening, about the suspicious black car crawling outside my flat, that I've a gut feeling that Nick is back.

"No," I sigh, quickly deciding against it. Because, let's face it, I was probably being paranoid. The flowers mightn't have been for me, there was no name on the card. And, as Daniel pointed out when I mentioned the suspicious looking four-by-four to him later that evening, there's no law against cars driving slowly along Dukes Avenue, particularly as it's lined with road bumps. The driver might've just been lost. "I'm just so used to living in my flat that's all," I admit, taking a glug from my wine glass. "Crouch End is lovely too. I must've misunderstood," I lie, but my mind is reeling – why did Daniel feel the need to exaggerate the truth? And why choose a house within walking distance of his ex-wife's?

"I've got some news, too." Tina announces, biting her bottom lip.

We both look at her expectantly. "You're not pregnant are you?" I grin into my glass.

She waves a hand. "Nooooooo!" Give me a flipping chance. We've only been back together five minutes."

"Well, what is it then?" Louise asks.

The washing machine plays an end of cycle tune – I think it's a concerto. Louise throws a glance at it, neatly rolling up her sleeves, and for some inexplicable reason, we all wait until the washing machine concerto stops before speaking again.

"Ronan has asked me to marry him and I've said yes," Tina trills.

We gaze at her in stunned silence. I'm not sure what to say. I knew they were getting on very well but didn't realise they'd become so close, and he is still married.

Louise speaks first. "Hey, that's brilliant news, love." She reaches out for her hand and gives it a light squeeze.

"Oh, wow, that's fantastic," I say almost at the same time, binning my cynicism. Who am I to judge? Ronan's separated, anyway, and he has filed for divorce. We hold hands around the table as if we're in a séance, grinning at each other stupidly. It's not often the room falls silent when the three of us are together.

"That's cheered us up, hasn't it?" Louise pours more wine into her glass and attempts to top up mine, but I pull it back and look at the clock above the kitchen door. "It's only half two and I'm working from home this afternoon." Louise looks at me as if I'm joking, laughs a bit, and goes to fill my glass. "No, honestly, Lou. I'm fine," I insist, closing my hand over it. "It's for a new client. Sam Knight, the body language expert. We had a board meeting about this morning."

 HER SECRET

"I've heard of him," Tina says excitedly, "He was on The One Show recently promoting his new book."

"Oh, right," Louise says, lips twitching with disappointment. "Well, let's drink to that too, then."

I can't believe we're all getting hitched. All we need now is for Gerry to make up with Louise. Unlikely, I know, but you never know, anything is possible. I smile, turning to Tina. "I'm really, really pleased for you. Say congrats to Ronan for me, too."

"To Tina and Ronan," Louise affirms, glass raised. "And Audrey and her new house. And Sam Knight."

Tina presses her palms flat on the table. "Well, you can congratulate him yourselves. I know this is a bit short notice but we're having a party to celebrate on Saturday. You're both invited, obvs." Taking a sip of elderflower water, she makes a circle with her hand. "Bring Jess, Louise. And I'm going to invite Vicky and George, Audrey. Feel free to ask Connie, too. She can come with you and Daniel if you like."

"She might like to bring her boyfriend," I offer. "If that's okay?"

"Oh? Is she seeing someone new?" Louise asks as her phone throbs with a notification on the table.

"Yeah," I check my phone too. 69 Groupon alerts and 7 Words with Friends. "She's all loved up." I slip the phone back into my handbag. "We're meeting him tonight, actually. Connie has invited us round for dinner." I raise my eyebrows. "It must be love."

"Yeah, sure, ask her to bring him." Tina's thumbs fly over her phone. "I wonder what he's like. She's quite stunning, isn't she?"

I agree. Connie does turn heads wherever we go. Naturally, Daniel insists that she gets her looks from him – and she does look like him. A bit. But my guess is that she's the spit of her mum.

"Yes, she's very attractive," Louise agrees. "Looks a bit like Daniel, doesn't she? But I wonder if she's more like her mum." I told you she can read my mind. "Jess is a lot like me but she's got her dad's eyes. He did have lovely eyes," she reflects, gazing up at the grey steel 3-light pendant hanging above us. "Even though he was a complete knob."

"Yes," I muse. "She's probably got her mum's green eyes, Daniel's are blue."

Connie lost her biological mum to a brain haemorrhage when she was only two. So we'll never know. Daniel doesn't like talking about Sophie, it upset him. All he's told me is that she was a doting mother, loved the ocean and was buried at sea. Sadly, only one photo of her remains. A family snap of the three of them taken when Connie was a baby. I found it while I was tidying up one of Daniel's drawers last year. It's tatty, discoloured and blurry. You can barely make them out. Shame.

"So," Tina says, snatching our attention. A magpie hops along the windowsill and we all salute it like soldiers. It pecks at the concrete slab a few times before spreading its wings and landing on the gutter of the house next door. "My engagement party."

"Yes," Louise and I say in unison, whipping our heads towards her.

"Audrey," Tina's eyes flit from me to Louise, earrings swinging in her hair. "I need a huge favour." Oh, no, I don't think I like her ominous tone. The last time Tina roped me in to doing her a big favour I ended up having to lie through my teeth to Patrick, a man she met on the Piccadilly Line. She made me answer her phone and tell him she was almost at death's door to avoid a second date. After going silent on me for what seemed like five minutes, he then asked me out instead – insisted that he liked the sound of my voice, as if that was the most important attribute when choosing a partner. It took me ages to get him off the phone; I think I just hung up in the end. "Would you be my maid of honour?" Tina

 HER SECRET

asks. I open my mouth to speak but her hand flies up. "No offence, Louise, but I've known Audrey longer."

"None taken," Louise groans, rolling her eyes

"Are you sure, Tina?" I gulp, pressing a hand against my chest. Tina's very popular, she's got lots of friends and close relatives she could ask. I can't believe she's chosen me. Tina nods eagerly. "Well, then yes." She pulls me into her arms and I get lost in a tangle of red hair and perfume. "I'd be honoured to be your maid of honour!"

"There's just one snag." We pull apart as if an electrical current has snapped between us.

"Well, spit it out." Louise moans, scrolling lazily through movehousenow.com

"It's Nick," she whispers in the tone of a spook on a secret mission.

My stomach clenches. I know what she's going to say. "He's back, isn't he?" I close my eyes briefly as the red tulips and the black four-by-four flash in my mind. Inhaling deeply, I tell myself that it's okay, I can do this. He was bound to return sooner or later. I can just avoid him. Our paths need not cross.

Tina nods, biting on a long, red fingernail, "Thing is, Aud…" I frown at her. Louise stops tapping on her keyboard, face dark. "Ronan has asked him to be best man." She cringes, hunching her shoulders, "So you'll probably have to liaise with him."

Oh, bloody hell!

CHAPTER 4

DANIEL PRESSES THE BUZZER then stands back, stretching his neck from side to side until it clicks before giving the knot in his tie a final jiggle, bottle of champagne in hand. I don't think I've ever seen him this nervous. In fact, I'm surprised he didn't chew off his entire thumb in the back of the taxi on our way here. I give him a small smile, open my mouth to speak, offer a bit of reassurance, but then Connie's voice crackles through the intercom, "Come up, guys." Another buzz and we're through.

My black stilettos sink into the luxurious fibres of the rose-coloured carpet leading up to the grand staircase. I always feel like I'm in a posh hotel whenever we visit Connie, which I must admit, isn't that often. She's not much of an inviter-over. She likes to visit, especially when she has her weekend sleepovers at Aliki's. Only these days she just drops Lily off on a Friday and collects her on Sunday afternoon so that she can spend time with her new bloke. She doesn't even invite us in when we drop her off sometimes. I think this is probably the third time I've actually been inside her Bayswater flat.

"Wait," I say, pressing a hand against the huge antique French limestone fireplace in the foyer. "There's something in my shoe." Glancing up at the majestic chandelier above my head, I pull off my red-soled *Louboutin*. They're new. Daniel came home with them this evening with a posh frock to match – a two-toned ivory and black dress, which, if I'm honest, is a bit daring for me with its low back and split up to my thighs. But I didn't want to hurt his feelings, and it is growing on me. Gifts, he said, for the misunderstanding over the location of the house. It appears that his interpretation of *around the corner* and mine are somewhat dissimilar. Still, Crouch End is lovely and familiar. Plus it'll be great to live within walking distance of Louise.

Living parallel to his ex-wife's house, though, is an entirely different matter. "It'll be good for the kids if we're all close by, Audrey," he said earlier, as I slipped into my daring new frock and he buttoned himself into a white Armani shirt in front of the full-length wardrobe mirror. Although I still can't get used to him calling a thirty-year-old woman a kid, I suppose he has got a point. Connie and Lily are forever flitting between our place and Aliki's, which often means I'm on taxi duties. "I didn't think you'd mind," he said, twisting his head to fasten the last black-thread button at his neck. "You and Aliki get on well, don't you?" And that was the end of that.

We take the stairs, Connie's flat is only on the first floor, and even I can manage that.

"Calm down." I squeeze his hand. "It's only a new boyfriend."

"Hmm..but she must be serious about him. The only other boyfriend she formally introduced me to was Lily's father and he turned out to be a complete dick."

"I'm sure Jake isn't like that." Lily's father disappeared the moment he found out Connie was expecting and they haven't seen him since. "Jake's got a good job with prospects." Connie told me he's a financial advisor – job in the city, drives a Porsche. "And he's very good with Lily," I add. Daniel doesn't answer. "He owns his house outright, Daniel. No mortgage. What thirty-six year-olds can say that these days, hmm? Stop worrying."

"Yes, but what if I don't like him?" We shift to the side as a young, posh looking bloke dashes down the stairs, mousey brown curls bouncing on his head.

"You will," I say, as we step onto the landing. "And if you don't, it won't be the end of the world, will it?" Technically speaking, it will be the end of Daniel's world. Although he'd never admit it, Connie and Lily are his life, his heartbeat. The thought of another alpha male muscling in and taking over doesn't bear thinking about. So let's hope they do get on, for all our sakes. We walk along the corridor hand in hand. "Anyway, what if he doesn't like you?" I tease. He gives me a look depicting *as if.* Modesty isn't one of my husband's traits.

Jake's got a Mediterranean look about him – dark, curly hair, caramel skin, soulful, big brown eyes and big lips; not Mick Jagger big, but plump and kissable, and he's very, very charismatic. And if that weren't enough, he's a bloody brilliant cook, too. Made everything for us from scratch tonight, from the sea bass with lime dressing to the warm, gooey chocolate orange sponge. He even made his own vanilla ice cream. I love a man who can cook.

"Another helping, anyone?" he says, in his estuary accent, moving his chair back slightly.

"Oh, not for me thanks. But it was absolutely delicious, Jake," I say, resisting the urge to pick up my plate and lick it clean. Connie throws Jake an adoring glance, then they grin at each other lovingly. A little too lovingly, actually. I suddenly feel uncomfortable. Clamping a hand over my mouth, I turn towards the door, wondering how long Daniel intends on standing in the corridor with that business call. Playing gooseberry to a couple of lovebirds on heat isn't my idea of a good night out. I'm missing a new BBC thriller for this.

 HER SECRET

I glance back, fingers tapping against my mouth, and catch Jake miming something (obviously obscene) to Connie across the table, which she laps up with lustful glee. Oh, bloody hell! I feel like I'm sitting in on a live porn show. Surely, they'll have plenty of time to seduce each other once we've gone. Picking up her spoon, Connie curls her tongue around it, licking off the mushy chocolatey remnants suggestively, as if I'm invisible, and I want to slit my wrists.

"And thank you too, Connie," I blurt out, digging my nails into her forearm a little too aggressively. Thank goodness she's wearing a long-sleeved grey marl cropped top. "It's all been lovely." I twist in my seat and stretch my leg across hers. I knew I should've broken my new *Louboutins* in at home. What was I thinking?

"S'okay," she replies with a small frown, rubbing her arm. Shit, I've hurt her. Well, I had to do something to break their amorous spell. It was too painful to watch. "You've cooked for me and Lily often enough." Well, I wouldn't call Waitrose ready meals cooking, but I accept the compliment with a little nod and a smile.

Jake leans back in his seat, head slightly tilted, all the while grinning at her. Well, at least they're not gazing at each other as if they want to rip each other's clothes off anymore.

Satisfied, I slip my shoe off and give my ankle a good swivel, feeling the tension lifting immediately. But as I let out a discreet sigh of relief, I feel the smoothness of leather caressing the length of my calf.

My foot finds my shoe within seconds, a little involuntary gasp seeps through my lips. "Er…that's MY leg?" For some unknown reason I say it in the manner of a teenager – as if I'm asking a question.

Jake straightens up in his seat, startled, then in a half stand, half sit motion he apologises profusely, scratching his stubble-bearded neck. I think he does a little bow, bless him. He's done so well up until now. I suppose hitting on his new girlfriend's step-mum, albeit accidentally, wasn't part of his 'impressing us' plan.

"You doughnut." Connie jumps to her feet, scrunches a napkin into a ball and throws it in his face. He catches it immediately. Quick reflexes, I'm impressed. I wonder if he's a rugby player, he certainly has the physique for it. I expect he spends hours in the gym honing that body and drinks lots of smoothies fortified with protein and flaxseed. "Sorry, Aud," Connie laughs theatrically, hand on my shoulder. "I can't take him anywhere."

I cut him some slack; it was an easy mistake to make considering my leg was outstretched over Connie's. We all cackle with laughter as Connie clears the table. I'm so relieved that Jake is everything we expected him to be and more. I don't think I've seen her this happy. Finally, Daniel will be able to sleep at night. I get to my feet, but my offer to help with the washing up is met with vehement protest. Connie pushes me back into my seat and heads for the kitchen, stack of plates in arms, tra-la-la'ing under her breath, then Jake and I are alone. We chitchat for a while about the weather – how cold it is for April. What a crap summer we had last year and how we had to put the heating on in June, and then he says:

"So, you and Connie's dad are newlyweds." He unwraps a toothpick, elbows on table. I can see why Connie's besotted with him. He is attractive. Very.

"Yes, we had a bit of a whirlwind romance, then tied the knot," I laugh, feeling relaxed after my third glass of wine.

"Were you married before?" he asks behind his large hand. His intrusive question throws me a little, but I suppose he's only trying to make small talk. I watch as he picks away and sucks his teeth. Mum would have a field day with Jake. She judges people on their table manners, and tooth picking during a conversation is one of her pet hates.

 HER SECRET

"No, this is husband number one," I joke, and he laughs behind his hand, his brown eyes twinkling in the candlelight as he tilts his head. "Not that I plan on having a collection," I add quickly, gazing at the bald gap between his thick dark eyebrows. He must wax them – very metrosexual.

"Connie said you were engaged to some bloke for years." Snapping the toothpick in half, he discards it onto an orange paper napkin, running his tongue over his teeth– veneers, I think. Large, even, very white and sparkly. "What happened?" My cheeks burn within nanoseconds and his eyes flicker. He knows he's overstepped the mark. His bulging muscles almost rip out of his tight white t-shirt as he folds his arms over the table in front of him. "I suppose you just drifted apart," he says, trying to redeem himself for being inquisitive.

I focus on the tattoo of four Latin initials encased within a large red heart on his left arm. "Yes," I say, twisting the stem of my wine glass. "We wanted different things." I take a deep breath to the ruckus of crockery and the slamming of cabinet doors traveling from the kitchen. Where the hell is Daniel, for heavens' sake? I know Jake is probably just trying to make polite conversation but I'm in no mood to talk about my past.

He leans back in his chair. A plate smashes, Connie shouts, 'fuck,' and he glances at the kitchen, smiling. "Break-ups suck, don't they?" he sighs, and I get the feeling that his heart has been ripped out of his chest and stamped on, too.

"They certainly do," I smile into my wine glass. Hopefully, that's the end of that conversation.

"Are you still mates, though?" he probes.

I stiffen in my seat, mentally writing 'nosey' under his list of faults, which was blank until now.

"No, we don't have any more contact," I say crisply, looking away. What's with the twenty questions? Connie must've filled him about my particulars. Is he really that stuck for conversation? Jake opens his mouth to speak again, but I'm saved by his mobile phone pulsating on the dark French-style table (Connie loves baroque).

"Sorry, Audrey." He gets to his feet, "I've got to get this." And he's gone, leaving me alone with my thoughts. I take a sip of wine. The smooth, yellow liquid glides down my throat, tingling my stomach. Why did he have to drag up my past, anyway? We were having such a lovely evening until now.

Getting to my feet, I walk towards the huge Georgian style window, glass in hand, and as I gaze down at the traffic swishing up and down the street in the darkness, my mind rewinds to four months ago. I'm in my lounge. It's my birthday. I was having a bit of a do with my family and friends, and Daniel, who'd turned up unexpectedly with a pair of *Jimmy Choos*. He was my ex at the time. We'd had a brief romance but had split up over an affair. Well, it was a one night stand, actually. He was trying to put things right.

Nick's first text pinged through as I made a wish and blew out the candles. The paternity test results were back. He wasn't the father of Louise's sister-in-law's baby. He was overjoyed – vindicated, at last. As the evening wore on the texts came through thick and fast. I knew I was being rude, favouring my phone over my guests, but I couldn't help myself. Nick's excitement was contagious. And this new piece of information put a new perspective on things. He wasn't the father of Francesca's baby. The only thing that was keeping us apart had vanished. I knew I wanted him back.

Much later, during a game of charades, well, I say charades but it was Daniel's version of charades. Instead of shouting out the answer, we had to write it down on a piece of paper and place it on a neat pile in the centre of the table. The winner of each correct answer gained points then won the sweepstake at the end, donated

HER SECRET

by Daniel. It's a brilliant game, actually. We've played it a few times since. Daniel is quite innovative and an excellent party guest.

I won a couple of the rounds but was too engrossed in my marathon text session to pay enough attention. My brother George won the fifty quid prize in the end. After several flirty texts, Nick went quiet, and my heart cracked a little. Perhaps he didn't want me back, I reasoned. Maybe he just wanted to share his good news with me. I returned my attention to my lovely guests. Then, at about nine o' clock, the all-important text buzzed through:

>>I love you Foxy – come away with me xx (Foxy was his pet name for me) Let's do it.

>>Do what?

>>Get married!

>>Don't b ridic – UR just overexcited by the news. Mad person.

>>I mean it. Let's just pack our bags and go.

>>Where? Shit, I thought, he really does mean it. I'd had a few glasses of prosecco and felt giddy, excited, adventurous.

>>Anywhere. Travel the world. Just the 2 of us. I miss U. xx

>>You're bonkers!

>>I know. Come on. We always said we'd to do it.

>>I can't just up and go travelling around the world. What about work? My flat? I was excited, tempted. The thought of finally becoming Mrs Byrne made my entire body tingle.

>>Take a year off – a sabbatical. I'll pay your mortgage for a year with savings, or we can get George or Ronan to rent it for you. Anything is possible.

>>You really are crazy!

Then twenty minutes later –

>>I've done something mad. I've booked 2 tkts to Rome. We leave tomoz at 1 pm.

\>\>No way! U seriously R mad!

\>\>Come on, Foxy. I thought you wanted me to be more spontaneous.

\>\> Not much notice tho. I was melting.

\>\> Just come as you are.

\>\>I'll have to check with work first. See if Raymond agrees. Can't risk losing job.

\>\> G8.U won't regret it!!!

I didn't hear from him for about fifteen minutes, so I texted him –

\>\> Where R u? Raymond said YES!! But only if I work online on location.

\>\> Sorry. Was booking cab & packing. Be at my flat by 10. Love you Foxy. X

\>\> Okay. X I paused, hesitated, then texted: Luv U 2. xx

Forty-five minutes later, his final text pinged through –

\>\> Brilliant, can't wait. X

The next day I arrived at his flat bright and early with my overnight wheelie case in tow. I rang and rang the doorbell, hammered the knocker, but there was no reply. I even opened the letterbox and yelled out his name. My voice lost in the dark, shadowy hallway. Still nothing. Then just as I was about to give up, a twenty-something girl stuck her head out of the first floor window, all wild haired and sleepy.

"Hello there." I used my hand as a visor against the bright autumn sun. "I'm sorry if I disturbed you. I'm looking for your neighbour."

"The bloke who lives in flat 1?"

"Yes, is he in? Only he's not answering the door and we're supposed to be -"

"Are you Courtney?" she cut in.

 HER SECRET

"Audrey," I corrected. "Have you seen him today?"

She rubbed her eyes. "Yeah, earlier, he helped me bring my stuff in. He was leaving as I was moving in. He said that if a lady called Courtney...sorry, I mean Audrey, came looking for him to give her a message."

My heart picked up speed, my mouth was dry. "What message?" Had he changed his mind? Had something happened? Was he ill? I knew he was having severe headaches after his motorcycle accident last September. He was in a coma for weeks. He even claimed he'd died for fifteen minutes and had an out-of-body-experience.

"He just said to tell you that he's sorry."

"Sorry?"

"Yeah, he said he can't do this. He's got to go off alone. Find himself or something."

"What?" I yelled incredulously, taking a clumsy sideward step.

"Well, don't shoot the messenger," she groaned, rolling up a cigarette.

My knees gave. I reached for the black dwarf gate to stop myself from collapsing on to the pavement. A young woman walking her dog stopped, asked if I was okay. The street traffic sounded louder, the wind colder, my surroundings out of focus. "I'm sorry," I managed, heart thumping, thumping, thumping in my ears, my stomach, my chest. "I...er...thank you...um..."

"Georgia." She ran her tongue across the length of her roll-up. "But everyone calls me Georgie." Then her face softened. "Look, Audrey, I know this is none of my business, but you're better off without a bloke like that. I mean, what kind of man dumps his girlfriend through a neighbour he's only just met?"

"Yes," I said faintly, tears stinging the back of my throat. The callous son of a bitch. I hated him with every part of me. "Thank you, Georgia........Georgie."

And I knew in that moment that it was over between us for good. That there was no way back. Ever.

"Sorry, Audrey," Jake's voice throws me out of my reverie. "That was my brother, girlfriend problems." He smooths down his grey waistcoat, "Family, eh?" He gestures towards the brown Chesterfield with his head, hands on his denim-clad trim hips. "Shall we sit there? It'll be more comfy."

"Yes," I agree, following him. "Daniel's been a while, though, hasn't he?" I look at my watch. He's been gone at least fifteen minutes. It's not like him to be rude and discourteous. "I'd better make sure he's okay first."

Daniel's not in his usual spot in the hallway next to the black traditional style radiator, where he claims is the only place he can get a good reception. I follow his voice to Connie's bedroom. My hand is on the doorknob, his voice is in short angry bursts. He doesn't hear me coming in. I stare into his back.

"Yes, well that's not my fault, is it?" he hisses into the phone. "No, that's not what I meant." He exhales loudly, rubbing the back of his neck. "Listen. I…will you just let me speak, for God's sake. I can't just drop everything, you know. I have got a life. No, not yet! Look, I told you. I'll-"

"Daniel?" I mumur.

He spins round, face red, mouth ajar. "Audrey," he gulps.

HER SECRET

CHAPTER 5

DANIEL RUNS HIS TONGUE along his bottom lip, chest heaving, face sheen with sweat. He's loosened his lilac tie and the top two buttons of his shirt are undone. It's not often I see my husband flustered. That person who was on the other end of the phone has done this to him. I take a step forward and he throws a glance at the phone in his hand as if were a grenade.

"We're waiting for you in the lounge." I sidestep Jake's unzipped leather duffle bag, and cross the room. "Who was that?" I ask, trying to curb the suspicious tone in my voice. As a rule, I don't do jealous wife. But there's something unsettling about Daniel's demeanour, something's not quite right. Curling my hand around the brown leather bedstead, my eyes flit to the scarlet throw. It's been folded back to the foot of the bed like they do in posh hotels; the crisp, white bedsheets are sprinkled with rose petals, a couple of deep red scatter cushions rest against the plumped up pillows. I bet Connie and Jake can't wait for us to leave.

"It was Matheus from the Larnaca office," Daniel huffs, blowing hard. I narrow my eyes as he slides his mobile into the back pocket of his tailored grey trousers. An orange light flashes through the window behind him. "I told him not to ring me in the evenings unless it was urgent. These people think that I live and breathe The Theodore Group," he complains, running a hand over cropped golden brown hair. His hair always looks sun kissed. Those regular Cyprus business trips give Daniel a year round suntan, but he still tops it up with a spray tan. I sometimes look like a corpse next to him, especially as I've got such dark features and fair skin.

"Oh, right," I say, beating down a second bout of suspicion. I mustn't jump to any conclusions. He is an active partner in the company. Work doesn't stop at 5.30 on a Tuesday afternoon for Daniel. I know that. This is quite normal. "What did he want? You sounded angry." I glance down at Jake's brown bag again, which looks as if two cats have had a fight in it. A grey towel, an Adidas shower gel and a Fendi shaving bag spill from the opening. There's a name fob with his initials JB embossed in gold hanging off one of the handles. I wonder if Daniel took a peek inside. I wouldn't put it past him. I resist the urge to drop to my knees, tidy everything up and zip it shut, but only just.

"You know those flats we're building, the ones by the seafront?" Daniel's voice averts my attention from the untidy bag. I nod, folding my arms. I remember him telling me about them the other day. Ten luxury two-bedroom apartments, each with an en-suite, in a very sought after area of Protaras. Six have already been sold. "Workmen are behind and the clients are giving him grief." I feel his hand between my shoulder blades as he ushers me back into the warmth of the narrow hallway with its taupe walls and coffee coloured carpet. "I told him I'll sort it out tomorrow morning, there's not much I can do on a Tuesday night is there? Come on, let's not let him spoil a lovely evening. Jake's great, isn't he? What do you think?"

A tinge of suspicion races into the folder marked Daniel in my brain and sits there, staring at me. "I think I really am married to a workhorse," I smile, wanting to believe it.

Back in the lounge, after much protest from Jake, I join Connie in the kitchen for a tidy-up and girlie chat while he and Daniel take

 HER SECRET

to the Chesterfield sofa with a bottle of cognac. Well, I can't expect Jake to cook us a lovely meal AND do all the washing up, can I? Besides, I know that Connie is bursting to talk about Jake.

"Well?" she asks excitedly the moment we're alone. Extending a slender, toned leg, she gives the door a light kick leaving a smear of her footprint on the white surface, several champagne flutes clamped between her fingers. "What do you think?"

I take the glasses from her hands and plunge them into the warm, soapy water. "I think he's lovely, Connie, I really do." And I mean it, despite his earlier probing. He was only trying to be friendly, find out more about his girlfriend's family. There's nothing wrong with showing an interest. I think I was just being a bit paranoid and tetchy.

"I knew you would," Connie says smugly. "I'm SO pleased." Flashing me a dazzling smile, she tells me that she hasn't been this happy in years – he's the best boyfriend she's ever had, takes her to all the swish restaurants, buys her lovely gifts. He spends hours playing games with Lily on his iPad. Lily adores him. They're planning a romantic weekend break away – Barcelona or Rome. They both adore Spanish and Italian food. She couldn't be happier. "Do you think Dad likes him?" she whispers, taking a wet glass from my hand. "They seem to have hit it off, don't you think?"

"Definitely." I grin into the soap suds wondering if I should buy a hat. "Your dad seems very relaxed with him. I think he's smitten, too." Although that might have something to do with the three bottles of wine we just consumed with dinner. Daniel does like him, I can see that, but that doesn't mean I won't get the post-mortem in the back of the cab on the way home. "He's perfect, Connie. I'm so happy for you." We're silent for a few moments, washing and drying side by side, shoulders touching, big grins on our faces, basking in Jake fever. "Will you be bringing him to Tina and Ronan's engagement party on Saturday?

"Y-e-ah, I'll ask him. I haven't had a chance yet, what with work and you guys coming over tonight. They're having it at her place in Palmers Green, you said, right?" She buffs a glass and it squeaks.

I tell her that they are, it's a small affair, they're only inviting about thirty people. Connie wipes the moisture off her forehead with the back of her wrist, careful not to spoil her three inch quiff, which no doubt took ages to perfect. A natural brunette, Connie's very innovative with her shoulder length hair. I never know what to expect each time I see her. Today she's sporting the blonde rock chic look.

"Should be okay, though," she goes on. "That's if Mum doesn't mind having Lily for a sleepover again. It's been every weekend for the last four weeks. Oh, and, oh my God, did Dad tell you?" she enthuses without pausing for a response. "I've got a gig in Cornwall next month. A FILM. The cast is A-MA-ZING! I can't wait." Connie's a musician and songwriter, but she's also a film and T.V extra, waiting for her big break, so this is excellent news. I'm surprised that Daniel didn't tell me. Unlike him to miss an opportunity to sing his daughter's praises. Matheus and the Protaras flats must really be stressing him out.

"That's fantastic, Connie," I say, "Well done."

She nods, eyes bright. "Mum's agreed to have Lily for that whole week, and she's got her tonight, too. So I can't push it." I think you can, I want to say, you've got your parents wrapped around your little finger, but in a good way. She and Lily mean the world to Daniel and Aliki. I sometimes feel a guilty pang of envy at their togetherness, their unit. I wonder what it feels like to be in their world. To be fair, Daniel does his best to include me, at least most of the time, but I can't seem to penetrate their rock hard cocoon.

I don't think I ever will, to be honest. They've got history, haven't they? Something I can never be a part of.

"I'm sure your mum and granny won't mind child-minding Lily. She's a little joy, and so well behaved. Anyway, I bet they can't wait to meet Jake, too." I tip the last glass onto the black plastic drying rail, throwing her a smile.

"Yeah, I've told them all about him, obvs, and I will take him round but....Well, there's just one snag, Aud." Connie's face suddenly darkens and I feel my anxiety antennae emerging. A roar of laughter erupts from the front room followed by a loud exchange of opinions about cars. With a quick glance at her phone she leans her tall, athletic body against the door until it clicks. I'd kill for her abs.

"You okay?"

"Yeah, yeah," she replies, running her tongue along her bottom lip quickly. A clear indication that she isn't, her father has the same habit. "It's just Jake....he...um...I mean, he loves me and everything...."

Ah, there's a 'but' coming on. I can feel it hovering between us. I knew this was all too good to be true. Walking towards her, I dry my hands on a fraying red and white tea towel. I do hope that she's not having second thoughts about Jake. Unlike the rough and ready men she usually dates, he seems like a sensible man – caring, kind, considerate.

"You don't feel the same way? Is that it? Is he moving too fast?" Like your dad, I want to say, because if it is, I know the feeling. Daniel whisked me down the aisle before I could draw breath. "Because if you want to take things a bit slower you should..."

"No," she cuts in briskly. "It's not that. I do love him. A lot. Christ, he's the best thing that's ever happened to me, but..." That ominous *but* again. Rubbing her chin, her eyes flit from me to her green Lanvin converse shoes. I've got an identical pair, Daniel says they look great with skinny jeans. I brush away a fleeting thought of why Daniel insisted we dress up for a clearly informal evening.

"Connie?" I lay a hand on her shoulder and look her in the eye. "You're not worried about what your dad thinks are you? Because if you are I can…"

"Jake's married," she blurts out, and my heart plunges.

CHAPTER 6

CONNIE AND I STARE at each other in silence. I can hear the tap dripping, I didn't turn it off properly - drip, drip, drip, almost in time to my heartbeat.

"Well, say something then." Connie does a little nervous laugh, her green eyes are moist, shiny. She's got to be fucking kidding me.

"You are joking?" I say finally, swallowing back what feels like a golf ball. I expected many things tonight but never, EVER this. Daniel will be mortified.

Shaking her head rapidly, she bites her bottom lip, as sirens start to go off in my head. My image of Jake switching from perfect boyfriend, possibly even marriage material, to lying, cheating, bastard in seconds. Okay, I need to calm down. Jake's married but then so is Ronan. Connie isn't a stupid girl. Jake is going through a divorce, that's all. They've been apart for months. His estranged wife and kids live in the family home and he's moved into a flat nearby, just so that he can see his children, help out.

"But it's over between them, right?" I quiz. Connie mutters something inaudible at the beige tiles of her state-of-the-art galley kitchen, shaking her head no, hands stuffed into the back pockets of her ripped skinny jeans. "Separated?" I ask hopefully.

She jerks her head up then. "Yes," she says quickly. Oh, thank goodness. I feel my muscles relax. At least that's something. "Well, sort of." Her tongue works her bottom lip again. "They're still living together, but they lead separate lives. And once the kids grow up he's going to leave her….and – "

"Oh, Connie, for heavens' sake," I interject loudly.

"Shhh…" Lunging forward, her cold, slim fingers curl around my bare forearm and her oversized silver bangles jangle on her wrist. "Keep your voice down, will you." Jake's laughter mingled with audience cheers from the surround sound TV fills my ears. "They'll hear us."

"How many kids?" I furrow my brows tightly and my head hurts. This is just getting worse.

"Four."

"FOUR?" I yell. At this, she pounces on me and covers my mouth, pushing me against the red gloss cabinet next to the sink. I grab a fistful of her grey top to break my fall and accidently kick the metal bin and it tumbles over and rolls along the floor, and then the door flies open. We stare at Jake, horrified. I know we're both thinking the same thing – how much has he heard and what does he make of his girlfriend gagging her stepmother in the kitchen.

Jake looks incredulous, which is understandable given that we look like we're in the middle of a women's wrestling match. "What's going on?" His eyes flit to the bin by his black trainers.

Connie releases me and I straighten up, panting. We face each other like street fighters, chests heaving, arms outstretched by our sides. I think I'm actually wheezing. She's bloody strong. I quickly regain my poise and tell him that she was just practicing a scene for her upcoming film role in Devon. I often help her with lines and rehearsals. Isn't she brilliant? Convincing? I laugh. Connie backs me up, throwing me a look of admiration. Actually, it may be one of surprise. I must say, I've shocked myself with my quick thinking. Maybe I should go into acting.

Jake's grin reaches his chocolate eyes. Phew, he's bought it. His dark curls shine under the spotlights as he bends down, picks up the bin and returns it to its position in the corner of the kitchen. "We got any more ice, babe?" he asks cheerily, wrenching the AEG black fridge-freezer door. Clearly, he didn't overhear anything.

"Er…yeah, behind the frozen chips." Flicking a strand of hair behind her ear, Connie goes to help him. "Audrey was telling me what a brilliant cook you are and how lucky I am to have found you. Weren't you, Aud?"

I give him a bright, wide smile. One of those false ones that make your face hurt, and his lips twitch. I wonder if he's suspicious. "Audrey?" Connie's voice again. My eyes flick from her to Jake then back again. I don't know what to say. My tongue feels as if it's been numbed with anaesthetic. I'm not going to sing his praises, that's for sure. He's a lying, cheating arsehole who is trying to hurt my family. My hands clench. He can't get away with this. Then as I open my mouth to speak, Connie gives me a warning look and I back down. "Yes," I say finally. "That's exactly what I said. The evening has been very….enlightening." I give him a tight smile. "Thank you, Jake, you're a fabulous cook, but you're not so bad yourself, Connie," I add, unable to allow him all the glory.

"Aww…" He fills a tumbler with ice. "Step-mummy/daughter love. How sweet. I'll give you girls some space." He drops a kiss on Connie's lips, touches my elbow lightly, and ambles out of the kitchen, whistling an unrecognisable tune as if he hasn't a care in the world.

"Four children," I hiss, the moment the door closes.

"What does it matter how many he has?" she hits back quickly, "I've got a child."

"Yes, but you haven't got a husband, have you? How old are they, Connie?" I know she's not my daughter but I suddenly feel very protective towards her and I dread to think how angry Daniel

 HER SECRET

will be. It doesn't bear thinking about. Our lives will be an absolute nightmare. Anyway, I can't just stand by and allow her to make a complete mess of her life with some jerk who plucks his eyebrows and wears eyeliner. No matter how gorgeous or successful he is, or how well he can cook. And, come to think of it, his lips aren't' all that kissable, after all. Mick Jagger's better.

Connie presses her hands against the worktop as if she were about to do a post run stretch, face down, arms outstretched. "The girl is eight, the older boy is six and the twins are toddlers," she pauses, head down. "They're about two, I think."

Jesus Christ. I run a hand over my face. What a mess. "Did you know he was married from the start?" She shakes her head no, and I'm glad. Glad she didn't set out to take another woman's husband. "Right," I start folding a tea towel furiously. "You're going to have to call it a day. You'll get over him, it's only been a few weeks and time's a great healer. I should –"

She jerks her head up. "What? Are you mad? Didn't you just hear what I said? I haven't been this happy in years. I love him. You've seen what he's like. You said yourself he's perfect. How can I give him up?"

"Connie, he's married, he's got a family. He can never be yours… not completely. He belongs to someone else."

Tearing off several kitchen towels, she starts wiping down the ring marked worktop furiously, arms working back and forth, back and forth. "She doesn't love him. All she wants is his money. She doesn't give a toss. And she's mean to the children. That's why he can't leave. He can't leave them in her care. I mean, they don't even have sex, he's in the spare bedroom."

My face burns. I can't believe what I'm hearing. I've always had Connie down as being savvy, streetwise. But obviously I was wrong. "Oh, come off it, Connie, I thought you were smarter than that."

"Oh, fuck! I shouldn't have told you," she snaps, wiping faster. "I thought you of all people would understand." I'm not sure what she means by this but I don't challenge her.

"So, why did you tell me then, hmm?" Because right now I *so* wish she hadn't. I rub my lips, staring at her shoulder blades moving as she works the surface. "You do realise that your dad is going to have a flipping fit, don't you?"

Suddenly she stops wiping and glares at me, green eyes expanding in their sockets. "You can't tell him."

"Connie, I…"

"I mean it, Audrey. Please don't spoil this for me. Promise me."

"You know I can't do that." Daniel and I promised each other when we got married that there'd be no secrets between us. "He's my husband, your father. I can't lie to him."

"But you won't be lying, will you? You'll just be keeping a secret. MY secret." For a moment I feel torn. It must've taken a lot for Connie to confide in me. But if I keep this from Daniel, wouldn't that make me a disloyal wife?

"No," I shake my head. "I'm sorry. I can't….I…"

"Oh, get off your high horse, Mrs Taylor, you're no fucking saint."

A sudden feeling of indignation rips through me. "Don't speak to me like that. I'm trying to help you here."

"Glass houses, Audrey."

Right, that's it. I've heard enough. I feel sick. I hate tonight. I want it to end. I want to go home. I make for the door.

"Don't," she pleads, grabbing my arm. Her fingers are ice-cold against my bare flesh. "I'm sorry I spoke to you like that." We look at each other, saying nothing, as if we're sizing each other up. Daniel laughs in the distance. The whir of the fridge freezer suddenly becomes audible, like a giant wasp buzzing around the kitchen. "Just don't tell Dad. Please," she says in a little voice.

And just then, I feel a bit sorry for her and my shoulders droop. I don't want her to be unhappy, but this relationship will end in tears. It's a no brainer. And if I keep this from Daniel I'd be breaking our 'no more secrets,' promise. My hand is still on the doorknob. "Okay, I won't say anything," I sigh, and she exhales loudly in relief, thanks me, goes to hug me. "But only if you assure me that you'll tell him yourself." Once she tells Daniel, he'll make her see sense. She always listens to him.

Backing away, she shakes head furiously, eyes full of annoyance, and my heart dives. "I can't…" Her voice is thick with emotion. "He'll freak out, you know that." Well, for once I can't say I'd blame him. "He'll confront Jake, he might frighten him off. I can't take that risk."

"Connie, what's all this about?" In my experience married men don't usually want anything to do with their lover's private life, especially their families. I wave a hand at the door. "I'm surprised he agreed to meet us."

She bites on a fingernail. "He didn't. It was my idea, and he made me promise not to tell you guys he's married."

I shake my head. "But why, Connie? Why introduce us to your married lover?"

"Because I want him to be a part of my life. I don't want him to be my dirty…" she falters.

"I'm sorry, Connie, I can't condone an affair." I twist the door handle.

"Okay, you go ahead and tell Dad," she spits, her fury returning. "Spoil it for me and I'll make sure everyone knows about *your* dirty little secret." My stomach clenches. What the hell is she talking about? "In fact, I'll announce it at Tina and Ronan's engagement party on Saturday night. How apt would that be, hmm? It's about time Tina found out what kind of a friend you really are. "

The room darkens. I close the kitchen door, drowning out the soundtrack of voices and laughter.

CHAPTER 7

"WHAT ARE YOU TALKING ABOUT?" I press my back against the door and it closes with a click, panic rising in my chest. There's only one thing it could be. The one thing that I regret more than anything in the world, that I want to highlight and delete, that I still hate myself for.

"You know what." Connie looks away, drawing in her lips, locking in her threatening words.

Taking a step towards her, I raise my hands out as if approaching an armed criminal. I'm going to have to tread carefully. This could ruin a lot of people's lives. "Whatever you think you know," I say trying to control the tremor in my voice, "You're wrong."

"No, Audrey." She opens the fridge door and pulls out some sort of homemade green health drink. I imagine one of Jake's concoctions. They probably drink it together. "I'm not wrong," she replies, holding my gaze.

My heart thumps hard against my ribs . Oh, fucking hell, she knows. I'm certain of it now. I can see it in her eyes. But then how could she? The only people I told were Daniel and Vicky. Daniel swore on his wife's soul that he wouldn't tell anyone, so it definitely wasn't him. And I know that Vicky would never betray me. She's like the sister I never had. We share our deepest, darkest secrets.

"Dad told me," she admits, and I feel my blood run cold. I can't believe what I'm hearing, just when I thought tonight couldn't get any worse she throws me her trump card. Why did I tell Daniel?

Why did I trust him with my secret? I shouldn't have. I should've just kept quiet and boarded the Eurostar train at Gare de Nord station on our way back from a day trip to Paris last November instead of caving in and confessing my infidelity like some sort of desperate, deranged loser who couldn't get a grip. And he'd have been none the wiser and I wouldn't be standing here now feeling like a pathetic fool.

Connie doesn't take her eyes off me as she takes a sip of green stuff. I twist my lips, cogs in my head turning furiously. I could deny it but what good would it do? It's obvious that she knows. So I may as well save myself a lot of heartache and come clean.

"Okay, Connie, I had sex with a married man, too, I messed up." Vicky's meme flashes in front of me; if I could turn back time right now and do things differently, I know, without a shadow of a doubt, I wouldn't have had sex with Ronan on my couch last year.

"But Ronan was..." I close my eyes fleetingly. "IS getting divorced.

My one-night-stand with Ronan was a random act of madness. It happened before I got married and, in my defence, before he started seeing Tina again. They weren't even on a break – they'd been apart for years. Although, he was still married to Catherine. Oh, shit, that just makes it sound worse. What I mean is, he was estranged - we both were. So that cancels it out, doesn't it? Sort of. I can assure you that I don't have sex with my friends' partners. My friends mean the world to me. They're like an extension of my family. Ronan and I....well, it just happened. We were both pissed, upset and estranged.

"Anyway, that part of my life is confidential. Your dad shouldn't have told you. He had no right."

Her top lip curls into a sinister grin. "He didn't. You just did." She takes a large swig of smoothie and swishes it around her mouth, cheeks blowing up intermittently. A bit of green liquid escapes from her red lips in a projectile motion, missing my *Louboutins* by millimetres.

I hone in on the spill by my feet, trying to process everything quickly, hoping, praying, that I misheard. "What?" I gasp. "But you just said…"

"Well, to be fair, Dad told me that you'd slept with *someone,* that's all." She pulls out a yellow pack of disinfectant wipes from the cupboard under the sink. "I guessed the rest."

"But how could……." I feel like such a fucking idiot.

"Look, keep your draws on, Aud." I step out of the way in a daze as she wipes the liquid by my feet. A bit has snuck into the grouting. She'll never get it out of there. "Dad didn't exactly spill the beans willingly. I prized it out of him. I wanted to know why you'd split up after you got back from Paris. Why you turned down his romantic gesture." Daniel proposed to me by the River Seine on his fiftieth birthday last November, but I turned him down. It was too soon. We'd only been going out a few weeks. We hardly knew each other. But I'd also missed a period after Ronan. My head was all over the place. Thankfully, it was a false alarm.

"He wouldn't tell me at first but I know Dad." Connie gets to her feet, face red, soiled wipe in hand. "But I know there's only one thing he won't forgive. Infidelity. He even walked out on a twenty-seven year marriage because of Mum's fling with one of the guys from the Cyprus office. But you know all about that, don't you?" Her foot rides the bin pedal and the manky wipe slopes into an abyss of darkness. I can't believe I've been so stupid. That I walked straight into her trap. It's the wine. I've had too much. "In the end, he confessed, said you'd cheated on him."

"Er..no," I say into her back, following her briskly to the sink. "It wasn't quite like that. Your dad and I weren't together when it

 HER SECRET

happened. We'd split up!" Albeit for twelve hours after a row but still.

"You can paint a pretty picture all you like, but at the end of the day, you had sex with a married man and you were unfaithful to my dad. End of." She pumps hand wash into her palm. "I thought you'd shagged Nick again," she muses, staring out of the window into the darkness. I wish she'd give me a break. "But then I thought, nah." She continues, soaping her hands. "I mean, how you could do it with that arsehole after all he'd put you through? When I started slagging you off, though, Dad put me right." She dries her hands and crosses the room and I follow her like a helpless puppy; heels clicking against the ceramic tiles. "He told me you didn't cop off with Nick - it was with a friend's boyfriend. Audrey, you're such a naughty girl. I didn't think you had it in you."

Jesus, how has she managed to pour her poison onto me? She's the mistress. I've done nothing wrong. I eye the crystal glasses on the drainer longingly. I want to scream, break things.

"No, it wasn't a friend's boyfriend," I growl, "He was her ex at the time. They'd been apart for over eight years. I'd never sleep with a friend's partner, Connie."

"Whatever." She rests her weight on one leg, drying her hands. "Anyway, I've seen the way Ronan looks at you. I reckon he's still got a thing for you."

Now she's just being ridiculous, spiteful. "No, Connie, you're wrong. Ronan's in love with Tina. They're getting married." I don't even know why I even bother to explain, defend myself, because I'm innocent in all this. Well, sort of. "Why did your father tell you all this, anyway?" I ask, feeling hurt by Daniel's betrayal. I know that she asked him, pressed him, even, but he could have lied. It's not as if he's never lied to her before, is it? He kept the identity of her real mother a secret for almost thirty years. What harm could another white lie do? Mind you, we had split up by then. I suppose he felt no loyalty towards me – he was probably still hurting, wanted to punish me.

"Well, because he needed to, of course." Her phone buzzes. She whips it out of her back pocket. "He had to say it out loud," she explains, fingers flying over the screen. I stare at her silver bangles chiming with each movement as Daniel's loud voice filters in through the door. "You broke him, Audrey. He loved you. Why do you think he took you back?"

"I don't know, Connie, you tell me, you're the clever one."

"Because I persuaded him to forgive you. I told him not to throw it all away over a drunken shag." Her smugness makes my blood boil.

"So, I've got you to thank, have I?"

She shrugs her shoulders and snorts. "No, not really. I didn't do it for you. I mean, don't get me wrong, I do like you, when you're not giving me grief, that is. But he was a miserable old sod without you. Flouncing around with a face like a wet weekend. I could see he was pining for you." Circling me, she regards me as if I were some sort of specimen. "I don't know what it is with you, Audrey, but you've somehow got under his skin. He was never like this with Mum." Her face darkens. She and Aliki are close. It must be difficult for her to see her dad happy with someone else. I cut her some slack.

"But what happened with me and Ronan isn't the same, Connie," I wrap my fingers around her wrist. "You're having an affair."

"Then you won't mind Tina knowing." She snatches her hand away, her anger returning. "Your call."

"You wouldn't." I stare into her cold, hard face and I know in an instant that she would. "Just think of the heartache it'd cause. How many people you'd hurt. Including your dad, you know how private he is. Do you really want to air his dirty laundry in public?

 HER SECRET

Humiliate him?" Uncertainty flashes across her face and I feel a slither of hope. I'm reining her in. I stir in a little more Foxy potion for good measure. "And it'd destroy Tina. She might even leave Ronan, the love of her life." She'd certainly never speak to me again, that's for sure. Tina's a bit territorial when it comes to blokes and friends. The two don't mix well with her – ex-boyfriends are completely off limits as far as she's concerned. "Do you really want all that on your conscience?"

"I'll do whatever it takes to protect my relationship with Jake," she says challengingly, cracking her knuckles.

Rubbing my chin, I study her as she opens and closes cabinet doors. Should I take a chance? Call her bluff? Surely, she doesn't mean it. She can't be that cruel. But then Tina will be devastated if she finds out. Our friendship would be over. It'd put a crack on her relationship with Ronan. I don't think she'd ever forgive us. And for what? Half an hour, not even, of drunken, rubbish, forgettable sex on the sofa in my front room.

I sigh loudly, combing a hand through my hair. "Why did you tell me, Connie? Why burden me with this secret?"

She spins round. "I thought I could trust you. I thought you'd understand. You know, because of the Ronan thing."

I stare at her in stunned silence. She can't seriously be comparing an affair with a married man to a one-night-stand. "Ronan had left his wife, Connie, and it was only the once." I swallow hard. "It's not the same thing."

"Oh, I KNOW!" Finally, a bit of sense. "I wanted to tell someone, I suppose. You know, a problem shared."

I take a lungful of herb infused, fishy air. "I don't know what to say to you."

"Just tell me that you won't say anything to Dad or Jake, that's all I ask. Forget I ever mentioned it to you." If only it were that simple.

"You're playing with fire. This will all end in tears."

"It won't. I know what I'm doing. Just promise me."

"You do realise that this is blackmail, don't you?"

"Please, Audrey," she says, voice cracking. "Look, I'm begging you, here."

"They're estranged, you say?"

"Yes!"

I mull it over. Despite everything I do feel a bit sorry for her, besides what choice do I really have?

"Audrey!"

"Okay, okay." I throw my hands up in submission. "You win. I'll keep your secret." I still can't believe that Daniel told Connie I slept with another man. I can't wait to hear what excuse he's going to come up with for betraying me. Even though we'd split up, it'd only been a few days. He obviously couldn't wait to dob me in. It'll be separate bedrooms tonight, that's for sure.

She presses her hands together, closing her eyes. "Thank you." Then she looks at me again, her expression a mixture of horror and confusion. What now, for goodness sake? "You can't tell Dad that you know he told me about you shagging another bloke either."

"What?" I exclaim, startled.

"He made me promise I wouldn't tell you." Brilliant. So not only have I been betrayed by my husband, I can't even have a go at him about it either. She really is something. "Promise me," she barks. I stay silent. "Audrey!"

"I promise," I hiss, furious.

Jesus Christ, as if my life wasn't complicated enough.

 HER SECRET

CHAPTER 8

ON THURSDAY, after wrestling with my conscience for over thirty-six hours, during which I cleaned the flat from top to bottom in the manner of a woman possessed instead of working on ideas for Sam Knight's new website (Raymond said I could work from home until Friday), I convince myself that keeping Connie's secret is the right thing to do.

I mean, Jake and his missus are on the brink of divorce, aren't they? It might happen soon. Absolutely no point in upsetting Daniel. It'll only set off his ulcerative colitis condition. Poor love suffers so badly when he has a flare up. I couldn't put him through it, not when he's been in remission for two months, and you know how I feel about Tina finding out. I'm not going to be responsible for ruining her relationship with Ronan.

So, with a semi-eased conscience, I arrange to meet Vicky at my local coffee haunt. I could do with a bit of respite from all that worrying and overthinking. Not to mention the cleaning, and Vicky could do with a break, too. Looking after three kids during the Easter Holidays in a tiny flat is no mean feat.

"I can't tell you what a relief it is to be getting out of that shithole," Vicky says once she's shrugged off her blue Parka coat and texted my brother; just to let him know where we are and what time she and Florian need picking up, which he stipulated has to be after he's fed the twins and done a bit of work – he's on Easter leave, too, and has tons of marking to get through.

"It won't be for a while yet, Vicks," I explain, breathing in the sweet aroma of freshly baked cakes, which I've promised myself to resist. I struggled to get into my jeans today. Lying flat on the bed, Daniel almost blew a fuse as he zipped me into them this morning. "These things can take up to six weeks to complete, then we'll have to do a bit of work on our new place before we can move in." A lot of work, actually. It needs complete renovation but I don't want to dampen her mood.

"Yes, but still." Vicky curls her glossy tresses behind her ears. She's looking gorgeous, as per, in a black v-neck sweater over a pair of high-waisted blue, skinny jeans and Ugg boots. "Just knowing that we'll be getting out of that pokey flat and the smell of that food. Did George tell you they're making doner now, too? Oooof." She waves a hand in front of her face. "I don't think I'll eat another kebab for as long as I live."

"I don't blame you," I concede, and we both laugh.

I study her face to the hiss of the coffee machine and the clatter of plates as she fills me in with their plans for the flat. There are a few crows' feet around her big, brown eyes when she smiles, which I haven't noticed before, and her vibrant, long, brown hair is threaded with a few strands of silver; pretty normal for a thirty-six-year old. It all quite suits her, actually. Vicky's one of those women who will age well and gracefully (unlike me). I can just imagine her in a sleek grey bob when she's older, just like my mum. Vicky's not big on make-up either. All she's wearing today is a splash of mascara and eyeliner but she still looks stunning – very Angelina Jolie-esque. And there's a calmness about her today that I haven't seen in ages. All traces of her post-natal depression seem to have melted away. I wonder if it's the news of my flat that's perked her up, or if it's something else.

"And I can't wait to get stuck into the gardening. I've been wanting to grow my own veg for years," she says, placing a hand on my arm gently. "It's like a dream come true. I can't tell you how grateful we both are." Her words of gratitude make feel all warm and fuzzy inside, as if I've had a few drinks. I know that I could get double the rent for my flat if I leased it out via an agent but money isn't everything, and knowing that I'm helping my brother and his wife is so rewarding. Family is just as important to me as it is to Daniel. I'd do anything for them.

"So, how are things between you and George?" I whisper, throwing a glance at Florian who's engrossed in a game on his mobile phone. George told me in confidence yesterday afternoon that the counselling sessions her GP set up for her seem to be working, that things between them are slowly getting back to normal. A giant relief, because for a while we all thought their marriage was over. Vicky opens her mouth to speak when the waitress arrives with our coffees and a chocolate sundae for Florian.

"A lot better since we got the news about your flat," she says as the waitress slinks off behind the Gaggia machine. "It'll be a fresh start for us." She tears a yellow sachet and pours it into her cup. I can't stop smiling. Her happiness is contagious.

"Yeah, Auntie," Florian pipes up, digging a long spoon into his dessert. "Your flat is awesome." And a great catchment for good, local schools; another factor my brother and his wife are delighted about.

I scratch the back of Florian's neck, careful not to spoil his new hairdo (shaved at the sides with a big, bouncy quiff at the top). At ten, he's at that age where he wants to look cool and grown-up. He grins at me, spoon in mouth, chocolate sauce at the corners of his lips. "Why, thank you, Florian. It'll be all yours soon."

"But we'll still be able to have sleepovers at your new, big house, right, Auntie? Dad said it's got a garden like a football pitch." Daniel couldn't get away yesterday afternoon, so he gave me the keys and I popped round there with George. It was actually a godsend to get away from Daniel, anyway, because every time he mentioned Jake I wanted to retch. And it was lovely to spend a bit of quality time with my brother, a rarity these days, and, of course, get an unbiased perspective on the property. George loved it as much as I did. It is stunning – lots of potential to build and expand.

Vicky and I exchange wry glances. "Yes, of course you will, my darling," I say to Florian.

"Cool," he beams, one hand spooning the ice cream, the other holding his mobile phone, thumb swiping the screen.

"He adores you, Audrey." Vicky gazes at her son, lips curling into a lopsided grin, and as she crosses her arms on the table, her long fringe escapes from behind her ear and falls onto her face, giving her the look of a sultry catwalk model. My brother is attractive, but he was definitely punching above his weight when he married Vicky. She a natural beauty. It's no wonder the man at the opposite table - strawberry blonde, early-thirties, good-looking in a rugged kind of way, keeps shooting her flirty glances. Not that she's even noticed, she's very humble when it comes to her looks.

"I know how much he loves me," I reply, to the drone of jazzy music. "And I adore him too." I tap Florian on the nose lightly and he twitches. "My favourite boy."

I admit I shouldn't have favourites and I do love the bones of the twins, but I can't help myself. Maybe it's because Florian was the firstborn, or maybe it's because he reminds me of my dad when he smiles.

We both ogle at Florian for a few moments. "What?" he demands, big brown eyes flitting between his phone and us, his frown taut against his young skin.

"Nothhhhing," Vicky whines. "I just love you, that's all." She drops a kiss on her son's head, then looks up, glancing at rugged man - finally. He gives her a bashful, sexy smile, one hand draped over the chair next to him.

"Oh, Mum," Florian exclaims, elbowing her away. "Get off. You're gonna spoil my hair." I can't believe how quickly he's growing up. It feels like only yesterday when I was pushing him to and fro on the park swing as he yelled 'Faster, Auntie, faster.' "Mum, where are my headphones?" he demands, "I can't concentrate with you two yapping all the time." He really is his father's son.

Vicky sorts Florian out with his headphones, then wraps her hands around her coffee cup, cosying up for a girlie chat. "So, how're things? Any juicy goss?" Oh, plenty, I want to say, plenty. I press my fingers firmly against my lips. Connie's affair has given a new meaning to *my lips are sealed.*

"Great," I mumble, fixing my gaze on her small silver heart-shaped pendant that's nestled against her skin.

A wicked grin spreads across Vicky's face. I know that look. She's going to ask me something personal. "Tell me what happened when you told Daniel about Nick," she says conspiratorially, and I frown. "About him being at the party on Saturday?"

Oh shit! My head has been so full of Connie and Jake, I forgot all about that. With a quick grin, I draw the cup to my lips, biding my time, squinting as the sun floods through the shop window. I feel Vicky's eyes on me as I drop a glance at a woman at an adjacent table tapping away on her MacBook, phone next to her white cup and saucer. She has coarse, grey, springy hair, which is jutting from a red scarf tied around her head. She's probably an actor or a screenwriter, there are lots of luvvies living in Muswell Hill. Eyes not leaving the screen, she pushes her bug-style *Prada* sunglasses up the bridge of her nose. Mum has the same pair. Dad bought them for her from Heathrow; she even wears them indoors sometimes, especially in Cyprus.

But Vicky's on to me like shot. "You have told him, haven't you?" Folding her arms, she chews the inside of her bottom lip. I don't answer and her shoulders sag. "Oh, Audrey," she says a little loudly, causing MacBook lady to look up briefly from her screen, annoyed. I shoot her a look – what does she expect? This isn't a frigging library.

"I was going to tell him yesterday," I lie, rubbing my mouth. "But he was in such a rush to get to the office. I didn't get a chance." She gives me a look that says 'nice try.' "I've been too busy," I flounder, avoiding her gaze. Not to mention being preoccupied with Connie's secret. I take a sip of milky coffee whilst I conjure up my next excuse. "I mean, I can't just spring it on him, can I? It has to be the right moment. You know how he feels about my exes, especially Nick."

I fumble with the vinegar bottle on the wooden table. It's been recycled into a vase, housing a single purple tulip, languid and limp. "Besides," I add, "there's something else." She furrows her brows, head inclined. I need to tell her this. I need to tell someone. "Look, I'm not 100% sure about this, but I found a bunch of red tulips on my doorstep the other day when I came in from work. I think they're from Nick."

Vicky's eyes shine. "Oh, my God." She twist the heart pendant between her thumb and finger, as if it's giving her some sort of insightful power. "Are you sure?"

"It's his trademark, he's done it many times before." I take a lungful of coffee infused air and blow it out loudly at the huge globe lights hanging over us like goldfish bowls. "Plus there's that incident with the black 4x4."

"What incident?" She slurps her coffee, MacBook Woman gives her a look.

  HER SECRET

I tell her about the black car, how it was on our tail end when Fearne gave me a lift home from work, and that later that evening I saw it hovering outside my flat.

"But you can't be sure that was Nick, can you? If there was no note, the flowers might've been for Margaret upstairs, and as for the 4x4." She pulls a face, the same expression Florian pulls when he thinks something is weird, and for a moment she morphs into him, even though Florian is the spit of George. "Where would he get a flash car like that from?" she snorts. "He's pot-less, isn't he?"

"Yes, there is that." Chewing my nail, I gaze out at the traffic on Fortis Green Road. "It's just that the whole episode freaked me out a bit." I do a little shiver. "Do you know what I mean? I'm happily married now. I don't want him hanging around me whenever the mood takes him like a bad smell."

Leaning back in her chair, she tuts, says I should put it all behind me and stop being so bloody paranoid, that it's probably all just a coincidence. I should concentrate on my marriage, tell Daniel that Nick is back and that he'll be meeting him for the first time on Saturday. Daniel's a reasonable man, he'll understand, and then, shaking her head, she adds in a headmistress tone, "I can't believe you've known since Tuesday afternoon, that's forty-eight hours. Why didn't you tell him when you first found out? Got it out of the way? Instead of dragging it out and torturing yourself. I know what you're like, Audrey."

"I couldn't," I murmur, pinching my bottom lip between my thumb and index finger. "We were having dinner at Connie's that night, remember?"

She nods. "Oh, yeah." Finally, a bit of compassion. "Well, what about on the way home then?" Oh, Jesus Christ. I wish I'd kept quiet now. I came here to get away from it all. "Or last night? Surely, you could've slipped it into the conversation somehow."

I shake my head no, catching a glimpse of rugged man's jean-clad thigh as he walks past our table. "He was working late last night. By the time he got in I was in bed nursing a headache." I wasn't. I was watching that new BBC thriller on iPlayer that I missed the night before. I say watching but I was just staring at the screen in a daze; worrying about Connie, obsessing about the flowers and the black car outside my flat. In all honesty, I'm surprised that my brain didn't detonate. "And I could barely get a word in on our way home in the taxi," I say. "All he kept going on about was how wonderful Connie's new boyfriend is, how much he reminds him of himself." If only he knew.

"Well, that's brilliant, isn't it?" Vicky smiles. I hesitate, take a sip of lukewarm coffee. A man's voice and a woman's laughter hum in my ears. "Daniel's always so protective of her, isn't he?" she goes on, obviously taking my silence for compliance. "It'll be peace of mind for him, I'm sure." She gives my ankle a light kick under the table. "And for you."

I want to scream that it's far from bloody brilliant. It's a catastrophe waiting to happen. I want to tell her that Connie is now a mistress. That the wonderful, successful Jake who has managed to charm the pants off my clever husband has a family. A wife. Children. FOUR of them. That each night after he sends his lover a goodnight text and brushes his teeth, he climbs into bed next to his prima donna missus and slips into the role of husband and father.

And worse still, I yearn to tell her how Connie has dragged me into her mess, blackmailed me into keeping quiet. I want to confess that when Daniel reached out for me in the darkness last night, I shrivelled into a ball of guilt, wanting to disappear into the denseness of the mattress. That I could barely look at him over breakfast this morning, because I've only been his wife for five

 HER SECRET

minutes and already I've betrayed him.

I look at Vicky and she squints at me fleetingly as she reaches over and wipes Florian's chocolately lips, who in turn vehemently protests – I'm not a kid, leave me alone, you're so embarrassing. I watch as they squabble, her face tight. She knows something's up. I pull my phone out of my bag and look at it absently, as she and Florian continue to rant. Should I tell her? Should I share Connie's secret with Vicky? She is very trustworthy. I tell her most things. Things I don't even tell Louise or Tina. Connie would never know. Vicky might be able to help, give me some advice. She's good at that. I've often thought that she should've been a therapist instead of a PA. I open my mouth to speak when my phone starts pumping out *Super Trouper* in my hand.

"Hello, darling." It's my mum.

"Hi," I trill, mouthing '*It's Mum*,' at Vicky and rolling my eyes. Vicky grins knowingly, raising her eyebrows as she pulls her phone out of her bag. "You, okay? How's sunny Cyprus?"

She coughs a few times before answering. "Darling." Her voice is heavy, throaty. "Thank God I've found you. I've been calling the flat all morning and your mobile's been ringing out." She pauses, takes a loud, catarrhy breath. "Does it ever make its way out of your handbag, dear?"

"Mum!" I warn, "What's wrong? You sound dreadful." Surely, she hasn't caught another virus.

"Oh, Audrey, my darling girl. Please…I…." More heavy breathing followed by loud coughing which almost punctures my eardrum. Jesus, I think she's having an asthma attack. I hope she's got her pump close by.

"Mum? What is it? Are you ill again?"

"Ill?" She laughs incredulously. "Darling, I'm dying."

CHAPTER 9

I CAN'T BELIEVE what Mum has said. I have to grab onto the rim of the dark wooden table, because I feel as if I'm going to faint.

"What?" I exclaim, causing Vicky to look up from her phone. "What's happened, Mum? Are you okay?" Silence. "Have you got your inhaler? Please tell me you haven't lost it." She tells me that her inhaler is right next to her on the bedside table, and instead of relief, acid swishes in my tummy. If it's not her asthma then it must be something far more serious. "Mum!!"

I'm on the edge of my seat now. A middle-aged couple who've just arrived turn and look at me as they shuffle chairs at an adjacent table. MacBook Woman glances up briefly with a tight face. I think I've annoyed her with my shouty voice. But I don't care. Alarming questions race through my mind like greyhounds at Walthamstow Dog Track – what's happening to my mum? Will I ever see her again? Why am I over two-thousand miles away from my parents? Why didn't I try harder to dissuade them from emigrating? I knew it was a bad decision. How will Dad cope if Mum needs care? How quickly can I get a ticket to Larnaca?

"Mum, please say something. Is Dad there? Put him on!"

"No, darling, he's gone to the food market with Mikalakis from next door." More heavy breathing. "I'm just so…so…" Oh, Christ, she sounds as if she's about to pass out.

"Mum, you're really scaring me now. Call an ambulance," I demand in a shaky voice. "What's the number? I'll ring them."

 HER SECRET

Vicky has stopped texting and is looking at me anxiously. I motion to her for a pen and she starts rummaging through her bag frantically. Florian, sensing the tension, pulls the headphones out of his ears.

"No, darling," Mum wails, deafening me. "I don't need an ambulance. I need FOOD!"

I push a hand through my hair and I notice that I've broken out into a sweat. WHAT?"

"Food, dear, food. I'm being starved to death by Maria."

Closing my eyes, I slump back into my seat. Vicky hands me a pen, face ashen, and I shake my head miming, 'It's okay.' The feeling of relief that slithers through me is quickly followed by a sudden urge to hang up. I wish Mum wouldn't do this to me, she knows I worry about them now they're living abroad, especially at their age.

"Oh, for goodness sake, Mum, you had me worried there." I roll my eyes and give Vicky and Florian the thumbs up and they go back to their phones. My mum is such a drama queen. She should've been an actress instead of a travel agent. She'd have made a lot more money from it, probably won a few BAFTAs, too. "What do you mean you're being starved by Maria?" Maria often cooks for my parents. She's housekeeper extraordinaire. In fact, if there were a prize for it, she'd win it every year hands down. Dad loves her moussakas and pasticcios, albeit neither is good for his cholesterol. But Maria has a family of her own, they can't expect her to be their cleaner AND their personal cook. She does have a life outside the Fox's Headquarters.

"I'm fasting, dear. FASTING. Have you ever known me to go without food?" Ah, now that's completely different. Mum is more of a frequent eater than a big eater. She's always munching on something strange-looking and healthy. Dad calls it bird food.

"For heaven's sake, Mum, why? Are you on a diet again?" Mum's a dietitian's dream, she's always on one diet or another. Not so much the slimming kind. Unlike the rest of the Fox clan, she's been blessed with a high metabolism. I've never known her to be overweight. She tends to go for those celebrity health fads. You know, the ones that promise to boost your immune while defying the cruel signs of aging, like kale and amaranth smoothies, or spinach and grasshopper muffins. She'll try anything. And, to dad's annoyance, at any cost.

"No, Audrey, it's not a diet. Aren't you listening? I said I'm fasting."

"For what?"

"For Easter, dear." She inhales deeply.

"Mum, are you smoking again?" No wonder she sounds so catarrhy. "You promised me you'd give up once you moved to Cyprus."

A pause while she blows out the smoke. "It's for medicinal reasons, darling, to calm my nerves. The doctor said it was okay to have the occasional one if it helps." I doubt very much that a doctor told her that. She must've read it in a magazine somewhere back in the eighties. But I'm not going to argue with her. I really don't need the grief.

As she continues to rant about her self-imposed starvation diet, it occurs to me that Easter is this Sunday. "Oh, Mum, it's only for another two days." I suck my lips in and shake my head at Vicky. Florian punches the air and yells, "YES!" Loudly. The middle-aged couple jerk their heads round, MacBooklady jumps, and all I want to do is howl with laughter. Vicky shoots an apologetic smile at them, then reprimands Florian by pressing a finger to her lips and widening her eyes while I give him a sly wink. It's not his fault. That's what happens when you're listening in on your headphones, you lose all sense of sound proportion.

 HER SECRET

"Not over here it isn't," Mum whines, "They're two weeks behind this year. Oh, Audrey, what am I going to do? I can't bear it."

"Mum, why are you fasting?" I hold my head. The Gaggia rumbles in the background, filling the air with a lick of caffeine. "You're not even religious." We never celebrated Easter in the traditional sense. Although Dad would come home with a carload of chocolate eggs and Easter bunnies when we were little, we only ever ventured into a church for a christening or a wedding. The heat must be seriously getting to her.

"When in Rome, Audrey. Besides, Maria has set me a challenge." Oh, no, Mum never backs down from a challenge. She's very competitive. She'll fight it to the bitter end. "I got fed up of her complaining about her Easter fasting. I mean, how hard can it be, darling? And do you know what she said to me? DO YOU?" She doesn't wait for me to answer. "That I wouldn't last a day. ME! Can you believe that?"

"So, how long has it been then?"

"Two days," she groans, taking another lungful of smoke.

"Out of?"

"Seven."

"Oh, Mum, you must be slacking, surely you can go without eating for a few hours a day." Glancing at the giant clock on the wall, I cover the mouthpiece with my hand as mum drones on about it being a vegan diet, that it's not a question of hours of abstinence followed by a feast. "Vicks," I whisper, and she looks up from her phone. "I'm just popping to the loo." I tap my watch, gently remind her that George will be here soon with the twins. "Ask for the bill, will you. I'll pay it when I get back."

Vicky nods, then to the backdrop of Mum's whiney voice – something about what she can and can't eat during Lent, I totter off to the ladies in a hurried, limpish, sticky-out-bottom gait as

MacBook lady and a tall, dark waitress in a tiny black apron, look on sardonically.

"Well, why don't you call it quits then?" I hover over the loo in the dimly lit cubicle, enveloped in the warmth of the wall to wall brown tiles.

"What?" she cries as if I've just asked her to sacrifice one of her grandchildren to save the NHS from privatisation "Quit? Me? Ha! Never. What's that noise, Audrey? Are you outside? Is it raining in drizzly, cold London?" she chuckles. I'm glad to hear her starvation hasn't affected her wry sense of humour.

Much as I love hearing from my mum, she's seriously starting to irritate me now. "Mum, look," I say, flushing the loo. "Have you just rang to tell me about your fasting? I'm out having coffee with Vicky and Florian. George is waiting outside to pick them up. I've got a ton of paperwork to get through this afternoon. I'm going to have to go."

Mum sighs loudly, tells me I've got my father's temper. "Anyway, I just rang to say that your father's done his back in again," she complains as I wave my hands beneath a powerless hand dryer, phone wedged between my shoulder and jaw. "We won't be coming to London next week, after all."

My heart plummets. "Oh, mum," I whine, pulling my sleeve over my hand before unlocking the door. Germs – you can't be too careful. "I was looking forward to seeing you."

"I know. We miss you too, darling. Look, why don't you come to us? It's 25c today and not a cloud in the sky."

To say I'm tempted would be an understatement. I could do with a nice break in the sun, but I doubt Raymond would give me time off work at such short notice. I've got a deadline to meet on Sam Knight's website. "I can't, Mum, work is solid."

She harrumphs and tells me, in a very unconvincing tone, that work comes first. She then quizzes me about our house purchase in Crouch End - she can't wait to see it, it's jolly good of me to offer my flat to my brother and his wife for a pittance, I'm a good girl and got the generosity gene from her side of the family – obviously. We end the call on the promise that she'll reschedule their trip once Dad is fit enough to travel.

Vicky is zipping Florian into his blue hooded Puffa coat as I return to our table, and George is honking the car horn outside. Repeatedly. Picking up the bill, I chuck fifteen quid into the plate. That should cover a good tip as well.

MacBook Woman glances up at us, one eyebrow raised, as we scurry towards the exit. Jesus, hasn't she got a life to be getting on with? At the door I turn back and give her a final glare, lips tight, because it's all I can do to stop myself from poking my tongue out and giving her the V-sign. But she continues to tap, tap, tap on her keyboard, completely unperturbed, no doubt working on some literary political masterpiece that will hit the Sunday Times Bestsellers list the moment it's published and be shortlisted for the Man Booker Prize – and probably win. Then just as I'm about to turn away I catch sight of Vicky's admirer. He gives me a leery gaze and a little wave. Clearly, prepared to give it a go with me now that Vicky's blown him out. He rather reminds me of someone I once went out with, actually. Jack Humphries in Accounts from my first job. We only had a couple of dates but I was completely besotted, often driving past his house with Louise at midnight to check if he was in, if his car was in the drive, if the lights were on. That's considered stalking nowadays, isn't it?

"Just saw your hubby across the road buying you a huge bunch of flowers," Vicky says as I hold the door open, ignoring her admirer who's sliding a hand into a worn out brown leather jacket. "How bloody romantic."

"Daniel?"

"Well, unless you've got any other husbands lurking around," she jokes as traffic hisses in my ears. We're halfway across the road, holding Florian's hand on either side. George has spotted us from his aging Grey Volvo estate parked outside the cinema.

"Are you sure it was him?" Suspicion creeps into my voice. George jumps out of the car, gives me a quick peck on the cheek, asks if we've had a good catch-up, then bundles Florian into the back of the car to the clamour of the twins calling out 'Mummy, Auntie, Flowian,' at the top of their lungs.

"Yeaaah," she says as I rest my hand against the doorframe of the car. "I think I can recognise Daniel. I tried waving but he didn't see me. He had his nose buried in the flowers in his arms. Besides, he double parked his white Audi right outside." She fastens her seatbelt. Josh smacks Florian on the head, ruining his quiff, and Florian retaliates with a loud snarl causing Nathan to wail in distress. "Well, don't look so shocked. I'd be delighted if George surprised me with a lovely bunch of flowers now and again." She gives George a wry sideward glance, the boys are fighting in the back seat. "Stop it now or no PlayStation," Vicky yells. "Or Spongebob DVD when we get home." Ignoring her, they continue to shriek. "I mean it," she says, swinging round in her seat to face them, eyes bulging. And they stop, faces sulky and wet with tears.

"You causing trouble again, sis?" George asks, turning the ignition on. "She'll be asking for a four-bedroom semi in Crouch End next."

"Buying flowers?" I mutter, searching Vicky's face worriedly. "Are you sure?" He never buys me flowers, says they don't last as long as shoes. Vicky must've got it wrong.

"A hundred per cent sure," she grins. "Gorgeous they were, too."

 HER SECRET

"Perhaps they're for a mystery woman," George jokes, and they both howl with laughter.

"Don't be so stupid." I click my tongue as an image of Daniel holding his phone in Connie's bedroom two nights ago flashes into my mind. "He never buys me flowers, that's all."

"Sign of a guilty conscience, then," George laughs, and Vicky slaps him on the arm. "Ouch, that hurt."

"Take no notice, Audrey," she says sternly, giving George the evils, "I'm glad one of us managed to bag a romantic man." And I don't miss the hurt in George's eyes.

"But why now?" I press on, as if Vicky is a prophet and knows everything. And then suddenly it hits me – it was because of the tulips that Nick left for me. Flowers my husband thought I bought for myself. Oh, fucking hell. I feel even worse now. Daniel is buying me flowers and I'm lying to him about his daughter's boyfriend. "I don't deserve them," I hear myself whisper.

"Oh, don't be ridic." Vicky pulls me down and plants a loud kiss on my cheek. Her lips are cold, moist. "It's not the end of the world," she remarks as George taps away on his phone. I bet he's checking the odds on Betfair. George likes a flutter and I'm sure he told me Man-U were playing at home tonight. "You can tell him about Nick and the party when he gets home from the office," she says, clearly thinking that's why I'm so upset. "He's going to have to get used to seeing him now that Tina has asked you and Nick to be a part of their bridal party. I saw quite a bit of Tom when Nancy got married. Church rehearsals, sorting out the seating plan, flowers. You remember Nancy Stewart, don't you?" I nod. Nancy was her best friend at school, got married last year, ironically to a divorce lawyer. "You'll be seeing quite a lot of Nick methinks."

"It's not that…it's just ….I." I want to say that if he knew that I was harbouring his daughter's sordid secret he'd be serving me with divorce papers via Nancy Stewart's husband, not buying me flowers. But I suck my lips in, swallowing the words as the brioche I had this morning stirs in my stomach. I've never been very good at lying. I'm going to have to tell him. Find a way.

"Audrey?" Vicky says. "You okay, love?"

"Oh, come on you two," George complains, slamming the car into gear and revving up the engine. "You've had over two hours of nattering I don't want to get a flipping parking ticket."

I stand up to the babble of goodbyes, air kisses from the kids in the backseat, the fizz of traffic on the street. "Oh, never mind." I smile, wrapping my arms around me. "I'll see you on Saturday at the engagement party, then. Don't be late." Vicky's always late. It's a thing. Always frustrates my punctual brother. And after a few quick parting pleasantries, they're gone, leaving me on the pavement with flowergate and my lethal secret.

CHAPTER 10

THERE'S A SMALL CROWD outside St James' church. I catch a glimpse of people in bright clothing in my peripheral vision as I scurry towards the crossing. I think it might be a christening, or perhaps it's just an Easter service spilling onto the street. A busker in a dark fedora is strumming a familiar tune on his guitar. On a normal day, I'd stop and take in all the atmosphere, search my purse for change. I like giving something back to struggling artists for cheering me up, especially when they're as good as this one. Daniel says I'm a soft touch – a lot of these singers are well off, have days jobs; Connie did a bit of busking years ago, just to play to an audience. I usually ignore his cynicism and make him empty his pockets for change, as well. But I can't stop today. I'm too wound up – Why is Daniel buying me flowers for no reason? Was it really Matheus from the Cyprus office he was arguing with last Tuesday? Is George right, is it a sign of a guilty conscious? What has he done?

I hurry along past Ryman's and onto Muswell Hill Broadway, and then just as I'm tying the belt of my mac into a knot, I get this mad feeling that I'm being followed. I dismiss the thought – who's going to mug me on the high road in broad daylight? I'm being ridiculous, paranoid. But instead of paranoia releasing its grip, it envelopes me, sealing me in its darkness, growing deeper and stronger with each step until I give in, stop, and look back. People are going in all directions, bypassing me. A blonde woman in dark clothing with hair piled on top of her head in a messy bun bustles towards me like a woman on skates. I step out the way to let her pass. We go in the same direction and scuffle a bit on the pavement. I apologise immediately, several times, in fact, even though it's not entirely my fault. Avoiding my gaze, she tuts irritably, then bashes my arm as she walks past and the strap of my bag slides off my shoulder. Why is everyone insistent of winding me up today?

Hesitantly, I give the area one final scan. There's no sign of anyone, or anything suspicious. No sign of Nick or Vicky's leery admirer from the café who reminded me of Jack Humphries from Accounts. Oh, Jesus Christ, no one is following me. I'm being stupid. It's because I'm so stressed out, that holiday in Cyprus is getting more and more appealing by the second. I dash past the coffee merchant, swathed in a mist of caffeine, hands in pockets, head down. I need to get home, pour myself a glass of wine and calm the hell down.

I turn into Queen's Avenue. Almost home, almost there. But instead of feeling comforted by the thought of my warm flat and a chilled glass of white, panic stirs in my stomach. Maybe Daniel hasn't got anything to hide. Maybe he's just being lovely and romantic and kind. I mean, buying your wife flowers isn't a criminal offence, is it? Any woman would give her right arm for a husband as lovely and generous as mine.

My mind is in knots. I can't live with Connie's secret. I can't keep lying to Daniel. I should never have agreed to it. It's too much, and Connie should never have burdened me with it. If, no, *when*, Daniel finds out, because Daniel will find out. Jake's a good actor but Daniel's too clever. He won't be able to pull the wool over his eyes for long. In fact, I wouldn't' be surprised if he's Googling him this very moment from his iPad at the office. And when he finds out the truth, like most protective fathers, he's going to do his flipping nut. I'm actually starting to feel a little frightened.

The junction at Muswell Hill roundabout is unusually busy for a Thursday afternoon. I wait alongside a young girl with her child, hands curled around the handlebar of a worse for wear buggy, fingers covered in gold rings, mobile phone jacked between her ear and jaw. Traffic swishes in my ears. The child whines and squirms in the buggy. I wonder if she's a single mum. If that baby's dad is around or if he's living with another family. If he has a wife tucked away somewhere in a leafy suburb. She glances at me briefly as her dark eyes flit from left to right. I offer her a thin smile but she ignores me and goes back to her conversation. Clearly, her only focal point is the person on the other end of that phone call. Oh, what I'd give for an easy life right now where my only problem was my boyfriend not answering my texts, or something equally trivial. She continues to jabber into the mouthpiece. Loudly. Something about a Tweet he posted and telling him to pack his bags and fuck off.

I secure the strap of my bag on my shoulder as a few more people join us on the crowded pavement, pushing, shoving, impatient to get across. Ahead of me, a crowd of faceless pedestrians morph into a blurry kaleidoscope as I sink back into deep thought. Maybe I should tell Tina about my one-night stand with Ronan. Put an end to all this misery. I'd be free to tell Daniel the truth about Jake, then. But then what if she leaves Ronan? I don't want to break up her relationship. Tina's a good friend. She was even talking about having ginger babies last Tuesday, said she asked Siri about the likelihood of having ginger-haired children if only one parent was a redhead (she's a bottle red, her natural colour is light brown). How could I ruin all that for her? For them? For the future of their ginger-haired mini-mes? I'd never forgive myself.

More pedestrians swamp the pavement like a mass of bees around me. My mobile phone throbs against my side in my bag. Probably Daniel to tell me he's on his way home so that I can get the pasta on. He often does this – especially when he's hungry. I'd better bin those tulips and wash out that vase before he gets in. It's the only one I own and Daniel's flowers will have to take centre stage on the sideboard. But as I reach for my ringing phone a lanky, dark haired young man with a long, sweeping fringe pushes in front of me with an urgency and I lose my grip. The phone drops back into my bag and strops ringing. Great. Why are people so impatient? I look up at the offender, willing him to turn around so that I can give him a look when suddenly I have the sensation of a hand on the small of my back and then I'm falling, falling, falling. Oh my God, I can't stop my gait. I'm off the kerb, hurtling into the traffic. A cacophony of screams, car horns and rubber squealing against tarmac fill my ears. It's all happening so quickly. It feels surreal, like an out-of-body experience, and then whoosh, I'm sucked back onto the pavement like a vacuum. A hand scrunches the clothes on my back, a tight ball in their fist. Not the same hand, this one feels smaller. I can't breathe, the collar of my dress is chocking me.

"Watch it, love," cries a voice as a car zooms by. I backtrack, the hand lets go of my clothes. I try to grab the girl by the sleeve of her black puffa-jacket, but I'm not quick enough and I hit the floor. The pain is instant. Oh, bloody hell, I think I've grazed my left bum cheek and my knee. Her hand is under my elbow, now, and someone else is holding me on the other side. It's lanky long fringe man. He's asking me if I'm okay in a foreign accent, eyes full of concern. I stare at them uselessly like a bewildered OAP on marijuana. What the hell happened? Did someone just try to kill me? I want to thank them, explain, but I'm paralysed with shock. "I…um…I'm…" I'm incoherent.

"Lady, have you got a deff wish or sommfink?" It's the puffa-jacket girl with the buggy and gold rings.

I finally find my voice. "Oh, God. I'm…I'm so sorry…umm… thank you. Both." I straighten up. My hair a mop in my face, knees shaking. I've torn my tights, there's a bit of blood on my knee. I feel a bit disorientated, stupid, embarrassed. The road has cleared now, people are rushing across, some give me curious sideward glances, probably wondering if I'm ill or just pissed. I push my hair off my face and catch my breath.

"Did you see that?" I ask the girl with the gold rings once lovely lanky-long-fringed-man is swallowed into the crowd ahead.

"Er..yeah, you almost walked under a bus," she says in an interrogative tone, as if she's asking a question.

"No, no…." I glance around me wildly. "I think someone pushed me."

The girl looks around, her chunky, gold earrings swing in her dark, shiny, corkscrew curls. Her child is now wailing in the buggy. She quietens him with a dummy and he sucks on it hard, big brown eyes wet and alert with curiosity.

"Um…I don't fink so. There were loads of people trying to cross, babe. Someone might 'ave accidently bumped you. People are so disrespectful these days, init? You okay?"

We walk across. Well, I limp; her hand on my upper arm in case I decide to throw myself under a bus again, I imagine. My knee stings. Ouch.

"Yes, yes, I'm fine now," I lie. I'm going to Google every ache and graze the moment I get home; just in case, because I am a bit of a hypochondriac when it comes down to it. "I was in deep thought, perhaps someone did accidently push me. Thank you for acting so fast." I look at her properly for the first time. She can't be more than twenty-three, kind smile, pretty. And then I feel sick with remorse. This girl, the girl that I was so judgemental about only moments ago has potentially saved my life.

"S'alright," she says, 'I'm used to looking out for people. I'm a carer in the home up the road, part-time, like." I'm not sure how to take this, although I'm sure she means well. "Most of them are housebound, bless 'em."

We pause for a moment on the pavement as she veers the buggy to the left.

"Oh, that must be quite a tough job," I offer as I pick wisps of hair that have stuck to my lip-gloss, knee aching. I want to rub my aching backside but I'm pretending that I'm not hurt – that I'm a toughie, that I took the fall well. I didn't. I ache from top to toe. I hope I haven't broken anything. I feel a bit dizzy and sick, now, too.

"Nah, not really. I love it," she says as her phone starts playing a muffled, tinny reggae tune. My cue to leave.

"Well, okay, thanks again." I smile as the wind throws my hair in my face. It's turned sunny but blowy. "You're a lifesaver. Literally."

She likes this appraisal of herself and gives me a wide, bright grin that reaches her dark eyes, and I notice that she has a jewel in her tooth. "You're welcome, and mind how you go, eh?" She presses the phone to her ear as she heads off down the road. "Ah, hiya, Rach. Yeah..yeah…no, it's all right. I was on the phone to……." Her voice fades like the end of a song as she melts into the crowd. I turn on my heel. I need to get home.

Two hours later, Daniel arrives home, minus the flowers, and in a mood. When I ask where he's been he gets a bit tetchy and I start feeling like a jealous, possessive wife. Where are the flowers? Did he forget them in the car?

"What do you mean?" he says. "I told you this morning that I was going to the gym after work." He didn't, or if he did then I've

 HER SECRET

no recollection of it. Perhaps I am going mad. Daniel is a keep-fit enthusiast, loves running but has also started going to they gym a lot, too. Maybe he did say something and I wasn't listening. I mean, I have got a lot on my mind. I need to chill out – relax. Join a yoga class. I'm sure Daniel said they do classes at the gym and we do have a joint membership at the *Jasmine Blake Leisure Centre,* although I've only ever been there once. I joined him in a spinning class back in January, but ended up not being able to walk for two days and that was the end of that.

"It's just that," I glance at my watch. "You're almost three hours late. Did you go anywhere else?" I'm curious about the flowers. I wonder if George was right, after all, if they were for someone else. But I don't want to ask him. I can't remind him about the tulips right now.

"What is this, twenty questions?" Unzipping his Adidas top, he gives me a little incredulous laugh as he shrugs out of it and chucks it onto the armchair. "What's got into you today?" And then his face softens. "Look, something did happen, actually." I follow him into the kitchen, he yanks the fridge door open and necks the milk straight from the carton. Another one of my pet hates. "I'm sorry, Audrey. I've had a shit day." Oh God, he's found out about Jake. He Googled him like I thought and discovered that he has a wife and four kids. I can just imagine his eyes widening, first with shock, then with indignation as he gazed in horror at Jake's family photo on Facebook. "A client's purchase fell through," he explains. "A big project. It's gonna cost us, and traffic was bloody heaving."

A swirl of relief mixed with disappointment cascades through me. If he knew about Jake, if he'd found out for himself, I wouldn't have to pretend anymore, lie.

"There must be something going on at Alexandra Palace again," he groans. Yes, there is, actually. I read about it the other day in the local paper. A Yoga festival. Tina and I went to it last year, they do classes and everything. It's very popular. That's probably why the Broadway was packed today. I didn't think of that. "And the gym was heaving. I had to wait half an hour to get onto a treadmill. Can you believe that? And now I've got a throbbing headache." He rubs his temple in circular motions. Poor Daniel, migraines must be dreadful. I don't suffer from bad headaches, apart from when I've necked one too many, that is. Hardly ever, these days. Gone are the regular girl's nights out now Tina's shacked up with Ronan, Louise is on night shifts at her new job in Soho and I'm a married woman. These days it's a couple of glasses with my food – very sensible, very grown-up.

"Do you want a couple of painkillers?" I root around in the drawer for some ibuprofen all the while wondering about the flowers. Perhaps Vicky got it wrong. He's not the only man in Muswell Hill who drives a white Audi. The roads are teeming with them. It's a popular car. Besides, he'd have been at the office at that time.

I place a hand on his yellow Nike clad chest as he swallows the tablets. I've had it with secrets and worrying about the future. "Daniel, there's something I need to tell you," I begin, in the tone of a woman about to inform her married lover that she's pregnant. I brace myself. It's now or never.

CHAPTER 11

"WHEN I SAW TINA at Louise's the other day," I say to Daniel. "When she told us about her engagement." My voice is casual, steady. I don't want him to think that this a big deal. "She told me something else, too."

Confusion flashes across Daniel's face, or is it indignation? "Go on."

"Nick's back from travelling," I blurt out, and, before I bottle it, I quickly add. "And he'll be at the party on Saturday." I brace myself for the backlash as he knocks back a glass of water thirstily. He glances down at me with a miniscule frown, his Adams apple bobbing in his neck and I know he's about to go into one – he'll refuse to go, or insist that I don't speak to Nick, slate Tina for agreeing to let him come.

"Oh, okay," he shrugs, wiping his mouth with the back of his wrist. "It'll be nice to meet him."

And now it's my turn to look confused. I stare at him aghast. I mean, I know that exercise releases endorphins but this is a flipping miracle. Maybe I should start going to the gym, too.

"Yes, it would," I say slowly, as if I'm not sure. Has my husband been abducted by aliens and replaced by a perfect replica? "I suppose we'll be seeing more of him now, because of the wedding and everything." I peer at him as he plugs his charger into his phone on the kitchen worktop. I've warned him not to leave it on there, countless times, especially when I'm cooking, but he won't listen. "He's asked him to be his best man." The charger buzzes. It's connected. "I'll probably have to have some contact with him seeing as I'm going to be Tina's maid-of-honour."

"Hmmm." He picks up a Pizza Hut coupon off the top of the microwave and turns it around in his hands, disinterested, as if I'm boring him. I fold my arms, shifting my weight onto one leg, and lower my head so that I can meet his eyes. "I was a bit worried you'd freak out, to be honest."

"Huh?"

"Daniel, have you listened to a word I've said?"

"Of course I have. Nick will be at the party and he's going to be their best man. Why would I freak out about that?" he asks, sounding like he means it. "He's no threat to me. You're taken now, anyway." Taken? I suppose that's a word for it. Available, engaged, and then taken. "We're all adults," he says logically. Goodness, he's taking this a lot better than I expected. A lot. "I mean, you made an effort with Aliki, didn't you?" I've been friends with his ex-wife from the word go. She's very likeable, easy-going, and definitely no longer has an interest in Daniel. But then, unlike Daniel, I'm not really the jealous type. "I'll try to do the same with Nick."

Gratification fizzes with bewilderment and all I can say is, "Thank you." I wish I'd told him sooner now instead of fretting over it for two days. I even practiced what I'd say in front of the bathroom mirror, rehearsed my lines like a script in a play.

I lay my head on his chest. I can hear the beating of his heart, lubdub, lubdub, lubdub. I don't question him about the flowers, not when he's being so lovely. Vicky must've got it wrong, that's all. Or perhaps he bought them to brighten up the office. I've often seen flowers on the shop floor – several long stems in tall, slim, elegant vases on the glass coffee tables with the twisty legs. Who else would he buy flowers for, anyway? There's no way he's seeing

HER SECRET

another woman. Daniel's not like that. It's not in his nature. He's very loyal, noble. I've probably had more lovers than he's had.

His hands slide down to my bottom. "I think someone tried to hurt me today," I say suddenly, feeling the pain under his gentle caress. The moment I got home, I showered and cleaned up my injuries. They looked and felt a lot worse than they were, just a grazed knee and a bruise on my left bum cheek and thigh – nothing broken.

"What?" he exclaims, holding me firmly at arm's length. "Who? Where?" His face tightens, nostrils flare. A cat cries outside. His phone buzzes with a notification.

"As I was crossing the road. I think someone pushed me into the traffic."

And now he has the same look in his eyes that the gold-ringed-girl had when I alleged the same to her – you're being paranoid, dear.

"Are you sure?"

"Yes, I felt a hand on my back on the crowded zebra crossing up the road." I wave a hand in the air as if the crossing is in my living room. "Near Barclay's, then a push."

He sucks his top lip in, eyes searching mine. "Are you sure it wasn't an accident? I mean, I've had impatient people shove into me at that crossing before."

"I dunno." I press my forehead against his chest and close my eyes, inhaling the smell of his sweat and Lynx deodorant. "Probably. I'm so tired, Daniel. I wish I could just go and see my parents in Cyprus. They're not coming over now. Dad's done his back in." He holds me in a bear hug, chin over my head, says I deserve a holiday, I've been overdoing it lately, asks if I'd like him to have a word with Raymond for me. But I can fight my own battles. "No, no, it's fine," I insist, bracing myself for the next question - round

HER SECRET

99

two. "Will Connie be bringing Jake to the party?" I pick at a loose yellow thread on his top, avoiding his eyes.

"Yeah," he sighs, and my stomach clenches. "They do make a great couple, don't they?" I feel a but coming on. "But he's a bit cagey, don't you think?" Didn't I say he'd be onto him? Didn't I?

"Really?" I look up at him, feigning surprise. "You said he was a decent bloke on Tuesday night. That he was a lot like…" I poke his chest, "YOU." My fingers trace his taught torso and trail over his chest and neck; when they reach his mouth he kisses them gently, sending an electric bolt through me.

"Well, he seems to be." He bites my fingers gently and I've a sudden urge to ravish him here and now on the terracotta tiles. It wouldn't be the first time we didn't make it to the bedroom. "I just hope he's sincere, that's all." More biting. "That he's not going to break Connie's heart, you know. She's really fallen for him."

Pulling my hand away, I lay my head back on his chest so that he can't see my face. All thoughts of rampant sex on the kitchen floor vanish. "Did you Google him?"

He laughs twirling my hair through his fingers lightly. "You know me so well."

My eyes widen so much they ache. "And?"

"Have you any idea how many Jake Brown's there are?'

"Hmm…" I murmur. It is a common name. "What did Connie tell you about him?"

He takes a deep breath, my head rises and falls on his chest. "Pretty much what you heard at the dining table – he's got a good job in the City, works hard, that sort of thing. He's half Egyptian, you know." Ah, that explains his dark features and olive skin. "Anyway, she never tells me much about her boyfriends. Thinks I might muscle in and spoil things for her - put them off. Can't say I blame her." That's true. We all know that no man will ever be good enough for Connie. "I mean what man wants an overprotective father-in-law? Well, potential father-in-law."

I feel every hair on my body stand on end. I don't like where this is going. Right now, theoretically, I'm not a liar, am I? I just haven't disclosed the truth about Jake. It's not as if Daniel's asked me and I've lied. I'm protecting him by keeping this to myself. The less he knows, the better. It'll all blow over soon, I'm sure of it. Connie will tire of playing second fiddle to his missus and ditch him.

"What were you two talking about in the kitchen on Tuesday night? She must've told you lots about him then? You were gone ages." Shit. I go rigid in his arms. I knew it. I knew there was a hidden agenda. That's why he was so nice to me about Nick. He's got bigger fish to fry – Jake.

"But you said you liked him?" I remind him, avoiding the question.

"I do." He rocks me gently in his arms. "But no harm in finding out who he is, where he comes from, is there?" He's beginning to sound like a game show host. "He might be gay for all we know."

"Gay?" I ask, unable to curb the shock in my voice. "What makes you say that?"

I peel myself away from him and his hands drop heavily by his sides. "I don't know. It's just something about him. Maybe it's those eyebrows."

"What's wrong with them?"

"They just looked weird. Do you think he plucks them?"

"Lots of men pluck their eyebrows, Daniel, it doesn't mean they're gay."

"I don't," he says sulkily, picking at a fingernail then biting it. "And his eyes, they were strangely dark, and his skin was sparkly. A bit like when you put that stuff on your face."

"Shimmer?"

"Yeah, that's it. I think he was wearing make-up."

I bustle out of the kitchen, grabbing an apple on the way, stomach grinding. He's making me nervous. I want him to stop. "He was sweating, Daniel. Probably because of you!"

He follows me briskly. "But what if he is?"

"Look, there's no way he's gay, Daniel." I buff the apple against my jogging pants hard and fast.

"Bisexual, then."

"No! And even if he is, so what? Connie might be cool with it – she's very open minded."

"So, you do know something then?"

"No, I don't."

"Then how can you be so sure he's not gay and using Connie as a smokescreen? His family must be strict about things like that."

Taking a bite from my apple, I fire up my laptop, anything to avoid his gaze. "I just know," I say through a mouthful of fruit. "Women's instinct." And the fact that he's fathered four children and has two women on the go might be a good indication.

Daniel goes quiet for a few moments and then, "Yes, but don't you think we should look him up on social media? He's bound to be on LinkedIn." He perches on the armrest of the sofa next to me, folding his arms. "There's something not quite right about it all. I can't put my finger on it," he muses into the fireplace.

Scrolling up and down my home page nervously, I swallow back a scream. "Just let them get on with it, will you? Stop meddling."

"Meddling?" he protests, jerking his head back. "I just don't want my daughter to make another mistake, that's all." Picking up the remote, he turns the T.V. on and starts flicking through the channels quickly. "Look, can't you have a word? Fish around for a bit of information at least; do a bit of digging so I can look him up?"

 HER SECRET

"Me?" I screech.I chuck the half eaten apple onto the coffee table; it rolls to the edge and then stops.

"Yes, she talks to you, trusts you." Yeah, only I wish she didn't. He continues babbling on and on about him – Connie's moving too fast. We've only got his word to go on about his background. What if he's broke, jobless, or on drugs?

And then out of nowhere I yell, "Stop it, Daniel, you're stressing me out." He looks at me, gobsmacked. "Connie's an adult, a mother. I'm sure she knows what she's doing. Besides, she won't thank me for interfering."

"But…"

My hands fly up like shields. "Daniel, can we please talk about something else? I've got tons of work to do for this client ahead of tomorrow's meeting and I'm way behind." Raymond has arranged for me to meet Sam Knight, the author and Body Language expert, at Olympia. He's doing a book signing at the Mind Body Spirit Festival. Although he's quite famous in his field, I had no idea who he was until last Friday. I've been given a brief, a description and a profile picture. I'm to meet him for lunch outside the exhibition centre by the railway. And I've no idea how to get there.

Daniel tuts, switches the T.V. off and gets to his feet. "Well, excuse me for being a concerned father."

I run a hand over my face. Oh God. I don't want to fight. I don't blame him for being concerned. He has every right to be. I want to tell him everything. "Daniel." I reach for his hand but he snatches it away.

"I'm going for a shower."

"Daniel…wait." But he's gone.

CHAPTER 12

THE NEXT MORNING, I leave my flat nice and early, giving myself just over two hours to get to my meeting with Sam Knight at Olympia, even though Daniel insisted it'll only take an hour and nine minutes from door to door. He knows the route well, done it loads of times. But you can't be too careful, can you? Besides, I like to keep on top of things. Mum has always praised me for my time-keeping, even as a child. Unlike George, I was always early for school and hardly ever missed a day, even when I was sick. He still managed to get more qualifications than I did, though, a natural academic which lead him into teaching.

I glance at my watch as the train soars towards Shepherd's Bush station, whistling and juddering, rocking the stony-faced commuters from side to side as if they're being hypnotised to whale music. Daniel was right, as per. I've got forty minutes to get from Shepherd's Bush to Olympia and it's only one stop. But I don't care because Raymond will be delighted to hear that I was waiting to greet Sam Knight outside the exhibition centre bright eyed and bushy tailed.

Getting to my feet, I discreetly check myself out in the reflection of the window inhaling the dusty, rubbery smell of the underground, and as the train hisses and squeaks, rocketing into the station, Daniel's face propels into my mind and my stomach clenches. Jesus, I don't deserve a man like him. He was so lovely to me this morning, even made me tea and toast as I was getting ready, without a mention of last night's conversation. And just before he left for the office, suited and booted, he folded me in his arms, wished me luck, told me how much he loved me, how gorgeous I looked in my navy Ted Baker trouser suit and cream flare-sleeved blouse, despite being sleep deprived. It never ceases to amaze me what a bit of concealer can do because I had the night from hell.

Daniel went to bed early, complaining that his migraine was getting worse while I sat in front of a flickering T.V. feeling like Judas. I couldn't even tell you what was on. By the time I climbed into bed next to him he was snoring for England, and I was a little bit relieved because it meant that we didn't have to discuss Connie and Jake again. But that didn't stop the guilt from seeping through every pore of my skin.

Tossing and turning to the backdrop of Daniel's grunting and whistling, thoughts battled in my head like an uncontrollable fire; insistent, burning, asphyxiating. Refusing to be ignored. But then at 4 a.m., twisted in crisp, white bedsheets like an Egyptian Mummy, the fire dwindled, leaving only a whiff of burning guilt behind and everything fell into place. What's the point in trying to fight Connie? She's too headstrong, she'll never listen to me. And who am I to judge other people, anyway? As Connie keeps reminding me, I'm not the relationships police, and I'm hardly a symbol of perfection. Perhaps she and Jake are deeply in love, even though they've only been together five minutes. I mean, how well do I really know Connie, anyway? Maybe she's like her dad, falls in love easily. And maybe Jake and his wife are estranged but living under the same roof for the sake of their children. Fearne told me that Melanie, one of her top clients, has this arrangement with her husband, said they haven't had sex in five years. So it's not as farfetched as it sounds. But if my hunch is right, if Jake is just using Connie, it won't be long until she figures it out and dumps him, and Daniel will be none the wiser. All I have to do is sit tight and wait.

The doors slide open and I step onto the platform, smoothing down my hair. I don't want a hair out of place. It took me forty-five minutes to straighten it to perfection this morning. I even nipped my ear with the straightners as I carefully slid the hot metal plates over each strand. I want to make a good impression on Sam Knight. Show him that I'm a sleek, well-groomed professional with a singed earlobe, but he won't notice that if I let my hair drop over my ear. I want to prove to Raymond that I'm capable of handling clients on my own. It took a bit of persuading to convince him that I didn't need hand-holding from Fearne or smarmy Callum. Besides, I'm tired of being Fearne's side-kick. Don't get me wrong, I love working with her but I want my own client list, and there's a promotion up for grabs with my name on it.

I'm outside Shepherd's Bush station, legs crossed, eyes skimming the area for a public toilet. Why, oh, why did I sip from my Evian bottle the entire journey when I know I've got a bladder the size of a pea? It's much hotter than I expected, too. The sun beats down hard on my face and chest. And oh, bloody hell, the humidity has welded my hair to the back of my neck like Velcro. I root around in my handbag for a tissue and pull out a McDonalds's serviette squashed in the zip compartment. Florian must've stuffed it in there whilst I was busy texting a few weeks ago. He often does that. I once walked around with a Darth Vander figure in my bag for weeks. Gathering my hair in one hand, I twist it forward and wipe the sweat off my neck hurriedly. Oh, God! I feel as if I'm melting. My hair will be RUINED. My weather app did say it'll be 25c today. Why don't I ever listen? But when has it ever been 25c in the middle of April? When? I thought they'd got it wrong. They always get it wrong!

I look around the unfamiliar surroundings like a wolf searching for its next prey, handbag strap over one shoulder, thick laptop strap over the other. It's bustling with shoppers, tourists, commuters, some spilling out onto the fashionable pavement cafes, making the most of the unseasonable hot weather.

I almost cry out with joy when I spot the public toilets ahead of me. But my glee is quickly replaced by a feeling of unease as its tired, magnolia entrance comes into focus, instantly giving me the impression of being sucked into an abyss of germs. I can't do it. I've got a thing about using public lavs. It might have something to do with the retching stench of wee and bleach that greets you at the door and the dread of an empty toilet roll. I know shop loos aren't much better but at least the busy ones are maintained regularly.

Dashing past the loos, my eyes flit from left to right as I make my way along the wide pavement in a hurried, slightly ape-style gait, taking in a colourful swarm of bikes on a tree-lined rack to my left and a fleet of shops to my right. Surely, there must be a fast food chain here somewhere, for goodness sake.

Westfield saves the day. I rush up the escalators of House of Fraser and leg it into the Ladies. I'm in, out, and back into the belting city sun within ten minutes – eyeliner and lipstick reapplied, cheeks dusted with a few strokes of blusher. Even the sweat on the back of my neck has lifted with minimal damage to my hair. Perfect. Thank you God.

Fishing for my ringing phone in my handbag, I make my way towards Shepherd's Bush Railway, anxiety bubbling away in my tummy. I tell myself that it's good anxiety, excitement, that it'll help me perform better. I'm sure I read that somewhere recently, and it had better be true because I can't let nerves get the better of me today. I really need to pull this off with Sam Knight. His appraisal could mean that promotion. A dark haired, faceless woman crosses in front of me and I look up, missing a near collision with a young, bearded, honey skinned man, white cables hanging from his ears, chin down. By the time I find my phone it stops ringing. Typical. Daniel says I should hang it around my neck. Two missed calls from Vicky. Probably about the blinds fitters – she texted earlier wanting to know when they can come round my flat to measure up but I didn't have time to respond. And oh, my dear God. My mother has learnt how to send picture messages on WhatsApp. A photo of a hunk of white crusty bread, olives, and a sliced beef tomato adorn my screen with the caption **FASTING FOOD!** and a fed up emoji. I'm going to have to reply to them later. I can't keep Sam Knight waiting.

I'm on the edge of the pavement about to cross the road when a woman's voice cries out, 'Helen.' I half turn, curling my hair behind my ear, and smile as two women fall into each other's arms, squeeing and giggling, and that's when I spot him and everything slows. I feel as if my heart has stopped beating. He's sitting at a pavement cafe, elbow on table, chin in hand, gazing adoringly at a young woman, their faces almost touching. I take a sharp intake of breath, closing my eyes. Perhaps I've made a mistake. Please let it not be him. Please let it be someone that looks like him – a doppelgänger. I open my eyes and he's still there, flirting, laughing, having a good time.

I can't believe this is happening to me, not today of all days. Today is about Sam Knight. Today is about securing my promotion. Today IS NOT about stressing over flipping blokes! I collapse onto a nearby bench behind a bicycle rack to the cacophony of car horns and the trudge of a bus leaving the station. My mouth is hanging open as if it's been permanently locked with a metal mouth clamp by a dentist that I've pissed off. I should go. Sam Knight is waiting. I'm running out of time. But instead of leaving. Instead of rushing for the train to Olympia. I sit and gaze at them uselessly. I thought I had it all under control but now everything is ruined. Unless I'm jumping to conclusions. Could I be? George says I'm always doing that. Oh, God, make it be a colleague, a friend, even. A billionaire client with houses scattered all over the world and cash stashed in Swiss bank accounts whom he must impress enough to sign on the dotted line.

He's on his feet now, picking up their empty Caffè Nero cups between his two fingers and thumb. When she joins him, he bends slightly and drops a few light kisses on her lips, and my stomach rips. The young woman grins up at him, cups his cheek in her hand and says something before disappearing into the depths of the coffee shop. Disappointment slashes through me like blades.

The lying, cheating, bastard. I get to my feet and take a few tentative steps forward then slide onto a smooth grey stone-block seat in *Colombo* style, just feet away from the coffee shop and I watch in disbelief as he charms the Barista. He's such a smooth operator. I thought that the very first time I clapped eyes on him. I want to punch him. Hard. The barista flutters her eyelashes at him as she reaches for a polystyrene cup. I often ask for a skinny cappuccino to go, even when I'm sitting in, especially during my lunch break, gives me the option to take the coffee away if I have to dash off. It isn't long before he glances in my direction, and then, as expected, his face falls.

CHAPTER 13

"AUDREY, WHAT A SURPRISE!" He's standing in front of me now, face ashen, a gormless smile playing on his lips. I get to my feet and he flicks his eyes to the people rushing past on the street, as if he doesn't want them to hear him, or perhaps he thinks I'm going to make a scene. I suppose he doesn't really know me. I could be highly strung. I could be like one of those women who go on the *Jeremy Kyle show*. I might start screaming, hurling abuse, right here in the street. "What are you doing here?" he asks, swallowing hard. Actually, he doesn't look as attractive as he did the first time I saw him. He looks like a pathetic wimp.

"Maybe, I should be asking you the same question, Jake?" I gesture at the empty seat his companion has just vacated.

"Look, I can explain. Please, just…" He throws a glance over his shoulder quickly, hands out. "Just not here, not now."

I look at my watch. Eighteen minutes to go. I should go. I'll make it if I leave within the next few minutes. A warm wind has picked up, lashing my hair onto my face. "I think now is good." I pull a few strands of hair that've glued to my lip-gloss. "Unless you want me to introduce myself to HER as your girlfriend's step-mum."

"Please, Audrey, don't. She's….she's…." With another glance over his shoulder, he licks his full (unkissable) lips and then the words spill hurriedly from his mouth. "Well, she's my wife."

"Oh, she's your wife is she?" Folding my arms, I shift my weight, balancing my laptop against my hip. Not letting on that I already knew he was married. I want to hear what he has to say for himself. What pathetic excuse he's going to give me. "Only I was under the impression that you were dating Connie? That it was serious between you two. I mean, you were all loved up the other night. I was half expecting a 'save the date' card to fly through my letterbox any day." I don't even try to keep the irony out of my tone.

"A what?" He looks incredulous, as if I've just made a ridiculous joke. "We've only been seeing each other a few weeks." A bolt of anger shoots through my veins.

"Really? Well, maybe you should tell her that, because she seems to think you're soul mates." Connie didn't use those exact words, but it's what she meant. It sounds good, anyway, and I need to pull out all the stops here.

"Look, I like Connie…a lot, actually…but it's…. it's…" He rolls his hand in the air as if trying to summon the right word from the depths of his philandering core. "Complicated," he concludes. I want to laugh at his cliché. I expected more from a clever City boy like him.

I raise an eyebrow expectantly. The breaks of the 237 to Brentford whistle and squeak loudly as it pulls up at the bus stop, its fumes creeping into my lungs. "So, what're your plans exactly, hmm? Divorce her?" I nod in the direction of the coffee shop. "Marry Connie and take on Lily?"

"Are you crazy?" he says, as if I'm barking mad. "I love my wife." Why am I not surprised? This is just what I anticipated.

"And Connie?"

Shoving his hands into the back pockets of his black denim trousers, he exhales loudly, watching me beneath thick, shaped eyebrows. I don't even think he's contrite. I can't believe I felt any compassion for this man – that I gave him the benefit of the doubt, entertained the idea that he could be trapped in a loveless marriage to a witch. "Connie and I have an understanding, Audrey, an agreement." My rage antennae goes from zero to a hundred in nanoseconds. I don't do public scenes but this has broken all my inhibitions. I'm ready to confront his wife.

I go to move and then he says, "Con and I have a good time together. You know?" I want to slap him so hard that my palm will sting for hours afterwards and leave a mark on his cheek. Shaking his head, as though bemused, he squints at the cloudless sky while I stare at his Adam's apple bulging in his throat, fighting the sudden urge to wrap my hands around it. How dare he treat Connie like a whore. "She's fun, vibrant. Sassy."

"Yes, thank you, Jake, I don't want a list of Connie's attributes. I want to know what you're going to do about THIS!"

"Look, she knows the score." Shrugging his shoulders, he gives me a look as if to say it's Connie's fault for sleeping with a married man. "I haven't been leading her on. We –"

But I don't let him finish. "I need to speak to your wife. I think she needs to hear a few home truths." As I make towards Caffé Nero he grabs me by the forearm, stopping my pace. His hand is big, hot. A young couple walking by glance at us as he propels me towards the bus stop, but they don't get involved. They don't even bother looking back. But instead of feeling threatened, all I can think about is the creases and possible sweat marks on the sleeve of my Ted Baker jacket and my looming meeting with Sam Knight.

"Audrey, DON'T. Please!" He lets go of my arm and I straighten my sleeve, regaining my composure. His chocolate eyes are moist, wide. There's a sheen of sweat at his low hairline. He's nervous, scared. But why should I care? He's deceiving my family, making me lie to my husband. I owe him nothing. "She'll leave me this time."

"This time?" I say, shocked, although I'm not quite sure why I'm surprised. My instincts were right from the onset. It was bloody obvious; but sometimes you just believe what you want to believe, don't you, because the alternative is just too painful.

"It was ages ago." His voice is shaky. I bet he's got a string of women on the go. "There was this girl I met at the gym. I took her out for a drink a couple of times. She said she was interested in a life insurance policy." He shakes his head as if she tricked him into bed. "Then she became infatuated. Kept following me around, phoning me on my mobile in the middle of the night. She was stalking me, Audrey!" He pauses, as if waiting for reassurance. I bet he strung her along, too. "Anyway, I managed to convince my wife that nothing was going on between us. But if she finds out about Connie." He runs a hand over his face. "I don't want to break her heart."

"And what about Connie, hmm? What about her heart?" Over his shoulder I catch sight of his wife who's now back at their table, looking around, bewildered. Jake's smart jacket is draped over an empty wooden chair. It isn't long before she clocks us. She's looking over now, on the edge of her seat, curious.

"I care about Connie," he admits. I fold my arms and do a little laugh that comes out like a soprano's aria. "I do! Listen, I'm going to level with you, okay? Cards on the table." He inches closer. I can smell the coffee on his breath. "I lied to Connie about my house. It's a three-bedroom terrace down the road, mortgaged to the hilt. I've got a bit of a habit." My eyes widen. Jesus, he's a cocaine addict. Daniel was right to be suspicious of him. Shit! Why didn't I just tell my husband the truth? What is wrong with me? Has he got Connie hooked, too? Is that why she's been behaving so erratically? Daniel is going to kill me when he finds out I knew all along. "Not drugs," he assures me, somehow sensing my fear, and my shoulders slump a bit. "I like a bit of a flutter, you know." He scratches his cheek and I notice that his fingernails are manicured, something I missed the other night. "Blackjack, a few quid on the gee-gees." And now the sirens go off in my head – flashing blue, red and yellow. Connie has a flat in Bayswater, okay, she's renting, but still. It's plush, prestigious, expensive and funded by her doting father who just happens to be a joint partner in a very successful property development business.

"And your high flying job in the City?" I say sharply, heart thumping against my ribs.

"No, that's true." I feel a pang of relief. Thank goodness, at least he's not after Connie's money. "I work for my brother-in-law. It's his company. David will fire me if he finds out I've been cheating on his sister." He pushes a hand through his thick, dark hair and holds the back of his neck. There's a wet patch under his arm. "Look, I'll cool it a bit with Connie, okay? My wife's already started asking questions. There are only so many fake leads that I can chase after work. She suspects every woman I frigging talk to. It's doing my nut in."

I throw another glance at his wife. She's looking at her phone now, probably killing time on social media, taking a photo of her coffee and using the FridayFeeling hastag. I'm about to look away when a feeling of dread comes out of nowhere and almost floors me.

"Shit," I bark, "I hope she doesn't think that I'm one of your floozies."

"Oh, God, no. She'd never think that. No way."

"What's that supposed to mean?" I yell. "I'm not that bad."

"No, no, no. It's not that. I mean because of your age and that."

"Hey?" I exclaim. How old does he bloody well think I am? "I'm not that much older than you, you know."

"Shit, this isn't coming out right." He closes his eyes briefly, hands out as if calming a feral animal. "Look, you're a very

 HER SECRET

attractive woman, Audrey, but the thought is just....well, weird, what with you being my girlfriend's..." he trails off.

"Just quit while you're ahead, Jake."

There are a few moments of silence and then, "Audrey, she'll kick me out if you tell her. I'll lose my home, my job. I'll never see my kids. Do you really want that on your conscience?" I give a little involuntary twitch. He holds my gaze steadily. I can see his heart beating through his fitted white t-shirt.

His wife is on her feet now – slim, smart in a black wide-legged trouser suit over a turquoise blouse. She must be on a work-break.

He follows my eyes. "Look, I'm begging you," he pleads. "I'll do anything."

It feels odd to have such power and control over Connie's over-confident, and dare I say, smug lover. "Anything?"

"Yes, anything. Name it!"

I throw another glance at his wife. She's strolling towards us. I can hear my heart beating in my ears, louder and louder with each step she takes - boom, boom, boom . I have to think fast on my feet. Connie's never going to give him up, is she? This affair could go on and on and on for years, forever even. What kind of example would that set for Lily? And it'll turn ugly when Daniel finally finds out. He might be fifty-years-old but he's fit, strong, fearless. Connie might take Jake's side if there's a showdown, as girlfriends often do. Daniel could lose his daughter, never see Lily again.

"End it with Connie," I blurt out.

He hesitates for a moment, clearly shocked, his wife is almost within earshot. "Are you serious?" My eyes widen. "Okay, okay," he says quickly.

"Say it!"

"I'll end it, I'll end it. Just keep your voice down will you?"

"Today." Silence. "Jake!"

"Yes, okay, today."

"But you mustn't tell Connie that I told you to end it," I add quickly, and he agrees. I pick at the hard skin around my thumb with the nail of my index finger, throwing glances at his wife, mouth dry. Am I doing the right thing here? This man is taking Connie for a ride but he's also deceiving his wife. If that were me, I'd want to know. Sisterly solidarity weaves through me and stamps its feet heavily on my conscience.

"Jake?" The woman places a hand on his back. "Is everything okay, honey?"

He looks at me imploringly and silently mouths 'Please' before closing his big, brown eyes tight.

"Hey, babe." Swinging round, he gathers her in his arms. "Yeah, everything's cool. You okay?" He rocks her against his hip, almost lifting her off the floor. "The Barista is just prepping our Flat Whites." Flat Whites. Isn't that just a hip name for a white coffee? "You're not due back yet, are you?" He flicks his eyes at his enormous brown watch. I was right about her having a work break, then.

"No, I've got another ten minutes." Her voice is soft, calm, posh. She smiles at me, her big blue eyes taking me in suspiciously. I reckon she's in her early to mid-thirties. Tall, almost as tall as Jake; blonde hair swept off her face and tied back in a ponytail, soft pink lips, silvery bags beneath her eyes, which she's tried to conceal with make-up. A young mum. A tired overworked wife trying to do her best. A far cry from the high-maintenance, materialistic diva that Connie described. About the only thing she's wearing that I know is pricey is a pair of purple cat-eye MK sunglasses that are perched on her head, and that's because I was eyeing up an identical pair in Debenhams during my lunch break last week. I suddenly feel sorry for her. Doesn't she have a right to know that she's married to a two-timing fuck-up?

"Audrey Fox." I offer my hand and she squeezes my fingers in her warm palm. "I mean, Taylor. Audrey Taylor." I still can't get the hang of using my new name.

Bewilderment flickers across her face. "Charlotte Bahar," she says slowly. He was lying about his surname. No wonder Daniel couldn't find him.

Jake looks at me wordless, arms folded, working his index finger along his chin.

"I'm an old client of Mr Bahar's," I say in a croaky voice, and he almost collapses with relief. In fact, I'm surprised he doesn't do a fist pump. I'm sure I see his arm flex a bit. "He sorted out my private pension plan," I lie, feeling awful. A woman holding a takeaway cup bashes into me while she's texting. She looks up briefly, apologises, but I'm glad of the distraction, anything to avoid Charlotte's innocent blue eyes.

Charlotte beams at him, proudly. God, maybe I should quit my job at Blue Media and take up acting. I haven't even got a private pension.

"He's very good, isn't he?" At lying? Yes. She brushes her long, slender fingers against his caramel cheek, and just then the sun catches her big diamond engagement ring nestled against her wedding band and my stomach constricts. "Always looks after his clients. David, my brother, says he's their top advisor." I want to shake her by the shoulders and tell her that her husband's a lying, cheating bastard thats shagging my step-daughter. "I'm not too happy with the long hours, though," she complains, elbow resting on his shoulder. "We hardly ever see him these days and we do miss his cooking. I'm useless in the kitchen." She waves a hand and rolls her eyes. I want to say that so am I, that I serve my poor husband microwave ready-made meals most nights, even though he's been slogging away at the office for twelve hours. Even on days when I'm working from home and have the time. But I don't think sharing mutual shortcomings with Connie's lover's wife is such a good idea. She pokes his strong abs and he pretends it hurts, cries out playfully. "You won't believe what a brilliant cook he is." Er...actually, I will, love, having sampled his culinary skills in his mistress's flat three nights ago. "The kids love his veggie burgers and his couscous Egyptian salad is out of this world. Have you got kids, Audrey?"

"No," I reply, then cough, smile at a woman walking her red cockapoo. This is starting to feel awkward. I want to leave now.

"A husband?"

"No." I throw a nervous reflex smile at an officey looking woman who ignores me. "I mean, yes." Oh shit. I don't know what I'm saying. "But he doesn't cook. Much."

Charlotte inclines her head, puzzlement skittering over her face again; she must think I'm a nutjob, and then she says, "I'm so lucky." Lucky? Ha. I draw my lips in hard, trying to hide the incredulity that rips through me. "Although, he has got an abysmal hobby, haven't you, babe?" Jake's eyebrows rise and fall, eyes shining. Blimey, does she condone his gambling? I bet she's a gambler, too. A poker player. No wonder I can't read her. For a moment I imagine them sitting side by side at a casino, a tower of chips in front of them – cool, calm, sophisticated. "Collecting penalty notice tickets," she laughs loudly. Perhaps she doesn't even know about her husband's addiction. Perhaps she doesn't really know her husband at all. "We've got a stack of them at home," she goes on, "all in dispute. Is the jeep okay where you've parked it?"

"Yeah, course...don't' worry. It won't get towed away."

"Bloody government. They're all scavengers," I offer, clearing my throat. "Do you work around here then, Charlotte?"

"Yeah, just around the corner. Howard Mavis?"

 HER SECRET

"Oh, you're a hairdresser," I say, touching my hair. Result. Now I've got a bit of insurance in case Jake goes back on his word.

"Been there years. Love it. You should come in some time," she offers, and Jake's face darkens. "I give friends a 20% discount."

"I'll bear it in mind. Thanks. Anyway." I point towards the railway station, adjusting the strap of my laptop bag that's making ridges in my shoulder. "I've got a meeting to get to. It's been a pleasure meeting you, Charlotte. And don't forget about that amendment on my pension plan, Jake," I add firmly. "If you could sort that out for me as soon as, please."

"Yes, of course, Audrey." A bus horn beeps, wind and traffic hound in my ears. "I'll do it as soon as I get back. Just leave it to me," he says with a conspiratorial wink.

I watch as he almost frogmarches Charlotte back to their table while she yells at me over her shoulder – "It was lovely meeting you too, and if you ever need any more financial advice...or a haircut..."

Six minutes later I arrive at the platform in a fluster, jacket over forearm, bag straps weighing me down like an overworked milkmaid. That confrontation with Jake has shaken me. It's 1203. I've got ten minutes left, but it's only one stop away. Glancing up at the passenger information screen, I'm relieved to see that the train is due in two minutes. I should make it just in the nick of time. Talk about cutting it fine.

I take a seat on a plastic red bench next to a smartly dressed young woman, her hand curled around a large smartphone. I bet she doesn't do any housework with those red varnished two-inch fingernails. I wonder if she varnished them herself, or went to one of those nail bars. The one near me is always choc-a-block. Jess, Louise's daughter, is a regular there. I run my thumb over my short, neat ones. Perhaps I should've varnished them for Sam Knight, especially as he'll be looking at my hands whilst I show him proofs of his website on my laptop. The young woman must sense my gaze because she looks up at me briefly from her phone and smiles, red lipstick vibrant against her dark skin. Taking advantage of her kindness, I ask if the next train is going to Olympia. Just to be a hundred percent sure.

"Kensington? Yes," she confirms, and I relax a little, tell her that I've a meeting in nine minutes. "I've got to be somewhere in fifteen, too."

We grin at each other complacently as we sit side by side in girl-power unison on the hard red plastic bench like a couple of contestants on *The Apprentice* waiting for Lord Sugar to call us in.

The sun is belting down on my head like a blazing rod. I'm going to get sunstroke at this rate. I should've smothered my face in Factor 50 sunscreen this morning instead of flawless foundation. I coat my dry mouth with a large gulp from my Evian bottle, then as I glance up at the destination screen, I almost spit out the entire mouthful. I blink, just to make sure I've read it right – *'Train Cancelled. Next train 1236.'* Surely, there must be some mistake. This can't be happening. The system must be on the blink. Any moment now the LCD panel will flash with the scheduled time. I turn to the girl with the long red fingernails for clarification.

"Yeah, it's been cancelled." She bites on her bottom lip thoughtfully, knotting her drawn-in arched eyebrows. Fear floods my stomach, mounting into my chest. I think I'm going to be sick. I half stand, panic stricken, cranky, yelling that I've got a meeting with an important client as if it were the red-long-fingernailed-girl's fault; and then, in a stressy voice, I ask her if Olympia is within walking distance. "Yeah, if you go through the houses via the shopping centre you could get there in ten minutes, if you hurry."

HER SECRET

I don't need telling twice. Tearing through the station, I'm onto the high street and into the shopping centre like a whippet on speed. Thank God I wore my black Prada pumps, a Christmas gift from Daniel. I flap up and down the shopping centre looking for the promised exit. Defeated, I accost a curly haired blonde man selling charity subscriptions for directions. Big mistake.

"Which exhibition centre do you want? There are two Olympia's. Olympia Exhibition Centre and Earl's Court."

What the fuck is he talking about? "Olympia! I need to get to Olympia and fast. I'm late for a meeting."

But as the words float from my lips to his ears they seem to metaphor into, *I've got all the time in the world*. He pulls his mobile phone from the breast pocket of his yellow polo top, says he'll find the directions on Google Maps. I tap my foot irritably as he moans about the slow connection, tells me how he's going to change his network when his contract expires in eight months.

"Waaaaaait," he cries into my back, "I've found it."

Outside, I stop a few passers-by, beg them for directions, and another five minutes flutter by. I wish that people who didn't know where a location was would just say so instead of pretending to be a top of the range human SatNav and sending me on a wild goose chase.

I rush up and down the street in a half walk, half jog pace, heart pumping, traffic screaming in my ears, hair flying around in the smoggy wind. Sweat pours down my back, my face, my cleavage. I'm officially five minutes late. Shit, shit, shit! Raymond is going to fucking kill me. Callum will have a field day with me when I get back to the office this afternoon. It'd make his day to see me fired.

I finally find a sweet Oriental lady with kind eyes and sensible shoes. "I'm on my way there now," she says warmly as my phone starts bleeping and ringing in my Birkin. "Follow me."

A ten minute walk, the long-red-fingernailed girl had said. Ten minutes! Perhaps she mistook me for an Olympic sprinter. Twenty minutes later I arrive at Exhibition Centre looking like an out of breath Flora marathon dropout with sunburn, and Sam Knight is nowhere to be seen.

CHAPTER 14

ON SATURDAY I wake up in my flat alone. I make myself a strong cup of coffee then fill the bath with hot water adding a splash of L'Occitane Lavande foaming bath that Jess bought me last Christmas. In a way, I'm glad I've got the day to myself, gives me time to prepare for Tina and Ronan's engagement party tonight, both physically and mentally. I know it won't be easy being in the same room as my ex after everything that's happened. I can't imagine what I'm going to say to him about the flowers he left on my doorstep, or what pathetic excuse he's going to give me for being such a twat. I just hope that Daniel turns up early as promised, he knows how much it means to me to have him by my side today.

Daniel drove me home from Connie's yesterday evening, then returned to spend the night with her. Jake had dumped her. Someone had to look after her, he said, make sure she didn't do anything stupid. She wouldn't, of course. Connie's as tough as old boots. But the fact that he mentioned it planted an unwanted seed of terror in my mind and I started to question my actions. But I did the right thing, didn't I?

"I'm glad she's not seeing him anymore, Audrey," Daniel seethed as he shoved stuff into his overnight bag, jaw throbbing. "I knew he was a shifty little shit. What kind of man dumps his girlfriend by WhatsApp, hmm?" My blood ran cold. I really didn't expect that. What a monster. I thought he'd have the decency to tell her face to face, or at least phone her, let her down gently. "Just wait until I get my hands on him." He zipped the bag angrily, as if it were Jake's throat, and I wondered then if Connie had told him that he was married, had children.

"Did he give her a reason?" I croaked, rubbing the back of my neck anxiously.

"Just that it's all moving too fast and he's not ready for commitment." I've got to tell him, I thought, confess that I put Jake up to it because I'd found out he's married. He'll understand. Thank me, even. I opened my mouth to speak and then he said, "No one hurts my daughter, no matter what." I took a step back; not because I was frightened but because I was a bit shocked. I know he's a doting father and expected him to be upset that his daughter had been ditched, but this was a bit much. "The shitting prick!" he barked. "If he ever shows his face around here again I'll…" And just then my knees gave a little and I sat on the bed heavily. "Oh, darling, are you okay?" Daniel rushed over and cuddled me; the smell of his freshly spritzed spicy cologne filled my nostrils and I sneezed, and then I began to sob lightly on his shoulder, feeling like a fake. "The last twenty-four hours have been hell, haven't they? First you lose your client and now this. I can't believe…"

He babbled on and on but I wasn't listening. The cogs in my mind were turning, faster and faster and faster – What if I didn't do the right thing? What if the distress causes Connie to become depressed? Jesus, she might need to go on antidepressants, might not be able to work. What if I've ruined her acting career? What did Daniel mean when he said he had to make sure she didn't do anything stupid? Oh, God, what if she takes an overdose?

"But she will be all right, won't she?" I jerked my head up and looked at his worried face, imagining Connie knocking back a handful of pills with a quart of vodka; Daniel finding her just in time, and then Aliki holding her hair back as she vomited violently into the loo.

"Yes, of course, she's a Taylor," he said, sounding as convincing as a local councillor pitching for our vote by promising that 9 million of our tax money will go straight into the NHS.

"But you said you wanted to make sure she didn't do anything stupid." My voice was trembling. He squeezed my hand.

"Yeah," he said, looking puzzled. "Like go running to him, beg him to take her back. What did you think I meant?

I step into the soapy, scented, warm water, now, to the milieu of children's voices, laughing, playing, giggling in the garden next door. Above me, the ceiling creaks, then Alan's voice bellows from the window, calling Mr. Gingernut to come inside, his voice shrinking as a motorcycle revs up in the street. Just another normal Saturday afternoon outside. Leaning my head back, I breathe in the scent of lavender as I gaze vacantly at the opaque steamy window while yesterday's events loop in my mind.

Raymond was furious when I returned to work after losing Sam Knight at *Olympia*. I know, how can you lose a person, right? But I had to feed him that lie. I had to say that I was waiting at the wrong entrance because if I'd told him the truth, if I admitted that I was running late because of a domestic crisis and then the train was cancelled, he'd have sacked me on the spot. Just like he did to Naomi, our PR girl, last January when she forgot to contact a client about his renewal. Poor Naomi. She'd only been with us a short while. She was devastated.

"My office, Audrey," Raymond snapped, as he stormed past my desk in his brown, tweed, three-piece-suit and pink bow tie. "Now."

My heart thumped so hard as I trotted behind him in my black *Prada* pumps, that I'm surprised it didn't protrude from my chest in the style of Stanley Ipkiss in *The Mask*, and knock Stacy out as she gawped at me at reception, phone in hand. Swallowing hard, I closed the door behind me giving Fearne a gormless, pleading smile as she watched in disbelief from the coffee machine, mouth agape, while Callum sniggered in delight behind her. Fearne's sympathy was almost tangible, bless her, she's always got my back.

As you've probably guessed, Sam Knight got fed up of waiting for me in the midday heat, and when I didn't bother answering my phone or replying to any of his text messages, he got the hump and buggered off. And who could blame him? I'd have done exactly the same in his shoes.

"Your first solo assignment, Audrey, and you screw up." Raymond's voice almost ruptured my skull. I actually felt the pain in my eardrums. "You're lucky Sam Knight is a decent bloke or we'd have lost this contract." A bit of spittle shot from his mouth and landed on my upper lip. I cringed but I was too scared to move.

Fearne, seeing my distress through the glass partition, was at my side like a greyhound. She pleaded my case to Raymond like a top defence lawyer, told him how well I was doing on this project, how invaluable my input has been. Explained that it wasn't my fault that I was waiting at the wrong entrance, said she didn't brief me properly, shouldered some of the blame. It did the trick, Raymond softened and gave me another chance. I think he's got a soft spot for Fearne. Or they've got history. Or both.

"One more fuck-up and you're out, Audrey," he spat, pushing his square rimmed glasses up the bridge of his nose, nostrils flaring, face red with rage. "Now get out of my sight."

Raymond is a lovely boss generally but goes all tight clothed and greenish (in the style of *The Incredible Hulk*) when angry,

  HER SECRET

which to be fair, isn't that often. And I did mess up. Big time. I eye my phone next to me on the wooden stall longingly. I should send Raymond a Whatsapp message, really, apologise again and thank him for being so understanding. He'll like that. The others do it when he gets cross with them – Fearne told me.

I dry my hands, pick up my iPhone and run a purple face towel over the steamy screen. Once I locate RayBoss in Chats, I activate speaker and dictate my message, then just as I'm about to close the app, I appear on the screen in nothing but my green face mask and shower cap. I sit up, water sploshes everywhere. Oh, my God, what's happening? What have I done? Have I accidently activated the camera? It's all such a blur. Oh, shit, the fucking thing is RINGING! Oh, flipping hell! I've got to end the call before he answers, and then just as I get my bearings Raymond's smiling face fills the screen. And now Raymond can see me stark bollock naked.

"Aaaaah, AAAARRRH…. I'm….I'm…I can't…" I stare at Raymond's face in horror. Where have the fucking controls gone? How do I end the call? I think I'm going to wee myself.

"Audrey, is that you?"

"Raymond, I'm sorry. I can't fucking switch the fucking thing off. Aaaaaaah!" I'm hysterical now. "Raymond, don't look at me. Oh, fucking hell!" I can't stop screaming and swearing. It's as if I've suddenly developed some sort of Tourette's. I think Raymond is saying something else now but his voice is distorted. I look at my naked image in a little box on the right hand side of the screen and I want to DIE. This can't be happening to me. Oh, God, please make it stop. Water is splashing everywhere; Raymond has now moved out of sight. I can just make out a cornice and the top of his head. I imagine that the last thing he expected on Saturday morning was a videocall from me in the fucking buff. The poor man must be traumatised. And then as I fumble with the phone in my water wrinkled, trembling hands, the controls appear and I quickly press the red circle – call ended.

Still holding onto the phone, I press my forearms against the bathtub, panting, trying to process what just happened. My heart is lashing in my chest. I think I'm going to faint. I can't breathe. I'm burning up. Oh, fucking hell! Raymond has seen me naked. I chuck my phone onto the wooden stool as if it's riddled with an infectious disease. I have actually sent my boss obscene images of myself, that's a sackable offense, isn't it? That's it, now, the end of my short career as a web designer. I want to cry. In fact, I'm certain that I'm going to need counselling sessions once I'm sacked. And just then my phone buzzes and lights up with a WhatsApp message.

RayBoss: Don't worry, Audrey. Easy mistake to make – done it myself, only I was fully clothed. See you Monday. Have a great weekend. And thanks for getting in touch. And an emoji smile.

"Oh, thank you Lord," I say at the ceiling. Naturally, I won't be able to ever look Raymond in the eye again but at least I've still got my job. I tilt my head back, arms hanging over the bathtub, phone in hand, as my heart slowly regains its natural symmetry. Jesus, I'm such a klutz. Still, it could've been worse, it could've been Callum. And the image was a bit distorted, maybe he couldn't see me properly.

The sound of chairs whine against the ceiling. Alan and Margaret must be sitting down for lunch. I haven't eaten a thing since last night but I'm not even hungry, especially not now that Raymond has seen me starkers. I bet he thinks I'm a bloody nutjob. I caress the silver taps with my toes, pushing the image of Raymond's face out of my mind and replacing it with Daniel's.

Why hasn't he returned my last two texts? I hope everything is all right. I hope they both turn up at the party as promised. It was his suggestion that Connie comes along, too, said that it'll be good for her to get out, mingle. Aliki said she'd have Lily for the night. And anyway, Tina did invite her, albeit with a plus-one. I sit up and the water sloshes around me. I'm being silly. Of course, they'll turn up, he'd have said if anything was wrong.

I dry myself off in front of a misty mirror, the humiliation of exposing myself to my boss taking a back seat to the self-doubt that is now trickling over my skin. Okay, I was expecting Connie to be upset, of course, but not to this extent. I mean, bloody hell! They'd only been together a few weeks and Jake IS married. There was no future for them. He as good as told me so himself. But dumping her by WhatsApp, really? What was that all about? I know Nick did a runner the second time around, which is much worse, I suppose, but at least he broke off our engagement face to face. The pain of being dumped shoots along my spine as Nick's face flashes in my mind. I can still taste the sourness of rejection as I stood outside his flat with my suitcase last December, almost as if it'd only just happened. It's an ache that bores through your skin and makes a hairline crack on your heart. One you have to carry around with you forever, I think. A bit like an unwanted tattoo. And, sadly, I'm going to see my unwanted tattoo in a few hours. So I'd better get a wiggle on.

CHAPTER 15

WHAT I LOVE about Tina's flat in Palmers Green is the ample free parking. Louise, Jess and I are the first to arrive. It's another warmish afternoon. It's hard to believe that it'll be chucking it down in an hour or two, according to my weather app. But, as my mother reminded me earlier today when she called to see how I was (the real reason was to remind me to ignore Nick at the party), "You can have summer, spring and winter all in one day in the U.K, darling. Get that gorgeous husband of yours and move over to Cyprus with us."

I glance at the clock in the dining room – 5.30. We've got an hour to help Tina and Ronan with the finishing touches before the guests start pouring in. The smell of freshly baked pastry makes my tummy rumble as I arrange a platter of food on the table. I only managed to wolf down a banana after exposing myself to my boss via WhatsApp, and can't wait to tuck into all this lovely grub.

Louise prepared everything at home, to save on time, and we transported it all in our cars in large silver domes – just puff pastry canapés, finger-food, that sort of thing, which she's now cooking in Tina's kitchen.

"You're fine about Nick being here, aren't you, love?" Ronan says quietly in a conspiratorial tone, placing a tray of mini olive pastries onto the busy table. Ronan has this air about him, a charisma that makes you feel completely at ease. We're so relaxed around each other, you'd never think we'd been intimate, that we

HER SECRET

share a shameful secret. I think that in another life he must've been a Tibetan monk.

Buffing a champagne flute, I hold it up to the light for inspection to the soundtrack of metal hitting the ground in the kitchen. It rattles to a halt in unison with Louise's voice yelling at Jess to be careful, that they're not in their own home and she'll have to pay for any breakages, which I must admit, is a bit harsh. Poor Jess. What other nineteen-year-old would give up her Saturday evening to help out in a sweaty kitchen?

I place the gleaming flute next to the others in the centre of the table by the ice bucket. "Sure, Ronan," I say with a tiny frown, my tone depicting, '*Why wouldn't I be?*' "That chapter of my life is over. I'm happy now." He gives me one of his cheeky smiles, face red, blue eyes twinkling. I think he's had a few already.

"That's grand, Audrey," he grins, running a hand over his cropped ginger hair that matches his designer stubble. He looks smart today in a white cotton shirt done up to the top, no tie, and navy DKNY blue suit (I saw the label on the inside of his jacket earlier when he was up on the ladder fitting the bunting). He's always been a snazzy dresser and is as fond of shoes as I am. His smart tan brogues look new and expensive, no doubt designer.

"Because…" he goes on, then pauses, grabs a champagne flute from the tray, unscrews a bottle of whiskey and splashes two inches of the golden liquid into the glass.

"Because?" I ask as he necks the drink in one. I wonder why he's so nervous. I hope he isn't having second thoughts.

"Well, because…." His pungent whiskey breath almost knocks me out as he inches closer.

And then just as he's about to speak a voice cries, "Audrey, babe." Jess is at my side looking gorgeous and gothic in a pair of black wool shorts and black short sleeved sweater, long limbs covered in black tights, glass of red in hand. "All right, Ronan?" She gives him a quick, polite grin. "Mum wants you in the kitchen, pronto." And before I can utter a word, she drags me by the sleeve of my cream cashmere cardigan, which I've worn over a pink and black illusion dress (to make me look thinner) and teamed with the black *Louboutins* that Daniel bought me the other day.

"Why didn't you return my calls last night?" Jess hisses in the dark corridor to the backdrop of Ronan whistling an unrecognisable tune. I think it's an Irish folk song. He sounds happy – a good sign. "I must've called you a dozen times." I got two missed calls from Jess on our way home from Connie's. She likes to exaggerate.

"I was driving," I lie, not letting on that I could barely hear the phone ring over Daniel's ranting. "And then, I'm sorry, but I fell asleep." I hiss back defensively, although I'm not quite sure why. I did read in Sam Knight's body language report that you mirror people that you like, and I do love Jess as if she were my own. "Why didn't you leave a voice message, anyway?"

Her lips tighten. "Because," she says through gritted teeth. "It's CONFIDENTIAL." She clasps my hand, scans the corridor, then quietly twists the latch and leads me outside, leaving the door open a crack behind her.

"You can smoke those indoors, you know." I nod at the Vapour cigarette in her fist as I straighten my sleeve, feeling slightly discombobulated by the sudden commotion. "Besides, I think it's a smoke zone area in there tonight." Ronan smokes like a chimney.

"Yeah, but Mum doesn't know I smoke these, reckons they're just as bad a habit as smoking fags, even though a report said that Vaping is 95% safer than smoking cigarettes. You know what she's like. And have you changed your makeup?" Her eyes flick over my face quickly. I tell her that I haven't. I've been wearing the same makeup for years. "Oh, you look different. Anyway, what was I saying? Oh, yeah. It's about Connie. She rang me last night."

"Connie?" A shot of acid swishes in my stomach. I know that she and Jess exchange Christmas and birthday texts, but didn't realise they kept in touch. "I didn't think you two were mates."

"We're not really. We only text on birthdays usually. But I messaged her last week about TV extra work. I need some dosh to help me get by until I finish uni. She gave me some tips and the name of her agent."

"Oh, right. Is that what she called you about, a job?"

"NO!" She takes a drag on her Vapour cigarette then blows an enormous cloud of minty mist in my face. I can barely see her "It was about her bloke. Well, her ex. You know that Jake dumped her by WhatsApp yesterday, right?" I nod quickly, waving the mist away. "Look, I shouldn't really be telling you this but I think he's married."

"Married?" I snap and she jumps. Shit. Jess is a clever girl, but surely she couldn't have guessed?

"Okay, I know he is. But PLEASE don't say anything. She made me promise not to tell." My stomach burns. So Connie didn't just confide in me, after all. Brilliant. If only Jess had told me all this before. "She rang me last night crying her eyes out – she was like manic. She wanted me and Sky to pick her up.

"Sky? I thought you two had split up."

"Yeah, but it's back on again," she drones, running a finger under her statement fringe, forgetting Connie for a moment. "Where was I? Oh, yeah." Her face is serious again. "You know Sky's got a car, don't you?" She doesn't wait for me to answer. "Just a second-hand battered Skoda. Anyway, she wanted us to take her to Jake's house to confront him and his wife!" Her words chill me to the bone. Daniel was right to think she'd go after him. He knows his daughter so well. "She was swearing and everything. She's a feisty thing, isn't she?"

My hand shoots to my chest in horror. "Jesus," I gulp.

"I know." She takes another lug of minty smoke, eyes wide.

"What time was this?"

"About ten past nine. I called you straight away." Shit, that was just after we left. Why didn't I pick up the damned phone?

"And then what happened?"

"I told her that we were out drinking and left the car at home. It was a lie, obvs, but I had to say something. Sky said not to get involved, wife might be a nutter."

"You did the right thing, Jess." I rub her back. "Thank you. And I'm sorry....sorry she involved you in all this…sorry I didn't return your calls. It was wrong of me…. I'll…"

"There's more."

"More?" I yell, and she shushes me, pulls me close.

"She kept saying that this was all your fault." The room spins. Oh, God. Oh, no. Jake told her. The bastard. That's it now. She must've told Daniel. That's why he didn't return my last two texts. He'll hate me forever. Divorce me. Never want to see me again.

"That you jinxed it cos you were against their relationship from the start, and how it's all right for you cos you've got a bloke that loves you and mad stuff like that." Oh, thank you, Lord. "She right jealous of you and her dad, Aud." Another inhale of minty smoke. "I think she was pissed."

I open my mouth to speak when the door flies open. Louise is in the doorway tied into a white apron. "What are you two doing out here?" She eyes Jess suspiciously, sniffing the air, then throws a glance at her arms behind her back. "Tina's looking for you," she tells me, eyes not leaving her daughter. "Wants your opinion on which shoes to wear with that apricot lace little number she's squeezed herself into. She's in her bedroom."

"Okay, I'll be in in a minute. We just came out for a mint." Jesus, what am I saying? Who goes out for a mint? Jess sucks her lips in, giving me a look that says WTF. "And some fresh air." I add quickly, waving my hand in front of my face. "It's hot, isn't it?"

"Oh? I'm all right." Louise does a little shiver. "Maybe you're having a hot flush."

"What? Already? I'm only forty-two." I touch my forehead for any signs of a temperature.

"I'm only winding you up, you muppet." Louise brushes past me, undoing the tie of her apron, yelling at Jess to put the Vapour cigarette away over her shoulder. "I do know that you smoke those things, Jess. I'm not senile. Well, not yet, anyway." She pauses at the gate and wipes something off the flare of her red knee length dress vigorously with a handful of the apron. "They're just as bad as smoking ciggies – you'll get addicted." Jess gives me a look depicting *I told you so*, then takes a final puff and blows it at her mum's back in protest before poking her tongue out.

"Put it away!" Louise warns as if she has eyes in the back of her head. "And stop making faces behind my back."

"Where're you going, Lou?" I call out. Across the road two cars have pulled up with glamourous looking guests, none of whom I recognise. "People are starting to arrive."

"Just putting my apron back in the car. It's my work one. Don't want to forget it," she yells to the backdrop of car doors thumping and the hullabaloo of voices. "I won't be a mo."

"And that's another thing," Jess says, eyeing her mother dubiously as she clambers into her car. "She's been acting strangely, too." She takes another lungful of mist, ignoring her mother's warning. "All weird."

"Weird?"

"Yeah, you know." She pulls a face. "Like she's on something."

"On something?"

Jess sighs and rolls her eyes. "Aud, babe, why are you repeating everything I say as if I'm teaching you a new language?"

I raise an eyebrow and twist my lips in mock exasperation. "She seems all right to me." Stepping out of the way, I fold my arms, smile at a stream of guests shuffling inside.

"Nah." She takes a drag then offers it to me as if it were a joint. I decline. "She's like okay one minute and then lashes out. Aggressive, like, you know."

"At you?"

"Sometimes, yeah, when I'm there. I've started staying with Sky in town again, saves on travelling, know what I mean?"

"Maybe it's the stress of the new job." I jump at the sound of a shrill bark. A Jack Russell Terrier is at the gate, yapping and growling at us while its owner pulls on its lead, and berates it for being a naughty boy.

"Hmmm." Jess sounds unconvinced. "And last night…." She hesitates, looks away as Jack Russell and owner stroll off down the street. "Oh, never mind." She chews her bottom lip.

"What is it, Jess? Tell me." I snatch her by the arm. I hope she hasn't been harassing her ex again. Gerry's made it very clear that he wants a divorce and a future with his new woman.

"Well, she didn't come home last night. She rocked in this morning at about 6 a.m. I heard a car pull up while I was Tweeting in bed, then the thud of a car door and her voice saying '*Thanks*'. By the time I got to the window the car had sped off. I think it might've been a cab. I just caught sight of her covered in a blanket."

"A blanket?" How weird. "Well, where was she? Who was she with? Where did she stay?" I ask, concerned. It's not like Louise to

HER SECRET

stay out all night. But then she might've gone out with a few of her new colleagues after the last service. She is a grown woman. We can't reprimand her for staying out one night.

Jess shrugs. "Your guess is as good as mine. Don't tell her I told you." Panic rises in her voice, blue eyes shining against her pale skin and jet black bob. I assure her that I won't and her shoulders soften. Jess trusts me, always has. "I think she might've met a bloke. You know, on one of those dating sites."

"Yeah, Trevor. He's sounds like a nice man."

"Who the hell is Trevor?"

"He's…"

Jess whips the Vapour cigarette behind her back again and waves her hand in front of us. "Oh, fuck," she cuts in. "She's coming back."

"Audrey!" A voice cries from inside. I spin round, Tina is standing barefoot in the corridor looking like a movie star in a beautiful figure hugging apricot crochet mini dress, a pair of shoes in each hand, big red curls tumbling over her shoulders in a chic forties style. "I've been waiting for you for ages. Didn't Louise tell you?" She shakes the shoes at me. "Which ones? The apricot or cream?"

"Cream," I say, "for the contrast." And Jess agrees.

Tina nods, scurries back into her bedroom and slams the door behind her. I take Jess by the hand. "Come on, let's get back inside. I'll speak to your mum later."

We step over the entrance to the soundtrack of banter and laughter, Louise's arm on my shoulder as she falls in line with us, and then, out of nowhere, the sound of his voice, his slight Irish twang searing into my back, opening old wounds. "Foxy?"

CHAPTER 16

"IT'S SO GOOD to see you, Audrey." Nick leans forward, hand on my upper arm. I always loved the feel of his lips against my skin when they were cold; after he'd just eaten an ice lolly or come in from the cold. Closing my eyes briefly, I take in his familiar citrusy-tobacco scent, the smell submerging me into a deep pool of memories. Memories I want to blank out forever.

I open my mouth to speak but it just hangs open uselessly. Standing rigid, like a mannequin, my hand is clammy in Jess's. When I got here, Tina told me he'd be arriving late; that he'd texted Ronan shortly before; had a photoshoot in Brighton, traffic was manic, there was a pile up on the M4. But he's here, EARLY.

"Great news about Tina and Ronan," Nick says, rubbing his hands together. "That pair should've got hitched years ago." Pot and kettle spring to mind immediately. The irony makes me want to laugh out loud.

Tina yells out to Ronan over *Jax Jones's Breathe* – her cousin Charlie's arrived, wants to meet him.

The kerfuffle of music, laughter and banter close in on me. This isn't right. This isn't the way I'd rehearsed it. Nick wasn't supposed to creep up on me like this. I was meant to be standing next to Daniel on Tina's garden patio by the warped fence with the nails sticking out, flicking back my freshly blow-dried hair, glass of fizz in hand, arm through Daniel's, and introduce my ex to my husband in a self-assured, civil manner, music and happy voices bellowing in my ears. He's ruined it all now. Why did he have to flipping turn up early?

"You okay?" he asks Jess as if he's just seen her. "How's uni?"

Jess's big blue eyes flit between me and Nick, finally settling on him, dark and vacant. I know that look. I've seen it many times before. She can feel my tension. She's ready to pounce. But as she opens her mouth to speak, I give her hand a light squeeze, like tugging on a lead of an agitated dog, and she backs off. Jess is always on my side, even when I'm wrong. She's probably more loyal than my family and friends put together. And I love her for it but I don't want any trouble, especially not today. The last thing I want to do is ruin Tina and Ronan's party. "Fine," she snaps, glaring at him.

"We're both fine, thanks." I finally find my voice, albeit croaky. "How're you? How was Italy?" I ask casually, making small talk.

Big mistake, because he spends the next five minutes telling us about his wonderful adventure. Rome was an incredible experience, he even squeezed in a day trip to Vatican City. The Sistine Chapel is a must see, but, sadly, no photography is allowed inside. The imp in me does a little summersault in my stomach when he says this, glad that he missed out on such a fantastic opportunity. It would've done wonders for his portfolio. He didn't stay in Rome for long – went on to Florence, regretted not going to the Uffizi gallery but he was strapped for time, jumped on a train to Pisa, on to France and then Spain.

"And then I ended up in America," he finishes.

"America?" Jess and I exclaim in unison. A man in blue jeans and a smart tweed jacket, stops chatting to two women by the lounge doorway, turns rigidly and glares at us, face full of botox, clearly irritated by our cacophony.

"Wow, what made you go there?" I ask, lowering my voice.

"Well, I –"

"Shall we get another drink, babe?" Jess cuts across him, clearly bored of his anecdotes. I look at her empty glass cupped in her hand, stem between her fingers, a double imprint of her crimson lips on the rim. I could go with Jess – escape this awkward chitchat with Nick, at least until Daniel arrives.

"You go ahead, honey." I've got to woman up and face the music or else my entire evening will be ruined. "I'll join you in a moment," I say quietly. She gives my arm a gentle squeeze, her eyes depicting *will you be okay?* I nod, and, giving Nick a final glare, she snakes her way through a sea of guests, disappearing into the lounge.

"Was it something that I said?" Nick laughs faintly, sliding a hand into his trouser pocket.

"You know what young girls are like these days."

"It's okay. I get it. I was a teenager once. She's a good kid. Clever." I look at him carefully for a few moments. He's lost weight, looks a bit gaunt, actually, as if he hasn't had a decent meal in weeks. He probably lives off takeaways and toast as a single man. He's worse in the kitchen than I am. He'd often eat an entire packet of biscuits rather than heat something up whenever I was out. His grey single-breasted suit, the one which we bought together from Selfridges for our wedding that never was, the one he looked so gorgeous in as he stood in front of the full length mirror to the admiring glances of staff and shoppers, the only suit he probably owns, is hanging off him. I was expecting him to look better after living it up in in Europe and America for several months. He rubs his lips, studying me with those kind, grey eyes of his, but I feel nothing.

"You look great," he says finally.

"Thanks," I reply in a staccato burst. Folding my arms, I gaze at my black *Louboutins*. I can't believe that's all I can say. I've rehearsed this speech for days. I was to tell him to never, EVER contact me again, no flowers, no DMs on Messenger - nothing. I'd be civil to him for the sake of our friends, for their impending wedding, but nothing more. We can't be friends, not after all that's happened. I'm married now. We're over. For good.

"Look, Nick," I begin. A few guests shuffle past us in the narrow hallway and we step aside. "About the flowers."

"Did you get them? he asks, eyes bright. He scratches his cheek and I noticed that he hasn't trimmed his nails. I'm surprised, he must be slacking. He used to spend ages grooming his nails in the bathroom, clipping them, smoothing down the edges with a nail file that he'd nicked from my washbag; he even used to push down the cuticles – said it was important that his hands looked good for his clients. I never complained, his touch was always smooth.

"So, they were from you then?"

"Yeah, course," he says as if no one else could possibly send me flowers. "I always bought you red tulips. They're your favourite." He bought me a bouquet on our first proper date. We were driving through Hampstead when he spotted a florist on the sidewalk, pulled up, jumped out, then came back with a huge bunch of them; and from that moment on they became my favourite flowers. "I bought them from that posh florist in Crouch End," he says. "I'm glad you found them first."

I stare at him, gobsmacked. I can't believe he's being so blasé about it all. He knows damn well that Daniel could easily have questioned me about the flowers – caused an argument even. But that was probably his objective. He's trying to ruin my relationship with my husband, but I won't let him destroy my marriage.

"You can't just bring me flowers, Nick. It's not on." A few glamorous women rush past us, giggling, leaving a trail of heady perfume behind them. Tina has some seriously glitzy friends. I still can't believe she chose *me* to be her maid-of-honour.

"Oh. It's just that…..Well….I wanted to let you know that I was back, that's all," he explains. I narrow my eyes. "I didn't leave a note in case your…your…" He rolls his hand in the air, throwing a glance at some guests who're are now spilling into the hallway in droves, pushing us out of the way.

"My husband," I confirm.

"Well, yeah. I thought it might offend him, you know. Your ex sending you flowers." I give him a miniscule frown and shake my head. Typical Nick, knows it's wrong but does it anyway. "It's just that I wanted to let you know that I was back home." WHY? I want to scream. He's really starting to fucking wind me up now. "I couldn't phone or text you because you'd changed your numbers." He looks at his shoes. They're scuffed. "Although I knew that, anyway. I tried texting you a few days after I went to Rome but they came back as undelivered." Too little, too late. He looks back up at me. "Tina refused to give me your new mobile number when I got back." A rush of gratitude tears through me. Bless her – so loyal, so trusting. If only she knew that I'd slept with her fiancé. I shake the thought away.

"I changed my numbers for a reason, Nick. I don't want you to contact me again. Ever." I pull my cardigan around me tightly and throw a nervy smile at two guests standing opposite as if they can hear every word I'm saying and will recite it all to Daniel the moment he walks through the door. I've got to calm down. Come on, Audrey, get a grip. "Look, I don't think we should even be talking like this."

"Like what?"

"Like nothing has happened. Like we're old friends. I want you to promise me that you'll back off. Let me get on with my life. Please, Nick, I'm happy for once. Don't ruin this for me."

HER SECRET

He looks shocked. "What do you mean?"

"How could you even ask me that question?" I say incredulously. I can't believe he's not the slightest bit contrite.

"But we've got history. Didn't our eight years together mean anything to you?"

My stomach tightens. He's got to be having a flipping laugh. I want to stamp my feet and scream at him. Tell him that I cried so much the second time he abandoned me, I thought I'd never stop. My eyes were so puffy, I looked like I'd done ten rounds with Nicola Adams. Fearne had to tell Raymond that I had the Norovirus. It was her idea, said it was the only way he'd let me have two weeks off sick.

"We need to talk," he goes on urgently, "I've got something to tell you. I..."

"Just give it a rest, will you?" I hiss, talking over him. A good-looking couple stroll through the front door, letting in the afternoon sun, illuminating the dark corridor. The man – short, early-forties, greying cropped hair, gives Nick a pat on the back, tells him it's good to see him while the twenty-something woman with long, LONG, blonde hair (probably extensions) gives me a small smile before hobbling off in her nine inch heels behind her partner.

"Look, we need to clear the air. We need closure."

I want to laugh. Closure? He's been watching too much day time TV. "Forget it," I snap. "I don't need closure, and whatever it is you want to say, I'm not interested."

His lips tremble; there's a sheen of sweat on his forehead. He looks broken, although I'm not quite sure why. Is it my fault that he left me? Is it my fault that he's alone again? He could've been standing in Daniel's shoes right now. Well, not his expensive *Santonis*, but you know what I mean. I'd have married him in a heartbeat if he'd taken me with him to Rome. But it's way too late now, and the sooner he gets that through his thick head, the sooner we can put all this behind us.

"Audrey, please, just hear me out, will you. I…" A few boisterous men having a play fight bash into him and he knocks against me. Our bodies collide. I hate it. I move away quickly. The corridor is crowded, music pounding, glasses rattling, people laughing. A man shouts, '*Get over it, you tosser, Arsenal are losers.*' Nick is so close to me now, I can feel the warmth of his breath on my skin.

"Just let me go. PLEASE!"

"I can't leave things like this, Foxy." Our eyes lock, then he drops his glance to my lips. Oh, shit, I think he's going to kiss me.

"What part of I'm not interested don't you understand, hmm?" I hiss, pushing him away. "My husband is due any moment now and if he –"

"But I –"

I've had enough. I need a drink. I'm about to walk away when suddenly a thought enters my mind and almost floors me. "Were you following me in Muswell Hill last Thursday?"

Jerking his head back, he pulls a face as if he's inhaled a bad smell. "Course not. I'm not a complete knob." I don't believe him. I think he was. Perhaps he even pushed me at the crossing. Not on purpose. He was probably just trying to get my attention in his heavy handed kind of way. He'd never hurt me physically. He's not like that. He was a good boyfriend – kind, gentle, thoughtful – he'd text me several times a day, even though I hardly texted him; make me tea and tidy up while I watched my soaps, fix me a hot water bottle when I couldn't feel my feet after a night out with the girls. He'd even buy me books by my favourite authors and leave them by my bedside with a note. But that was then. Now he's an unreliable, annoying pest whom I may have to take out an injunction on.

HER SECRET

"Stop stalking me, Nick." A loud woman's shrill laughter tears through the flat and I wince. Throwing a quick glance towards the lounge, I mumble that I've got to go and find Jess, that she'll be wondering where I am. I go to walk away, this is getting out of hand, but he grabs me by the wrist.

"Wait. I...."

"Get off me." I snatch my hand away. We've only been in each other's company for ten minutes and already we're fighting. And there was me warning everyone else to stay calm. Oh, God, why, oh, why, did I agree to this? I'm going to have to ask Tina to find another maid-of-honour, for her own sake as well as mine. She'll understand once I explain that Nick is harassing me.

"Foxy, please....."

"Stop it." I bark. "I don't need this today."

His hand flies to his forehead. "Look, I'm sorry, okay? Oh, God, this is all going horribly wrong." He pauses, filling his lungs. "I am happy for you." Well, that's a blatant lie for a start. "I mean it, Foxy." Oh, God, I wish he'd stop calling me that, pet names are for lovers and friends, and most definitely not for estranged girlfriends, especially married ones. "Ronan says your husband's a top bloke. I just can't get my head around how we ended up like this, that's all." Well, let's start with you leaving me on your doorstep and fleeing to Rome on your own to find yourself the moment you discovered you hadn't knocked-up your best friend's sister.

"My head," he says, rubbing his temple.

A shot of compassion shoots through me and I soften. I wonder if he's still having all those headaches and nightmares. Imagining things, like coming out of his body and seeing the future in his dreams. All crap, obviously – a side effect from his motorbike accident last year.

"Look, are you okay?" I ask.

And then out of nowhere a voice cries, "Nicky. An attractive woman rocks up and tickles his waist and he jumps. "I thought you were meant to pick me up?"

The woman is smiling at me kindly, hazel eyes twinkling. I'd say she's mid-fifties - fit, confident, slim, in a figure hugging red knee length dress and incredibly gorgeous red sling back heels, similar to the *Louboutins* I was wearing when I first met Daniel at that Greek taverna in Cyprus. And she's tall, almost reaching Nick's six foot frame. One of his ex-model friends, I presume.

Nick looks like he's seen a ghost. "Oh, SHIT!" Then he looks at her, shoulders limp. "I was running late and completely forgot. I'm so sorry." How could you forget to pick up your date, for heaven's sake? I bet he just stood her up.

"Good job I had the address, then." She gives him a sideward glance, slapping him playfully on the arm. "I waited over an hour," she complains to me. "And why don't you ever answer your mobile phone?" Because he's an unreliable prick, love, I want to say, but decide to chew the inside of my bottom lip instead.

"Sorry, I was on my bike. I couldn't hear it." Then he looks at me. "Came straight from a shoot in Brighton."

"Honestly, he'd forget his head if it weren't screwed on." She grins at him wickedly.

"Well, you're here now, boss." He's brought his boss with him to a party? Talk about Billy no mates.

Shaking her head, she rolls her eyes, then mimes *men*. And we grin at each other in girly harmony. I like her. She's open, friendly, cool. Ballsy.

"I'm Audrey," I say, offering my hand.

"Sorry." He straightens up. "Audrey," he says, pointing his hand at the woman. "Katrina Rickman." He gives me a tight grin, head bowed as he slips his hands into his pockets. He's nervous as hell.

 HER SECRET

I know him so well.

Then to my utter surprise she throws her hands up in the air and gathers me in her arms as if we're old relatives being reunited by Davina McCall in an episode of *Long Lost Families*. "Well, why didn't you say?"

Squashed in her arms, I respond with a gentle pat on the back while Nick looks on, eyebrows raised, rocking on his heels. I know he wants to laugh because he knows that I'm not very good at touchy-feely stuff with strangers.

Over Katrina's shoulder I spy Louise walking up the path, texting, Daniel and Connie in tow. Oh, thank God. The sight of my husband gives me an instant rush of adrenalin.

"Audrey, I've heard so much about you," Katrina says when we finally disentangle." I feel as if I know you, for heaven's sake. How the hell are you?"

"Yeah, I'm good," My smile is frozen. My head buzzing. I wasn't really expecting Nick to bring a plus-one. Not that I mind. In fact, I'm relieved. It makes everything so much easier. But filling his boss in on our relationship is a bit…well, weird.

The house is teeming with people, the air dense with voices, perfumes, cigarette smoke.

"Audrey?" Louise is at my side, hand protectively on my back. She looks at Nick carefully beneath knotted thin blonde brows, then back at me. "Everything okay?"

Nick leans forward and gives Louise a hug before introducing her to Katrina, and she responds, thank God, in a cheery manner. I'm glad Louise is being civil, as promised. That she's making an effort. I throw her an appreciative glance, which she reciprocates with a wink.

"Oh. My. God." Connie's giving Nick the once over. She looks good in a mint flared dress (my favourite shade of green. I love green), and pink slingbacks, and, thank goodness, much happier than when I last saw her. "Where've you been?" she says to Nick. "Boot camp? You look like death warmed up."

Finally, I'm in my husband's arms, safe, secure. His lips close over mine. I can taste his minty breath, seductive, clean. "You look stunning," he whispers. "Sorry I'm late, darling. Why do women take so long in the bathroom?" He gesticulates at Connie with a quick flick of his head, then gives me a gentle squeeze and I melt into him, kissing him back, giggling, happy, content, feeling like the luckiest woman on the planet, because I know I was being paranoid about the flowers that Vicky saw him buying last Thursday. I know they're for the office, because he told me, without me even asking, as we drove past the florist's last night. I know he'd never lie or cheat on me. We're forever, he and I.

Nick and Katrina look at us with baffled amusement. I suppose we're acting like a couple of love-struck teenagers, but I don't care. I want to show off my gorgeous new husband. I want to shout my happiness from the rooftops and plaster it all over social media.

"Where are my manners?" I say after a few moments, clearing my throat. I catch Tina's silhouette in the background walking towards us, Ronan behind her. "This is my husband Daniel," I say loudly above Tina's voice telling everyone to get into the lounge and get the party started. "And Daniel, this is Nick and Katrina, his…" I wait for her to fill in the blank. A roar of thunder booms in the distance, the sky crackles with lightning.

"Wife." Katrina says, squeezing his arm with glee.

 HER SECRET

CHAPTER 17

THE HOURS SLIP BY quickly. Ronan gives a boozy heartrending speech, punctured by a few jestful jibes from Nick, which go down exceptionally well with the guests, particularly their buddies who flew in from Dublin for the weekend, and Tina's uncle Vernon, who doesn't approve of Ronan because he's still married, despite knowing that Ronan has filed for divorce.

We all oooh and ahhh as Ronan gets down on one knee and presents a blushing Tina with a diamond engagement ring the size of an almond, and cheer loudly when she says 'YES!!!' Again.

Once the rain stops, most of the guests escape the humidity of the small lounge and scuttle into the garden with their drinks, taking the fug of cigarette smoke, perfume, and, unless my smelling senses fail me, a waft of marijuana with them. But amongst the celebratory chaos, all I can think about is my warm bed. "Just a small get together," Tina had said, just the other day in Louise's kitchen. "Family and a few friends. No biggie." This is more like a flipping rave. I don't think I've been to a party like this since I was in my twenties. It's official. I'm getting old.

My aching limbs almost cry out in gratitude as I sink into a cosy leather armchair in the front room by the bay window behind a group of giggling women taking selfies with a long stick and posting them on social media, which I know they'll regret deeply in the morning because, gorgeous as they are, their Sex and the

City image is now slowly morphing into an Alice Cooper tribute act. It's been a long day for all of us.

"Take one of me necking the bottle," cries one of the women, stumbling against the fireplace, bottle of Smirnoff in hand while Post Malone's *Rockstar* fades in the background.

"Aaaarghhh," cries one of her friends, almost bursting my eardrum. "Don't you dare put that up on Instagram without a filter."

Leaning my head back on the armchair, their voices become a distant, whiny buzz in my ears. I'm not going to sleep or anything, I just need to rest my eyes for a bit. The drone of voices is slowly breaking up, Stomzy's *Blinded by Your Grace* is almost an inaudible lullaby. I'm slowly drifting, drifting, further and further into darkness when a loud voice shrills in my ears like a Claxton, "What the HELL are you doing here all alone, for heaven's sake?"

My eyes snap open, body rigid, hands squeezing the leather armrests as if I'm about to fall off. Katrina is looming over me, hands on hips, looking just as glamorous as she did the moment she arrived, and for a moment I wonder if this woman is actually human.

"She's sixty-five and loaded. Big house on Primrose Hill," Tina had said earlier, as she, Louise and I stood like Charlie's Angels eyeing Katrina from the kitchen window as she chatted to Daniel, Ronan, Tina's sister Paula and her partner, grumpy Steve, in the garden, our wine glasses pressed against our chests as if they were loaded guns. "It was part of her divorce settlement, apparently. I wasn't going to let Ronan get away without him giving me her full C.V., not when he kept their marriage a secret from me." Apparently, Nick wanted to tell me himself and swore Ronan to secrecy. "She's a travel writer, grown-up kids, always jetting off somewhere. Met Nick in a bar in Barcelona while she was working on a piece for *Travel Lightly*. And the rest is history."

I look at Katrina, now, through bleary, tired eyes, and then she says, "Come on, you, on your feet." Her soft hands are warm around my wrists. "You'll have plenty of time to sit around in an armchair when you're ninety."

Before I can protest, she hauls me up by the hands and shoulders her way through the Alice Cooper lookalikes, then half walks, half dances her way through a melee of people, dragging me by the hand. I trot behind her wondering what on earth she's on and wishing she'd give some to me. Not if it's drugs, obviously. But her vitality should be bottled and sold on QVC or John Lewis. Or both. No wonder she married a much younger man, no one over the age of sixty-five could possibly keep up with her. She has the stamina of a thirty-year-old athlete.

The heavy fug of rain fills my lungs the moment we step onto the patio, and I'm pleasantly surprised to see Daniel on the damp lawn chatting with Nick and Ronan, beer in hand, blades of grass smothering his *Santoni* shoes. He really did mean it when he said he'd make an effort tonight. My poor husband. I bet his socks are soaked through. I told him not to wear the woven toe brown leathers for a garden party in April, but would he listen? The moment he sees me, he raises his arm, then pulls a face, points at his shoes, then wags his finger warningly. I don't need telling twice. My *Louboutins* don't do sodden lawns – the idea is unthinkable. So, while Daniel chats with Nick and Ronan (quite loudly, drink does that to him) about the property market and the Cypriot economy, I acquaint myself with Katrina from the safety of the patio.

I quickly find out that she's a grandmother to three children under the age of ten, was a professional makeup artist for ten years before becoming a travel journalist; worked on lots of popular TV dramas and films. But journalism is her vocation, she loves it, and can't wait for her next project – an all-expenses paid for gig at a luxury five-star Spa hotel in Mykonos for herself and Nick. Clearly, I'm in the wrong job. I've always fancied Mykonos. She tells me that she adores being called Mrs Byrne but has kept her maiden name for professional use.

"You're lucky," she enthuses, "landing a gorgeous, successful hunk like Daniel." And I agree, gazing adoringly at my husband while Nick blows cigarette smoke over his head, which I know is annoying the hell out of him, because Daniel's very anti-smoking and will jump into the shower the moment we get home to rid himself of the stale scent of tobacco, which he often says reminds him of a bitter childhood with his father – something he's always reluctant to talk about.

At eleven-thirty, all giddy with booze and euphoria, Ronan sticks his retro playlist on and turns up the volume, "Come on, everyone," he cries, "One final jig before the music goes off." Uncle Vernon and his wife Ruby, who refused to join the rest of the older members of the family in the kitchen, cover their ears from the safety of the black leather sofa as we all stomp into the middle of the room. It's a good job Tina was savvy enough to invite all the neighbours or we'd have had a visit from the noise pollution team by now.

Daniel swirls me around to one of my all-time favourite Abba tracks, *Super Trouper* and we all drunkenly sing along to the music, out of tune and out of sync. In my peripheral vision, I spy people watching us. He's still a great mover. Daniel and his ex-wife Aliki were ballroom dancers back in the day; not just hobbyists, but regional champions. He taught me a few moves for our wedding dance, which I'm executing now, quite bravely and quite impressively by the look on people's faces.

Before I know it, everyone is on their feet. Cheering, stomping, singing. Tina stumbles towards me as Ronan spins her around

HER SECRET

energetically to *Blue Suede Shoes*, and, much to the amusement of my brother who is jiving clumsily nearby with Vicky, I almost land onto uncle Vernon's lap.

"Enjoying yourself?" Daniel whispers into my ear once I regain my composure. Blowing a few stray hairs off my hot, sweaty face, I tell him that I am, that I think we all are. I wave a hand and he throws a glance over his shoulder. Behind him, Jess is teaching Katrina how to *twerk* while Louise slithers against a silver-haired fox in a pink shirt. Whatever he says to her must be hilarious, because her drunken laughter tears across the room like a missile. Clearly, the last straw for uncle Vernon and Ruby who're now hobbling towards the exit, wincing. Poor things, they've lasted well. It is almost midnight. Pausing at the door, they say their goodbyes to Tina, as Nick and Connie slide past them and hit the dance floor. I was wondering where they'd got to – probably outside having a sneaky fag and a chat.

Connie doesn't like smoking in front of her dad because he always has a go at her, and, despite all his faults, Nick can be a real tonic when you're down and he is a great listener. She looks much happier, and I truly hope this means Jake is becoming a distant memory. Unsurprisingly, Connie is throwing some impressive shapes (that girl can shuffle; dancing is in her genes) while Nick breaks out some dad dancing moves. He hasn't really got much rhythm; apart from *The Twist*, he's pretty much useless at anything else.

So when *Gabriella Cilmi's* cover of *Warm this Winter* booms through the amplifier, Nick lets go of Connie and the next thing I know his hands are around my wrists. He's pulling me towards him. I back away, dragging my feet, but he's like a persistent terrier.

Glancing over my shoulder, I try to catch Daniel's attention but he's now twirling Connie around to the music. Despite his bravado,

I know he was a bit apprehensive about today, about Nick being here. Unlike Nick, Daniel is a bit more clingy and possessive, but in a good way. So I'm quite sure that dancing with my ex will upset him. I've got to grab his attention so that he can stop dancing with Connie and come and save me.

I strain my neck towards Daniel, willing him to look round as I struggle to get out of Nick's firm grasp. "Come on, Foxy," Nick says, face red and sweaty. "For old times' sake." Nick's hands are damp but strong, tenacious. My eyes flit from his mouth to the patches of sweat under the arms of his white cotton shirt, he's undone the top buttons and a bit of chest hair is showing through.

"Nick," I warn, "Don't. I can't, my..." I glance at Daniel again, music pounding, voices yelling; and then Nick, seeing my distress, loosens his grip. I'm about to wriggle free, but then Daniel looks over, and, surprisingly, gives me a little nod and a wink. Maybe I was wrong about him feeling insecure, and I do bloody love this song. I spin back round, "Oh, go on then." I kick off my shoes, throwing the bitter past with them. Why can't Nick and I be friends? We're both married now. We're both in love with other people.

Our feet twist against the wooden flooring. Our sync as perfect as ever. We've danced to this song so many times over the years. It's like second nature.

Imprisoned in the moment, high on adrenalin, drunk on the resounding boom pounding in my ears, I swing my hips, rocking back and forth to the music, and then we go down low, twisting, twisting, twisting. It's only when I look round that I see that the floor has cleared and everyone is cheering, clapping, woohooing. Everyone apart from Daniel and Connie, that is, who are huddled together by the doorway chatting like a couple of espionage agents.

"What's up?" I pant, heart racing. Did I overdo it with Nick? Is that why Daniel has a murderous look on his face? I push a hand through my damp hair, which I know has doubled in size since I arrived. The music has stopped, voices clatter in my ears. It's been a while since I danced so energetically.

"Connie wants to go home," Daniel scratches his chin, lips tight.

"Home? Why?" I ask with a little yelp that makes me sound like a Chihuahua. A young woman knocks into me and I grab ahold of Daniel's arm for support. We all watch as she staggers towards the front door in six-inch heels, arm slung around her friend like *Stretch Armstrong*, slurring her undying love for her. Loudly. "I thought you were staying with us tonight, Connie." That was the agreement – Lily stays with Aliki and Connie stays with us. "I've already made up the spare bed." I glance back into the living room searching for my shoes, sweat trickling down my lower back and descending into my knickers. "Daniel, have you seen my shoes?" I'm certain I saw a figure reach down for them when I took them off earlier. He shrugs, tells me that they must be in the living room where I abandoned them, and I'm sure I detect a hint of acid in his tone. I was right. He's grouchy about Nick. I shouldn't have danced with him. Daniel's nod of approval was probably just a test to see if I'd go through with it. And, like a fool, I did. I'm going to get the silent treatment for the rest of the night now, maybe even tomorrow. I don't suppose he'll ever really be okay about my relationship with Nick, no matter how much he wants to be, no matter how hard he tries. It's a cross I'll have to bear.

"I just want my own bed, that's all," Connie complains sulkily. I follow her eyes to my shoes under a chair a few feet away. She must've put them there for me for safe keeping. Good girl. She knows how expensive they are. A pang of remorse hits the pit of my stomach. Did I spoil her dance with Nick? Is that why she wants to leave? I motion my head at Daniel and mouth '*I'll sort it*' before bending down to pick up my shoes. He looks at me hesitantly, then nods and he's gone, swallowed into the boisterous crowd like quicksand.

Tina's bedroom door is slightly ajar. Sliding two fingers inside my shoes, I incline my head towards the bedroom, and that's when I notice that one of the heels has snapped. Damn. I've only worn them twice. But right now, I've more important things to worry about. I take Connie's hand. "Come on."

We're sitting on Tina's bed amongst a heap of jackets, cardigans, fluffy pink pillows and cuddly toys. Anyone would think this bedroom belonged to a young teenager girl, not a thirty-six-year-old woman. "I take it you haven't heard from Jake, then?" I ask, examining my shoe. How on earth could the heel snap off so easily? Daniel will have to take them back.

"No." She exhales loudly, dropping her head into her hands, elbows on knees. "I wouldn't mind, Audrey, I mean, I know he's married and everything, but –" She looks up at me and a rush of guilt slithers along my spine. I hate feeling responsible for her pain but I did the right thing, didn't I? What any stepmother would do, right?

"You'll get over him, Connie." I rub her back soothingly, gazing at a set of starry fairy lights draped along the length of the wooden headboard. Tina left them on, good call. It's getting dark outside, and the warm glow is filling the room with a soft blue hue. "There's plenty more fish in the sea." I berate myself inwardly the moment the words leave my lips, but I can't think of anything more comforting to say, and I want her to stop hurting.

"You don't understand. It's not that." Rubbing her chin, she stares at the door vacantly. I've never seen Connie this cut up about anyone, or anything, for that matter.

 HER SECRET

"What is it then?" I probe. Silence. "Connie?"

She sucks her teeth loudly. "Look, I lent him some money, okay." A bolt of acid rockets into my stomach, and for a moment I envisage Jake pushing a tower of casino chips on *black* as the ball thunders and rattles in the wheel before landing on *twenty-seven, red.* "But, don't tell my dad," she adds quickly, grabbing my hand and squeezing it.

"Connie, were you out of your mind?" My shoe slides out of my hand and lands by my bare feet, and suddenly I'm aware of a coolness beneath my right sole. I must've laddered my tights while doing *The Twist* with Nick. "How much?" Please God let her tell me that it was just a couple of hundred quid to pay for one of their lavish meals at The Ivy or Nobu.

"Because he begged me to, that's why. People think that I'm just heartbroken but they don't know the half of it. He won't answer his phone. I don't know where he lives or works. He lied to me about practically everything." She runs a hand over her face, forgetting that she's heavily made-up. "I don't know how I could've been such a fucking moron."

I look at her lipstick smeared, sad, little face and an unexpected burst of maternal love almost knocks me out. "Well, how much did you lend him?" I ask softly. Reaching out, I rub the lipstick off her chin with my thumb, then tuck her hair behind her ear. "I can help if you're short, just until - "

"You don't understand, Audrey. I gave him THOUSANDS."

Oh shit. My instincts were right. "How many?" I gulp, my voice going up an octave.

"Ten."

"Oh, fucking hell, Connie." Thrusting a hand through my hair, I gape at the lilac walls, feeling them closing in around me, encasing me in a cocoon of terror. This is all my fault.

"I know," she whimpers, as if my annoyance has made this all real for her. Pressing a hand against her chest, she takes short, sharp breaths, as if she's in labour. I wrap my arm around her shoulders. Jesus, I hope she's okay. "The thing is," she pauses, exhales loudly and gazes up at the pretty purple chandelier. "Well, I need that money for Lily's school fees. I don't know what I'm going to do. I mean, I can't tell Dad that I gave Lily's school fund to Jake, can I? He'll go mental." I can just imagine Daniel, fists balled, jaw throbbing, and then, once all the shouting is over and done with, calmly firing up his laptop, tracking Jake down on social media, because I'll have to give him his real name, of course, then turning up at his office and getting him sacked on the spot.

I stay silent as she takes a few more labour style breaths, shaking a hand in front of her face as if drying freshly varnished nails. "He'll find him somehow, you know what he's like, then he'll find out I was having an affair with a married man. I couldn't bear that. I don't think I could cope with his disappointment. It's just all such a goddamn mess. I'm such a stupid fuck. ARGHHH!"

"Can't you borrow the money from someone? What about your mum?"

"No bank will lend me that kind of money. I haven't got a proper job. And Mum will want to know what it's for." She's right. Daniel told me once that Aliki tells him everything. I'm not helping.

Stroking her hair, I try to calm her with platitudes while she sobs quietly onto my chest. "Shhhh, it's not your fault, honey. You were blinded by love, that's all. Anyone would've done the same in your shoes." Well, anyone with ten grand to spare. "The bloody lying, cheating, prick." I groan. She snuggles to me and the motherly bond grows. I really feel as if we're finally connecting, albeit under dismal circumstances. Inhaling the scent of her hair, a concoction of perfume and fags, I say, "You'll never see that

 HER SECRET

money again. He's probably gambled it all away by now." I'm going to have to help her. I know where Charlotte works. I'll turn up, tell her everything. But what if she hasn't got £10K, or refuses to hand it over? No, that's a bad idea. I've got a few thousand saved in the bank. I can give her that and borrow the rest. Sign up for one of those zero percent credit cards and transfer the money into her account. "Don't worry, Connie, I'll –"

But suddenly she pulls out of my embrace and fixes me with a long, hard stare. "How do you know about that?" she asks, inhaling teary mucus.

"About what?"

"The gambling? You just said he gambled it away." She wipes her nose with the back of her wrist, tears drying as fast as they came.

"Well, you must've told me." I laugh feebly at the lilac walls, this time hoping that they'll part, suck me in like a vacuum, and teleport me to the safety of my flat on Dukes Avenue.

She's on her feet now, looking down at me pointedly, arms folded, head tilted. "No, I didn't."

"Well, he must've then, over dinner at yours last Tuesday." I scratch my neck and regret it immediately. Sam Knight says it's a sign of lying in his Body Language report.

"Uh-ah." Connie shakes her head, face like thunder. She knows I'm lying. Fuck. "He couldn't have. I didn't even know about it then. He asked me for the money the next day, gave me a sob story about his gambling habit, said he couldn't keep up with his wife's spending. He even cried, said he was in arrears, that he was on the verge of losing his house."

This can't be happening to me. It's got to be some sort of dream. I take in the room; Ronan's jacket is draped over a green, leather chair, the dressing table is strewn with makeup and half-filled bottles of perfume, a tray with two empty mugs and a small plate with crumbs beneath it. Tina's never been much of a neat freak. I want to swoop it all up and take it into the kitchen and disappear. "Well, I….I…" I feel as if I've just developed a speech impediment. The clock tick, tick, ticks on the bedside table next to Tina's kindle. I hadn't noticed that before. Voices and the scuffle of commotion feed through the door, and she just looks at me, waiting.

"Audrey, have you spoken to him since that night? Have you seen him?" The lethal look on her face tells me that she's already guessed that I have. She's worked it out, because she's sharp. Just like her father. My face is burning. Panic rises in my chest. I think I'm going to vomit. I should confess. She'll understand, because if she could read my mind right now she'd know that I did it out of love. To protect her, because she's my family now, and you don't have to share the same DNA to care about someone, do you?

"No," I lie, wimping out. "Course not. "Grabbing a pink fluffy cushion, I begin to stroke it as if it were a fluffy cat; the soft, velvety fibres strangely giving me some sort of comfort.

"Audrey!"

"Okay, OKAY." I'm not going to be able to get out of this. Oh, God, why did I do it? What was I thinking? I didn't do the right thing, did I? I did the wrong bloody thing. Again. But I can't undo what I've done, or unsay what I've said. I'm a selfish, thoughtless bitch, and when my husband finds out what I've done to his child he will leave me. I'll lose everything and it's all I deserve.

I toss the pillow aside and take a deep breath. Connie sits back down, face tight, and listens intently as I tell her everything. I bumped into Jake on my way to Olympia. I met his wife. He begged me not to tell her, told me he was in love with her, that he'd never leave his family, not for Connie, not for anyone.

"You bitch," she whispers, eyes narrowing. "How could you?"

"I did it for you," I swear, truthfully, "to protect you." I reach out for her but she snatches her hand away, catching the sharp edge of her ring on my finger. Blood oozes from the tiny wound, but I'm too wound up to feel any pain. "You should've seen him with his wife, Connie. They were all over each other." I suck my finger, the warm metallic taste makes me feel bilious and giddy, or it might be the fumes of Connie's hatred seeping into my pores and stirring my gut. "There's no way that marriage is over."

"Oh, so you thought you'd play God, did you?" she spits, throwing a glance at my bleeding finger with uncaring venom.

"What was I supposed to do?" Reaching across her, I snatch a tissue from the box on the dressing table and wrap it around my finger. "He begged me not to tell his wife about you."

"Oh, this just gets better and better. Where are your loyalties, for fuck's sake?" A bit of spittle shoots from her mouth and lands on my cheek and I wipe it away angrily. "You should've told me right away. Let me deal with it." Yanking the brown translucent claw grip off her hair, she secures it between her teeth. "I'm not a bloody child," she mumbles through the clip, pulling her hair back into a ponytail angrily. "I'll never see that ten grand now, thanks to YOU!"

Right, that's it. I've had enough of Connie's fury and tantrums. Okay, I shouldn't have got involved, but their relationship, at least on Jake's part, was nothing more than convenient sex. How was I to know she'd given him her life savings?

"Yes, well, I didn't know about the loan, did I? If you'd told me then – "

"You're not my goddamned mother, Audrey," she cuts across me. Her words pierce my heart like long, sharp needles. That mother-daughter bond we shared just moments ago seems as if it never happened. I can almost see the hatred pouring out of her.

"Look," I yell back, "If you just let me explain a few…"

"Oh, just piss…."

There's a loud knock followed by a rattle, then the flick of the lights. We both freeze like a couple of startled cats. The bright light hurts my eyes. "What's going on?" Tina's at the door. "I thought I heard voices."

Connie drops her head, and, to my surprise, convulses with laughter. "Talk about perfect timing. Shall you tell her or shall I?"

Oh, fuck. She's going to tell her about me and Ronan. She wants to hurt me. It's written all over her face. "Connie, don't," I say quietly, pleating the hem of my dress. A tear rolls from the corner of my eye and slides down my cheek, and I don't even bother to wipe it away. She's finally broken me.

"Tell me what?" Tina takes a step forward, brows furrowed.

Connie looks up at her, then at me, her lips curling into a sinister grin. I close my eyes, squeezing in the tears, as I brace myself for an imminent explosion. This is it. The moment I've been dreading for months. The end of my friendship with Tina.

CHAPTER 18

"IF YOU'VE GOT something to say, Connie, then just say it." Tina edges closer, closing the door behind her with a click.

My eyes flit nervously from Tina to Connie, my entire body is trembling. What am I supposed to say to my friend? What excuse can I give her for shagging her fiancé on my couch five months ago? The usual clichés charge through my mind like horses at the Grand National – 'We were both very drunk.' 'You weren't together at the time.' 'I don't know why I did it, I don't even fancy him.' But no, that might imply that I think he's a minger. 'It didn't mean anything.' Is that even a valid excuse?

"Well?" Tina probes, tucking her auburn curls behind her ears. I stare at her gold heart-shaped earrings – an engagement gift from Ronan. She told me so just the other night, said the little blue velvet box fell out of his jacket as she was hanging it up, or was she suspicious? Was she searching his pockets, looking for clues? She did seem to make a big thing of her discovery. Oh, God, what is wrong with me? Of course she's not suspicious. I'm being stupid, paranoid. There's no way she knows about me and Ronan. "I'm waiting," Tina says to Connie.

"Well, Connie wants – "

"Shh..Audrey, let her speak."

There are a few moments of silence punctured by Ronan's voice shouting '*You bastard*', then a roar of male laughter and Irish accents. I'm not sure how much more of this I can take. My heart feels like it's about to rupture through my chest. I eye the window longingly, wishing I could whip it open, climb out, and disappear into the darkness. "What's going on between you two?" Tina's voice again. "Come on," she demands, one eyebrow raised, "Spill."

I close my eyes, every hair on my body is on end. "Go ahead, she may as well – "

"We accidently spilt some…."

We've spoken at the same time. My eyes snap open; Connie looks at me as if to say, 'What the fuck?' The air is thick with trepidation. All I can hear is the knocking of my heart and the clamour of voices and laughter seeping through the lilac walls. I thought she was going to tell Tina, almost certain of it. Connie and I continue to gawp at each other inanely. A scraping at the door followed by a woman's voice shouting '*Steady on, Maya,*' makes me jump. Connie wasn't going to drop me in it, after all. She was just trying to frighten me. Get back at me. Why did I speak? Why didn't I just keep my big trap shut?

"Blimey," Tina groans, "you two wouldn't make very good detectives, would you?" Silence. "Look." Folding her arms, she crosses her legs, as if she needs the loo and can't be arsed to go. "I know, okay, so quit with the Gestapo looks."

Our heads jolt up. Shit! What does she know? That I copped off with her fiancé, or that Connie was having an affair with a married man? Oh God. She must've been eavesdropping at the door – she heard everything.

"Tina, it's not what you think," I say guardedly, palm out as if warding off an armed intruder who's threatening to blow my brains out.

She edges forward. "Oh really? I know all about your little secret."

"What do you mean?" Connie gulps, a slight wobble in her voice. Then she looks at me, eyes full of hurt. "You promised me…"

 HER SECRET

"Oh, no, no, no, Connie…I didn't…you're barking up the wrong tree. I – "

"I've known about you and Ronan for a while, Audrey. I've just been waiting for you to tell me."

I can almost feel Connie's body slump with relief. But I'm bloody well in for it. A spit of acid dances in my stomach. "Tina, please." I get to my feet. Any moment now she's going to grab a handful of my hair, drag me along the passageway and kick me out onto the street. Everyone will know what I've done. Daniel will be so ashamed of me. Katrina, who's only just met me, who's heard so many lovely things about me, will be mortified.

The miniature mushroom tart that I ate greedily an hour ago, because it was the last one in the tray, ascends towards my chest. I swallow it back. "It happened long before you got back with him," I explain with a shaky voice. "I was drunk." Tina's eyebrows rise and fall. "VERY drunk." I scan her face but it's unreadable. "And so was he," I clarify quickly. "I wasn't thinking straight. I'd had a shit day. I wasn't coping. I couldn't. I didn't…I…" I can't stop blabbing. I'm not making any sense. "I was in a state. I…I…" I can't breathe. I can almost feel invisible hands around my neck, squeezing, squeezing. And then the room is moving. Connie and Tina seem to be turning, as if they're on a carousel. I grab the bedstead for support.

Connie leaps to her feet. "Enough, Tina, can't you see how upset she is? You okay, Audrey?" I feel her hand on my bare arm. It's warm and moist. I sink back onto the bed in a daze.

Tina is at my side, on her knees. "Quick, get her a glass of water. Shhhh… It's okay, Audrey," she says gently. And then I start to cry. Big, loud, hiccupy style sobs.

"Oh, come here." Tina pulls me to her and I sob into a mass of red hair. I feel her arm stretch over my shoulder, then I hear the puff of a tissue being plucked out of a box. "I'm not angry with you, so stop with all the crying, okay?" She dabs at my eyes, then glances up. "Thanks, Connie. Here." I take the tumbler of water from her hand, take a few sips and immediately start choking. Fuck. It's gone down the wrong way. Tina pats my back, Connie looks up at me worriedly.

"I'm okay now," I manage, feeling like the worst friend in the world. "I just had a moment." How can Tina be taking this so well? "I'm so sorry, Tina," I blub, throat stinging. "I wanted to tell you, but I thought you'd freak out. I thought I'd lose you."

"You don't have to apologise."

"Wait," Connie says bluntly, pointing a finger at Tina. "How did you find out? I didn't tell her, Audrey."

"Ronan confessed," she says, matter-of-factly. I wonder if that's what he was trying to tell me in the lounge earlier. Warn me that Tina was on the warpath; even though she wasn't. Although you can forgive him for imagining that she was. "We were having a heart to heart after polishing off three bottles of prosecco, and he let it slip," she explains. "I think he was quite relieved, to be honest. He said he wanted us to start with a fresh slate. No secrets." Connie snorts with sardonic laughter and Tina gives her a look. "He knows we're besties and he didn't want it to ever be a problem. He did the right thing."

Pulling her phone out of the side pocket of her dress, Connie sighs in exasperation as she taps at the screen. I'm surprised she's lasted this long without looking at her phone. It's like a life support for her. Tina grins at me as I blow my nose into the tissue in the manner of a trumpet. I don't think I can bear her being so nice to me about it. I expected fireworks – swearing, shouting, hair pulling. But she doesn't even seem pissed off.

"So you don't hate me then?" I ask hopefully.

 HER SECRET

"'Course not, you loon. How could anyone hate you?"

"Are you sure it won't be a problem?" I say shamefully into my lap. "In the future, I mean. I know how much you hate this sort of thing. And I wouldn't blame you if you never wanted to see me again."

Inhaling loudly through her nose, she rolls back on the balls of her feet and stands up; her knees creak. "If you'd copped off with him whilst we were together, it would be a different matter." It's not the end of the world, is it? I know it was just a drunken, stupid, one-night stand. We've all been there." Actually, I hadn't until then. My first time was at the ripe old age of forty-one. But now is not a good time to clarify this fact.

"And Ronan?" I ask carefully. Connie's phone buzzes with a succession of notifications. She must've just switched it on. "Are you okay with him about it?"

"Yeahhh." She pulls a face depicting '*Are you insane?*' "He's the love of my life. I'm not going to chuck it all in because of this." She shakes her head at the window behind me. "Not a second time. I love him too goddamned much, Audrey. I get a flutter right here whenever I look at him." She taps her taught stomach hard. "I've never felt like this about anyone before. I'd do anything for him. I'd kill for him." Connie and I laugh feebly, but Tina's face is deadpan. I stare at her, mouth slightly agape. Connie gives her a long, sideward glance as if she were an escapee from a high security psychiatric unit. Well, Tina's background is a bit colourful. Her dad and two of her uncles were part of an underworld scene for years. I think they still are. I fold my arms and shudder, suddenly feeling cold. Surely, she doesn't mean it, it's just a figure of speech.

"Well, not literally," Tina laughs, clearly sensing the tension. Phew, thank God for that. "But you know what I mean." She rolls her eyes, the old Tina resurfacing. "And I don't want to lose

 HER SECRET

you either. Our friendship means the world to me." The knot in my stomach slowly starts to untangle. I hope she means it. She's dumped friends in the past for a lot less. Like the time she discovered that Hannah, a childhood friend, was texting one of her exes; apparently, to invite him to a birthday bash. Tina insisted that she couldn't possibly trust a snake that went behind her back and made a move on her ex. But that was years ago; she's older now, and wiser. I hope.

"You of all people have shown me how to be forgiving," Tina sighs, reapplying red lipstick in the Venetian mirror on the wall. "I mean, you forgave Louise." She presses her lips together. "After all that palaver over the baby business." I did but I held onto a grudge for weeks.

"Thank you," I say softly at her reflection in the mirror, then look away quickly. I'm glad she knows and has forgiven me, but now I feel as if something has shifted. I can't bear to look her in the eye. I feel so ashamed.

"Oh, per-lease," Connie grumbles, clearly miffed with our soppy interaction.

"Where are your shoes?" Tina looks at my bare feet, ignoring Connie.

I pick them up and sway the broken heel under her nose. "My new *Louboutins*, no less."

"Another gift from Prince Charming?" Tina laughs. Taking the black shoe from my hand, she examines it under the light and the smile dies on her lips. "This is a clear snap, Audrey, looks like it's been pulled off." She throws a glance at Connie. I know that accusing look, but Connie wouldn't do such a nasty thing. She's hot-headed but not spiteful, she proved that tonight. "Look, some of the red sole has come away with it."

Tina and I peer at the shoe, heads touching. "No, I don't think

 HER SECRET

so, Tean." I look fleetingly at Connie, but she's busy scrolling through her phone, smiling. "I chucked them in the doorway, someone must've trodden on them," I lie. I don't mention the figure I thought I saw picking them up, because she'll be convinced that it was Connie, insist that she tampered with my shoes.

"Or maybe one of the guests had a go at trying them on," I suggest. This is actually more likely given that most of the guests are wasted and behaving like unruly teenagers. "Someone with size ten feet, probably," I giggle.

"Oh, stop winging and get Dad to buy you another pair," Connie groans, eyes not leaving her phone. "It's not as if he can't afford it. Besides, you need to go on a shoe shopping binge to fill up that wardrobe he plans to build in your new luxury house."

"A walk-in shoe closet?" I sniff, forgetting our dilemma for a moment. This is the first I've heard of it.

"Ooops. It was meant to be a surprise. Soz." And then under her breath she mutters, "Not."

Tina raises her eyebrows at me. "Lucky girl," she says, then drops to her knees, pulls out a pair of strappy black sandals from under the bed, and hands them to me. "Good job we're the same size."

I take the shoes from her outstretched hand. "Oh, are you sure?" She tells me that she is, that I can't walk around barefoot all night. I can return them anytime. They're an old pair. She hardly ever wears them. "You're a lifesaver," I say, slipping them on.

"No, probs. Anyway, I'm glad we got that business with you and Ronan sorted."

"Oh, so am I, Tina." I glance fleetingly at her warm, green eyes, highlighted with smoky make-up and fake lashes. "And thank you so much for being so understanding. You're a true friend. And if...."

"Oh, stop it you two," Connie interjects, shoving her phone back into her pocket. "You're making me want to vom."

"Anyway," Tina squeezes my forearms, albeit a little too tightly, must be the drink. "I'd better go find my fiancé," she smiles, peeling herself away from me, "Close the door behind you when you're done. I don't want anyone creeping in here for a shag."

The moment the door closes, Connie turns to me. "If you believe that then you'll believe anything,"

"What?" I frown and my head hurts. That confrontation with Tina was like competing in a triathlon. I'm shattered.

Connie perches on the edge of the bed. "That she's okay with you fucking her bloke."

"Oh, don't be ridiculous." I hate it when Connie's so crude. "Tina and I go back a long way, you heard what she said, it's in the past," I retort, although I'm not sure who I'm trying to convince, her or me.

"Well you know what they say, keep your friends close and your enemies closer. Don't blame me when she comes after you the moment Ronan winks at you. I bet she's the one who broke your shoe."

"You're being absurd." I remove the blood stained tissue from my finger, ball it up and bin it. Thank goodness it's stopped bleeding.

"You're making a habit of ruining people's lives, aren't you? I'm surprised you've got any friends left."

"What's that supposed to mean?" I demand, "I haven't ruined anyone's life."

"Er…Louise?"

"What about her?"

"Hah," she huffs in fake amusement. "Don't think she doesn't blame you for ruining her marriage."

 HER SECRET

"WHAT? How dare you!"

"Gerry only left her because of that hoo-ha over adopting his sister's sprog." Gerry was furious with her for keeping the adoption process from me, but that's not the reason their marriage crumbled.

"Don't be so stupid. Gerry and Louise's marriage was on the rocks. They wanted different things, they –"

"If it wasn't for you sticking your oar in, as per, they'd still be together now. Bringing up a family. And Louise wouldn't be spending random nights with blokes she met on the internet and coming home wrapped in a blanket. Yes, Jess told me everything."

I look at her aghast. "Louise is the one who lied to me! Going behind my back to adopt my ex's baby," I protest, truthfully.

"Only it turned out that Nick wasn't the father, didn't it? You ruined any chance that woman had of happiness. I'm surprised she's still talking to you."

I swallow back my anger. She's obviously still furious with me and itching for a row. But I'm not going to take the bait. I've had enough drama for one night. I reach out for the doorknob. "I'm not having this conversation with you, Connie."

"Oh, whatever," she barks into my back.

And then out of nowhere, the guilt returns and wraps itself around me like invisible ivy. I can't just leave her. I turn around and take a few steps forward. I've got to explain, make her understand that I did what I did for her own good. "Connie, I know you're upset about Jake. Let me just –"

"What? Give me ten grand?" she says, her tone full of sarcasm. Actually, that's exactly what I was going to say. But before I can answer, she leaps to her feet. A brown leather jacket slides off the bed. "I'm going home."

"No, Connie, please. Wait," I stand in front of her like a shield. "I was only trying to help you. Jake's a snake."

"Help me?" She throws her head back and laughs at the chandelier. "You made my boyfriend dump me."

"No, I –"

"We were planning a life together. He was going to leave his wife for me before you got involved and fucked it all up!"

"Connie, he was playing you, for goodness sake. Surely you can see that now." But she's having none of it. Huffing furiously, she goes to bypass me, but I manage to block her. "Look, I'll lend you the money, okay?"

"I don't want your charity," she snaps, her face so close to mine that I can smell her cigarette breath. "You can stick it up your fucking – "

The door flies open. Daniel is standing there looking horrified. "Is everything okay?" He's taken his jacket off and loosened his tie, his neck looks red, sore, probably shaving abrasions. He must've used one of Connie's razors this morning.

"Get out of my way, Dad." Connie pushes past him. "I've had enough shit for one night."

"Connie, wait." Daniel gives me a look as if to say, 'What've you said to her?' before stalking off after her without even giving me a chance to respond.

Grabbing my *Louboutins* off the floor, I barrel after them, fighting my way through a crowd of people, their voices like wasps buzzing in my ears. Daniel yells out Connie's name repeatedly. Tina stops me – causally asks what's wrong. I can't leave yet, it's too early, they've only just cut the cake. Then suddenly, George is at my side looking stressed. He wants a word, something's happened, Vicky's upset.

"Not now, George," I say irritably, my eyes not leaving Daniel and Connie.

"Fine," George blasts above the blather of voices as I go after them.

When Connie claps eyes on me, she goes to leave. "Con, wait." Daniel grabs her by the arm. "You won't find a cab at this time of the night." He looks at his watch, then at me worriedly. I know what he's thinking. He shouldn't have forced her to come out tonight. It was too soon. She's still pining for Jake, and now she's had a skinful, too. But he doesn't know the bloody half of it. "Our cab will be here in just over an hour. We'll take you home if that's what you want," he offers gently.

"I can't wait that long," she yells. "Oh, just leave me alone, will you!" At this, she marches off, knocking into Nick and Katrina who are gathering to leave.

"What's wrong, love?" Katrina stops buttoning her black double-breasted coat with huge collars, and takes Connie by the shoulders. Connie turns her face away and stares at the ground.

"She wants to go home," I explain, unable to hide the desperation in my voice. "But none of us is in a fit state to drive, and our cab won't be here for another hour."

"I'll call you a cab, Connie." Nick slides his arm into his jacket and goes to pull out his phone while Connie leans her back against the wall, arms folded, shaking her head at the ceiling, as if she's being held against her will in a flat by a bunch of drunken pensioners.

"Don't you think I've already tried that," Daniel laughs incredulously. "It's Saturday night, mate. They're all booked up solid."

"You can give her a ride home on your bike, darling, can't you?" Katrina suggests kindly. "You haven't been drinking." Nick's been on alcohol free lager all night; but it's too much to ask, it's too far, and he must be knackered after riding home from Brighton.

Connie's eyes light up. "Would you?"

"Don't be ridiculous," Daniel intervenes. "He can't take you home on his bike for crying out loud. It's too far. Besides, how will Katrina get home?"

"I don't mind," Nick offers, giving me a fleeting look. I know he's trying to help. Trying to be nice, make amends. "If you're okay with that, babe?" he says to Katrina, "I can come back for you."

Then they all start talking at once - arguing, debating, making unfeasible suggestions. Katrina tells Nick that it's fine to drop Connie off, she'll jump on the night bus. Daniel objects again and again. Connie tells her father that he's getting on her tits and to back off, which, under any other circumstances, I'd have found hilarious.

I stare ahead as they continue to rant. People are starting to leave. Car doors thud. The front door is wide open. Outside, a girl is being sick on the pavement. Two young women cower over her, one holding her hair back as she retches beneath an orange street light. A woman bashes into me, knocking me sideward. It's Vicky. "Vicks," I cry into her back. "Where're you going?" She turns briefly with a teary face. "Vicky?" She looks through me as George charges along the hallway, coats folded over his arm. Oh, God, I hope they haven't had another row. At the door, Vicky says something to him, he hesitates, then stomps back over.

"Oh, you've got time for us now, have you?" George growls. What's got into him? As if I haven't got enough problems of my own.

"What? Hang on. George!" I see the back of his bald head bobbing as he snakes his way through a herd that's assembled in the doorway, shepherding Vicky outside like a body guard. "George, wait!"

"I don't want you riding on the back of a motorcycle after all the booze you've knocked back tonight, Connie." Daniel's voice is suddenly amplified, officious.

"I'm not pissed, Dad. Get a grip."

"She'll be perfectly safe, Daniel." Katrina tries to reassure him. "He's an excellent rider." But I know Daniel is thinking about the accident Nick had last year. The one that put him in a coma. But that was an isolated incident. We'd just separated. He did have a drink inside him then, but it's different now. He's sober.

"We can't expect you to wait here until Nick gets back, Katrina." Daniel explains, sweat trickling down his face. "It's a lovely gesture. Thanks, but, no thanks."

"I'm going, Dad," Connie insists, shouldering her bag. "Come on, Nick."

Nick shrugs his shoulders at me then says, "Connie, wait, maybe you should…."

She spins round. "No! Either you take me home now, or I'll hitch a ride on the street." She points at Daniel. "Don't you look at me like that, I mean it."

"Connie, you're not going on that bike and that's final," Daniel says sharply, hands balled by his sides. I give him a look. It amazes me how patronising he can be towards her sometimes, as if she were nine-years-old. "What." he says to me, annoyed.

"You know what!"

"Maybe we should go, Nicky," Katrina suggests, clearly wanting out of our public domestic. I don't blame her. They've done all they can. Far more than expected.

"Are you sure everything is okay, Foxy?" Nick twists towards me, dragging his feet as Katrina hauls him by the hand. "If you want me to stay – "

"Come on, Nicky, let them sort it out themselves, sweetie. Don't interfere."

"Dad, leave me alone, I'm not a child, for fuck's sake."

"Then stop bloody acting like one!"

Oh no, here we go again. This is getting us nowhere. "Look, stop it all of you," I scream at the top of my lungs. And they all fall silent. A few people look round at me. They must think I'm an unruly drunk. I rake a hand through my hair, mouth dry, face hot. "Nick why don't you take Connie home?" I turn to Daniel. "We can drop Katrina off on our way, there's plenty of room in the cab." We booked a mini bus for us, Louise and Jess, but with Connie refusing to come, that leaves an extra seat. "Where do you live, Katrina?"

"Nelson Road. It's in Crouch End."

"Still at my rented one-bedroom," Nick smiles, and I nod. I'm not surprised to learn that they don't live in her prestigious home in Primrose Hill. Nick loves Crouch End and doesn't do airs and graces.

"Great," I blow my long fringe off my face, hands on hips. "That's sorted then."

CHAPTER 19

THERE'S A BUZZING noise in my ears. Is it a fly? I'm not sure. It stops. I close my eyes, heavy with sleep. The buzzing starts again, only this time with a familiar tinny jingle – *Super Trouper*. Shit! It's my phone. What day is it? Have I overslept? Am I late for work?

I force my eyes open and peer at the alarm clock. A horizontal red blur sways in my vision. My mouth feels like the inside of a Greek ancient vase that's just been dug out of a ruin – dry and lined with hairline cracks, and probably rancid. I need some water – fast. The phone stops ringing just as I remember crawling into bed at 3.30 a.m. without removing my make-up. Not a good move. Daniel will think he's climbed into bed with the *Bride of Chucky* when he wakes up. I gaze at the red digital numerals through narrowed eyes – 6.27 a.m. Fuck. I've only had about three hours sleep. The phone starts ringing again, demanding my attention. Who the bloody hell is calling me at this ungodly hour on a Sunday?

As I clumsily reach out for my phone on the bedside table it slips from my hand, hits the floor and stops ringing. Oh, bloody hell, I hope I haven't broken it. The sudden ruffle of a bird on the window sill makes me jump then merges with the tinny Abba tune coming from my phone on the carpet. Phew, it's working. I bet the determined caller is mum checking up on me from Cyprus. She'll never get to grips with the different time zone. She'll want the post-mortem on last night, no doubt, make sure that I adhered to her strict instructions to stay away from Nick. I sigh in exasperation as I dangle my arm over the mattress rooting around for my phone as if swishing my hand in warm bath water. The moment my fingers curl around it, it stops ringing.

"Daniel?" I turn to him in haste and almost vomit onto my pillow. My stomach feels as if it's been kneaded by an energetic baker and shaped into plaited bread. I shouldn't have necked that Guinness shot that Ronan concocted before we left – God knows what was in it. "Daniel," I croak, "someone's keeps calling …" I reach out into empty space. He's gone. On the pillow there's a yellow post-it. I heave myself up on my elbows, feeling like crap, and peer at his large, neat writing.

Gone for a run then gym. Be back before you even surface! X

"Cheeky bloody sod," I groan out loud as I punch my passcode into my phone. Three missed calls from Connie. Probably wanting to apologise for the way she spoke to me last night. She's got a habit of doing this. She'll blame it on the booze, as per, and I'll tell her to forget it, as per. Six missed calls from Unknown ID – probably a nuisance call, someone trying to sell me a kitchen, or insist that I've been involved in a car accident. There's nothing from Vicky or George. Damn. What was wrong with them last night? Anyone would think I'd committed a felony the way they were going on.

Staring at the ceiling, I try to evoke yesterday's events. I'd had a fair bit to drink but I don't recall saying anything offensive to Vicky or George. A scene of me and Vicky chatting on the patio plays out in my mind. We're all smiles, happy, content, gazing at the pink, blue and yellow sky as the sun dipped below the horizon, glasses in hands. I'm babbling on about my new house between sips of prosecco, telling her I'd been to a couple of kitchen and bath centres for inspiration, that I'm thinking of converting the loft into a leisure room to help me get back in shape. I hold my phone to my chest like a bible. She seemed happy for me, excited about moving into my flat when I leave. Oh, God, I hope I didn't overdo it. I hope the drink didn't make me sound ostentatious and braggy. The sheer thought of it makes my skin crawl. I dangle a leg out of the side of the bed as heat spreads through me like wildfire. I'll give George a call, find out what exactly happened, then arrange to meet Vicky for coffee at our usual haunt in Muswell Hill. Explain. Grovel. Apologise. That's if I've got anything to apologise for. I'll do that just as soon as I muster the energy to crawl out of bed, neck a cup of coffee and a couple of painkillers.

Still holding onto my phone, I close my eyes to the soothing sound of birds chorusing away in next door's enormous evergreen. Daniel put away more booze than I did last night, and he spent at least half an hour in the bathroom the moment we walked through the door.

"I can't sleep with the smell of tobacco in my hair," he insisted when I told him to come to bed. Although I'm pretty sure he had a Colitis flare-up, possibly due to the stress of Connie, because his visits to the loo were quite frequent and he seemed a bit out of sorts. He'd never admit it, of course, wouldn't want a fuss. But I know. I always know. "I'm just going to jump into the shower," he said, sounding irritated when I rapped on the bathroom door to see if he was okay. "I'm having a shave as well, my face is all itchy. Go back to bed."

How he can have the energy to exercise on a few hours' sleep is beyond me; especially after spending half the night on the toilet. That man is a machine. Nothing will stop him. My phone starts vibrating in my hand – Unknown Caller.

"Hello," I croak.

"Oh, good morning. Is this Audrey speaking?"

"Er, yes, it is," I reply as if I'm not quite sure.

"Audrey, I'm so sorry to disturb you but I was hoping you'd be able to answer a few questions for me." A cold caller? At 6.30 on a Sunday morning? Oh, for fuck's sake. Anger rips through me.

"Have you any bloody idea what time it is?" I growl into the mouthpiece, plumping the pillows behind me with my elbow.

"Oh, God. I'm so sorry. I didn't think…. umm.." I hear a shuffle then her voice murmuring *'Jesus Christ is that the time.'* "Look, forgive me, Audrey. I……..I'll call you back when –" Cold callers aren't usually this apologetic, not to mention yielding.

"Who is this?" I cut in.

"It's Cat." Who the bloody hell is Cat? I rack my brain, then it suddenly occurs to me that one of our client's is called Cat. Mrs King's new secretary. "Audrey?" It wouldn't be the first time a new, bushy tailed secretary called me out of hours with a new 'vision' for their site. "Can you hear me?" They've no real concept of time. "Audrey?" All they want to do is score brownie points with their new boss. "Are you still there, hello?"

"Hello, yes, I'm still here. Sorry." I can't ignore a work call. Raymond would kill me, especially after the starkers episode on WhatsApp. "Cat, you say?" I grab a pen off the bedside table and root around the drawer for a scrap of paper. I'm going to have to take notes.

"Yes, that's right. You haven't forgotten me already have you?" she laughs.

"No, of course not. I was just thinking about your company, actually," I lie. Raymond's marketing ploy. It always works a treat.

"Oh?" She sounds confused – a newbie thing.

"Yes, if you could just remind me of your surname then – "

"Well, it's Rickman. Katrina Rickman, or Byrne, but – "

Oh, shit. It's Nick's wife. "Katrina!" I whip the duvet back and swing my legs around the bed a little too quickly and the room dances. I think I'm going to vomit. "Sorry, I'm still half asleep. No, of course I don't mind you calling. Umm…" What on earth does she want with me? Doesn't this woman sleep? And how did she get my number? I've no recollection of exchanging numbers with her last night.

"I hope you don't mind but I got your number off Ronan," she says, right on cue. "I know it's ridiculous o'clock, and I wouldn't call if it wasn't urgent." She pauses for a moment. "I'm in a bit of a pickle, you see."

"No, no, it's okay. I don't mind." I slide my feet into my purple *Prada* slippers. "What exactly is the problem? How can I help?"

"Well, Nick's the problem."

"Oh." I reply simply, catching a glimpse of my reflection in the mirror and wanting to scream. Nick's wife calling me for a girlie chat about him isn't what I'd class as urgent.

"He's still not home, you see," she goes on, as I tie the belt of my dressing gown into a knot at my waist, phone fastened between my ear and jaw. "I dozed off on the sofa while I was waiting for him to return from your step-daughter's." She sighs loudly and I wince. "I've just woken up, and he's still not here."

"Oh, I see, Kat." Clearly, she likes this abbreviation of her name. "I'm guessing that he's not picking up his mobile."

"It just goes straight to voicemail. I think it's switched off. I've left him several massages but nothing. I thought you might've heard something."

I'm not quite sure why she says this. I'm not my ex's keeper. "No, I haven't heard a thing. He didn't go back to Ronan's then?"

There's another deep, crackly sigh. "No. No-one's heard from him. I'm really worried now, Audrey. Maybe I should ring the police, the hospitals. I – "

"Calm down, Kat. It's only been four and a half hours."

"Yes, I know but…well…."

"You didn't have a row or anything, did you?" I interject, padding into the bathroom. Nick did have a habit of taking off during a barney when we were together – he hated confrontations.

"No," she replies pragmatically. "Quite the contrary, actually. We had a great time at the party. The last thing he said to me before zooming off on his bike with Connie was, '*Won't be long. Wait up for me.*' I mean how long does it take to drive to Bayswater and back?"

"At that time of the morning?" I examine my teeth in the bathroom mirror, definitely need whitening again. My dentist told me this would happen. "On a bike, about an hour. An hour and a half, tops."

"That's what I thought."

"Look, I'll give Connie a call, find out what time he dropped her off."

"Oh, you are a love." I can almost feel her relief.

"It's okay. It's the least I can do after you gave up your ride for her last night. Did you get home okay?" Paula and grumpy Steve gave her a lift in the end, said they were passing through Crouch End.

"Yes," she says brightly, "I was home by ten past two. Tina's sister is lovely, isn't she? But has her partner got a problem with flatulence?"

"No, I don't think so," I chuckle, "Why? Did he let one off?"

"That's an understatement," she says miserably. "He spent most of the time stretching to one side. One of them sounded like a door that needed oiling in a horror movie. I had the window open the entire journey. Poor Paula couldn't look me in the eye when I climbed out of their little Fiesta."

"Oh, dear," I say, and we both laugh. I'm liking Katarina more and more. I'm really glad Nick found her. She's good for him.

HER SECRET

There are a few moments of silence as our laughter peters out, and then, "You don't think he stayed the night, do you?"

Feeling a sudden sting on my shin, I slump onto the toilet seat, slide off my slippers, and extend a leg onto the bathtub. "What do you mean?" There's a red mark on my skin – something must've bitten me in the garden last night.

"Well, maybe she invited him in for a nightcap and….." she tails off. I know what she's implying, but Nick wouldn't do that. Not to his new wife. He was only unfaithful to me once during our eight years together, and that was when we were on a break.

"No, of course not," I say, as if it's the most ridiculous thing I've ever heard.

"Only she was getting a bit raunchy with him last night, wasn't she?"

"Really? I didn't notice," I lie. Connie was bumping and grinding against him at one point, but we'd all had a bit to drink. She was just having a bit of fun, that's all. She's already been hurt by a married man. There's no way she'd make the same mistake twice. "I wouldn't worry, Kat. I'm sure there's a reasonable explanation to all this. He might've run out of petrol, he did have that long ride from Brighton."

"But he'd have called to let me know, surely."

"Maybe he ran out of juice," I offer.

"Juice?"

"Maybe his phone died." I take a deep breath, amble back into the bedroom, and start rooting around in my drawer for some ibuprofen. "Got a flat battery."

"Oh, I see. Yes." She suddenly sounds distant, as if she's not really listening to me anymore.

I ease two pink tablets out of the blister pack. I wonder if the age difference is proving to be a problem for Katrina, after all. I reach for the tumbler of water on my bedside table. Nick and Connie were only having a friendly dance. We all were dancing with each other's partners, including her. I thought she was going to snog Daniel's face off at one point. I knock back the pills. "Look, if you're worried about him and Connie, don't be. Nothing happened between them. I'm certain of it. Nick isn't into..." I stop before the words 'young women,' leave my lips. I don't want to offend her.

"Into what?" Oh bloody hell, this is what happens when I've not had enough sleep. My mouth isn't in sync with my brain. "Oh, wait," she says suddenly. "I've just looked out the window and his motorbike is parked out front." My shoulders sag in relief. "Still no sign of him though." Shit!

I'm saved by a call on the landline. "Look, Katrina...KAT! I'd better go, my other phone is ringing. I'll get back to you with any news as soon as I can, once I've spoken to Connie. Yes, yes, of course. Try not to worry. I'm sure Nick is fine. And let me know if he turns up."

I leg it into the lounge, stubbing my toe against the coffee table in my haste. The pain sears through me as I snatch the phone from its cradle. It's Connie. Thank God.

"Audrey, why aren't you picking up?" she demands without preambles. "Where's my dad?"

I hobble around, screaming inwardly in pain. "I've just woken up, Connie," I manage. "Your dad's gone to the gym."

"Already? But I've been calling him since 5 a.m." Why on earth would she call him so early? I hope nothing's happened. "What time did he leave for Christ's sake?"

"I'm not sure, Connie. He was gone before I woke up." I collapse onto the armchair and rub my toe. "Listen, is everything okay? You sound upset." I hope she hasn't been in touch with Jake. "Can I help at all?"

 HER SECRET

"I'll try him again," she says, sounding dreadful. "Hang on, Audrey, will you?" I sigh into the receiver, drumming my fingers against my lips. Within a few moments Daniel's phone starts ringing. I follow the sound into the kitchen.

"Connie, he's left his phone charging on the kitchen worktop. I'm sorry."

"Fuck," she mumbles.

"Look, are you okay?"

"No," she says tearfully. "I'm not okay. Not okay at all. Something terrible has happened." Terrible? Oh, no, please don't let her tell me that they've been in a road accident. Daniel was dead set against her climbing onto the back of Nick's motorbike, pleading with her not to go, even up until the very last moment when she put her helmet on. And they do say you attract what you fear, don't they? My stomach constricts. "Audrey, could you please pick Lily up from my mum's and bring her to yours? My mum's on her way here now and Nan can't cope with Lily on her own for too long."

The hairs on my arm spike. Aliki's on her way? God, it must be serious. "Yes, of course I can. What's wrong, Connie? You're scaring me now."

"I've been attacked, Audrey."

"Whaaaaat?" I leap to my feet as if I've been sparked with an electric volt. She doesn't answer. All I can hear is her heavy, teary breath. "Connie. Are you okay? Who attacked you? Where? How?" That's why Nick didn't go home. Katrina will be devastated. "Is Nick with you?" Knowing Nick he probably tried to take them all on. Jesus, I hope nothing terrible has happened to him. No wonder he's not picking up his phone. He must've borne the brunt of it. He's probably lying unconscious in a hospital bed. The police must've transported his bike back to his flat while they carted him off to A&E. "What kind of an attack, Connie?" I pace around the coffee table clockwise, anticlockwise, clockwise, anticlockwise. I wonder if it was a random act of violence by a gang of youths. Druggies, maybe, after some cash to feed their addiction. Knife crime is on the up in London. I hear about it all the time on the news. Oh, God, has Nick been stabbed? "Do you know where Nick is?" I almost scream out the words. The phone shakes in my trembling hand. "He didn't go home. Katrina is worried sick."

"Oh, shit, that's my door," she huffs. There's a buzzing sound and then, "Come up, Mum." Then another buzz and a crackle. "Look, I'm gonna have to go, Audrey. Please just pick Lily up and tell Dad to contact me as soon as."

"Yes, I will….But."

"Thanks."

"Connie, wait." And then there's the dialling tone.

CHAPTER 20

"WAIT HERE," I say to the taxi driver over the grunt of his diesel engine. "I may need a lift to Crouch End."

"Okay, but I'll have to charge the standard waiting rate if you're longer than fifteen minutes, love," he replies, elbow hanging out of the window, belly like a balloon over his trousers.

I thunder across the concrete car park, packed with Range Rovers and BMW 5 Series, and through the automatic doors of *Jasmine Blake Leisure Centre* as fast as my legs will carry me, clutching my mobile phone as if my life depended on it. I'm waiting for a call back from George. I must've rang his mobile and landline at least a dozen times before the cab arrived but my calls all went straight to voicemail. So I ended up leaving him a teary message in the back of the taxi to sympathetic glances from the balloon-bellied driver in his rear view mirror:

"George, please. It's me. Pick up or...or...or ring me. I need to talk to you. It's urgent. Something's happened to Connie and I think....I think Nick, too. Something really bad. Look, I don't know what I've done to you guys. I need to talk to you. Please just call me back as soon as you get this message."

A blonde girl with rosy cheeks at reception taps away at her keyboard behind her workstation with long, purple fingernails embellished with glittery stars, eyes darting up and down the screen. "Mr and Mrs Taylor, you say?"

"Yes, it's a joint membership." I shoulder my bag and exchange a small smile with a lycra-clad forty-something lady that brushes past me, gym bag slung over her shoulder.

"And your full name is?"

"Audrey Taylor." The girl taps at the keyboard again, then shakes her head. I lean forward, resting my elbows on the black worktop. A phone goes off in the background. "Can you please try Fox?" Daniel sometimes uses my maiden name for business. "Audrey Fox?" More tapping followed by more head shaking and murmuring. It's quite busy in here for a Sunday morning. I can barely hear the girl speak above the bustle of voices, tapping keyboards, and swishing synthetic fabric.

"Can you confirm the address for me please?" She raises her voice, drowning out some of the cacophony. Finally, we're getting somewhere. As I tell her the first line of my address, my phone starts vibrating in my hand. "Oh, I've found it," she announces brightly.

I look at my phone. It's George. "I'm sorry," I say, backing away, "I've got to get this."

I'm sitting on the edge of a squishy, brown, leather sofa, very posh for a gym. It must cost Daniel a fortune in subscription charges. "George, where the hell have you been?" I breathe heavily down the phone through my nose. "Why aren't you answering my calls?"

"It's," crackle, crackle, "what's," crackle, hiss, "to," crackle, "because."

"Oh, George, you're breaking up. I can't hear you. Hello?" I walk along a short corridor and through a set of automated doors, my satin navy *Manolo* pumps clicking against the white tiles. The doors close behind me, sealing in the noise. "George? Can you hear me now?"

"Yes! Can *you* hear me?" I wince at the boom of his voice.

 HER SECRET

"I can now," I say, gazing up at the notice board in front of me – Swimming Lessons for Adults, Burn Off the Calories with Bootcamp Every Friday, Hatha Yoga for Beginners. "Why haven't you been picking up? I've rung at least a dozen times." The doors slide open and a middle aged man in a yellow t-shirt and blue shorts trudges past me, dripping with sweat and looking like he's just endured three hours in the chamber of torture. Why do they do it?

"Er…some of us do sleep, you know," George groans.

I look at my watch. Shit. It's still only 8 a.m. What was I thinking? I run a hand through my hair and hold it at the top of my head. "I'm sorry, George. I didn't think."

"Hmm…" he murmurs. "Anyway, where's the fire?"

"Huh?"

"The emergency?" He exhales loudly down the phone, clearly exasperated. "What's all this about Connie and Nick? Don't tell me he smashed his bike up again."

"Oh, I see. No, no, it's nothing like that." I pace up and down the small area and in my haste activate the automatic doors. I stand still. "Connie's been attacked. I don't know the full details yet, she wouldn't tell me on the phone but she sounded delirious. I'm at the gym now looking for Daniel. He…he left his phone at home. He doesn't even know about Connie. Aliki's gone to her." I raise my hand in frustration and let it drop heavily by my side. I'm at my wits' end. But George is here now. He'll know what to do. "I've got to pick Lily up from her Nan's. I can't even drive because I've still got alcohol in my system from last night. I'm all over the place, George. Katrina's having kittens. Nick didn't go home last night. Well, this morning, yet his bike is parked outside. And – "

"Whoa…whoa…calm down," he says in a sleepy voice. "How bad is she?"

"I'm not sure. I'm really scared." Closing my eyes, I fill my lungs with warm, stuffy air and exhale loudly. "I mean, it sounds like they may have both been assaulted. Nick must've taken the brunt of it because he's not home yet. Probably still waiting in A&E for a once over. You know how short staffed the NHS is. He'll probably be there all day." My fear of him being stabbed dissipated the moment I put the phone down from Connie. She didn't sound worried when I asked about him; she'd have said if he were seriously hurt. "Nick was probably trying to protect her," I go on. "You know what he's like." George doesn't answer, but he knows Nick has a protective nature. I bite my bottom lip thoughtfully – should I call him? I know his number by heart. That's if he hasn't changed it.

"Well, what sort of an assault was it?"

"What do you mean?"

"Was it a sexual assault?"

A feeling of dread sluices through me. I didn't think of that. "No, I don't think so," I say, terrified. "I mean, if Nick was with her that couldn't have happened, right?"

"Yes, that's true." He breathes loudly again. He's thinking. Trying to work out what to do. I know my brother, he's good at sorting things out. He'll have a plan, a strategy. "Well look, I hope you sort it out."

Sort it out? He can't be serious. How can he be so blasé about it? Connie's been attacked. Nick is missing. Why isn't he anxious? Why he isn't offering to come over and help me like he always does? George always looks after me. We're close siblings, everyone says so. "George, did I say something to offend you or Vicky last night?" I gulp, tears stinging my eyes.

There's a brief silence and then, "Audrey, what do you want me to say?"

"I don't understand… I – "

 HER SECRET

"Vicky had her heart set on your flat." I can hear the annoyance in his voice. "You know that."

"Yes, of course." I wipe a tear off my face sharply. "So?"

"SO?" he tuts. "Is that all you have to say? You of all people know how vulnerable she is right now."

"What do you mean?" I furrow my brows, twisting my face into a scowl. George isn't making any sense. "Has something happened?"

Another loud, lingering sigh that seems to travel through my ear and into my brain, setting off alarm bells. My mind races through Saturday night's events but I can't think of what I might've said or done. "You don't know, do you?" he says finally. The doors open and two young women breeze in. "Look, I think you should speak to Daniel."

"And I was like, are you shitting me," says one of the women to the clank and hiss of the second set of doors opening.

"God, if that were…" replies her friend, as the doors close behind them.

"Speak to Daniel?" I gasp, confused. "Why?"

"Audrey, now is not the time. I feel like shit, you're stressed. Just go and sort out your family. We'll be all right." His words trample over my heart, digging their heels in for good measure.

"MY FAMILY? What's that supposed to mean?" I demand.

"Well, you always put them first, don't you?" His cold, harsh words dig into my skin like sharp icicles, and I shudder as I steady myself against the wall. I can't believe he just said that. "You've changed since you became Mrs Taylor." My mouth falls open. What is he saying? They're my family, too. Him, Vicky, the kids. They're my world.

"George, what's –"

But he doesn't let me finish. "Listen, the twins are wailing." I can hear them babbling in the background but they're not crying. My brother doesn't want to speak to me anymore. "I'm gonna have to go. Hope no one's seriously hurt. Good luck and see you when I see you."

"George, wait. You can't just leave me hanging on a thread. I want to know what happened. What has Daniel said? You can't go around throwing accusations like that without an explanation. I've got a right to know….George? George?" Silence. "George, are you still there?" I look at my handset. Screensaver. Shit. SHIT!!

I dash back to reception, knocking into two fit looking girls with tight ponytails and white bandanas. One of them calls out into my back, "Look where you're bloody well going." But I don't break my stride. There's a lady in front of me talking to the blonde girl with the rosy cheeks, elbows on workstation, one leg tucked behind the other as if she has all the time in the world.

After several moments, that feel like minutes, of irritable exhales and tutting, I finally get to talk to blonde-rosy-cheeks. "Did you find it?" I say hurriedly. The sooner I get into the gym and find Daniel, the sooner I can get back to George. Find out what the hell has happened.

"Er…yes, Mrs Taylor." She glances at my fingers drumming against the workstation. I stop. "Your trial membership expired a month ago and hasn't been renewed." She slides her chair back and goes to stand up. "I can get someone in Sales to talk to you about a permanent membership. It'll only take - "

"What?" I cut across her loudly as a faceless silhouette of a woman passes through the barrier on my right. "It can't have. There must be some mistake. My husband comes here regularly – definitely every Sunday!"

"Not to this gym, I'm afraid." She glances at me quickly with a twitch of a grin. Her eyes depicting, 'Your husband is shagging someone else, love. "But I could get Sales to…."

 HER SECRET

When the fresh air hits me, my legs give slightly. I hold onto a blue light pole outside the gym for support, taking short, hot breaths. A young woman sitting on one of the benches on the right looks up from her mobile phone with a reflex frown then goes back to her call, chewing gum, talking loudly in a foreign language.

If Daniel hasn't been coming here then where the hell has he been going for the last month? Vicky's word echo in my ears '*Yes,*' she'd said in the coffee shop only three days ago when I returned from the loo. '*I saw him buying you a big bouquet across the road.*" Were they for some mystery woman, after all? An image of Daniel in Connie's bedroom last Tuesday flashes into my mind. He's shouting into the phone, '*I told you, I'll sort it.*'

A feeling of dread passes through me like a scanner. What is Daniel up to? Who were the flowers for? What did he say to my brother and his wife? And, more importantly, is my husband of two months cheating on me already? My stomach flips. I don't think I can keep the sickness at bay.

CHAPTER 21

"YOUR HOME IS all nice and clean," Lily announces as we shuffle through my front door. "Not like Yiayia Aliki's. It's all full of old rubbish and it smells of poo. I hate it there now." She straightens the pink mini dress on her doll and pouts her lips, as I press my back against the door firmly.

"Don't be like that, Lily, she just likes collecting things, that's all. It doesn't mean her house isn't clean." You could eat off Aliki's kitchen floor but her hoarding is getting out of control. I thought the towers of old newspapers and magazines in the large square hall were going to collapse as Despina, her elderly mother, guided me through a maze of overflowing boxes and bulging bin bags to where Lily was sitting crossed-legged on the lounge floor, staring up at *Shaun the Sheep* comforting his crying offspring on the 52 inch screen.

"Can I play in the garden, Audrey?" Lily asks, skipping into the hallway, blonde curls tumbling over her narrow shoulders.

Sliding my bag off my shoulder, I glance at the modem on the second shelf of the tall table in the corridor. I turned it off to reboot before I left. It hasn't been switched back on, which means Daniel hasn't been home. Where the hell is he? The flat is quiet, eerie. It's almost as if the bricks and mortar can sense that something has gone horribly wrong in our lives.

My eyes dart to my watch. It's only just gone nine and already I'm exhausted. "Yes, of course you can, Lily. But aren't you hungry?" I follow her into the kitchen and immediately spot that Daniel's phone is missing from the worktop. There's a cup of half-filled black coffee in the sink. He's been and gone. "I can make you a boiled egg and soldiers," I go on, opening the fridge to check for supplies. I need to make things as normal as possible for Lily. Shit – no eggs. "Or how about some toast and strawberry jam?"

Pausing by the hob, she rubs her little tummy, twisting her pink, bow shaped lips in contemplation. "I'd better not, Audrey," she says in a very grown-up tone. I'm so glad that despite Daniel's protest she still calls me Audrey and not Nan, or the Greek equivalent, Yiayia. "Yiayia Despina made me koulouri toast and halloumi. I'm still quite full. But Millie might want some."

I crouch down to Lily's eye level and gently tuck her hair behind her ear, and suddenly I'm overwhelmed by how much she resembles her mother. Not so much her features, Lily's blue-eyed and naturally fair-haired, but her expression and demeanour, right now, is so like Connie's, it's uncanny. I straighten the short sleeve of her blue cotton dress, taking in the big red roses and the red silk bow at the neck. Connie is almost as fussy about Lily's wardrobe as she is of her own. I was with her when she bought her daughter this Ted Baker dress in the January sales. We had champagne afternoon tea at Liberty's afterwards. We talked and laughed and gossiped, and I really felt like we were bonding.

I smile sadly now at Lily. "Shall we ask Millie if she's hungry, then?" I say, looking at the doll clasped in her little hands.

"Don't be silly, Audrey," she giggles, swaying from side to side and at looking at me shyly. "Dolls can't hear."

My knees creak as I get to my feet. Outwitted by a child. There really is no hope for me, is there? I open the back door to a loud thud and crash as Mr Gingernut, who was sunbathing in his usual spot on our patio, legs it over the fence like Usain Bolt. "I think Florian left his football in the garden if you want to have a kick-about."

"On my own?" Lily juts out her bottom lip and looks at her doll. "Mummy always plays football with me," she says sulkily. "She's rubbish so she always goes in goal. What time will she be here, Audrey?

The sunlight catches her eyes as she squints up at me, and I fight the urge to bend down, scoop her up in my arms and hold her tight; tell her that mummy won't be picking her up today, that she's had a little accident but everything is going to be all right. But instead, I ruffle her hair. "I've got a few things to sort out and then I'll join you," I promise, "How's that?" She nods happily. "I'll just get you a juice out the fridge."

"Okay," she says over her shoulder as she skips onto the lawn. "And one for Millie, too. I think she's thirsty now."

I look at her from the kitchen window with a heavy heart. Poor little thing, stuck in the middle of all this mayhem. It can't be easy for her growing up without a dad. Daniel is a great substitute and a good father figure, but how can it be the same? "Oh, Daniel," I murmur, "where the hell are you?

Then as I curl my hand around the handle of the fridge, I catch sight of a note pinned onto the door with a Cyprus magnet, a souvenir I picked up when I was there last September.

'Gone to Connie's – just found out the news. Tried calling you but no reply. Call me asap. D. X'

I'm in the hallway, rummaging through my bag for my phone. Lily squeals in the background, a helicopter thrums in the sky. Three missed calls from Daniel. Damn.

The floorboards moan beneath me as I pace up and down the corridor, hand on hip. "Come on, Daniel, pick the bloody phone

HER SECRET

up." He answers on the fourth ring. "Daniel, it's me. Where the hell – "

"Oh, God, Audrey. I'm so glad to hear your voice." He sounds dreadful. "Connie said she told you what happened."

"Yes, she did but – "

He doesn't let me finish. "Did you pick Lily up? Is she okay? It's all kicking off down here."

Kicking off? What does he mean? "Yes, I did." Clipping my Bluetooth earpiece on, I walk back into the kitchen, and reach for one of the coloured plastic tumblers from the cabinet. Daniel bought them especially for when the kids visit. Lily always likes to drink out of the green one; takes pride in the fact that it's our favourite colour. "She's in the garden playing." I say. "I'm just pouring her a glass of orange. Where have you been all morning? – I"

"I went for a swim. Didn't you get my note? I left it on the pillow."

"Yes." I hesitate. "Erm…you said you were at the gym."

"Yes, that's right."

"In Finchley?"

He breathes heavily down the phone. "Yes, in Finchley," he confirms, annoyed. My stomach tightens. Why is he lying to me? "What's with the Spanish Inquisition, anyway? My daughter's in a right state here."

I focus on the green washing up liquid on the sink, biting the inside of my bottom lip, and decide very quickly not to pursue GymGate. At least not right now. "I can't believe this is happening. How's Connie? Do you – "

"Black and blue, Audrey," he cuts across me. "Awful, just awful." My heart cracks, poor, poor Connie. "God, why doesn't she ever listen to me?" he goes on, his voice thick with emotion. "I did warn her. I had a bad feeling about this."

I take a lungful of air as Lily squeals in the garden at Mr Gingernut who's reappeared over the fence. Why does everything have to be so complicated? Why do bad things happen to innocent people?

"Is there anything I can do?" I ask as calmly as I can, replacing the carton of orange juice in the fridge. "Has Nick been badly hurt, too? Only he didn't go home last night. I – "

"Hurt? I bloody well hope so!"

"Daniel!" I can't believe he's blaming Nick for this. "None of us could stop Connie from leaving the party. You saw what she was like." There's a shuffle, then I hear him say, "Yes, please." I sigh heavily, rubbing my forehead. Maybe jumping to Nick's defence wasn't such a good move. What the hell am I doing? My stepdaughter has been hurt. "Look, I'm sorry, Daniel," I say softly. "I know you're upset. And so am I. It's all such a shock." I look up at the spotlights, eyes stinging with tears. "I don't want us to fight, okay? What do you want me to do?" Silence. "Daniel? Are you listening?"

There's a rustle, and then, "Yes, I am. Sorry. Aliki just made me a cuppa."

He blows loudly down the phone. I'm not sure if it's irritation, or if he's blowing on his hot tea. "Just stay put for now. I don't want Lily to see her mum like this. It might frighten her." Jesus, Connie must be in a terrible state. What kind of monsters could do this to her? The bloody savages. "I'll talk to her later, explain what happened. That might soften the blow."

"She's only six, Daniel." I glance out of the window at Lily. She's crouched down next to the cat offering him a sniff of Millie's bottom.

"Yes, but she's a clever girl, she'll understand." He's right about that. Lily's got her mother's strong genes – gutsy, brave, says it how she sees it. Unlike Florian and the twins, she never complains or

HER SECRET

cries over a scraped knee, or an unfair tackle. She just gets up, dusts herself down, and carries on. But I still think this is too much for her.

"Yes, but even so," I say. "You don't want to scare her, she's only little."

"Well, we'll think of something to tell her. Anyway, we've talked about it and think it's best if she and Connie stay with Aliki and Despina for a few days." Lily won't be happy with this arrangement given that she thinks her Nan's house stinks of poo.

"Okay." I slouch against the sink and the lip digs into my back. "How's Connie doing?"

"She's bearing up."

I tell him to send her my love, that I'll be over to see her later this evening at Aliki's when I drop Lily off, and he agrees, says she'll appreciate that. He can't believe how unlucky she's been lately. First she gets dumped by that good for nothing Jake, and now this. A shiver whisks along my spine at the mention of Jake's name. "Perhaps we should all go on holiday," he suggests. "Get away from all this madness for a while. Cyprus is great at this time of year. It'll be nice to spend some time with your parents, too." And I agree. I miss them so much, especially now.

"By the way," I add as casually as I can, "what did you say to Vicky and George last night? They've got the right hump with me."

"Oh, Audrey." I can hear the irritation in his voice. "Not that. Not now."

So something did happen between them then. "Please, Daniel. George was really narky with me earlier, said something about my flat." I need to know what happened. I can't bear any bad feelings between me and my brother.

His loud sigh crackles in my ear. "I told Vicky the flat was Connie's."

"WHAT?" I cry, straightening up. She's living in a luxury apartment in Bayswater while my brother and his family are roughing it in a tiny flat above a flipping fish and chip shop. "Why would she want to swap her swanky flat for mine?" My eyes dart around my *barely enough room for two people to stand in* kitchen. Is Daniel mad?

"Her term is up. The landlord has doubled the rent. We only found out the other day. She and Lily can't afford to stay. End of."

"I thought you helped out with the rent."

Another long sigh. I picture Daniel holding the bridge of his nose in exasperation. "Business isn't doing that well, you know that. The current climate is crushing us. We've got to make cutbacks or we'll go under."

"But I promised this flat to my brother and his wife. I can't go back on my word." Despite everything, I can't seem to hide my frustration.

"I know, I know." There's a brief pause. I hope he's rethinking. "Look, I'm sorry, but she and Lily have nowhere else to go." Shit. "I can't turf my daughter and grandchild out onto the street. You've got to understand that, darling. It's not as if your brother and his family are homeless, is it?"

"Can't you find them somewhere to else live? You are an estate agent," I groan.

"Not in an area with such a good school catchment. I'm sorry, darling."

I shake my head. I can't believe he promised my flat to Connie without discussing it with me first, but now is not the time to argue. "What a mess," I sigh heavily. "Vicky and George are well pissed off with me now. And I don't blame them. I don't know how I'm going to make it up to them." No wonder my brother thinks I put my new family first.

 HER SECRET

"I'll speak to them, see if we can sort something out." There's a pause then I hear Aliki's voice, a hiss and a scrape as Daniel covers the mouthpiece followed by mumbling. "Audrey, can we talk about this later?" I'm going to have to go. We're ready to go down to the station."

"The station? I take a sip of water. "Didn't you drive there?"

"The police station." He raises his voice, annoyed that I'm not keeping up. But this is all too much for me on only a few hours' sleep and a hangover. "Connie needs to make a statement."

"Didn't the police go round there? Someone must've called them."

"Yes, but she was too distraught, then she had to go to A&E to get a once-over. The police said she could go down to the station with a family member later on today. They might want a statement from me. They'll probably want to talk to you at some point, too."

"Me?" I ask, astonished. "What for?"

"They'll want to question you about Nick."

"Where is he?" I suddenly remember Katrina. "I've got to call Katrina."

"Behind bars," he barks, "and I hope they bloody well throw away the key after what he did to my daughter." A shiver tears through me and I feel my blood run cold.

"What do you mean?" I gasp. "Are you saying Nick was involved in Connie's attack?"

"That's exactly what I'm saying. He beat her up." My hand flies to my mouth. He can't be for real. There must be some mistake. "The bloody nutter. People like him should be on a lead. Just wait until I get my hands on him, I'll ….."

The room darkens. I feel as if I've been hit by a bulldozer, everything seems surreal. I go to move but my legs feel like lead. I steady myself against the sink. Lily is at my side, whining. She's thirsty, where's her drink? Had I forgotten? "You've got to be joking," I mumble through trembling fingers. He tells me that he wishes he was, why am I so surprised, didn't Connie tell me? "No…no…Connie didn't say, she was in a rush…..she -" I pull Lily close to me and she clings to my thigh. She knows something's wrong.

"He's in custody. I don't know how long they'll detain him for but we'll be prosecuting. I've already called my lawyer. I'll make sure he does time for this. The fucking PRICK."

CHAPTER 22

CONNIE LOOKS UP AT ME. There's a bit of dried blood on her top lip; the skin around her right eye is red and starting to go a bit purple. I press my fingers against my lips as this evening's spaghetti pomodoro somersaults in my stomach. Giving me a meek smile, she draws Lily closer to her, then stares ahead at a barely audible T.V. in the corner of the living room.

"Oh, mummy," Lily says, gently pushing Connie's hair off her face. "Don't be sad. You should be careful on the slippery floor." Daniel warned me earlier that they'd all agreed to tell Lily that Connie had a fall at home, which is just as well. I'm not sure how she'd have coped with knowing the truth; however smart, she's just a child.

"I know, baby," Connie sniffs, stroking Lily's cheek with the back of her fingers. "Silly mummy."

"And you won't be able to wear your red lipstick now on your cut lip," Lily points out, inclining her head. "Maybe we should give it to Millie. She likes red lipstick." Daniel, Aliki and I exchange glances and smile. Lily is such a great kid – smart, bright, and incredibly cute. Connie's done a wonderful job as a single parent.

A loud bass beat from a speeding car fills the brief silence, and then I say. "So, how are you feeling, sweetheart?" It's a stupid question, because clearly she's feeling like shit. But I can't think of anything more helpful to say.

Connie points at her face. "It's not as bad as it looks. The doctor said it'll fade in a few days." She's being stoic. Playing it down. I'm sure of it. Jesus, how could Nick have done this to her?

I gaze at her in stunned silence, one hand covering my mouth, my other arm wrapped around my waist, as she goes on to say that it was the fear of losing control that was the worst part of it.

"I thought I was going insane," she says wiping a tear from the corner of her eye.

I frown, look at Daniel for clarification but his eyes are fixed on Connie, balled fist pressed against his mouth, almost as if he's chewing his knuckles off. Aliki puts a protective arm around her daughter, comforting her with soothing sounds and platitudes – it was the drink that caused it. You heard what the doctor said; it's very common, nothing permanent, nothing to worry about.

I clear my throat. "What do you mean?"

Connie looks at her dad sharply, then at me. "The alcoholic blackout," she says, as if I'm supposed to know this. But I don't even know what it means. "Mum looked it up online when we got home."

Aliki confirms this with a quick, sharp nod and a tight smile. She looks older today somehow. I'm not sure if it's because of the inch of white roots in the centre parting of her short, dark, layered hair, or the severity of the orange lipstick against her olive-skinned face. Or maybe she's just suffering from 24-hour-manic-stress-syndrome. It can age you by twenty years overnight, and I should know because when I looked in the mirror before leaving the flat this evening, a weary double of my mother stared back at me. Only a much fatter version, because mum is skin and bone.

"Shall we go and make everyone a cup of coffee, Lily?" Aliki asks. Lily carries on stroking Connie's arched eyebrows, as if her grandmother hasn't spoken. She must be able to feel the tension.

HER SECRET

I always knew when something was up at home, especially when my parents had a barny, because George and I would become their speakers – *'Tell your father dinner's on the table.' 'Tell your mother I'm not hungry.'*

"Go on, Lily," Daniel says encouragingly, leaning forward. His small smile looks as if it's causing him physical pain. "I'm dying for a cup."

Lily doesn't answer, instead she looks at Connie intently and then flings herself at her mother. See what I mean? She knows. Unlike most adults, children are very in tune with their sixth sense. At least that's what I read on Sam Knight's report as I was typing up his notes on Friday morning.

"You can help Yiayia Despina with dinner if you like," Aliki offers, and as she gets to her feet and folds her purple long jumper over her leggings, I notice that she's lost a little weight. Connie told me a few weeks ago that her mum's on a diet, wants to slim down to a size fourteen. It must be working. "Come on, agape mou," she says to Lily, and my lips twitch. I always want to laugh when Aliki ends sentences or people's names with *mou*. I always thought it had something to do with cows. But Maria, mum's Cypriot cleaner, told me that it means *my* in Greek. It's often used as a term of endearment – my love, my Lily. "Uncle Vas and Auntie Elena will be here soon," Aliki goes on. I inhale the smell of Mediterranean cooking wafting from the kitchen, still perplexed by Connie's alcoholic blackout. I'll Google it when I get home. It must mean that she collapsed from too much booze, or something.

Lily untangles herself from Connie and looks up at Aliki, eyes bright. "From Cornwall?" Aliki nods happily, arms open, and Lily hops off her mother's lap and slides a hand into her Nan's. "Will Alex and Kyri be coming too?" Connie's cousins. They're a close knit family. "And Boo?"

"Yes, they're all coming to see us, including the dog," Aliki says, steering Lily gently out of the lounge.

Their voices taper off as they disappear into the kitchen. Daniel cups my knee, smiling sadly. "She won't get rid of it," he whispers, gesturing at the heaps and mounds with his head. "It's getting out of control. It's unhealthy, unhygienic."

"Oh, leave her alone, Dad," Connie snaps, jumping to her mother's defence. "She is trying. She took three bin bags to The North London Hospice last week. Give her a break." Pulling a scrunchie out of the pocket of white *Nike Air* jogging pants, she pulls her hair back and secures it into a tight ponytail and immediately looks like a teenager. She's got her father's youthful genes.

"No, I know, honey," Daniel says, scratching his five o'clock shadow. "I wasn't having a go…it's just that…" He looks at me for support but I just pull a face. I know he's got a point, but what am I supposed to say?

They carry on discussing Aliki's hoarding, as I gaze around the living room wondering how Aliki will sleep eight people and a cocker spaniel in this four-bedroom cluttered house. "Looks like a full house tonight," I say once they stop talking, to the thud of car doors followed swiftly by two central locking beeps. Surely, they can't be here already. "You could stay over at ours if you like?"

Connie shakes her head as she half stands, edging forward. "I want to be with Mum and Nan," she says, peering curiously out of the bay window.

"Have they arrived?" Daniel jerks his head round.

"No," Connie sighs. Flopping back down, she curls one leg under the other and reaches for her phone. "It's for next door but one."

I let her settle, read her texts, and then I say. "So, what happened, Connie?" I lean forward, forearms resting on my thighs. I need to

HER SECRET

make some sense of this. I need to understand why Nick did this to my stepdaughter – what made him lose it.

Leaning her head back, she stares up at the crystal chandelier, a bespoke piece from Harrods. Aliki told me they bought it when they first moved in. Daniel chose it. It's striking and sparkly and grandiose, and far too big for this room.

"You don't have to, Con," Daniel says, giving me a look.

"Oh no, of course, you don't…" I feel my cheeks redden. "I just – "

"No, it's okay, Dad. I want to."

Connie spends the next ten minutes recounting her ordeal, and I listen silently as Daniel shuffles and grunts next to me.

She invited Nick up for a nightcap. It was the least she could do after he gave her a ride home in the middle of the night. Feeling sticky after a long day, she quickly changed and tied herself into a dressing gown, before opening a bottle of red. It was all going well. Everything was pretty normal. They were talking, having a laugh.

"He told me about his bizarre wedding in Vegas," she laughs faintly, rubbing her palm with her thumb. "Said a boozy whirlwind romance was the only way anyone would get him down the aisle." Well, I can vouch for that. "Anyway, we finished the wine and then got the vodka out." Unscrewing a bottle of Evian, she takes a large glug to a racket of clashing saucepans and Greek dialogue drifting in from the kitchen. "Yes, Dad, I know it was a dumb thing to do, so quit with the looks, okay?" Connie's not a big drinker. No wonder she had alcoholic blackout, whatever that is. "That's when I started to feel weird. I'd had too much to drink. I knew it was wrong but I couldn't seem to stop." I nod knowingly. The thing about telling yourself you'll only have a couple of drinks is that after the second glass you no longer care. "I was just drowning my sorrows, you know? I told him all about Jake." My stomach tightens. I wonder if she told him he's married. "He was really lovely – kind, sympathetic, even told me not to give up hope, that we might get back together again." She didn't tell him, then. "And then I…I.." she stammers and Daniel tells her to stop, she doesn't have to go on, we're not the damned police, for heaven's sake.

"I'm okay, Dad," she snaps, "I want Audrey to know what happened. She's family." I love her for saying this. It makes me feel all warm and glowy and like I belong. "Besides, I've got nothing to hide."

"Go on, Connie," I say warmly, "you're doing really well."

She nods, caressing her knee in circular motions. "We started arguing. I must've upset him because he suddenly went all cold on me. I remember calling his wife an old fucking cunt." A pink tinge sweeps over her face. I'm not sure if this is because she's used the C word in front of her dad, or because she knows it was a shitty thing to say. "Things were getting out of hand, and I……I….." Her voice cracks and this time Daniel insists that she stops. "Oh, Dad, will you please stop FUSSING," she says, throwing her hands out like an overenthusiastic orchestra conductor. "I'm okay. JESUS."

Daniel sinks back into his seat and looks away, grimacing, while she fishes for her Evian bottle around her seat. I know he's trying really hard to keep it together.

"He grabbed me by the arms." I feel Daniel tense up next to me. The plastic bottle dents a little from the pressure in her hand. "We were both shouting, talking over each other. I can't remember much of what happened after that. It's all such a blur. A slap… there was a slap…a hand coming at me and then I was out." The alcoholic blackout, I was right. "I must've been unconscious for about five or ten minutes. When I woke up I was on the sofa, alone. I kind of sobered up right away. It was really weird. I could taste something like copper in my mouth. I thought I'd lost a tooth at first but then realised that the bleed was coming from my lip and nose. I managed to get to my feet and call the police." I stare at her agape. All this from a squabble, really? It doesn't sound like the Nick I know. He usually runs for the hills at the sniff of an argument.

"But when you started arguing, why didn't you tell him to leave?" I ask, concerned. I feel Daniel's eyes on me. How dare I question his daughter.

She exhales loudly, shaking her head. "I don't know. I think I did. Things are coming to me in flashbacks. I just remember snippets - loud voices. Shouting. A hand flying towards me. Oh, God, I'm never drinking again." She covers her face with her hands.

Daniel throws me a glance, face dark, and I swear I see a fleeting look of accusation in his eyes. But this isn't my fault, is it? Or maybe it is. After all, I was the one who agreed that Nick should take Connie home. It was I who brought him into her life. I who made Jake end their relationship, which resulted in her getting off her head at the party. Maybe I'm responsible for all of this – for everything.

"Didn't anyone hear you shouting, try to help?" I press on, mouth dry. I wish Aliki would hurry up with those drinks.

Shaking her head, she draws her legs in and wraps her arms around her knees. "I don't know. I don't think so." She pauses. Daniel's phone pings in his pocket. It's been going off all evening and it's now seriously starting to piss me off. "A lot of the residents were out, or asleep, I suppose. There was a party going on upstairs." She raises her eyes to the ceiling. "That probably drowned out our voices."

I lick my dry lips. Daniel is going to hate me for this and I'll probably get a mouthful for it, but I have to ask her this question. "And you're sure it was Nick that slapped you?"

Her eyes flash with confusion. Daniel's phone pings again. "Um...yeah....I'm mean, who else was it?" There's a hint of uncertainty in her voice that makes me catch my breath. "It was just the two of us in the flat."

Daniel leaps to the edge of his seat, fist clenched on the armrest. "What are you insinuating?"

"Nothing. I'm just trying to get a clear picture, that's all."

"I know I can't remember much of what happened, but he definitely hurt me. I mean, look at me!" She gestures her hands at her face and I nod slowly. Poor Connie. I want her to stop now. I've heard enough. I can see how distraught she is.

"He's as guilty as fuck," Daniel yells.

"You do believe me, Audrey, don't you? I wouldn't make this up...I.." she falters.

"Of course she believes you," Daniel jumps in before I can answer.

I run a hand over my mouth, my mind reeling. Why would Nick do this to her, to anyone? It's so out of character. I wonder if his accident had anything to do with it. A severe head injury can have side effects. I Googled it last year when it first happened. The victim can change; become angrier, lash out.

"I'm so sorry, Connie. I shouldn't have let him take you home. I feel so responsible." Guilt almost chokes me. I swallow it down and it burns my stomach. Daniel shoots me a look of approval. Clearly, glad he's got me onside.

"It's okay, it's not your fault." Her voice cracks and Daniel tells us that's enough now, and I agree. I should go. Leave her in peace. Her family will be arriving soon and I don't' want to overstay my welcome. I gather myself and get to my feet. "We'd better get going before your guests arrive." Daniel stands up too.

"It's okay, baby, daddy's here." He's sitting on the armrest, cradling Connie in his arms, his cheek squashed against the top of her head. I watch as they cling to each other. She's so lucky to have such a caring, loving family.

"He's been released," I croak, and they both look up at me, startled. "I spoke to Katrina a while ago."

"Have they charged him?" Daniel demands, leaping to his feet, arms outstretched like a heavyweight boxer.

"I don't know," I say wearily. "Katrina said he was in a terrible state. He just showered and went straight to bed." I twist my wedding band, my eyes darting to the flickering T.V. A rerun of *Antiques Roadshow* is on. An expert is telling an astonished middle-aged woman the price of a strange looking wooden object. "He didn't want to talk about it." I shrug, feeling numb.

I don't tell them that he did have one question for Katrina – *'Does Audrey know and what did she say?'*

"I'm going to ring the station." Daniel thunders across the room, yanks his mobile phone from his jacket pocket and starts jabbing at the screen. "Find out what the hell is going on."

"I could speak to Katri – " I begin.

"Yes, can you please put me through to sergeant – "

We've spoken at the same time.

"No," Daniel howls at me, covering the mouthpiece. "I don't want my family anywhere near him or his wife. No contact, Audrey, okay?"

I nod, twisting my ring round and round and round as if somehow it'll turn off the thoughts that are swimming around in my head. Why would my kind, gentle, ex-boyfriend give my stepdaughter a lift home and then knock her out flat? Why?

CHAPTER 23

MY PHONE THRUMS on my desk and then starts vibrating. I glance at the lit up screen quickly and my stomach stings.

"Him again?" Fearne asks, throwing me a quick glance from the adjacent desk. I nod, staring at Sam Knight's intro page on my screen without even taking in the words. We're working on his website and have a tight deadline to meet. It's tough, and it doesn't help that my head is full of Daniel and Connie and Nick. But I am enjoying the challenge, and it's a distraction – sort of.

"Persistent, isn't he?" Fearne remarks. I pull a 'whatever' face, scrolling up and down the page and frowning, as if I'm really concentrating on what I'm doing. "Maybe you should answer it before it goes into meltdown, it has been ringing all day." Fearne laughs, but I'm sure it's been driving her insane. It stops ringing and we go back to our work. Maybe I should switch it off, or at least put it in my bag. But as I pick it up it immediately starts buzzing in my hand. Fearne twists her lips and looks at me over her cat-eye glasses. "Don't you at least think you should hear him out?" she asks, a hint of exasperation in her tone. "Connie had her say yesterday, it's only fair, given the circumstances. This isn't going to just go away, Audrey. You're going to have to face the music sooner or later."

"I can't." I take a deep breath and look at the gold band on my finger. "I promised Daniel I wouldn't have any contact with him." My eyes flit from Fearne to the ringing phone in my hand.

"Since when have you let a man tell you what to do?" Her words resonate with me like a loud shrilling bell. "You're Audrey Fox, remember." She's right. Perhaps I should speak to him. It'll get him off my back, if nothing else. Nick's the most stubborn person I've ever met.

Rolling back in her office chair, Fearne gets to her feet. "Coffee?" I nod. "Yes, please."

"And answer that phone." She squeezes my shoulder as she passes by. "Or I will!"

I watch as Fearne walks gingerly towards reception then slide my phone to answer.

"Hello," I croak, as if I'm on fifty fags a day.

"Foxy?" Nick gasps, "Oh, at last. Thank God." There's a pause and then a click. I think he's lighting up. "Did you get my texts?" I hear him blowing out smoke.

"Yes," I say, clearing my throat. They all pinged through last night and this morning. All nineteen of them – it's a good job Daniel was asleep.

1.I need to see you. Can we meet?

2.Okay, maybe a bad idea. Can we talk?

3.I'll phone u now.

4.Ur not picking up – guess ur asleep.

5.Look, I didn't hurt Connie.

6.We had misunderstanding.

7.She was pissed. Told me her secret. (I gasped at that and Daniel stirred, grunted, then turned on his side and started snoring again.)

8.Made me promise not to tell anyone, doesn't want dad 2 find out, but said u know.

9.Said they were planning future together and U scared him off. Got Jake 2 dump her. Good move, Foxy. (thumbs up emoji)

10.Got angry cos I told her u did right thing.

11.I defended u & she went for me. Crazy like - feral. Was drunk tho.

12.I held her arms 2 stop her hitting me. When I let go, she tripped on naked Barbie doll on floor – fell. Helped her up and made her a coffee. Went home – police outside.

13.She was ok when I left. Don't know what happened after that.

14.Maybe she hurt herself when she fell.

15.Did have a bit of blood on lip – prob scratched it with nail when falling.

16.Foxy, are you there?

17.Why won't you reply?

18.Are you getting my messages?

19.Look, I'm gonna phone u.

"You didn't reply," I can hear the hurt in his voice.

"What do you want from me, Nick?" I smile at Stacy nervously, half covering the mouthpiece, as she hands me a yellow file, feeling as if she knows who's on the other end of the line and will immediately ring Daniel and tell him.

"I just want you to understand what happened. I did spend a night in a cell, you know," Nick says indignantly. "Cops found a bit of blood on my shirt cuff, probably from Connie's scratched lip when I tried to help her up." My stomach clenches when I hear this because it makes it all seem so raw, so real, when all I want is for it to go away, for it to never have happened. "They took fingerprints and samples from under my nails, and swabs from my mouth, too. Jesus, I can't believe this is happening to me." Neither can I, I want to say. It sounds like something out of *Line of Duty*. "And the thing is…" he hesitates.

"What?"

HER SECRET

"There's something else."

"Something else?"

He pauses and then. "Well, I've got a previous conviction."

My hand flies to my mouth, Callum looks up at me from his desk a few feet away. "Since when?" I gasp, turning my back on him.

"It was a long time ago. I was only about twenty-two. I punched a guy at a club." I shake my head at the yellow file on my desk. "He was harassing one of my friends, a girl, feeling her up, so I decked him. Woman aren't there for the taking. You know how I feel about that." Yes, I do. Nick's very protective and respectful of women. It's one of the things I loved about him, and is one of the reasons why I'm find all this impossible to deal with. "The bloody maniac went to the police and I spent a night in a cell. I forgot all about it, to be honest. But I didn't assault Connie, I promise you. On my mother's soul," he says, and I picture him standing with his hand on his heart. He adored Coleen and only swears by her when he's telling the truth.

"I don't know what to say to you."

"Just say you believe me."

I pause for a moment, holding the inside of my lip between my teeth. "So, how did she get the black eye and the fat lip, then?"

"God knows." He takes another lug on his cigarette and blows loudly. I can hear traffic hissing. He must be outside. Shit. I hope he's not here. I run to the window and search up and down the street. All clear – phew. "I'd never hit a woman, you know that." I stay silent, because agreeing with him would mean we were on the same page, and I can't go against my own family. "Anyway, I just wanted to explain," he says sulkily. "I mean, come on, Foxy, what do you take me for? You still mean the world to me. I'd never do anything to hurt you or your family." Tears prick my eyes. I can hardly bear to hear anymore. "But I can't force you to believe me, obviously." Silence. "Ronan and Tina have been a rock. Audrey, are you still there? Hello?"

"Yes, I'm still here," I sigh, leaning my back against the window sill. Tina told me that she and Ronan will give Nick character references, if necessary, urged me to do the same, but I can't stand up in court and testify against my own stepdaughter. That would be mad – my marriage would be over. And besides, I don't know what really happened, do I? "How's Katrina," I ask, veering off. Poor woman must think we're all bonkers. I bet she wishes she'd never set eyes on us.

"Bit shaken but okay. She's at Sas's until tomorrow night," he says, as if I'm supposed to know who Sas is.

"Sas?"

"Saskia. Her daughter. She's in Canterbury with her husband. He's the lead singer of The Smokes, they're recording their latest album."

"Judas Keyes?" I say loudly, and Callum looks up at me again, irritated. "Wow," I whisper. "I didn't realise Katrina had a celebrity son-in-law. What's he like? I'm a big fan."

"I know," Nick sighs, disinterested. Obviously, the last thing he wants to do is exchange anecdotes about Judas Keyes. What was I thinking? "Look, can we just meet up for a coffee?" he pleads. "I can come to your office if it's easier. We could go to that pub around the corner."

Straightening up, I look across the office, suddenly aware of the shuffle of papers, ringing phones and tapping keyboards. Fearne is back at her desk talking to Raymond. When she clocks me, she holds up a Starbucks cup, which I know has my name written on it in thick, black marker, because it always does. Fearne is very efficient. I give her the thumbs up.

"Look, I'm going to have to go, another call is coming through,"

  HER SECRET

I lie.

"But – "

"I'm sorry, Nick. Please don't call me again, okay?"

I hang up before he can speak, and as I walk a little unsteadily back to my desk, feeling as if I've just had a couple of drinks, heart belting against my ribs, I wish I'd never answered that call, because now that I've spoken to him, now that I've heard his voice, now that he's sworn on his mother's soul, I feel more confused than ever.

"I'm sorry, love," Daniel murmurs later in bed. "I'm just all stressy and tired."

I tell him it's okay, not to worry. The last thing I expect him to be feeling after everything that's happened is frisky. He turns the bedside light on, picks up his mobile phone from the table, flicks through a few Apps then turns it off.

"I'd better get some sleep," he mumbles before turning on his side. "I've got to be in Brighton by 8.30."

"Brighton?" I say, almost accusingly. "I thought that fell through." It's a big project Daniel and Aliki were working on – thirty 1, 2, and 3 bedroom luxury apartments on the seafront. Daniel's been trekking back and forth for weeks trying to sort it out.

"No, it's back on. We've had the go ahead from the council."

"Oh, that's great news." He doesn't answer. Any other time we'd be planning a celebration, an overnight stay with dinner at the Savoy, or a weekend away somewhere warm and sunny. I'd be sitting in bed right now with my laptop checking out hotels on TripAdvisor, ignoring the 534 five-star reviews and only paying heed to the lone one-star that complained of scratchy bedsheets. But now our world is cloaked in darkness, sealed in all four corners without a glimmer of light.

"Na night, Cinderella," he says after a few moments, settling. "Love you."

"I love you too."

I shut my eyes tight, yearning for sleep to come, but I can't stop thinking about my earlier conversation with Nick. According to Connie, Nick grabbed her arms and then slapped her, yet she admits that most of it is a blur. Nick says he tried to control her during an outburst, that she slipped and fell when he let her go, scratching her lip, yet he didn't bother calling for help. Is it possible that Connie sustained her injuries from a fall? Mum tripped in the garden a few years ago and hit her face on the concrete patio; ended up with two shiners for weeks. Dad refused to go out with her because he said people kept giving him funny looks in Waitrose. Is that what happened to Connie, or did Nick just lose it for a moment? But then why would he even do that to her? There's no reason. He's not a violent man. Connie was a bit hesitant when I asked her if she was sure it was Nick who thumped her. Is she having doubts? Could Daniel be putting pressure on her to prosecute? He does have a jealous streak and he's never been comfortable about me and Nick. I take a deep breath and turn on my back. I'm being ridiculous. Daniel is a decent bloke, he'd never go that far. Turning the pillow over, I give it a few punches. I can't seem to get comfortable, and it's so damned hot in this room. I can even feel the heat radiating from Daniel's body. It's like a flipping sauna in here. I kick the duvet off and dangle a leg over the mattress, staring at the silhouette of my clothes strewn over the wicker chair in the darkness. My brain feels like a bundle of tangled cables. Why does everything seem so much worse at night? I exhale loudly.

"You okay?" Daniel asks, turning on his back and pushing the duvet away. "You haven't stopped moving."

 HER SECRET

"I'm sorry. And no, not really." I think about my visit to *Jasmine Blake Leisure Centre*, about the girl with the big rosy cheeks telling me Daniel hadn't renewed his membership. I wonder if I got it wrong, if Daniel did tell me and I've forgotten, or wasn't listening. I do sometimes forget things, especially when I've got a lot on my mind. Two weeks ago I went out and left the bedroom window open. We're lucky we didn't get burgled. I exhale loudly. Oh, what the hell am I thinking? Daniel confirmed he was at the gym in Finchley on the phone to me yesterday. I can't think straight. My mind is like a mass of tangled up wires.

"It's a difficult time for all of us." His hand is warm on my bare thigh. "I'm exhausted. The sooner this is over, the sooner we can get back to normal."

"I know," I exhale loudly, gearing myself up to question him about the gym, in a matter-of-fact style and not like some loon, possessive wife. I have a right to know where my husband disappears to three times a week, haven't I? "Perhaps you should give the gym a miss for a few days if you're so exhausted," I suggest, stroking the outline of his smooth, firm pecs. He murmurs something gobbledegook. "Daniel?" I shake his arm.

"What?"

"Did you hear what I said?

"Yes."

"Will you give it a miss then? The gym, I mean. At least until this business with Connie is sorted out?"

"Business? You make it sound like some sort of contract." His phone pings on the bedside table. Who the hell is texting him in the middle of the night? Rolling on his side, he hitches up on his elbow, reads the message, then drops the phone back onto the table.

"Who was that?" I ask. The backlight of his phone is still on, I can see the worried look on his face.

"No-one. Just a sports notification."

"At this time of the night?"

"Yeah, tell me about it," he says, yawning. "I'll change my settings tomorrow." He rolls on his side and pulls the sheets up to his neck.

I blink, horrified. I don't believe him. I hoist myself up on my elbow and peer at him. "What about the gym then?"

"Look, it's my mind that's exhausted not my body. Exercise helps me to unwind."

I sigh loudly. This isn't working. I'll have to try another tactic, because now that he's getting texts in the middle of the night, I feel more concerned than ever. I cuddle up next to him, pressing my body against the curve of his toned back, inhaling his scent. He finds my hand under the sheets and draws it close to his hairless chest, making me feel safe, warm, loved. "You could try a gym nearer home," I suggest casually, laying my face between his shoulder blades. "There must be a few in Muswell Hill or Crouch End. *Jasmine Blake* in Finchley isn't exactly our local, is it?" Silence. I hope he hasn't fallen asleep. "I could call and cancel for you if you like."

"No, there's no need," he murmurs. My heart leaps with joy, as if tearing through golden hills in the style of *Maria Von Trapp in The Sound of Music*. He's going to tell me that it expired. That he's joined a new gym, one closer to home, or the office. That he just forgot to tell me. "I'll ring them myself in the morning and cancel."

Shit. SHIT! I turn on my back and focus on the red standby light shining from the T.V. opposite our bed, as my dancing heart slumps into the pit of my stomach. Not only has my ex-fiancé been accused of assaulting my stepdaughter, my husband of only two months has just told me a big, fat fib. I want to howl.

CHAPTER 24

"HERE," LOUSE SAYS, splashing a tawny liquid into my coffee, voice croaky with sleep. "You look like you need it." She screws the cap back onto the *Five Kings* brandy that I bought her from Cyprus. "Is Tina still trying to park her car in that space across the road?" She gesticulates her head at the door and I nod. Poor Lou's eyes are just as puffy as mine, and that pillow case crease along the left hand side of her face makes her look like an extra from *The Godfather*. I must've woken her this morning when I called in a semi-hysterical state while Daniel was shaving in the bathroom, pleading for an urgent coffee morning in hushed, hurried tones. "You could fit a bus in that space," she goes on, shaking her head and laughing.

The sudden shrill of the doorbell makes me jump. It's as if someone has pressed their finger on the ringer and won't let go. "Finally." Louise rolls her eyes. "I'll just let her in. Won't be a mo."

I close my eyes to the clamour of footsteps in the hallway, the clank of the front door, and then voices; and as they begin to argue about car spaces and parallel parking, my mind spins back to my earlier conversation with Daniel.

"Why aren't you dressed? You're going to be late," he said, swishing his razor blade in a sink of murky water, white towel wrapped around his taught waist, skin glistening with moisture.

"I'm not going in today," I replied hesitantly, one hand on the doorframe. "Can you call in sick for me?" I rubbed my tummy for effect.

HER SECRET

He stopped shaving and twisted stiffly towards me, and I didn't miss the flicker of fear in his blue eyes. "Are you okay? You didn't stop moving in bed all night. Do you want me to call the doctor?" No, I wanted to scream, I want you to tell me why the bloody hell you keep lying to me.

I shook my head, folding my arms, inhaling the steamy, mango infused air. "I've just come on, that's all." The look of relief on his face was almost laughable. Would it really be so catastrophic to have a child with me? Not that I want a baby, or anything, but still.

"You should lay off the sauce for a few days." He dipped the razor in the water again.

"I only had two glasses of wine last night. It's not the drink," I protested, picking at the hard skin around my thumbnail.

"Why don't you take a couple of paracetamol, then?" And why don't you state the bloody obvious, Daniel?

"I already have," I groaned. "Look, I can't go in today. I'm going to Louise's. Tina's called a coffee meeting. It's…it's urgent. She's," I faltered, he stopped shaving and looked at me in the mirror. "Oh, something to do with Ronan," I said, absently.

"Trouble in paradise?" He gave a little laugh, then twisted his face to get into a groove with the blade.

"Will you ring work for me, then?"

"Can't you do it?" he said, sounding really put out. "I'm in the middle of shaving, and I'm seeing my solicitor in half an hour."

"Oh, come on Daniel, you're better at lying than I am."

He held my gaze in the mirror, razor blade in mid-air, and then his eyes crinkled at the corners. "Okay, let me just finish up here. What's up with old Ronan, anyway?"

I shrugged my shoulders, avoiding eye contact, because I knew that if Daniel could see my face, he'd be onto me like a shot, know I was lying. "I'm not sure. I think it's something to do with his

HER SECRET

ex-wife." My hand found the back of my neck. I hated myself for lying about Tina and Ronan but it was the first thing that sprang to mind. "Don't say anything to them though," I added hastily.

The sound of the blade scratching against his skin in quick succession followed by the splosh of water filled the few muted moments. "That Ronan seems like a bit of a character to me," he said finally.

"What do you mean?"

"Well, he's still married for a start."

"Divorcing." I picked at my nail again.

"Still married now, though, isn't he? What's to stop him going back to his missus, hmm? And if you're having to take a day off work to sort out Tina's relationship problems." He paused and pointed the razor at me in the mirror. "Then I'd say she should run for the hills." Damn, I thought, why did I use that lie? He's going to go on about it for days now, because we both know that this isn't about Tina. It's about my one-night stand with Ronan. Daniel can't bear the thought of me being intimate with any other man. He wants our romance to be a fairy-tale, he doesn't call me Cinderella for nothing, you know. In fact, I'm sure he'd have all the men I've slept with erased from my subconscious with a laser if he could. Dipping the blade in the sink, he swished it around nosily. "Don't get me wrong, darling, I do like him," he said, sensing my tension. Daniel's a sharp as the blade he held in his hand. "I'm sure she could do a lot better, that's all. They've only been back together five minutes, haven't they? What's the rush?"

Hypocrisy bounced off the walls and did a few cartwheels in the bath. I looked up at him sharply. "She's known him for years," I said loudly, getting to my feet. "He loves her, probably always has." I continued to watch him as he puffed out his cheek and ran the razor over his skin. "But I suppose men can't help lying, can they?" I said coolly, eyes fixed on his reflection in the mirror. "It's in their DNA."

"Shit." He dropped the razor blade onto the side of the sink. Blood mingled with the white foam on his face. I'd hit a nerve. At last.

"I really feel for you, mate." Louise says now, drawing air between her teeth in the manner of a dodgy builder who's about to fleece you with an exorbitant estimate. "Your ex accused of roughing up your stepdaughter." Shaking her head, she stretches her arm across the table, Tina stops texting and quickly covers her cup with her hand.

"Not for me, thanks," Tina says, "I've got a job interview in…" Her eyes flit to the door and we all look up at the clock above it. "An hour and forty-five."

I turn to Tina. "An interview? Where?"

"I thought you were happy at that P.R. firm," Louise says.

"Yeah, I am, but this one's got more prospects," she explains, then looks at me. "P.R. and digital media officer at Farlie Elton & Kyl." She looks at us, all smiles and shiny, straight, white teeth.

"The publishers?" I say in a shrilly voice. I love reading. "Will we get free books hot off the press?"

"Yeaaah." Tina nods furiously and her big hoop earrings swing in her glossy, auburn curls. "And you two can be my plus ones at all the glitzy events." She rolls her eyes, "That's if I get it, of course."

I can barely contain my excitement, they're one of the top publishers in the UK. We'll probably get to meet loads of authors and celebrities. "Wow, that's brilliant. Good luck. Not that you'll need it."

We all grin at each other stupidly.

"Thanks," Tina beams. "So, no brandy for me, sadly. I need a clear head. Anyway, I'm driving." I feel instantly irresponsible. But

HER SECRET

a drop of brandy won't harm, will it? Besides, I'm sure it'll wear off by the time I leave, especially after a few more neat coffees.

"You're allowed one, aren't you?" Louise protests, picking up on my vibe. Tina shakes her head defiantly as she slips her phone into her maroon Mulberry handbag on the kitchen table. "Suit yourself." Louise groans. Taking a sip of boozy coffee, she noisily pulls up a chair next to mine, and I suddenly remember that she's on night shifts. Shit. She probably didn't get to bed until gone 1 a.m. I immediately feel selfish. What was I thinking, dragging my friends away from their work, their lives? "What?" Louise demands, eyebrows furrowed.

"Nothing.…." I pull the neck of my grey long sleeved t-shirt over my chin like a nervous, awkward teenager, and notice that the collar of her white shirt is sticking upwards. I wish she'd tuck it back into her yellow sweater. I'm finding it incredibly distracting. "I just hope I didn't…" I don't finish. Louise won't take kindly to being asked if she's only just got out of bed at ten-thirty. She used to bite my head off in the past when I'd ring first thing with a cheery, 'I hope I didn't wake you.' I stick to clichéd preambles these days.

"Didn't.…?" Frowning, she tucks her collar back into her sweater and I feel an instant slither of relief. I do sometimes wonder if she can read my mind.

"Well, didn't…" Our eyes lock, but I'm saved by the chime of her phone ringing on the table.

Louise looks at the flashing screen and her face creases into a grin, "Hellllooooo." She gets to her feet and mimes, 'Sorry,' at us, then sits back down again. She's nervous as hell. She's gone red. It must be that bloke Trevor that she met on that dating site. "Yes, I enjoyed it, too," she says, all breathy and flirty. It's definitely that bloke Trevor from the dating site.

"Is that Trevor?" Tina hisses, and I nod, tell her it must be. Leaning forward, she folds her arms over the kitchen table. "Good that she's started dating again, isn't it? Though I've always been wary of meeting blokes on the internet. You hear so many horror stories."

"I know what you mean," I reply honestly. "But it's through a verified site, and he sounds like a really nice man. They've already been on a couple of dates."

"Seriously?" she says with a wry smile. "The slut. Look at her." Tina shakes her head, as Louise pushes a hand through her hair and agrees to another date, face pink and shiny. "She's all loved up."

"Well, that's good, isn't it?" I smile up at Louise as she mouths, '*Sorry,*' again with lots of eye rolling and blushing cheeks; and then, holding up a finger signalling that she'll only be a minute, dashes off into the hallway, giggling and playing with her hair as if Trevor can see her.

Shifting in her chair, Tina runs a finger along the inside collar of her navy, floral, sheath dress. It never ceases to amaze me how easily Tina can switch from casual hoodie girlfriend to P.R. professional. She looks stunning. I've no doubt in my mind that she'll get that job today at Farlie Elton & Kyl. I'm definitely keeping everything crossed for her, anyway.

"What's wrong, Aud?" Tina curls her fingers around my hand. They're cold but I'm too numb to flinch. I close my eyes briefly as Daniel's handsome face flashes into my mind. Why do I keep letting men mug me off? "You look terrible," she says gently. "Is there anything I can do? Has something else happened? Is Connie okay?"

"I spoke to Nick," I admit, and she gasps, averting her eyes to the door as if Daniel is standing in the corridor listening.

"What did he say?"

"Pretty much what he said to you and Ro."

"You do know he's not pleading guilty, don't you?" I nod at the fruit bowl on the table containing two red apples and a bunch of black bananas. Louise's loud laughter feeds through the half open door. "And once it goes to court, Connie will have to testify." Tina sighs loudly through her nose, squeezing my forearm. "I don't think he hit Connie, Aud. It must've been an accident, like he said. Either that or something else happened."

"What about the slaps, though?" I insist, searching her eyes. "And the black eye?"

Tina shrugs. "A dream, maybe? Or what about that boyfriend of hers, perhaps she let him in and can't remember? She did have a blackout." Tina does have a point. When I Googled alcoholic blackout, it said that the victim doesn't pass out, like I imagined. In fact, they're very much awake but just can't remember much of what happened, if anything. By her own admission, Connie did say everything was a blur. But then she was pretty damn sure about the slap. I doubt Jake would risk it. He's got too much to lose. But I can't tell her that because then I'd have to tell her about Connie's secret. And I can't, because I promised. "This may sound mad." She hesitates, biting her bottom lip. "But it's almost as if he's been set up."

I shake my head at her, laughing faintly. She's been watching too many episodes of *Happy Valley* on Netflix. Unless Connie's memory comes back, which is unlikely, there's nothing she nor I can do. Daniel is intent on sending Nick to the gallows and will stop at nothing. "Let's just leave it to the professionals," I say, and she agrees.

"Bloody cheek!" Louise's voice booms in my ears.

"What's happened?" Tina and I say in unison, as Louise sits heavily onto the chair. Surely, they haven't fallen out already.

"He hung up first," she says indignantly, staring at the phone in her clenched hand. Tina and I grin at each other. I'm glad she's lightened the mood.

"So, come on then," Louise probes, plugging her phone into the charger. "What's the crisis? Why have we all been summoned to a meeting that couldn't wait until tonight? Is it ConnieGate? Has there been a new development?" she says, as if she's a DCI. "You poor love. You must be going through shit – stuck in the middle of it all."

"It's not just that," I say tearfully, "It's Daniel. I think he's having an affair."

I fill Louise and Tina in on recent events and they listen intently, faces grave, elbows on table as if we're at some sort of conference discussing Brexit. We go through all the possibilities.

Option One: He's doing charity work incognito and doesn't want me to find out (a thought that fills me with a warm, fuzzy glow, but I know it's a long shot. Daniel's very open about his charity donations – NSPCC, Cancer Research, and recently, Crohn's & Colitis UK).

Option Two: He's got another wife tucked away somewhere (Louise's idea, a bit implausible but stranger things have happened).

Option Three: He's a DCI on a secret mission and his job as a property developer is just a cover up (Tina's brainwave. Farfetched but not entirely impossible).

The options are endless, but the most likely one is staring us in the face like an elephant in the room. He's seeing another woman.

Over our third cup of coffee, we agree, after much protest from me, that the best course of action would be for me to keep schtum, put my Sherlock cap on and follow him. Find out where he disappears to every Sunday morning, come rain or shine.

"I can go with," Tina offers excitedly. "Drive you."

"Don't be an imbecile," Louise retorts. "Anyone can spot you a mile off with that red mop." She flicks Tina's long curls playfully. "Besides, he'll recognise your car. Who else is bold enough to drive a bright green Corsa?"

"I could wear a disguise," Tina says sulkily, wrapping a strand of red hair around her index finger. "I've still got that black wig from when Ronan and I went to my cousin's fancy dress party as Uma Thurman and John Travolta from that film…" She frowns, tapping her fingers against the table. "What was it called? The one where he's got that long, greasy hair….um."

"Pulp Fiction," Louse confirms, glancing at her phone as it tinkles then lights up with an alert.

"Yeah, that's it!"

Panic tightens in my chest and dives into my stomach. I cover my face with my hands. "This is all mad. I don't think I can do it." I look at them through the gaps between my fingers.

"Don't be silly, Audrey, of course you can. But don't go alone," Louise warns. "If he is seeing someone else it might be too upsetting for you."

"She's right, Aud." Tina lays a hand on my shoulder.

"Is there anyone you could trust that he hasn't met yet?" Louise asks.

"I can't think of anyone, no."

"What about someone from work?" Tina suggests, taking a sip of lukewarm coffee. "That woman whose husband left her with his teenage daughter."

Louise takes a sharp intake of breath. "The bastard."

I narrow my eyes and twist my lips to the side. Actually, he hasn't met Fearne yet. She's always been away from the office when he's popped in. "I could ask her but I don't know if she'll agree. It is a big ask. I mean, we are only colleagues. We're not mates or anything."

"But you can trust her, right?" Louise pours more coffee into my cup from the cafetière. I'm not going to get any sleep tonight.

I nod, wrapping my hands around my warm mug. "Fearne is a loyal and trustworthy person. But…"

"No buts. She's your girl." Louise insists. "And if he is having an affair then you can confront them both there and then. With Fearne."

I nod quickly, putting on a brave face in front of my friends, but I know that news of an affair will break me into a thousand pieces.

CHAPTER 25

SUNDAY CAN'T COME ROUND quick enough. I tell Daniel that I'm meeting Louise and Tina for an early-bird breakfast in Crouch End, and slip away as he's preparing his holdall for the gym. He's a stickler for punctuality and routine, so won't set off until eight, which gives me about fifteen minutes to meet Fearne and get back here to spy on him before he leaves.

I head off towards the Broadway, arms folded, chin down as the cool breeze licks my bare chest. Why didn't I bring a jacket? Plunging necklines are for high summer not nippy spring mornings. But it's too late to go back for my mac now – timing is everything.

At the crossing on the Broadway, I'm accosted by the young chatty girl with the big swingy earrings and pram who saved me from being thrown into the traffic a couple of weeks ago. She's amazed that fate brought us together again so soon and insists it's a sign, that her clairvoyant told her that a chance meeting with a dark haired woman will bring her luck. I try to edge away politely but she won't stop talking – her nan's been poorly, her toddler's teething, that waste of a space of a boyfriend is fucking useless.

"I ditched him on the day I met you," she says, shaking her head and sucking her teeth.

"Oh, I am sorry," I offer. Traffic hounds in my ears. I think I need the loo. It must be my nerves.

"Nah, don't be," She waves a hand. "He was a total knobhead."

She carries on talking – pink lips moving, huge rose gold crucifix earrings swinging in her hair whenever she moves. But I'm no longer listening. The cogs in my brain are turning wildly. I'm going to be late. What if Fearne thinks I've changed my mind and goes home? I hope Daniel doesn't leave before we get back to my flat. Because then I'd have to persuade Fearne to come with me again next week. But what if she can't? What if she's busy? "I'm sorry," I blurt, glancing at my watch absently. "I don't mean to be rude, but I've got a meeting and I'm late." And before she can answer, I'm gone.

Fearne is waiting for me on Princess Avenue, face like thunder, double parked in front of the Montessori Nursery. After she scolds me for being seven minutes late, reminding me that it is she who's doing ME the favour and not the other way around, we drive the short distance to my road where she parks up on the corner of Elms Avenue; close enough to get a good view of my front door but far enough to be inconspicuous. Then while she messages away like an overenthusiastic teenager, sniggering and grunting intermittently as the responses ping through, I sit in wait like a lioness waiting for its prey in the back of her red Fiat 500.

At eight o'clock on the dot, Daniel steps onto the pavement wearing a black tracksuit with white stripes along the sides, holdall in hand. I suppose he's doing it all for effect. Clever man, my husband. But he's not going to pull the wool over my eyes. The betrayal of my last relationship has set me up for life. It's as if I've been fitted with a micro 'suspicious' chip in my brain; even though Nick shagged Louise's sister-in-law while we were on a three week break, so technically we weren't together, it still hurt like hell. And now this. I do a little shake of my head, closing my eyes, Fearne chuckles at another message. What kind of a man cheats on his new wife? The whir of the ignition makes me jump.

HER SECRET

"He's getting into the car," Fearne announces in a panicky voice, locking in her seatbelt, "Make yourself scarce." I lay flat on the back seat, adjusting my yellow bobble hat and huge dark glasses (my disguise provided by Fearne, kindly donated by her teenage stepdaughter).

We drive over several road bumps then inch along in traffic. The small car space is muggy, humid, and reeks of food - onions, thyme, roast meat, which Fearne has clearly tried to cloak in a gallon of what smells like Opium. My aunt Jacqui used to bathe herself in the stuff. It always made me heave as a child whenever I sat next to her in her black shiny Merc, as she droned on and on about my clever and high achieving cousins. It's having a similar effect on me now. I think I'm going to puke. I wish Fearne would open a window. I cough a few times, hoping that she'll ask me if I'm okay, but my efforts are met with silence. We start moving again, she turns a corner and my stomach turns with it. A few moments later she pulls up.

"Why've we stopped?" I ask, lifting my head and feeling a little woozy. I hope she hasn't lost her nerve. I gaze out of the window as the bookshop slowly comes into focus.

"Shhh," she hisses, "get back down! He might see you." She glares at me in the rear view mirror, blue eyes wide and wild.

"Where is he?" I whisper, mimicking her tone, although I'm not quite sure why, because unless Daniel has suddenly developed superpowers it's very unlikely that he'll be able to hear or see me from fifty feet away, or, dare I say, recognise me in this Ali G disguise.

"He's gone into that posh florist." Oh, my God, he's buying her flowers again. I want to cry. Fearne pops a Starburst sweet into her mouth then extends the tube over her shoulder. I shake my head. The last thing I want is to choke on a sweet in the back of a Fiat

500 whilst spying on my husband. "And put your glasses back on if you're going to leap up like a jack-in-the-box. I thought you didn't want him to see you."

I slide on the oversized glasses as per Major Fearne's instructions. The sweet aroma of strawberry flavour Starbucks fleetingly masks the pungent smell of food and Opium.

"Quick." Fearne turns the ignition on and revs up the engine with the gusto and determination of a getaway driver on a jewellery raid in Hatton Garden. "He's getting back in the car, get back down," she snaps, chewing madly. And I get the odd feeling that she's quite enjoying this little adventure.

We drive to the tinny sound of Smooth radio for the rest of the journey, remaining three cars behind him; the silence only punctured by Fearne's moment of panic when she thinks she's lost him.

Fifteen minutes later, the music fades and we slow down to about 5 mph. "Well, I think we've arrived," Fearne announces to the tweet, tweet and ruffle of birds.

I gaze up as we cruise beneath an arc of trees. We must be in a woody park or forest. Or maybe in some swanky manor hotel. My stomach twists. "Where are we?" I gulp, not daring to get up and see for myself. I pull the yellow bobble hat tightly over my head, wishing I could climb inside it and disappear. Oh God, why did I let Louise and Tina talk me into doing such a stupid, stupid thing? WHY?

"We're at Southgate Cemetery; following a hearse, actually," Fearne says nonchalantly. A cemetery? What the fuck? "Which is quite handy as it goes, cos he'll just think we're part of the group of mourners." My phone chimes loudly in my bag. I fish it out quickly. Oh, dear God, my mother has sent me a picture of her sun-kissed thigh on WhatsApp. "Oh wait," Fearne's voice again.

 HER SECRET

I turn my phone to silent and shove it back into my bag. "He's parking up. Stay down."

I feel sick, panicky. I can't do this. I've had enough. "Fearne… I've…I've…I don't think I'm feeling very well. It must be last night's takeaway. Can we just go home please?"

"And now he's getting out of the car," she says, ignoring me. I feel my heart pounding in my ears.

"Did you hear what I said? Fearne? Why have we stopped?" I gulp. "What's happening?"

"Traffic. The hearse has stopped." She looks in her rear view mirror, eyes glinting. "I can't even reverse, we're sandwiched in."

"Well, overtake it, then," I say hurriedly, waving a hand.

"I can't," she hits back. The windows are steaming up, she buzzes the driver's one down an inch, letting in a little air. "It's a one-way system. Unless you want me to drive over the tombs."

"Of course, I don't," I say indignantly.

Then suddenly she hunches into her shoulders and slides down her seat. Oh, God, I hope she hasn't fainted! "Fuuuuuuk," she whimpers in the manner of an inept ventriloquist speaking from the side of her mouth. "He's looking at me."

"WHAT?" My eyes widen so much they hurt. I draw my legs to my chest. I think I'm going to pass out. Surely, he hasn't rumbled us. How could he? He's never met Fearne. Then in a moment of horrific clarity it dawns on me that he did see her once, fleetingly, when he came to pick me up from work on our first date. Dread crawls over my skin and I shiver, as an image of me sitting in the back of a black cab with Daniel flashes into my mind. He's asking me what I fancy eating. I tell him something simple, a pizza or pasta. Then as I turn around to wave at Raymond at the entrance of Blue Media, Daniel turns too, and just as we lift our hands to wave, Fearne appears at Ray's side clutching a yellow folder. Oh, fucking hell! My cheeks feel like they're on fire. Oh, my God. What if he's recognised her? I focus on the green air freshener in the shape of a *Converse* boot that's dangling from the rear view mirror. I need to keep calm. Stay grounded. Come on, Audrey, deep breaths. He can't have recognised her, it was too quick, it was from a distance. It's impossible.

"Shit! Shit!" Fearne cries.

"WHAT NOW?"

"He's coming over," she gulps, face ashen. I close my eyes. I want to die.

CHAPTER 26

"QUICK, DO SOMETHING," Fearne says through gritted teeth. Holding onto the steering wheel tightly, arms outstretched, she stares ahead as if she's been frozen by an evil villain with a cryogenic gun.

"Like what?" I cry, curling into a ball behind her in the backseat. Any moment now I'm going to be outed – and what am I supposed to bloody well say? Because somehow I think that leaping up and shouting, 'Surprise,' isn't going to go down too well.

"Phone him," Fearne snaps.

"But…"

"NOW!"

I empty the contents of my bag onto the back seat, snatch my phone and, with trembling fingers, start jabbing at the screen. He answers almost immediately.

"Darling, I was just thinking of you," he says. I can almost hear his smile down the phone.

"Oh, thank God. He's turning around." Fearne crunches the car into first gear hurriedly and we start moving. I can hear Daniel's voice but I'm not listening. "Panic over." Fearne's hand flies to her chest, eyes flitting to the rear view mirror. "Phew, that was close." She takes a corner quite sharply and I almost puke into my empty bag. "Keep him talking until I find the exit."

And suddenly I'm lost for words. "Umm…..um…" I start shoving things back into my open bag hurriedly – tissues, mini umbrella, make-up bag, keys, antibacterial wipes (for emergencies), a bunch of old receipts, hand gel (for my numerous Howard Hughesy moments).

"Darling…can you hear me? Are you still – "

"Yes…yes..sorry. I…um…" I drop a squashed, ancient *Snickers* bar into my bag in disgust. Jesus that must've been in there for months. "Umm…Where are you?" I ask, rubbing a bit of toffee off my fingers.

"What do you mean?" he says incredulously. I can just imagine his face darkening. He hates being quizzed. "I'm at the gym, of course, silly. Have you forgotten already? Just about to go for a swim, actually. You okay?" I clench my jaw, curbing in the word LIAR from spilling from my lips.

"You sound like you're outside," I reply, pulling an antibacterial wipe out of the blue packet angrily. I did say they're good for emergencies.

"Yeah, I've just arrived. I'm walking in now," he fibs and my eyes sting. The bloody bastard! "Just parked up." I hear the beep of central locking. He's obviously doing it all for effect. "Darling, are you okay? You sound breathless."

"What? You're cracking up," I lie. A tear leaks from the corner of my eye and slides along the side of my nose. "Daniel….Daniel? Can you hear me?" I hang up, furious.

"Don't worry, love," Fearne says as we inch in traffic. "I'll get us out of here just as soon as this lot clears."

"No," I say, shifting around on the back seat. I don't think these cars were made for amateur spying. I'm going to have sciatica for a month. "I want to stay."

"But, I thought you said…"

"No, I just panicked. I'm okay now." I sniff. Dragging my purple sleeve over my hand, I wipe my wet cheeks. "I can't give up now.

 HER SECRET

Not when we're this close to finding out the truth."

Fearne looks over her shoulder at me briefly, a smile dancing on her lips, eyes shining with glee. "Hope you're okay behind there." I tell her that I'm fine, which, of course, I'm not. I've got cramp in my leg and I can't feel my left arm. "Look, I'm going have to follow the hearse," she says excitedly, changing gear. "In case he spots us again and gets suspicious. We can spy him from the other side of the graveyard." I agree and wonder if she's in the wrong job. Fearne is very good at playing detective. I didn't think she'd be this proactive.

I rock around in the back seat of the car, eyes closed, using my hands as a pillow, my body numb with sadness. Okay, so the flowers aren't for a mistress, that's good news; and he's not bonking some twenty-something lovely in a smart boutique hotel in north London, that's great news. But he's still lying to me – blatantly. Why? Why lie about visiting someone's grave, for crying out loud?

The car engine purs, we're reversing, then I hear the crunch of the hand break. "You can get up now," Fearne says brightly, unbuckling her seat belt. "I've parked behind the church. If we just walk round we'll be able to see him. Come on, hurry up or we might miss him."

I climb out of the back of the car feeling frazzled and nauseous and in desperate need of a wee, and follow Fearne to the front of the church in a zigzaggy gait, like a drunk who's just been chucked out of the local boozer. We tread along the gravelled path noisily as we make our way to a green lined with hundreds of headstones. And as we begin our journey, I take in the fresh mounds covered in beautiful wreathes and heady bouquets; memorials splashed with white pebbles and wilted flowers in urns. Grey, stained, lopsided tombstones, old and forgotten – a bit like me. Foreign voices murmur in the background. I snap my head up and see three people dressed in black behind a mist of smoke. They must be Greek. Maria, mum's cleaner, used to wander around the house with a smoky urn when I was in Cyprus. She once waved it over my head while I was still asleep. "It's to keeping diávolos away, Audi," she said when I woke up with a start, gasping and flapping my hands in front me like a scene from *The Birds*, demanding to know who diávolos was and why she thought he'd come to my room. "Is the devil," she snapped, eyes wide. "I blessing this house and you."

"Come on, Audrey, keep up." Fearne throws a quick glance over her shoulder. A crow squawks above us, a police siren wails in the distance. Inhaling the waft of incense, I up my tempo, feeling some sort of association comfort from the lingering smell. I must visit my parents in Cyprus soon. I'm missing them more than I can say. Including Maria and her smoky urn.

"I'm trying my best," I say defensively. I slip onto the concrete edge of the track to save my suede three-inch *Miu Miu* stilettoes from digging into the dewy grass, slowing me down.

"Look, there he is," Fearne announces suddenly, waving a finger. "Let's stand behind this tree, he won't be able to see us from here."

Fearne pokes her head around the huge trunk as I hold onto her back, peering over her right shoulder. My heart feels like it's bouncing around in my chest like a basketball. In fact, I'm sure it's reverberating against Fearne's spine.

Daniel has his back to us, head bowed over an unkempt, weed infested grave. Poor thing, he looks lost, broken. Did I really accuse him of shagging another woman behind my back? I swallow back a ball of guilt. Although, to be fair, you can't blame me for thinking the obvious, can you? What with all the lies and the caginess.

"Well, there's your answer, Miss Marple," Fearne says, half turning. A black crow sits on a stone cross, chimes tinkle in the soft wind, the smell of burning olive leaves waft under my nose. "Your bloke isn't having an affair. He's just visiting some poor old soul's grave." She takes a deep breath and lets the air out loudly through her nose. "Crikey, what's that stench? It's making me feel queasy."

"Burning grove leaves," I reply, feeling like a bit of an expert, "It's a Greek religious thing."

There are a few moments of silence as we swap positions, and then, "I didn't have you down as being the cynical type." Fearne holds onto my upper arms lightly, chin hovering over my shoulder.

"I'm not!" I elbow her lightly and she yelps in fake agony. "Anyway, whose grave is it? And why is he staring at it like that?" I turn and press my back against the tree, folding my arms. "Why would he lie about this?"

Fearne shrugs her shoulders. "Maybe it's an ex-girlfriend? Perhaps he thought you might get jealous if he told you."

"Of a corpse?" I ask flatly. "Besides," I turn back and peer at him on tiptoe as he walks around the grave, flowers in arms. "I'm not the jealous type."

"Er…Me. You. Here. Spying."

"This is different," I hiss, "It's because he lied to me about the gym. It made me all tetchy and suspicious." I give her a quick glance to gauge her expression, and as I turn my head back, I catch a glimpse of a figure in my peripheral vision rustling in the woods - dark glasses, hands in pockets of a black ski coat, hood up.

"Who the fuck was that?" I gasp, taking a few steps towards the woodland.

Fearne follows behind me, concerned. "I can't see anyone, love."

I point a finger, waving it nervously. "There was someone watching us just there," I say, mouth dry, heart fluttering, "Between those two trees. Didn't you hear the rustle?"

I watch as Fearne runs towards the trees, then she stops, hands on hips, looking this way and that, "No one here," she sighs, lifting her arms up and down. "It must've just been a mourner."

"She was staring at us, Fearne."

"How do you know it was a she?"

"I don't. I'm just guessing. The figure wasn't bulky enough to be a man."

Maybe it was a ghost," Fearne jokes, ambling back, hands in pockets. "We are in the middle of a graveyard."

She's being absurd. I don't believe in ghosts. I tut, give her a light tap on the arm. "Very funny," I say, and we return our attention to Daniel. "This may sound nuts, but I think someone's been following me."

Fearne throws her head back and laughs. "I think you'll find that you're the one doing the following, dear." I give her an exasperated look. "Look, there's no one there, I checked. Maybe it was one of the caretakers or something."

I nod, she's right. I'm being paranoid again. Stupid. "Yes, it could've been a young lad…or a mourner. I'm sorry, I think this is all getting a bit too much for me."

We're quiet for a few moments, and then. "Your hubster's a bit of all right, isn't he?" she remarks, plunging her hands into her pockets and eyeing Daniel approvingly. "I thought he'd be….I dunno…more mature, given that he's quite a bit older than you."

"He looks after himself," I reply. He's kneeling by the grey, faded, gritty, headstone, now, reading the inscription. I wonder if he's talking to the deceased. Stacy from work once told me that she often talks to her mum when she visits, says it somehow gives her some comfort. "Anyway," I say, inhaling deeply. "I doubt it's an ex-girlfriend."

"What about an ex-wife?" Fearne dabs her nose with a tatty tissue, sniffling. "He's been married a few times, hasn't he?"

  HER SECRET

"Twice. Well, three if you include me. Sophie, his first wife, died years ago but she was buried at....UNLESS!" I clamp my hand around Fearne's forearm as a string of questions charge through my mind. What if his wife wasn't buried at sea? What if he lied about that too? What if this is actually HER grave. But then, why would he lie? He knows I wouldn't stop him from visiting his wife's grave.

"Unless what?" Fearne asks, her blue eyes flitting from mine to my tight grip. I let go of her arm, and notice for the first time today that her eyes are slightly bloodshot, and the skin beneath them looks as bruised and puffy as mine did this morning. Poor Fearne. She works so hard as a single parent. I shouldn't have asked her to do this today. It was thoughtless and selfish. I'm going to have to make it up to her. Take her for lunch at that new Italian place around the corner from our office next week, buy her something lovely and smelly from Jo Malone, she's always raving about their stuff.

"Oh, it's nothing," I lie, waving a hand. Fearne must go home now. I've taken up enough of her time. She's got a daughter to get back to – a life. "I'm just being silly again. Look, I'd better go to him. Find out what the hell is going on. I'm sorry I dragged you here today. There's probably some reasonable explanation to all this. I overreacted, as per." I pull a silly face and rock my head from side to side in an attempt to lighten the mood. Fearne is looking at me as if I've just escaped from Broadmoor. "It's just all this business with Nick and Connie," I explain, "Getting used to being Mrs Taylor, the impending house move. It's all a bit overwhelming, that's all." And I'm not lying. All the upheaval has taken its toll on me. I'm not sleeping well, or eating properly. We've been living off takeaways for the last week. I can't even remember the last time I washed my hair.

"You can keep that until Monday," Fearne says, as I hand her the yellow bobble hat and tell her to thank her daughter for allowing me to borrow it. "And ask Raymond for some compassionate leave," she suggests. "I'm sure he'll understand if you explain." I tell her that I can't. I'm already on a warning and we need to crack on with Sam Knight's website. "Don't worry about that. I can work on it on my own. I'll have a word with Ray for you on Monday."

I look at her, my eyes filling with gratitude, and for a moment I imagine a white halo hovering over her head. This woman is a saint. I can't believe what she's done for me today – what I've put her through. Her blood pressure must've gone through the roof.

"Thanks, Fearne. I could probably do with a few days respite." I hug her gently and her dry, wiry hair scratches my cheek as I watch Daniel over her shoulder, crouching in front of the headstone. He's probably saying his goodbyes. "Look, I'd better get a wriggle on before he leaves and I'm left stranded in a cemetery," I laugh lightly.

"But what will you say to him?"

"Don't worry, I'll think of something." Only God knows how I'm going to get out of this one; how I'm going to explain why I'm in the middle of a cemetery on a Sunday morning when I told him I'd be in Crouch End with Louise and Tina.

Smiling at me, she takes a few backwards steps. "Sure you'll be okay? Because I could always…."

"Yes, Mum," I cut in, sarcastically. "Perfectly sure. I'll go home with Daniel now. I'll just tell him everything. Come clean. I'm sure he'll understand. Eventually." I cross my fingers and look up to the sky. "You've been an absolute star, Fearne. I couldn't have…."

But she doesn't let me finish. "It's fine," she whines, "Stop thanking me, for heaven's sake. That's what friends are for."

And as she makes her way towards her parked car, a feeling of gratitude almost floors me. I've never really thought of Fearne

HER SECRET

as more than a colleague; someone to have lunch with, to share anecdotes about the weekend with. But she's gone above and beyond the call of duty today. This act of kindness has really sealed our friendship. I owe her – big time. Two crows fly above our heads, squawking. We instinctively gaze up at them as they soar across the blue sky, then as she twists her body into a half turn to give me a final wave, her smile dies on her lips. "Wait," she says, hurrying towards me. "Who's that?"

I spin around on my heel. A forty-something slim woman in an oversized coat slides up to Daniel. He pushes her long mousy-blonde fringe off her face and presses the flowers against her chest, and as she dips her nose into them, smiling up at him, my heart stops.

CHAPTER 27

FEARNE PULLS OUT a bunch of keys from her black cross-over handbag. "Come on, they're walking towards the car," she announces briskly, "Get back in the Fiat."

I hurry behind her, eyes stinging with tears, then suddenly I stop and cover my mouth as this morning's coffee ascends towards my chest. Oh, God, this can't be happening to me. Please make it stop. Please make it be some big misunderstanding. I balance myself against the chapel, pressing my hand against the limestone. I think I'm going to be sick.

"Audrey?" Fearne stops, hair wild, face red. "What's the matter?" She's walking back towards me, keys in hand. "We're going to miss them if we don't –"

"I don't think I can do this, Fearne," I cut in. My bottom lip starts to go. I swallow back a queue of tears that are marching up my throat. "I mean, I know I said I wanted to know…but….but…" I rub the palm of my hand that's stinging with the imprint of the limestone.

"Oh, come here." Fearne pulls me into her arms and I breathe in a mixture of food and Opium perfume, and, if I'm not mistaken, a whiff of bleach in her dry, blonde hair. "There, there, my love." She holds me tightly. I'm sobbing uncontrollably onto her shoulder, definitely bleach. "I know what it's like. I've been there and done it, remember?" I open my mouth to reply but I can't seem to string a coherent sentence together; hiccuppy moans tumble from my

HER SECRET

trembling lips. "He's not worth your tears, love." She curls my hair behind my ear gently. "Come on, don't let him win. You're Audrey Fox – strong, independent, smart."

Pulling away, I fish for the pocket tissues in my bag, which have somehow managed to crawl under all the other essentials. "Audrey Fox isn't feeling very strong today," I say in a nasally tone, slightly baffled that I'm referring to myself in third person, as if I were some sort of superhero. "It's just that he seemed so genuine, so loving. I can't believe he's done this to me. To us. And so soon!" My voice cracks. "I feel like such a bloody idiot." I faff about with the packet of tissues then pull the entire contents out in anger; they fly around us like confetti before landing on the ground, one sticks to a tombstone.

Fearne drags her bottom lip along her teeth, then her eyes soften. I can see she's heartbroken for me but I can also sense her determination. She doesn't say anything but it's written all over her face. The thud of car doors echo in the distance. They're leaving.

"Look," Fearn fastens her hands onto my shoulders firmly, ducking her head to meet my eyes. "I can either take you home right now or we can follow them, find out what's going on, what the hell he's playing at." I gaze at her wordless. I can see the little red veins on her eyeballs, feel the warmth of her breath on my nose, the smell of Opium and food and woodland. I know what she wants me to say. I've got to make a decision. Fast. The roar of Daniel's Audi pounds in my ears.

"What's it gonna be?"

I nod quickly. "Let's follow them."

"That's my girl."

We're three cars behind them. I insisted on sitting in the front with Fearne this time, and, after a bit of oohing and ahhing, she agreed, but only if I wore her daughter's huge dark glasses and yellow bobble hat.

In the distance I can see their heads. She's sitting in the passenger's seat. My seat. How dare she. How dare THEY! I wonder if he buys her shoes or if he just sticks to flowers. Some Prince Charming he's turned out to be. I hate it when he calls me Cinderella, anyway, as if he saved me from a life of misery. I bet he thought he was doing me a favour by marrying me, perhaps he assumed that my expiry date as an eligible woman had run out at the ripe old age of forty-two. I pick at my thumbnail as we cruise along the High Road in silence. Why did I marry him so quickly, anyway? What made me think that having a ring on my finger would make me happy, make my life complete? Define me? Marriage isn't the be all and end all, and I've quickly come to realise that I'd rather be single forever than be in an unhappy relationship. I don't want half a loaf. In fact, right now I don't want a loaf at all!

Folding my arms, chin in hand, I stare ahead at the familiar Audi. Fearne is talking to me, I can hear her voice, but I'm only half listening, something about Ed Sheeran, a concert, her stepdaughter and her friends. I know I'm being rude, but I can't help it. I can't stop imagining what he'll say to me when I confront him – *It's not what you think. I don't love her, it was just sex. Please don't leave me, I'll end it now.* Or maybe I'm being overconfident, perhaps he'll tell me that he is in love with her, that he made a big mistake marrying me, wants a divorce.

"Oh, I love this song," Fearne says abruptly. "It's my favourite." Reaching out, she turns up the volume and the small space is instantly filled with Ed Sheeran's voice telling us about his *Perfect* love. His words filter through my ears, gathering momentum in my heart until I am filled with an uncontrollable rage.

HER SECRET

"He can't get away with this," I mutter under my breath. I unbuckle my seatbelt and it flies over my left shoulder. My hand is on the door.

"Audrey!" Fearne stretches her arm out and grabs a fistful of my cotton top as the lights change from red to amber. "What the fuck are you doing?" Her eyes dart from me to the lights and then back again. "Close the fucking door."

I'm taken aback by her fury and abundant use of expletives; she's not usually this sweary. Pressing my back against the seat, I sink into my shoulders, face on fire, heart slamming against my chest like a squash ball. I throw a glance at Fearne, she still has my top in her rather large hand, revealing my size 38C bra-clad breasts to the world.

We move about a hundred yards, then stop at a zebra crossing. People shuffle across. Fearne swears again, loudly, complaining that she's going to lose them now, one hand on the steering wheel, the other still holding me down, as if I'm some dangerous criminal under her arrest.

I give her a worrying sideward glance, stiff in my seat. I daren't move. Her face is tight, angry, the veins on her neck looks as if they're about to burst from her skin. It's official. Fearne is *The Incredible Hulk's* sister. *The Incredible Hulkess*. Only a red version.

Okay, I admit I behaved a bit erratically, but I wasn't going to throw myself from a speeding car. I was going to get out when she stopped at the next set of lights. I was just prepping myself, that's all.

The crossing almost clears, and then a couple step off the kerb, hand in hand, and Fearne exhales loudly, as if they're being completely unreasonable and taking their time on purpose to wind her up. The man, not bad looking, actually, mid-thirties in brown jeans and a brown leather jacket, catches sight of my almost bear chest and eyes my boobs enthusiastically, turning back for one last look as his partner smiles and chats to him, completely unaware of her partner's mental philandering. Bloody men. I hate them all! I want to buzz my window down and yell, 'Leave him now before it's too late, love.'

We start moving. I look at Fearne. "Okay, okay." I push her arm away, "Just let me go will you?"

Fearne releases her grip and I straighten my top, feeling the sting from her nails on my skin. I rub it gently. It hurts like hell, but I don't say anything.

We drive the short journey from New Southgate to East Barnet listening to *Heart* radio in silence. On Cat Hill, Daniel takes the second right. Fearne slows down, gives him a little time to go ahead, says she doesn't want him to spot us, then she follows suit just as Daniel takes the first left. When we reach Vernon Crescent, we spot them parking up on the right.

Fearne pulls up behind a silver VW Polo and pulls on the hand brake nosily. In fact, I'm quite amazed that it hasn't come off in her hand.

We peer at them in conspiratorial silence as they climb out of the car and head towards a house. The mistress first, flicking back her long fringe and laughing, as Daniel follows close behind. At the front door, he puts a hand on her back as she pushes the key into the lock. Any onlooker would think they were a normal, happily married couple going home after a swift one at the local pub. Fresh, hot tears fill my eyes, I blink them away, my vision blurs.

Fearne looks at me sadly. The poor woman looks as if she's aged ten years after a morning with me. "What do you want to do, my love?"

I shake my head. I feel like I've just had my guts wrenched out of my stomach and chucked into the heaving skip across the road.

  HER SECRET

"I don't know," I say into my lap, wiping my wet cheeks with the back of my hand.

"We could wait here, see what happens." She licks her lips loudly, glancing at her large, white wristwatch.

"I don't know what to do." I run a hand over my face. "He could be in there for hours. We can't wait here all day."

"Hmmm… well, you could just go and knock on the door, I suppose. Confront them. Have it out with him." I don't answer. "I know that's what I'd do, but it's entirely up to you. I could come with you. Hold your hand? Or I could wait here. I'm easy."

I shake my head. "I don't think I can do that, Fearne."

"Well." She undoes her seatbelt and leans back in her seat as if settling down to an episode of *Silent Witness*. "Let's just sit here for a while until you decide. I'll just give Kylie a quick call, see if she's taken the roast out of the oven. You know what teenagers are like, she's probably still in bed with her phone. I'd be better off sending her a Tweet than ringing her. Yes, hello, Kylie…."

I lean my head back against the headrest. My thoughts drowning out her voice. I can't believe I've been so stupid. Dad warned me about the dangers of rushing into this marriage. His words of wisdom, wasted on me, hum in my ears:

'Daniel seems like a nice enough chap, love, but don't you think you're rushing into it?'

'He has got a lot of baggage – an ex-wife, a full on daughter, a granddaughter. It's a lot to take on.'

'There's just something about him Audrey, that isn't quite right. I can't put my finger on it. Just slow down a bit, eh?

Why didn't I listen to him? WHY? My own father, who's been there and done it. Who had my very best interests at heart.

"Audrey, look!" Fearne's voice breaks into my thoughts. I whip my head up. Daniel is getting into his car. Fearne starts the engine and just then, his mistress rushes out of the house, laughing and waving something in her hand. I think it's his mobile phone. He's making a habit of leaving it behind lately. Not like Daniel to be so careless, it must be the stress of Connie's assault. He reaches across the passenger seat for the item, they exchange a few words, then she turns on her heel and runs back into the house, a sprint in her step. I'm sure she's flooded with endorphins after a quickie with her married lover. That's IF she knows about me. She might think he's single, that there's a future for them. The thought bubbles in my mind.

Fearne puts the car into first gear, the indicator clangs like a time bomb – clack, clack, clack.

"Fearne. Wait." I curl a hand around her forearm and she looks at me, puzzled. "I'm going in." She turns the ignition off and immediately goes to unbuckle her seatbelt. "No," I say firmly, putting a hand out to stop her. "I want to go alone."

She pauses, hands still holding the seatbelt. "I'll just wait for you here then."

"No, Fearne. Please. Just go home now."

"What?" she says, horrified, "And leave you here on your own?" She gestures at the house with her head. "With 'er? I don't think so."

"Please, Fearne. I'll be okay. I'm sure she's not an axe murderer or anything." I give a little laugh that sounds like a hiss.

"How do you know?" Fearne peers at her front door, one eyebrow raised. "She might put arsenic in your tea, get you out of the way."

"Look, if I go missing then call the police and tell them to dig up her garden."

Fearne smiles softly. "But how will you get home?"

"I'll get a cab or jump on a bus. Don't worry about me." Stepping onto the pavement, I lean over the passenger door. "I really, REALLY appreciate what you've done for me today. I'll

HER SECRET

never forget this." I blow her a kiss.

She exhales loudly, shoulders sagging. "Only if you're sure."

"A hundred per cent sure."

"Okay." She turns the ignition on and the Fiat 500 drones. "And whatever you do, don't drink any tea!"

I'm standing outside a red door with a small triangular stained glass window. Number 43. I brace myself before pressing my finger on the doorbell. It rings loudly. Brrrrrrrr. I take a deep, heartfelt breath, shuffling from foot to foot, arms folded. I can't believe I'm about to come face to face with my husband's lover. Blood pounds in my ears. My heart is hammering against my chest. I should go. This is a daft idea. What am I even going to say to her? But I wait and wait and wait. Every second seems like a minute. I press the doorbell again, hard and long this time. Then I hear a woman's voice, shouting, followed by a thunder of footsteps down a stairwell. The door flies opens.

"Hello." The young, stocky man, late twenties, in jeans and a Spurs football shirt gives me a broad, warm, friendly smile. "Can I help you?" he asks in a measured, nasally voice.

I gaze into his blue, almond shaped eyes and my breath catches in my throat. I don't know what to say. This isn't the scenario I was expecting. "Umm…is…um…your…" I swallow hard and look over his shoulder.

"Ryan," a woman's voice cries in the distance. "Who is it, love?"

"Muuuuuuum," he hollers. "It's a lady." And as he turns his back on me, an out of focus silhouette appears in the distance; and then, as if in slow motion, my eyes flit from the dark figure to the name and number on the back of the lad's football shirt, and my legs give way. TAYLOR – 7.

CHAPTER 28

HER HAZEL EYES sweep over me quickly. She looks as if she's seen a ghost. Clearly, she's recognised me. I hate her immediately. I wonder how many times she's snuck a look on Daniel's phone to check out the competition in his photo album. He always showers after sex, she could've done it then, or maybe when he was fast asleep in her bed. Naked. The thought of them together makes me heave and it takes all of my strength to stop myself from decking her. She licks her wide, thin, pale pink lips, then she finally finds her voice.

"It's okay, Ryan, you can go back up now." Her eyes don't leave mine.

"When's lunch ready?" Ryan whines, stomping back into the corridor. "I'm starving Marvin."

"In a bit, love. Just go up to your room. I'll give you a shout when it's ready."

"Can I water the plants in the garden?" he asks, one hand on the banister. "Please, Mum. I'll put the hose away."

"Yes, okay, Ryan," she says, a tinge of irritation in her voice. "But make sure you use the watering can for the pot plants, we don't want any more accidents."

"Yay!" He does a fist pump, beams at me one final time, then is swallowed into the darkness of the corridor.

"Can I help you?" she asks, pulling her red cardigan around her and looking around wildly. I imagine she doesn't want the neighbours to bear witness to this. I take a few moments to digest her as she stands in the doorway like a security guard – middle class, well-spoken, attractive in an ordinary kind of way, not beautiful. Not much taller than me, maybe 5'8. Her skin is pale, as if she's never had a holiday in the sun. The crow's feet around her deep set eyes and the slight sag in her jowls suggest she's older than I originally thought. I'd say mid-fifties but looks after herself. I spy a few pairs of bright coloured running shoes against the wall in the left hand corner beneath her oversized coat hanging on the rail – pinks, yellows, electric blues; all different shapes and sizes. I wonder if she runs with Daniel, if it's a shared interest. I bet that's how they met! I can just imagine them chatting at the starting line of one of those half marathon charity runs he keeps signing up for. I can't count the times he's tried to coax me into joining him on one of his morning runs. But I'm no runner, never will be.

"I don't know," I reply confrontationally, hands on hips. "You tell me."

Furrowing her dark, thin brows, she inclines her head. "Excuse me?" I stare at her in stunned silence, and then she tuts, frustrated. "I'm sorry, but who exactly are you?" She tucks her long, wavy fringe behind her ear and then folds her arms.

My face is flaming. Who exactly am I? I'm your fucking lover's wife, I want to say, that's who I am. But I don't want to antagonise her. I've come here for answers not a slanging match. I need to keep my cool so that she can invite me in, and then I can interrogate her – make her tell me everything. Taking a deep breath, I fold my arms, and as I shift my weight onto one leg it suddenly occurs to me I'm mirroring her. Sam Knight says this is a sign that you like someone. And I definitely don't like her. I immediately change position and shove my hands into the pockets of my jeans. Her eyes flick a few times, darting to my balled fists in my pockets. I can almost feel the tension emanating from her slender body. The body that was in my husband's arms just minutes ago. I want to scream.

"I'm Audrey," I say flatly.

"Audrey?"

I click my tongue and roll my eyes. "Audrey. Daniel's wife," I clarify in exasperation.

She looks at me aghast for a few moments, feigning shock. I'll give her ten out of ten for her acting abilities, I almost believe her.

She purses her lips. She's gone a bit red. Good! "Oh, I see." She fastens the top two buttons of her cardi. "Well, you'd better come in then, Audrey Daniel's wife," she says wryly, and I'm sure I see a smirk on her lips. How dare she make fun of me. I resist the sudden urge to turn on my heel and leave, and I follow her along hallway. It's neat and tidy, as if everything has just been polished and vacuumed.

"I'm Sarah, by the way," she says, smoothing the back of her knee-length black dress, before sinking into the worn brown leather armchair. We're in her small sitting room, facing the patio doors that lead into the neat, square, well-kept garden. I don't bother acknowledging her, instead I watch Ryan splashing the pot plants with a big metal watering can. I wonder how he feels about Daniel, the intrusion. It's never easy when there's kids involved, whatever their age. "So," her voice again. "How long have you known about us?" Her words slice through me like rotating blades. She's not even bothering to deny it, or at least humour me with a few excuses.

"Not long." I look her in the eye, rubbing my wedding ring with my thumb. "A few days." She looks surprised, or perhaps it's just shock. Looking away, I take in the sizeable dark but homely room – red walls, mahogany furniture, colourful bric-a-brac on every

HER SECRET

surface. Daniel must be a magnet for hoarders. A bookshelf takes up the entire wall behind the Chesterfield sofa. The rest of the walls are covered with family photographs and canvas paintings, mostly of flowers – lilies, roses, tulips and one that looks like a replica of *The Sunflower*. She's obviously an artist. They're bloody brilliant, actually, which only makes me loathe her more. Above *The Sunflower* replica is a taxidermy of a deer's head wearing a Spurs scarf, which I find a little disconcerting. I'm not into stuffed animals.

"I see," Sarah says again. They must be her favourite words. An awkward silence hangs in the air, and then. "Oh, God," She half stands. "Where're my manners? Would you like a cup of tea?" Fearne's voice rings in my ears '*And whatever you do, don't drink any tea!*' I give her a blank look, twisting my lips. You can't be too careful. "Okay, no tea then." Sitting back down, Sarah raises her eyebrows, as if I'm the most awkward visitor in the entire world. Then as we lapse into silence, my stomach makes a loud, gurgling noise, which I'm sure she hears but politely ignores; and I'm suddenly overwhelmed by a need to fill the silence to stop an encore. I haven't eaten a thing since last night.

"Have you lived here long?" I blurt loudly, and she jumps; I've started her.

"Um..Yes, several years," she says absently, then looks at me as if I'm a door-to-door marketing agent wasting her time. "Look, am I allowed to ask why you're here? How you found us?"

"That's none of your business," I say confidently. I cross one leg over the other and rest my elbows on the armrests of the chair, steepling my fingers. Sam Knight says this is a sign of self-assurance; politicians often do it to show they're confident, as do barristers and chess players when they want their opponent to know they're about to destroy them.

She gives a breathy little laugh at the ceiling. "Was that you following us? In that little red bubble car?"

SHIT! Fucking fuck! Fearne was certain that we'd got away with it. She'll be devastated when I tell her we were rumbled by the mistress.

"Did you see us?" I say in a voice that sounds as if I've just inhaled helium. "What did Daniel say?" My bum finds the edge of the seat and she laughs. Damn it, this isn't going as planned. I was supposed to be the one making HER feel uncomfortable not the other way around.

"I don't think he noticed, to be honest. At least, he didn't say anything to me. I saw you through the sun visor mirror first, and then in the wing mirror. You were wearing a yellow hat and sunglasses. And you were at the cemetery too, weren't you?" Jesus, this woman should work for *Scotland* flipping *Yard*.

I rub my forehead. I'm bloody well sweating now. She looks like the cat that got the cream. I suppose she thinks she's clever – first she snatches my husband and then she unravels my secret escapade. As we eye each other like a couple of poker plays, a scene plays out in my head where I reach inside my handbag, pull out the ancient, gloopy Snickers bar and smear it all over her smug face.

"Are you sure you don't want any tea? Or coffee, even? I've got fresh if you prefer or something cold. I made some fresh lemonade this mor –" She goes to stand up again and my hand shoots up like a buckler.

"Look, please," I butt in. "I'm not here for a tea and pleasantries. I need to know what's going on."

Confusion flickers over her face. "Okay." She clasps her knees. "Fire away."

I clear my throat and kick off with a cliché. "How long has it been going on?" I bite hard on my top lip to stop the tears that are stinging my eyes. I can't believe I'm doing this.

She looks at me as if I'm the local nutter. "Going on?"

I sigh loudly. This woman really does like to play games, doesn't she? No wonder she gets on so well with Daniel. "Do you really want me to spell it out?" I bark. She pulls another face, throwing a glance at Ryan in the garden, lips curved downwards in surprise. Anger ripples in my heart. I've held onto my wits for long enough. If she wants war, she's going to get it. "Screwing my husband," I leap to my feet. "Having an AFFAIR." She jumps when I say the word *affair*, fastening a hand over her mouth. I think she wants to laugh. The cow.

"Mum?" Ryan has appeared at the door, face dark. Giving me a daggered look, he rushes to his mother's side and swings a protective arm around her shoulders, eyebrows knitted together.

"Are you alright, Mum?" He shoots me another furious look. "You should go, now, lady. You're upsetting my mum."

"I'm sorry, Ryan," I say, suddenly feeling awful. Poor lad. This isn't his fault. "I didn't mean to…"

"Just go," he yells. "And leave us alone."

I swoop my bag off the zebra rug. It looks like real hide. Jesus, what is it with this woman and dead animals? I need to get out of here. I've found out all I need to know, anyway. My husband is a two-timing arsehole. A lothario. A cheat. Cross examining Sarah isn't going to make any difference. I need to get home. Have it out with him. Tell him that it's over between us.

"No, wait." There's a shuffle and then I feel a hand on my arm. "It's okay, Ryan. The lady can stay. She didn't mean it." She looks at me pointedly. "Did you?"

I shake my head quickly, wordless. Ryan's grip tightens around Sarah's shoulders, his deep blue eyes, Daniel's eyes, not leaving mine.

"Why don't you make me and the nice lady a cup of tea, hey?" She smiles round at him, cupping his left hand. "He makes the best cuppa in East Barnet."

Ryan likes this. He releases his mum and lets his arm fall by his side, his anger dissipating just as quickly as it came. "Do you take sugar?" he smiles. I tell him that I don't as I sit back down, and he's gone.

"I'm sorry about that," Sarah says to the pelting sound of a kettle being filled at the kitchen sink. "He thought you were going to hurt me. He doesn't like arguments, you see." Her voice drops to a whisper. "Very protective." I look at her blankly. I'm not sure what she wants me to say. "It's a part of his condition. He's terrified that I'm going to die and leave him." Rolling her eyes, she smiles, as if that's never going to happen, as if she has some kind of superpower that will enable her to choose a timely death.

"I'm sure that bringing up a child with…" I falter.

"Down's Syndrome," she says crisply. "You can say the word, you know. It's not contagious. It's just an extra chromosome."

I feel my cheeks flush. It's not what I meant. "I'm sorry…I didn't mean to –" I hesitate, and as I focus on the spiral base of the glass table in front of us, it strikes me that it's similar, if not identical, to the ones scattered around Daniel's office in Hampstead. I wonder if it's a gift. It definitely doesn't fit in with the rest of the décor. It's too modern, too blingy for this oldie worldly room.

"It's okay," she sighs, shoulders slumping. "I'm used to it. People don't know what to say. But yes, you're right - bringing up a child with special needs is harder, but worth every moment. I love the bones of him – he's my world."

She touches her chest, and I notice that her neck has come up in red blotches. I wonder if it's an allergy from the tiny silver crucifix around her neck, or if she's just nervous because I've discovered that Daniel is Ryan's dad. Daniel is the father, isn't he? He must be – the eyes, the name on his shirt. I fold my arms, my anger returning. I want to know how my husband was leading a double life right under my nose and why he's kept Ryan a secret from me and Connie. "Look, I'm not –"

"I don't –"

We've both spoken at the same time. "Go ahead," I say, lifting a hand, "You first."

"I'm not having an affair with your husband. This isn't how it seems." Finally, the clichés. Next she's going to tell me that it's over between them and now they're just good friends. "We did have a bit of a thing," she says into the cobble stoned surround of the open fire. "But that was many years ago," she adds firmly, looking at me.

My stomach tightens. I was right. Daniel has a mistress and is leading a double life. He and Sarah have been lovers for years and Ryan is their lovechild. "Look, don't bother with any more excuses." I rub the back of my neck. It suddenly feels stiff. Probably from being curled up in a ball in the back of Fearne's Fiat 500. "I'm going to leave him. You can have him. He's yours."

"So easily?" Her voice drops to a whisper. "You've only been married five minutes. Daniel will be devastated. He's been through so much." Jesus Christ, this woman is absolutely barmy.

"What are you suggesting, hmm? That I just put up with it? Put up with YOU?" I growl.

"No, look, you've got it all wrong…. You don't understand. I – ".

"What's the matter? Don't you want him now that you can have him?" I snap.

"Why would I want your husband when I've got my own?" she says defensively. I follow her eyes to a photograph on the wall. She's standing in the middle, Ryan is on her left and a middle-aged man with thinning hair and thick rimmed square glasses is on her right – arms slung around each other, all teeth and smiles. The perfect happy family.

"Oh my God," I say quietly. She's cheating on someone, too. That's why she's so tetchy, nervous, denying the affair; she doesn't want her husband to find out. "How could you?" I whisper. "With Ryan in the house?" I get to my feet. I've heard enough. "I can promise you one thing, I will find your husband and I will tell him."

"Oh no, please, wait," she pleads, standing up too. "Let me just explain."

"It's too late." I shoulder my bag. "I don't want to hear anymore."

"Where are you going? I've made you tea." Ryan is standing in the doorway holding a tray of French Fancies and an expensive looking tea set. The kind my mother would only bring out if a VIP was visiting, like the Chair of her Bowls club.

"I'm sorry, Ryan." I shoulder past him in the doorway. "I've got to go. "

"Audrey, please." Sarah follows me into the corridor urgently, and I notice for the first time that she's barefoot – she is bloody tall, after all. "I promise you that Daniel and I are NOT having an affair."

"I'm sorry, Sarah," I give a little laugh, "but I don't believe you."

"Are you talking about my new uncle, Mum?" Ryan is behind her, crockery rattling in his unsteady hands. We've upset him again.

A bolt of acid hits the bottom of my stomach. "Uncle?" I stammer.

"Shit! I knew this would happen. Why doesn't anyone ever listen to me?" Sarah says angrily, raking a hand through her hair. "Look, I thought you knew about us, but clearly you're clueless. I

HER SECRET

didn't want you to find out like this. Daniel promised me that he'd told you about me."

My heart is in my mouth. "Told me what?"

She wrings her hands, and I notice that they're small, veiny. "Well, that I'm Connie's auntie, of course."

CHAPTER 29

SARAH AND I sip our tea in unison. The warm, sweet liquid glides down my throat, cascading into my stomach. I don't take sugar in my tea but Sarah insisted, said it'd help with the shock. And it has.

The news that Sarah is Connie's aunt and that Daniel has a son we knew nothing about, almost floored me. It's a good job Ryan put the tray of tea down the moment my legs buckled or I'd have hit the floor. In fact, I'm sure I heard him say something about calling 999. I take another sip in silence, giving Sarah a side-eyed stare, as if she's just announced that she's won the Euromillion Jacketpot and donated it all to The OAPs Lap Dancing Foundation. I'm very open minded as a rule, few things shock me, but sleeping with your sister's husband and having his child is way, WAY off limits. Unless it happened after Sophie died, that is. One of my mum's friends married her husband's brother when he passed away, said they just fell in love; she didn't even have to change her name, or her in-laws.

The prattle of water hitting a fence makes me glance out at Ryan, hose in hand, sun on his back, spraying the garden with glee. Ryan took his tea outside, just to cool down, he said, while he watered the plants. Then, as if he can feel my eyes on him, he turns around and waves. His big, infectious smile whooshes over me like warm, foamy seawater, and my heart melts. I wave back. I expect Daniel kept him a secret because he was trying to protect Princess Connie, as per. I imagine she won't be too happy when she finds out her dad shagged her mum's sister the moment she died and got her pregnant. On the other hand, I'm sure she'll be thrilled to bits when she finds out she's got a beautiful brother.

"He's a lovely young man, Sarah, you must be very proud," I say.

"Yes." She smiles into her cup, a big, wide smile that reaches her eyes. "He's made my life complete."

Sipping my tea, I gaze around the room, the cogs in my brain turning faster and faster and faster. I really ought to leave now, go back to my husband, tell him that I know all about Sarah and his secret love child. But now that I'm here I want to find out as much as I can about Daniel's past, and Sarah is the only person who can provide it. I can't let this golden opportunity slip through my fingers.

"So, is that what he calls him then? UNCLE? When are you going to tell him the truth?"

"What do you mean?"

"Well, that he's Daniel's son."

"Daniel's? Whatever gave you that idea?"

I look round at her, shocked. "Umm….Taylor on the back of his shirt?" And Daniel's blue eyes, but I don't say that.

She puts her cup down and leans forward, cupping my knee. "I'm not sure if Daniel has filled you in about our past." Filled me in? I didn't even know you existed until half an hour ago. "But I wasn't married when Ryan was born. His real dad scarpered when…" She looks at the door as if she can see him walking through it. I take a gulp of tea. "When Ryan was a few weeks old. He couldn't cope with…" she falters. He sounds like a complete knob. "Anyway, Taylor is our maiden name, not Daniel's," she says, and I almost spit the tea in her face. "Audrey, are you okay, love?" She takes the cup and saucer from my trembling hands and puts it next to hers on the table next to the empty plate of French Fancies.

"He….he…" I stutter. "He said that Sophie's maiden name was Cooper."

"Cooper?" She shakes her head, bewildered. "Look, I don't know what he's told you, but Taylor is my family name – his name is Daniel Armstrong. Jesus, no wonder we couldn't find him all these years."

I press my hand hard against my mouth to stop myself from screaming. I can't believe what she's saying. I open my mouth to speak but nothing comes out, it's as if the words are frozen in my throat. If Daniel Taylor isn't his name then who the hell am I married to?

"But you said you had a fling with Daniel years ago… and I…I…I thought that…..Ryan…was…was – "

"Yes, but it wasn't a relationship. We had a few snogs at the back of the local Odeon, that's all, and then when I introduced him to Sophie I was history." She pats her lips nervously, she knows she's disclosed too much. "Anyway, that's water under the bridge," she says quickly, looking away. "I really don't know why Dan's using our name. Maybe he got caught up in something illegal." She turns her palms up and her shoulders rise and fall. "But I do know that he adored Sophie. She was everything to him. And he was a good husband and father. Well, you know what he's like." I don't answer. I don't even know who he is, let alone what he's like.

"So what happened after Sophie died?" I probe. "Why did you lose contact?"

"Well, it wasn't on purpose," she says in a tone that suggests I was accusing her of that very thing. "At least not on our part. Daniel told us he'd been offered a job in Cyprus – a great opportunity, a fresh start for him and Connie. He promised he'd be in touch once they'd settled down. But we never heard from him again." I'm speechless. I know Daniel can be quite controlling at times, and clearly he's got a lot of issues, but it's not like him to be so cruel. "Well, not until a few weeks ago, anyway," she adds, placing her cup and saucer down next to mine. "I suppose seeing us reminded him too much of Sophie, his." She air quotes. "Burning love." I swallow back the bitter saliva that's formed in my mouth and it hits my stomach like sharp needles.

"Why didn't you ever try looking for them?" I press on, trying to keep my voice level.

"How?" she yells, and I jump. "We had no idea where they were in Cyprus. I mean, I know it's only a tiny island, but still. There was no internet or Facebook in those days. And by the time there was, he'd changed his flipping name." She throws a hand out. "Oh, I could swing for him, I could." Her face reddens and she pauses, takes a deep breath. "My parents moved to Spain when they retired. They're still there now. We visit often. Beautiful country." She smiles. "My mum's Spanish."

"Spanish?" I gulp, as Daniel's voice echoes in my ears – '*Are you sure you haven't got a bit of Spanish in you?*' "Really?" This is really starting to freak me out now. I swallow hard. I know I should leave, but I can't go now, not when I'm this close to finding out the truth about my husband.

"So how did Daniel find you then?" I ask. "Why now?" I know why, it's because Connie is obsessed with finding her real family but I want to hear her side of the story. So I sit back while she tells me that six weeks ago Daniel tracked her down, wanted to meet up, said he thought it was time Connie met her real family. They met at a local pub, and he told her everything. How he'd lied to Connie about her mum, how I'd stumbled across Connie's birth certificate and discovered Aliki wasn't her biological mother. The lot. "At first I was bit miffed. How could he take off with Connie and wipe us all out of her life? But then when he explained how he met and married Aliki, that he thought he was doing right by Connie, how she needed a mother, stability in her life, I understood. I'm a parent, too. I know what it's like. You always put them first."

I nod slowly. "Desperate times, desperate measures." I'm not here to judge anyone. I'm here to find out the truth about my husband. I need to know who I'm married to because it clearly isn't Daniel Taylor. "So, why are you still a secret? Don't you want to meet Connie?"

"Of course I do," she exclaims. "But according to Daniel, she's not ready." Another lie. "He said he needed a few weeks to break the news to her." She waves a hand. "It's been a month. I keep going on at him. But I guess she's just not ready," she says sadly. I shake my head in disbelief. I don't tell her about Connie's attack, about Jake, which is probably the real reason why Daniel hasn't told Connie yet. "Dan's been visiting us here every Sunday after he pops to the cemetery. I haven't been to Sophie's grave in ages." Sophie's grave. I knew it. She wasn't buried at sea. Daniel has lied to me about practically everything. "But today was the anniversary of her death – twenty-nine years. Where does all the time go, eh? I must say, it's been great getting reacquainted. Dan and I go way back. And we all can't wait to meet Connie and Lily."

I clear my throat. I need to find out why he didn't tell me that Sophie was buried at Southgate Cemetery, but it's a delicate issue and I need to tread carefully. I don't want to upset Sarah, open old wounds. "Sophie's grave…it's…" I want to say a complete mess but I don't want to upset her again.

"Her grave's is a bit untidy, I know." She nods, picking up on my vibe. "Mum and Dad were going to buy a headstone, just something basic to keep it tidy. They weren't well off. But Daniel wouldn't have it, said she deserved something grand, that he'd sort

HER SECRET

it once he had enough cash. I think he had this idea of some sort of shrine, and then he disappeared, of course."

"He told me she was buried at sea," I say quietly, feeling numb with shock.

"Still fibbing, then, is he? We used to call him Danny Liar back in the day." Unsurprisingly that the most sensible thing I've heard all day. "But they were only white lies," she adds, clearly sensing my tension. "Just to get himself out of tricky situations." Not anymore, I want to say, he's moved on to premier league now.

We sit in silence, as I try and fail to digest everything, and then I hit her with another question in the manner of *Colombo*. "So, what was Sophie like?"

"As a person, you mean?"

I nod. "As a person. What did she look like? Have you got any photos? I'm sure Connie would love to see them if you have." And I mean this, because as soon as I get home I'm going to make Daniel ring Connie and tell her everything, or else I will.

Sarah takes a deep, heartfelt breath, a smile creasing her face. "She was a sassy and vibrant little minx, and very good looking." Sounds a lot like her daughter. "I haven't got many photographs, I'm afraid. Most of our pics got lost in our last house move. But…" She sucks her lips in and narrows her eyes, regarding me, as if trying to decide on whether to let me in on a family secret. "Wait here." Leaping to her feet, she thunders up the stairs.

I close my eyes to the backdrop of creaking floorboards. What a bloody mess. Daniel Armstrong has lied to me about practically everything about his past. It's almost as if his life ended when Sophie took her last breath and he rose like a phoenix from the ashes and reinvented himself. But why, Daniel Armstrong, why? A loud, angry thrash tears through the room. I open my eyes, startled. Ryan has splashed the patio doors and is standing there laughing. I smile back at him and give him the thumbs up.

"I've found a few." Sarah's back with the photographs, face red, panting. She perches herself next to me on the armrest. "This is one is of me and Sophie." I smile at the black and white photo of two little girls. They must've been about eight or nine. "And this was taken in Brighton. Look, this one is of me with my friend Jenny on the Pier." Smiling at the photo, I imagine the smell of salty sea, fish and chips, and fresh doughnuts; the sea lashing against the pebble stone beach, of good times. "Daniel must've spoken about Jenny, right?" She looks at me and I shake my head no. "Oh…." She hesitates for a moment, frowning. Oh, Christ, I think I'm going to get the history of her friendship with Jenny, now. I glance at the clock on the mantelpiece. I've been gone hours. I need to go home, have it out with Daniel. Tell him that I know everything and that I want a divorce. "It's just that she was part of the gang, that's all. Anyway, that's me there." She points at a young, attractive Sarah, windswept hair, laughing, holding down her billowing dress. "And there's Daniel, and a side profile of Sophie." Her eyebrows rise and fall. "She liked her fags." I look at Daniel; he's leaning against the railings on the pier, hair standing up in the wind, gazing adoringly at Sophie as she blows smoke over his head. "And here's one of her with Connie. Dad took it at the hospital the day Connie was born."

And as I take the photo from her hand, my smile dies on my lips. Every hair on my body is on end. "Oh, wow," I manage after a few moments.

"I know." Sarah enthuses. "I saw the resemblance immediately. I can see why Daniel is so taken by you. It's always Audrey this, Audrey that," she whines playfully. "You're just his type."

Heat prickles my skin. "Jesus," I gulp.

"You could be sisters, couldn't you? Twins even."

 HER SECRET

A wave of fear washes over me and mergers with the incredulity that's swishing in my mind at what he's done to me, what he's done to his own daughter. I start fanning myself with the photograph. I get to my feet, shuffle from foot to foot. "Look, I'd better go." Sarah takes the photo from my trembling fingers.

"Are you sure?" she asks, startled. "Why don't you stay for lunch, there's plenty to go around. Brian will -"

"No," I cut in frantically. How on earth can she suggest such a ludicrous thing? She knows that Daniel has lied to me. Maybe Fearne was right all along, she is a maniac. "I've got to get back," I croak. "Daniel will be wondering where I am." I laugh nervously, folding my arms to stop my hands from shaking.

"Oh, okay," she says, looking confused. "But, Brian should be back any moment. If you wait a while I could give you a lift to Muswell Hill. It's really no bother." The confirmation that she knows where I live fills me with a sudden incomprehensible unease. "It's getting nippy out there and you haven't even got a jacket. Look at you." She touches my arm. "You're shaking."

"No, really." I edge away from her as if she's holding a grenade that's about to detonate. Taking backward steps, I feel for the door frame with my hand. I need to get out of here, get back to reality. "I'll be fine. I've got an Uber account." I feel my pocket for my phone. "I'll call a cab."

At the door she hesitates. "It was lovely meeting you, Audrey. You will tell Connie about us now, won't you?" I nod, gulping. "Perhaps you can all come over for dinner, bring Lily, too. I'll cook us something nice." I do wonder why people say 'something nice.' What's the alternative, knocking up something unpalatable?

"Sure..um...that sounds great." I take a step back and in my haste forget that there's a step on the porch. I land in the safety net of the bushes, Sarah is helping me up. "Are you okay?"

Staggering to my feet, I dust myself down furiously, face flaming, sweat trickling down my cleavage, my temples. "Yes, I'm fine," I mutter, grateful that she isn't laughing. "Say goodbye to Ryan for me, and thanks for the tea."

"Okay, love," she says worriedly. "Mind how you go now."

I head off down the road, breaking into a run, and then I hear her voice. "Audrey, wait…." I spin on my heel. She's rushing towards me, behind her a black four by four with dark windows is turning into her drive. I want to run, run, run. "You dropped your phone in the bushes," she says breathlessly. "You won't get very far without it." And as I take my iPhone from her hand, I swear I see a flicker of hatred in her eyes.

CHAPTER 30

MY PHONE STARTS FLASHING with notifications as soon as I pull it out of my handbag in the back of the cab.

A missed call from Daniel. No alarm bells. That's quite normal.

Five missed calls from an unknown number – probably the gas company wanting to fit a smart meter, they won't leave me alone.

Three missed calls from Vicky and a voicemail. It must be urgent. I'll pick it up just soon as I've read my texts.

Daniel: Where are U? Home now. X

Tina: How'd it go today, DCI Fox?

Daniel: Tried calling U. No answer. Ring me. Hungry. Miss you.X

Louise: All okay? Ring me when you've finished. ☺

Fearne: How was it? Hope ur ok, luv.

I don't bother replying to the text messages, instead I go straight to Vicky's voicemail.

"*Audrey, hi. It's me. Look, can you ring me when you get this please. I've got some news for you. Umm….*" Her breathy sigh crackles in my ear. "*I think you ought to know ….Josh, stop hitting your brother. Nathan give it back to him. NOW!*" The wail of the twins almost perforates my eardrum and I pull the phone away. "*Oh, look, Audrey, I've gotta go. The twins are driving me mad. Ring me. Yeah? Laters.*"

I ring Vicky back immediately. It goes on to the answering machine. I wait out the automated reply and start blabbing into the phone. "Vicky, it's me. I hope you're okay….I..um..Look, I'll."

"Hello, Audrey," Vicky's voice. "Sorry, didn't get to the phone in time. I've been trying to get ahold of you all day. Where've you been?"

"It's a long story," I sigh to the milieu of Capital Gold drifting from the car radio. I didn't tell Vicky I was spying on Daniel today because she might've told George, and I know he would've tried to stop me. "Look, I'll tell you all about it later. And, about the flat. I can explain…I…" I hesitate. "Look, is everything okay with you and George? Are the kids okay?" Please God let them all be all right. I can't take any more anguish today.

"Yes, we're all fine," Vicky says blithely, and I let out a sigh of relief. Thank you God. "Look, I don't want you to get cross with George or anything but last night he told me something." She pauses as if in two minds, but then carries on. "Something I think you should know…about Nick….something that happened at Tina and Ronan's party."

My heart picks up speed. "Go on."

"Well, remember when you were texting Nick at your birthday party last year?" My mind spirals back to my forty-second birthday party. I'm in my lounge. Nick has sent me a text saying the paternity test results had come through, he's not the father of Francesca's baby. We're both elated, especially him. Texts fire back and forth.

"Yes, of course. We were talking about going away together, eloping." I roll my eyes.

"Yeah, that's right. The plan was to meet at his place, wasn't it? Then you said you turned up and he was gone."

"Yes, the bastard," I say dryly. "I still can't forgive him for being such a coward, especially as it was his suggestion to get back together."

"Well, that's the thing. Apparently he said you sent him another text…..No Florian, we're having lunch soon…" I hear Florian's mumbled whines. "When Daddy gets home… Sorry about that, Audrey, he wants a bar of chocolate. Anyway, where was I? Oh yes, he said that you texted him saying that there'd been a change of plan and to meet him at Heathrow Airport instead."

"No, that's a complete lie," I say firmly, and the driver gives me a sharp look in the rear view mirror, eyes dark and wide. "He's just making excuses to get out of it, Vicks, that's all."

"George said he seemed very convincing," she muses. I don't answer. Vicky's always liked Nick. "The thing is, Audrey, apparently Nick went to Heathrow Airport and waited and waited. He almost missed his flight. He said he was about to call you but then some young bloke with a long, wiry, ginger hipster beard and a Russian accent turned up in your absence, said he had a message for him – from YOU."

"Well, that's insane," I cry, the driver looks at me again and buzzes down his window a fraction, perhaps he thinks the fresh air might calm me down. "I don't even know any ginger bearded Russians." Jesus, what a day. Blood beats in my ears. I wonder if my phone was hacked. I'll need to call the police. Change all my passwords. "What kind of message?"

"A hand written note." Now I know he's definitely lying. What is it with me and lying arseholes? I must be a magnet for them. "In your writing," she adds. "Apologising or something. Anyway, as far as he's concerned you stood him up!"

I laugh at that. "Oh, that's complete bollocks." I rake a hand through my hair and shake my head at the driver, and he nods, as if he knows every detail of my complicated life and is on my side.

"But George said he showed him the texts on his phone, Audrey," Vicky explains. A flicker of dread rushes up my spine. I hope Nick didn't show my brother the intimate, flirty texts I sent him.

"That's just crazy. None of this is making any sense. Besides, he left me a *Dear John* message with his new neighbour upstairs. Georgia, I think her name was. My brother did have a few at the party, Vicks. Maybe it was just a trick text. I mean, did he say he saw dates and everything, my number? And as for a hand written note. Pffft." I shake my head at a stream of houses as we speed past them.

"No, I don't think he mentioned dates. Oh, wait, he's just walked in now. George, it's Audrey. She wants to know if you saw dates on Nick's text messages. What? You didn't tell me not to tell her!" Oh, bloody hell, what a time for them to have a row. "George, she's your sister, she has a right to know."

There's a shuffle and then George's voice. "I'm sorry, Audrey. I told her that in confidence," he huffs, as if she's just leaked the MI5 security protocol on terrorism and espionage. "She shouldn't have told you."

"George," I hiss through gritted teeth, "If this were true, which it isn't, then why wouldn't you want me to know, hmm?" I actually feel quite hurt that my brother would keep something like this from me.

"Because you're happily married – at last." Am I? He doesn't know the half of it. "Nick's your past. Let sleeping dogs lie."

"So are you saying that Nick showed you a text from me saying that I wanted to meet him at Heathrow instead of his flat?"

George's breath is loud and hissy down the phone. I can just imagine him knitting his thick, dark eyebrows and scratching the back of his shaved head. "Yes," he says eventually as we ride over a road bump. "But I didn't want you to find out. I made him promise not to tell you. I said that if he really did love you, then he'd leave well alone."

"Why would you even do that, George?" I manage in a croaky voice. "You're not my keeper. I can make my own decisions, you know."

"Because I knew you'd react like THIS," he says loudly. "Because I know how impulsive you are. That you act before you think." He's right. I've always been a bit impetuous even when we were kids. But this is different.

"I want to speak to Vicky," I demand, exhaling loudly through my nose. "Put her back on, please."

"Audrey, look –"

"Now, George!"

There's a bit of shuffling, then his muffled voice, "She wants to speak to you."

"Vicky, can you please do me a massive favour?"

"Yes, of course, anything." There's a cackling noise and I know she's wedged the phone between her cheek and shoulder, as she always does while attending to the kids or housework. I've seen her do it countless times with other callers.

I hesitate. What the hell am I doing? George is right. I do act before I think. Vicky's got enough on her plate, a family, a husband. I can't involve her in this. I've got to sort out my own mess. "Audrey?" she says in a strained voice. She's picked up one of the twins. I can hear his congested breath down the phone. Poor little thing must have a cold.

"It's nothing. Forget it."

"George, take Nathan, I need to talk to Audrey in private," she says firmly. "And give him some *Calpol*." George's deep voice murmurs in the background. "Where it always is," she hisses. "Yes! In the medicine cabinet in the bathroom. Honestly," she tuts, "Go on, Audrey, fire away."

"No, Vicks, it's nothing, honestly."

"Audrey, please, you sound dreadful. I want to help. Do you want me to come round? George can look after the boys. In fact, you'll be doing me a favour, I could do with a bit of air." Did I say that Vicky is the best sister-in-law in the world? But that doesn't mean I should take advantage.

"No, no, I'm fine. I'll just – "

"Right, that's it. I'm coming round whether you like it or not. See you in about fifteen minutes."

There's a scrapping noise. I think she's about to hang up. "No, wait!" I scream and the taxi driver jumps. I quickly mouth 'Sorry,' at him in the mirror. "I'm not home," I say to Vicky, glancing around the small space. "I'm in a cab. Look, I'll tell you all about it when I see you. Could you come with me to Nick's, please? I want to see this so called text that I sent him, and I don't fancy going there alone. I can come straight to you." I lean forward and ask the driver if he would take me to Archway instead, and, after quickly negotiating a new price, he agrees. "I could be there in fifteen minutes."

"George," Vicky cries, "you're on child-minding duty. I'm going out with Audrey." After a light domestic where she doesn't bother to cover the mouthpiece, she comes back to me, and, in a breathless voice, agrees.

Vicky has several near collisions as I bring her up to speed on recent events.

"I knew there was something dodgy about, Daniel." She slides the car into fourth gear and speeds along Fearne Park Road, seemingly in much more of a hurry to get there than I am. My heart flutters in my chest like a trapped butterfly. We're almost there. I'm starting to get cold feet. I wonder if I was hasty. If I got my priorities wrong. Shouldn't I be at home with Daniel discussing the breakdown of our short marriage? "The lying bastard," Vicky spits, curling her lips as she takes the corner sharply, wheels spinning.

I feel a sweep of loyalty, my defence antennae emerging. Daniel's done some very stupid things, and God only knows why he changed his name to Taylor, but, now that the fog has lifted, I'm starting to see it all a little more clearly. Perhaps he couldn't face the Taylor's because it was a painful reminder of his past. Had to hide the truth from Connie because he was too ashamed, too weak to admit that he ran away, that he couldn't cope, and then things just spiralled out of control. "He was in a difficult position, Vicky," I shuffle in my seat, something hard is prodding my backside. I fish beneath my left buttock and pull out a plastic toy part. "He was heartbroken, shocked, confused," I say, staring at the red and blue plastic limb in my hand.

Vicky raises her eyebrows as we drive along Nelson Road. "He sounds like a bit of a control freak to me. First the house, then your flat, and now this flipping bombshell." I know this is chiefly about my flat, about Daniel promising it to Connie behind my back. She feels betrayed, but, actually it's all worked out for the best, because Mum and Dad have offered to help them out with the rent on a new place they've found. A three-bedroom garden flat in Winchmore Hill, close to shops and a great catchment for schools. Much more spacious and accommodating than mine. She glances at me quickly as I wave the plastic toy part at her. "Spider Man's leg," she grins. "Sorry, just put it in there."

"I think he meant well," I insist, forcing the plastic leg in the overflowing glove compartment. "He must've been suffering from depression when Sophie died. He should have gone for counselling instead of soldiering on."

"Do you know what, Audrey? For an intelligent woman with an impeccable taste in shoes, you can be quite daft sometimes."

"None taken!"

"You're too soft with Daniel, that's your problem. If George ever lied like that to me," she growls, jabbing her finger at the dashboard, as if it were George's face. "I'd commit a crime." She glares at me briefly. "I mean it!"

"George wouldn't, he's not like that. He thinks the world of you."

"Well," she says miserably. "I'm just saying, that's all."

I can see Nick's flat in the distance now. "Look, I'll deal with Daniel later. Let's just see what Nick has to say about these hoax texts first. I want to see them for myself."

We pull up across the road from Nick's flat. I notice immediately that his red Yamaha isn't in its usual spot on the small yard outside the house and my heart sinks. In my haste, it didn't occur to me that he'd be out. But there's a gap in the top sash window. Someone is in. Maybe he just popped out for a takeaway or something, he always loved his Sunday takeaways. We can wait with Kartina until he gets back. Sadly, she will have to hear everything, but there's not much I can do about that. She needs to know the truth about her husband, too.

"Do you reckon they're home?" Vicky asks, ducking her head across me and eyeing up the three-story period building. "I'd kill for a flat on this road."

"Well, there's only one way to find out." I undo my seatbelt hurriedly before I change my mind.

I'm standing in front of the royal blue door, heart pounding, mouth dry. I press the buzzer of Flat 1 and stand back. Nothing. I press it again repeatedly, rapping the gold knocker at the same time. Still nothing. "Anybody home?" I push my hand through the large gold letterbox and call out his name, then Katrina's. But there is only stillness in the empty hallway and a bicycle propped up on the side.

"They're not in, Audrey," Vicky says, holding onto the black metal dwarf gate. "Let's go, babe."

I shuffle along the concrete path, hands in cardigan – Vicky's. It was on the back seat of her car. "They must've forgotten to close the window," I point out. And just then there's a rustle followed by a loud thud.

We both look round. Georgia is at the window on the first floor. "They're out," she calls, can of lager in hand. "Oh, it's you," she smiles, recognising me. She pushes her long, brown soft curls off her face. "Hello again."

"Hi Georgia. Sorry to bother you. Have you any idea what time they left?"

She shakes her head and her dishevelled hair falls into her pretty oval face. I think she's a bit pissed – or stoned. "I was asleep. Sorry." She takes a swig from her can. "But Kat said something about going to stay with her daughter the other day." She must be looking after her grandkids again. "And Nick had a gig somewhere, a job in town, I think." She takes a glug from her can. "Asked me to keep an eye on their flat. Lots of burglaries round here lately." Well, I don't know how to tell you this, I want to say, but leaving a ground floor window open isn't the best way to deter burglars. But I keep my observations to myself.

I face Vicky. "He won't be back for ages then." Maybe it's just as well. Maybe it's fate. George's words ring in my ears, '*You're happily married woman now. Let sleeping dogs lie.*'

"We could come back tomorrow," Vicky suggests kindly, folding her arms.

"No, it's okay. I think I just got caught up in the moment." I rub a hand over my face, feeling a dull ache in my lower back. "I've had such a shit day. Do you mind dropping me home?"

She puts her arm around me. I look up at Georgia. "Thanks,

Georgia, and sorry to have bothered you. Again!"

"S'alright," she shouts back. "You got a thing about the blokes that move in downstairs, haven't' you?" She laughs and goes to pull down the window.

"Wait?" I cry, "What do you mean?"

"Oh, Jeez." The window flies open again and she almost tumbles out from the force. "Oh, nothing. I didn't ….umm…shit, bollocks. I don't mean you're a slag or anything. I. OMG. I'd better shut up. It's this." She rattles the beer can. "I've had too much."

She pulls the window almost shut this time then. "Georgia! Please." I pull my phone out of my handbag. "I need to show you something. Can I please come up for a moment?"

I rush up the dark stairwell, it smells of ale and cigarettes and bleach. Vicky's in tow, asking me questions hurriedly. Why are we going up? What if she's a serial killer? My kids will be orphans. George will have a meltdown. What do you need to show her for crying out loud? You should've asked her to come down onto the street.

Georgia's door is on the latch. We creep in like a couple of undercover agents and stare around the large room suspiciously, thick with a fug of stale beer and what smells like weed. The brown worn carpet is speckled with stains, the yellow and orange walls, bright enough to bring on a migraine. They must've decorated while they were off their heads.

"Sorry about the mess." There's a duvet and several pillows on the large brown sofa, covered with an orange throw. At least the furnishings match the décor. "A few mates stayed over last night. "Can I get you a can?"

"No, thanks, I'm fine." I say.

She looks at Vicky. "I'm driving."

 HER SECRET

The silence is peppered by a loud, male voice screaming, 'Fuck off, you cunt', followed by two beeps of a car horn and a dog barking. Georgia pads to the window, nudges the seventies style drab orange, green and white patterned curtains and frowns until the loud, sweary voice becomes a hum in the distance.

"Look, Georgia," I say urgently, and she returns her attention to me. "Remember when I came round last time, you said that the bloke downstairs left a message for me."

"Yeah." She picks on a scab on the inside of her forearm. "The day I moved in. He helped me bring my stuff in from the van." She gestures at the small round kitchen table in the corner of the room and we sit. Vicky's on the edge of her seat, checking out the flat wide-eyed, hands limp in her lap.

"Was it the same man who lives downstairs now?"

She shakes her head and my breath catches in my throat. I want to cry. "No, no, it wasn't Nicky Byrne," she says, looking at me carefully. "This bloke was a bit older but fit, good looking though. I wouldn't' kick him out of bed."

Vicky and I exchange glances. I look up at the crooked yellow lampshade, swallowing back the bile that is rising in my chest, then I start scrolling through my photographs, hands clammy. "Is this the man you saw?"

I hold my phone under her nose with a shaky hand. She squints at the image of Daniel smiling into the camera. "Yeah, yeah. That's him."

Outside, it's started to rain, droplets are spitting onto my hair, shoulders, face. I walk towards Vicky's car in a semi-trance. What kind of a monster have I married? I feel numb. Cold.

Vicky unlocks her car in silence, face fraught. We haven't exchanged a word since we left Georgia's flat. This is serious, mind-blowing stuff. Daniel is totally screwed up.

"Come on, Audrey, let's go back to mine, have a drink, talk to George."

I open the car door, wordless, then just as I fold myself into the passenger seat, I see it - parked across the road.

"Audrey, wait! Audrey, where are you going?"

I sprint towards the black four by four. The sound of the ignition thrums loudly in my ears. He's seen me, he wants to get away. I pick up speed. "Wait," I cry, Vicky is behind me, crying out my name but I can't stop my gait. The car's indicator blinks. I'm in front of the huge, black vehicle as it starts towards me. "Audrey," Vicky's cries echo in my ears. "Get out of the way!"

CHAPTER 31

THE SUN IS DROWNING beneath a hue of pink and blue when I turn the key in the lock. I find Daniel on the sofa, staring ahead stiffly, glass in hand, bottle of Jack Daniel's on the table in front of him, T.V. off. It's never off when he's home alone. He knows, of course, he does. Sarah must've phoned him the moment I left. So much for sisterhood solidarity. I begged her not to ring him, to give me a chance to talk to him first, and she promised that she wouldn't. Some people's promises are worth nothing. I should know that by now.

"Where the hell have you been?" Daniel says at the fireplace. "I've been worried sick?" He knocks back the liquid, the colour of autumn leaves, and grimaces.

"I've had a shit fucking day. I need a drink," I say, letting my bag slide off my shoulder and onto the sofa. The familiar sound of a WhatsApp message trills on my phone as I pad into the kitchen. It's from Jess, asking how I am and when I'm free for a drink. Sky wants to meet me – at last. She's put two kisses at the end and a double heart emoji and a red pouty lips one. Jess always signs off her messages with kisses. I'll text her back later. I yank the fridge door open, and as I pour myself a large glass of Sauvignon Blanc an image of the driver in the dark grey, almost black, Range Rover parked outside Nick's flat flash before me. He must've thought I was a complete nutter, standing in front of his car, screaming at him to get out, accusing him of all sorts.

The driver kept his hand on the horn so I could get out of the way, but I wouldn't budge. Then when he buzzed his window down and stuck out his head, face pale and distraught, I realised that I'd made a mistake. My heel bent a bit as I took a clumsy step back and Vicky caught me, straightened me up, urged me to go back to the car with her. My ankle hurt. I think I may have sprained it. Then the man started speaking but I couldn't take in what he was saying. His lips were moving, twisting in anger, eyes like steel bullets but all I could hear was a scrambled sound, as if he were speaking in slow motion. I took a step closer towards his window. He must've been in his mid-thirties, dark floppy hair, amber eyes and small features; a mousy moustache curving downwards, very urban, very seventies. I imagined him at home with his children watching Disney films while his wife cooked their evening meal – an ordinary, happy family.

"I'm calling the police," he said in a northern accent, pressing the phone to his ear, "You're a flaming psychopath. My girls are terrified."

"Girls?" I peered over his shoulder like a woman on crack. Two horrified little faces strapped in on the back seat stared back at me, vibrant blonde hair resting on their narrow shoulders, and I felt sick. One of them called out Daddy, said she was scared of the lady. What was happening to me? When did I turn into this mad, paranoid shadow of my former self?

Thank God Vicky was with me. I'm so glad I wasn't alone. She gently managed to calm the driver down and, reluctantly, he hung up. I think flattering her eyelashes at him and giving him her Angelina Jolie look clinched it, because he asked her for her number before we left in hushed tones, as if I were some batty, deaf old dear. Vicky flashed her wedding ring at him and with a rueful smile took several steps back, slung her arm around my shoulders and ushered me quickly towards her car.

I take a sip of wine now as I pad back into the lounge. Daniel hasn't moved. I stare at his balled fist on the armrest. The sleeves of his black knit polo top are scrunched up to his elbows. He looks a bit darker – tanned, and I wonder if he popped in for a spray tan on his way home. He likes them, says their good for his professional image. But I think they just make him look fake.

"Okay, do you want to tell me what's going on?" I breathe loudly, collapsing onto the armchair with a thump and kicking off my shoes.

"What're you talking about?" He unscrews the bottle of JD and fills almost half the tumbler; the ice clinks against the glass.

I wonder for a moment if Sarah kept her promise after all. It is all mind games with Daniel. That's how it's always been. "I was with Vicky, "I sigh, "We went round to Nick's flat. I know you tampered with the text messages on my phone at my birthday party last year." He stays silent, jaw throbbing, lips a thin, tight line. "And that you went to Nick's flat, on the day I was meant to go to Rome with him, just before I arrived; told the new tenant upstairs that you were him. Why did you do that, Daniel? Hmm?"

He closes his eyes, fist tightening, rubbing his knuckle with his thumb. "It was the only way to get rid of him."

A confession, just like that. My eyes fill with tears. He's not even putting up a fight. "But why?"

"Why do you think?" he snaps. "You were going to run off with him. Leave me. Ruin your life." He takes a large glug from his glass. "He was an obstacle. He had to be removed."

"REMOVED?" I hit back. "You're not a flipping gangster, Daniel. And how did you get into my phone?" I demand. "I've got a passcode."

He gives me a little huffy laugh. "Do you know how many times I've watched you unlock it?" Damn. I didn't think of that. But I suppose you're not going to shield your handset from your partner every time you use it like you do at the Waitrose counter, are you? It's called trust. He takes another swig. "Fortunately, his last text buzzed through while you were in the kitchen. I read them all then sent one myself, told him to go straight to Heathrow. Within seconds he replied, agreeing, no questions asked. I then deleted the transcript from your phone just as you were making your way down the corridor with the tray of coffees. Perfect timing. Kismet. My impromptu plan worked."

I look at him, mortified. "What about the hand written '*Sorry*' note, did you write it?" I imagine Daniel up all night in his study practicing my handwriting until he got it down to a T.

The side of his mouth curves upwards into a cocky smile. "No, of course not. I don't do bodge up jobs. I can't copy your handwriting. It's too beautiful." He leans his head back and stares at the ceiling as if admiring a star studded sky. "Remember that game we played at your party?"

I frown. "Charades? Yes." Well, it was his version of Charades. We all had to write the answer to his clue on a piece of paper and sign it.

"Do you remember the clues of game three?"

I shake my head. "No…umm…" I try to think but my head is buzzing, there were so many.

He smiles. "The clue was, *In which T.V. sitcom did Ronnie Corbett play the part of Timothy Lumsden?* That's one of your favourite comedies. I knew you'd get it right."

My hand flies to my mouth. "Sorry," I whisper through cold fingers. The image of the yellow post-it note jumps to the forefront of my mind in an instant – *Sorry. Audrey. X.* I even put a kiss at the end. It was meant for Daniel. More fool me.

I watch him, mouth agape, as he recites his masterplan in detail.

 HER SECRET

He slipped the piece of paper into his pocket while I was talking to my mum about her trip to Cyprus, and left the rest on the table for me to bin. The next morning he sent a cabbie to Heathrow Airport armed with a photograph of Nick, which he'd nabbed off my phone. He told the driver he wasn't to leave until he saw Nick read the note. He paid him a hundred pounds upfront with the promise of another hundred when he texted him a photo of Nick going through Departures. But, of course, he wanted to make sure Nick left his flat on his own that morning, that there weren't any last minute changes. So he parked up opposite Nick's flat and waited until he saw him get into the taxi.

"I started the ignition as the cab drove off," he explains, "I was going to follow him, wait outside until my driver texted me the photo of him leaving, but then a van pulled up outside and a young woman got out and started walking towards the flat."

"Georgia from upstairs," I say, bewildered.

"I wasn't expecting that," he says in the manner of an excited schoolboy. "It was a stroke of luck. I ran up behind her as she struggled with some gear, grabbed a bag from her hand, told her I lived downstairs, I was her new neighbour, explained that I was going travelling for a while; then I asked if she'd do me a favour. She wasn't bothered at first. You know what young people are like." He rolls his eyes. "But when she clapped eyes on the fifty quid I pulled out of my pocket, her eyes shone. I told her that if a lady called Audrey came looking for me to give her a message. I pressed the money in her hand and she agreed." The minx, she didn't tell me that. No wonder she was singing Daniel's praises.

"What if I'd phoned or texted him to find out what was happening, what would you have done then?"

"Did you?" he asks. I clench my jaw. "I know you better than you think."

"And what did you think was going to happen when Nick got back, hmm? Didn't you think I'd ever find out?"

He shrugs, taking a sip from his glass. "With any luck, he'd have stayed away. But even if he returned, you'd have been married to me by then, might never have clapped eyes on him again with any luck."

I laugh incredulously, shaking my head. "You thought it'd be that simple? Really?"

"Oh, I dunno," he barks, face red. "I panicked, okay? How was I to know you and Vicky would turn into *Cagney and* flipping *Lacey*?"

I feel winded, as if I've been punched in the stomach. "I can't believe you'd do such a crazy thing, Daniel. You're not all right in the head." I jab at my temple.

"Why not?" He gets to his feet and starts drawing the curtains. Why is he drawing the curtains? It's not completely dark yet. A flicker of fear shoots through my veins. "I was in love with you. You were going to go away with him. I had to get you back. He'd have ruined your life, the unreliable son of a bitch." He squats in front of me and gives me a long, hard stare. "You'd have been a battered wife if you'd gone with him, you do know that, don't you? Look at what he's done to our –" he pauses, closes his eyes. "MY daughter. I was protecting you. I know what men like that are like." His covers his hand over mine and I feel my skin crawl.

"No, Daniel." I snatch my hand away. "Nick's not like that. I was with him for eight years."

"He beat Connie black and blue, you can't deny that. It's a fact." He's pulling out all the stops, even using Connie's assault as bait. He's pathetic.

"If it was Nick," I say, because that is still questionable given that Connie admits to an alcoholic blackout. "It must've been an accident. Connie can hardly remember what happened that night."

HER SECRET

"He's been charged," he says firmly, jaw throbbing.

The swish of a car and a roar of an aeroplane fills the muted moments, and then he says, "Did you ever love me, Audrey?"

"What kind of a question is that?" I say, pulling a face. "I wouldn't have married you if I didn't."

"But not as much as you loved HIM, hmmm?" He gets to his feet, hands loosely on hips.

"Don't be ridiculous. It was different with him. It was…."

"A burning love," he cuts in, bending to my eye-level. "I bet that deep down in the depths of your heart you can still feel the flames licking at the edges."

I study him for a few moments, wordless. Burning love. Those were the exact words that Sarah used to describe his love for Sophie. I know what he's doing. He's trying to be clever, manipulative, turn the tables, wriggle out of it. Make this all seem like it's my fault. That I married him on the rebound – ruined HIS life.

"So, your answer to this meddling is that you did it to protect me from a monster, is it?"

He slides his hands into the pockets of his grey chinos. "As I said, you were going to run off with him, marry him. Someone had to stop you from making a fool of yourself again."

My cheeks burn. "Don't you think that should've been my decision?"

He pulls a face that makes him look as if he's just inhaled the whiff of a sewage. "But you were about to make the wrong one. You were confused. Can't you see that now, darling?"

A feeling of dread comes out of nowhere and I almost scream. It's him. He's been spying on me. "Have you been following me?" I say accusingly. He's seriously freaking me out now.

"Me?" he laughs, sitting back down. "Of course not. Why would I follow you?" A knot forms in my stomach, telling me not to trust him. "You've been watching too many late night movies. Oh, come on, don't look at me as if I'm some kind of nutjob. I admit, I'm a bit of a control freak." A bit? That's a bloody understatement. "But I'd never hurt you, or anyone else for that matter, you know that." Yes. I click my lips, they're dry, flaky with dried lipstick. He's right. I'm overreacting. The knot slowly untangles. "Look," he rubs his chin, giving me one of his lopsided smiles. "This all sounds a bit bonkers, doesn't it?"

Ironically, that's the most sensible thing he's said all afternoon. "You could say that," I agree, knocking back the last dregs of my wine. His cue to refill. Getting to his feet, he takes my empty glass and saunters off to the kitchen, all the while keeping up a monologue of how he was trying to protect me from a distance, he did what he thought was right. I was an emotional wreck when he met me and he saved me. He didn't want to see me broken again. I'm happy with him, aren't I? My life is good, I want for nothing.

"I admit, I overdid it and I'm sorry," Daniel says, walking back in. "What can I say? I didn't want to lose you, okay." I take the glass from his hand. "Look, I love you more than you can ever imagine, but if you don't want me." He spreads his arms out, glass of bourbon in hand, the liquid swishes and I will it not to spill onto my freshly cleaned Turkish rug. "If this is all too much for you, I'll understand. I'll leave. I promise. I'll pack my bags right now and go to Connie's."

I'm not sure if it's his reassuring words, or the effects of the wine, or perhaps it's the fear of being alone, but I'm suddenly unsure. Daniel may be many things but he's not a psychopath, and I don't think he's inherently cruel. Getting rid of Nick was a dirty, manipulative trick but, as Aliki often tells me, he always gets what he wants in the end – he's proactive, a go-getter. And okay, I am the spit of his wife, and that is a bit weird, but maybe he likes that look, Sarah did say I was his type. He's right – I feel safe with him, protected. My life is good. I want for nothing. "Yes," I say, nodding vigorously. "I think you should go, Daniel." Because money isn't everything and I am neither desperate, nor a mug. Well, not a complete mug, anyway.

His eyes close, one hand balled by his side, the other tight around his bourbon glass. This wasn't the answer he was expecting. "Okay, I'll give you some space, time to think." But there's nothing to think about. It's a no brainer. I rushed into this marriage, made a mistake and I now want a divorce. "I'll pack a couple of things now and come back in the morning for the rest. Look, I really am sorry, Audrey. About everything." He sounds like he means it, but we both know it's too late for apologies. At the door he turns and looks at me. "I do love you, you know, my Cinderella." The floorboards creak as he walks along the corridor. But he can't go. I haven't finished with him yet.

"Daniel, wait," I shout. He pads back in, hands on the doorframes. "You keep saying how much you love me, but you don't. You never have, not really."

He's on his knees in front of me. "I messed up big time. I know. But I love you with every part of me, Audrey. You're here." He taps his chest. "And in here." He jabs his right temple. "All the time. Just think," he says breathlessly, eyes shining with adrenalin. "We could be in our new home in a few weeks. We complete at the end of this month. It'll be a new start. A clean slate. A new beginning. Just the two of us." He looks at me pleadingly.

"No more secrets?" I ask quietly.

"No more secrets." He swallows hard and his Adam's apple bobs in his neck. "I promise. If you give me one more chance I'll prove that -"

I clear my throat. "So, when you look at me, Daniel, whose face do you see?"

He furrows his brows, scrunching his face. "Yours, of course."

"Not Sophie's? Not your dead wife's?" His face pales in seconds. "I've seen her photograph. I've spoken to Sarah."

"Whaaat?" he says quietly, getting to his feet.

"And I've met Ryan too. Your nephew. Remember him?" I say, standing up, too. "Oh, yes, I've met your wife's family, the ones you've been visiting every Sunday for the last few weeks when you were supposed to be at the gym. And I know you lied about the membership, by the way. You're not the only clever one around here." I face him. "But I never for the life of me thought you'd stoop this low. How could you?"

Taking a few back steps, he covers his head with his hands. "Shit. SHIT!" He kicks the wastepaper basket and it flies across the room, scrunched up papers, sweet wrappings, an empty Coke Zero can, and bits of debris cover my freshly cleaned Turkish carpet. "How the bloody hell did she find you?" he says furiously. But all I can think about is my Turkish carpet and whether any dregs of cola will saturate the fibres. "I told her to leave it to me. I'd tell you."

"I found her," I say coldly. "Anyway, it doesn't matter how we found each other, the important thing is we did, and now I know the truth." Bending down, he starts picking up the mess and putting it back into the brown leather bin. "So, when were you planning on telling me, then?"

"Soon. This weekend." Yet another lie.

I shake my head as I walk towards him. "You just can't help yourself, can you?" My face is close enough to smell the sweet aroma of bourbon on his breath. "Lie after lie after lie. You're a pathological LIAR," I scream, "Aren't you?"

He bites the top of his lip and holds it between his teeth. "I only hooked up with Sarah a few weeks ago. I was going to tell you,

 HER SECRET

but then this thing with Connie kicked off and I couldn't think straight." Sweat slides down his face. "So, give me a sodding break, will you."

"What about Sophie's grave?" I hit back, following him across the room. "Why did you tell me she was buried at sea, hmm? Answer me that Daniel ARMSTRONG!"

Daniel spins round quickly and I backtrack. "The fucking bitch," he murmurs in a whiny tone. "Did she have to tell you that?" We're silent for what seems like an eternity. The boiler judders. The heating's come on. The temperature must've dropped to below 15c. No wonder I'm feeling so cold, and then I hear his voice again. "I had to tell Connie her mum was buried at sea," he sighs, pulling out a chair at the dining table. "Sophie was an artist," He looks up at me sharply. "And that's the God's honest truth. Sarah's got her paintings all over her living room wall." The flower canvases, they're Sophie's. I am both overwhelmed and sad. It's probably all Sarah has left of her sister. I can't even begin to imagine a life without George in it. "If Connie knew that her mother was buried at Southgate cemetery, she'd have wanted to visit and ..." he tails off.

"She'd have seen her real name on the grave?" I say, and he nods.

"Everything would've come out, the secrets, the lies." I know he's hurting and I want to hold him, comfort him, and yet I can't, because it would only give him false hope.

"But why run away and cut the Taylor's out of your lives, Daniel? Disappear off the face of the earth?"

He swallows hard. "I dunno. I had a bit of a mini breakdown when Soph died. I couldn't stay in our house, couldn't bear seeing all her things – not just clothes and stuff but memories. Like the pink wall she painted in the guest room, which I hated and she loved, the flowers and shrubs she planted in the garden, even the fixtures and fittings reminded me of her. She bought this blue glass doorknob – ordered it from Italy. Cost me almost a hundred quid." He laughs faintly. "Everything reminded me of her. Our road, the local park, the Taylor's. I couldn't stand it."

"Yet you changed your name to hers," I point out, fairly.

"I wanted to keep a little piece of her with me and Connie forever." Plus they'd never be able find you, I want to say, but he's in enough pain. I sit down next to him, tell him to stop, that I've heard enough. "No," he says, throwing a glance at my hand on his shoulder. "I'm okay. I want to tell you. I need to." He takes a deep breath and presses his hand together as if in prayer. "We went to stay with my folks in York while I was grieving, recovering. Mum suggested a holiday abroad. They chose Cyprus, and that's where I met Aliki. She saved my life. I owe her – big time."

I lay my hand flat on the table and look at my wedding band. "You've got to tell Connie everything now, Daniel. She might want to visit her mother's grave," I say gently, "Take flowers, maybe even build a little memorial for her." The garden security light comes on and we both look round – probably a cat, or someone next door. It's so sensitive.

He nods, wordless, snorting back tearful phlegm, and then covers my hand with his. I can feel the coolness of his wedding ring against my knuckle.

There's a rustle at the door. Our heads jerk up simultaneously. Daniel leaps to his feet, rushes into the corridor. "Fuck!" he yells. "Connie, wait! CONNIE!"

I'm standing behind him. "How the hell did she get in?"

"I cut her a key!"

"Oh, for fuck's sake, Daniel. Why?"

"I've got to go after her. I'm sorry."

And he's gone.

CHAPTER 32

DANIEL TEARS across the street after Connie like a greyhound out of a trap. His voice growing bigger and louder until it morphs into a cry, "Connie!"

Jesus, how long was she standing there? How much did she hear? My heart is pounding like a drum in my chest, my stomach, filling my ears with panic. I watch Connie belt around the corner to the sound of a distant hum. And for a few fleeting moments I feel disorientated, fuzzy, everything is happening so fast. I can't decipher the sound, then the tinny tune of *Super Trouper* snaps into my mind. I slam the front door and leg it into the living room searching for my phone like a woman on speed. Shit. Where did I leave it? I root around behind the sofa, then empty the contents of my handbag onto the coffee table – nothing. It stops ringing and starts again within seconds. I follow the sound to the kitchen. My eyes dart around the worktop, the sink. Where the hell is it? It stops ringing.

I've lost my phone in my own flipping flat. I don't think I can cope with any more drama today. I need another drink. And as I yank open the fridge door, my phone starts ringing again, only this time I can see it, next to the tub of butter. How could I leave my phone in the fridge? How?

"Audrey?" It's Nick. "I've been ringing for ages, it kept going to voicemail." He sounds breathless, fraught. "I got your message. Are you okay?"

I pour myself a glass of wine and knock back half of it in one gulp. I need to feel anaesthetised – fast. "I'm sorry, Nick. I was… Oh, never mind. Listen, thanks for getting back to me. I need to see you. Can we meet?"

"Ummm…." I can hear the swish of traffic, the cackle of commotion in the background. He's still not home. "Yeah, sure. I can meet you at mine in about an hour. Is that any good?"

"No," I say urgently, almost choking on the wine. "I don't want anyone to see us together. North London is too risky, and I think someone is following me."

"Following you? What do you….." A police siren shrills, drowning out his voice. "Seriously?"

"Yes!" I sprint into the living room, flick the light switch off, and yank open the curtains, filling the room with a dim light. "I think it might be Daniel's sister-in-law." I peer through a gap in the nets. A car swishes by. A lad thunders past on a skateboard. "Look, I'll tell you all about it when I see you. Where are you?" The rumble of the skateboard echoes in the distance and then dwindles into the afternoon. "Holland Park. I can..main.." There's hissing and scraping. He's breaking up.

"I can't hear you. Nick, are you still there?"

"Yes, I…" More hissing and crackling.

"Look." I glance at my watch. "Meet me by the main entrance in about forty-five minutes, okay? Nick? Hello? Can you hear me?" I look at my phone – call ended. Bloody, shitting, brilliant!

"Here all right, love?" asks the taxi driver over the rumble of his diesel engine.

"Yes, it's perfect. Thanks."

I dash through the white arch, past the woodland and along the Kyoto Gardens. By the time I reach the tennis courts I'm breathless. I really ought to start going to the gym.

I hurry along the path, scanning everyone on the benches. I can't see him. Where the hell is he? He said he'd be by the benches near the tennis courts in his text, or have I got it wrong? I pull my phone out of my bag and punch in my new passcode. A lady, middle-aged, blonde bob, well dressed, looks up at me and smiles. "Are you looking for someone?" she asks kindly.

"Yes," I glance down at my phone and, because I can't be arsed to fish out my glasses, hold it at arm's length and squint at the screen. "I'm meant to be meeting a friend here but…."

"Tall, good looking, in a dishevelled kind of way?" She rocks from side to side. "Irish twang?"

I nod fervently. She must be psychic. "Yes, how did you – "

She gesticulates with her head. "Behind you."

I spin on my heel in a half daze. "Audrey," Nick says softly. I look into his sad, grey eyes for a few moments and then throw my arms around his neck. He can't reciprocate the gesture because he's holding two polystyrene cups and has a rucksack slung over his left shoulder. The lady smiles at us, and Nick gives her a cheeky wink as he guides me with the inside of his forearm to a nearby bench.

"Extra milky, no sugar." I take the cup from his hand and take a sip. It burns my lips. "What's going on, Audrey? Why is Daniel's sister-in-law following you? Is she some kind of mentalist?"

"Where do I start?"

I realise I've been talking non-stop for almost ten minutes, only drawing breath to take sips from my polystyrene cup.

"Shit, man." Nick rakes a hand through his hair. "I can't believe it." A bee buzzes near my ear and he waves it away. He knows I'm scared of them. "I just thought you'd had a change of heart. I didn't blame you, You could do a lot better than me," he laughs faintly.

"But I'm glad you know the truth now. I can't believe you thought I'd leave you, and in such a cowardice way."

"I know," I say, feeling awful. "I'm sorry. Daniel is so damned clever."

"You're telling me. Wow, man. He really is something. Have you reported him to the police yet?"

"No, of course not," I say irritably. "The last thing I want is the police involved in this, too. Besides, what am I supposed to say, my husband sent bogus texts to my ex on my phone? Is that even a criminal offence?" I scratch my cheek and look at a mother chasing her son along the wide path.

"Even if it isn't, you can still have him for harassment, or something. He's a bloody nutter."

"Oh, Nick, stop it. You don't know him like I do. Daniel's ruthless in business but not with the people he loves. He's just used to getting his own way, that's all." And he's a pathological liar, but Nick doesn't need to know all the details. I pull Vicky's long, black cardigan around me, keeping out the early evening chill. I didn't think to grab my Mac before I left the house and now I'm frigging freezing. I don't say anything, though, any hint of being cold and Nick'll whip his denim jacket off and make me wear it. He's only got a light blue polo top underneath, he'll freeze.

"You saying it's all bravado, then?" he says incredulously. I glance up at a family approaching. The dad yells at his boys on their scooters to slow down.

"Yes. No. Well, kind of. He's a strong character, yes, but he does have a heart; he helps a lot of charities and loves his family to bits." We draw our legs in as the boys ride by, their mother smiles at us and mimes 'Thank you'. "He may appear to be ruthless, and, I suppose, at times he is, but he just knows how to hang onto his sangfroid." Sam Knight said you can do this with body language.

Certain body poses make you look and appear more confident to others even though you may be a screaming mess inside. It's what people see that counts. "Deep down he's very insecure, especially where women are concerned." I don't tell him about the wife lookalike thing because it'll freak him, and I can't deal with a freaked out Nick right now.

"I didn't like him, anyway," Nick groans.

I give him a sideways glance. "Why am I not surprised?"

"No, not because of you, of us. I got a bad vibe, that's all."

"A vibe? Since when have you been into all that stuff?"

"It's not just stuff, Audrey, it's fact. We all give off electromagnetic waves, which affects other people in a positive and negative way. That's why we feel down with negative people and good with positive ones. We feel each other's vibes."

"Well, Daniel's not very positive at the moment. He's been through a lot."

"You're very understanding," Nick grins. "Ever thought of being a therapist?"

I smile. One thing that marriage has taught me is that if you're not understanding, accommodating to someone else's flaws and weakness, your marriage is over. "None of us is perfect, Nick, you of all people should know that."

We're silent for a few moments, and then, "We'd have been married now if he hadn't had stuck his oar in." Nick picks at one of the several loose threads on the tear in his jeans. "I even bought you a ring." I arch an eyebrow. Yeah, right. "I did," he protests, reading my expression. "Well, one of those plastic ones so that I could propose to you properly in mid-air. A luminous green one, actually. You like green." More thread picking. "Then we could have chosen a ring together in Rome…or Venice." A plastic ring and an inflight proposal. My tummy flutters, how bloody romantic. "I love you," he says, his eyes not leaving his bare knee. "Always have, always will."

I cup my hands over mouth and nose, closing my eyes briefly. I can't do this. This isn't why I'm here. "Stop it, Nick. We're both married."

"I know. I'm sorry. But I can't help how I feel. I care about Katrina – a lot. But it's always been you, Audrey. I don't think I can love anyone else, not in the same way." I look at him for a few moments taking in the grey threads in his hair, his strong jawline, his unshaven face. Nostalgia stirs inside me, or is it longing? I'm not sure.

I turn away quickly and focus on a middle-aged lady walking a sparkling white Westie tied into a vibrant red coat. "Daniel texted me while I was on my way over here," I say, diverting, anything to stop myself from looking into those grey eyes. "He's at the flat with Connie, they're talking, so that's good. At least she's calmed down." I glance at my watch and decide to stay here with Nick a while longer, give them time to talk. "I just had to tell you about what Daniel had done, that's all. Apologise for being so harsh with you at the party. If I'd know…" He holds a hand up to silence me, tells me that I don't need to apologise for anything, none of this is my fault. I rub my eyes, feeling like crap. It's been a long day. "Anyway," I say, after a few moments. "How're things with you? Any news about your case?"

Pulling a cigarette out of the box, he lights up, then blows the smoke out from the side of his mouth, closing one eye. I wish he'd stop smoking. "My solicitor has advised me to plead guilty. My DNA is everywhere," he says, smiling up at an old couple in hats, scarves and winter coats. "Says it might reduce my sentence." I watch the orange tip of his cigarette ignite as he takes another drag.

"You should stop. It's bad for you." Grinning, he takes another lungful of smoke. He knows I still care. I was always nagging him to stop smoking when we were together, he never listened, of course, and he won't now. "I don't think you hurt Connie on purpose." I blurt.

He looks round at me sharply then. "Thank you. That means a lot."

I nod, fold my arms and stare into the middle distance. "Has a date been set for the hearing?"

"End of the month."

I tut, shake my head and cross one leg over the other. The well-dressed lady whom I met on my arrival gives me a little wave as she saunters off with a good looking man, mid-forties, dark, in jeans and a leather jacket. Must be her husband. She looks like she's married with kids. Unlike me, she probably did all the right things – two years dating, a year engaged, then married. I bet she lives in a lovely semi with a neat lawn in a leafy part of London. I imagine a huge tree in the corner of her tasteful living room at Christmas; colourful, sparkly gifts beneath it, a roaring, big fireplace. A real one with logs, not like my gas one. They've probably both got great careers and teenage children in private schools, too – they look like professionals. "How do you know her?" I ask.

"The bench lady?" he says, and I nod. "When I first got here she thought I was her date."

"Date?" My image of her perfect life dissolves like salt in warm water.

"Yeah." Nick's mobile phone pings with a message. "Said it was an online dating thing. Tinker, I think she said." He reads the message then pops the phone back into the breast pocket of his denim jacket.

"Tinder."

"Yeah, that's it."

We lapse into silence and I lean my head on his shoulder, elbow on his photography bag between us. We used to do this a lot when we were together; sometimes we'd bring a flask of coffee with us and sandwiches, and eat them on a bench while we watched the world go by.

"Do you want me to go round and have a word with him?" Nick says suddenly.

I snap my head up. "What? No! I can handle Daniel. He's not Hannibal Lector. Anyway, he's staying with Connie for a few days, so you needn't worry."

A huge Saint Bernard appears in the distance and Nick's face lights up. I know that look. Within moments he's snapping away at the dog with his camera.

"Awesome, isn't he?" He sits back down heavily, holding the camera under my nose.

"Might be a she," I say, squinting at the screen.

"Yeah…" He scrolls through the photos and I coo over the dog. "Oh, and that's it. The rest are of Ronan and Tina's engagement party." He rolls his eyes; it's a day I'm sure he'd sooner forget.

"Oh, can I see them?" He hands me the camera and I start flicking through the photos. Lots of selfies of him and Cat, him and Ronan, all smiles and one of them pulling faces, tongues out; and then one of me and Daniel fills the screen looking happy and content. I want to cry. I pinch the screen to enlarge it. "Jesus, I look so old. You should put a filter on it."

"Don't be daft," he laughs, "you always look gorgeous." And then he looks up at me and our eyes meet. Oh, shit. I can't have a moment with Nick. He's not mine – not anymore. I look away quickly and continue scrolling through the photos – unknown faces, several of Tina and Ronan, and a few of Cat on her own looking glamorous.

"She's stunning, Nick. Looks great for her age too. Not that she's old," I add quickly, "A news report said that sixty-eight is middle aged nowadays." I skim through a few more photographs. Nick is such a talented photographer, knows just when to take the shot. "I'm glad she got the green plastic ring," I grin, giving him a quick sideward glance.

"It was a spur of the moment thing. Her idea," he says, inhaling deeply. "I'd just found out from Ronan that you got married. My head was all over the place." I frown at him. What is he saying, that he married Katrina on the rebound?

"You did the right thing. She's good for you," I say, meaning it, and he nods kindly. "Georgia said she's at her daughter's again."

"Yeah, she's looking after Sas's kids."

"Another Judas Keyes recording?"

"Nah, it's work related this time – a course."

Poor Katrina. She must be devastated. Exhausted. We're quiet for a few moments, and then I say. "So, what does Sas do?"

"She's a vet."

"Oh," I say, liking her immediately. "She sounds nice."

Nick smiles at me for the first time, a proper smile that reaches his grey eyes. "She's is. She's very caring; takes after her mum." There's a hint of resentment in his tone. I suppose Katrina's family didn't welcome him with open arms, given that he's much younger than her. Bar Sas, that is, because she's a vet, and all vets are nice. It's in their DNA. But if they think Nick's after their mother's money, they couldn't be more wrong. He's the least materialistic person I know on this planet. I bet his loose fitting faded jeans are from *Tesco*.

My phone rings in my handbag, probably Daniel. "We should get going soon," I say, sounding as if I want to stay here forever.

"Who is it?" Nick peers at my handset.

"Unknown – they've been ringing me all day. Probably a call centre." I go to end the call but he snatches the phone from my hand.

"Give it here. I like winding them up. Hello? No, this is Audrey's secretary." I slap his arm and giggle, leaning forward, trying to listen. I miss these times so much. "She's unavailable at the moment. Can I help at all?" He laughs and then his face goes a bit serious. "Her office gave you her number, you say?" Bloody Callum. He's working overtime on that health and leisure website today. He gave them my number on purpose, so they can pester me all day. Just wait until I see him on Monday. "I see, it's urgent. May I ask who's calling please?" Nick says, then covers the mouthpiece and whispers, "Charlotte Bahar?"

I screw my face up, shaking my head, and then it suddenly hits me. "Oh, shit! It's Jake's WIFE!!!"

"Talk to her," Nick mouths. I draw back in horror, shaking my head, as if the handset has been dipped in a tub of germs and will contaminate me on contact. She must've found out about the affair. Jake has told her that Connie and I are related, and she's after my blood like a hungry, wild wolf. I can almost see her licking her lips. "No, I'm not her husband," Nick says, waving his hands at me manically and shrugging his shoulders – he doesn't know what to do, what to say.

"Tell her she's got the wrong number," I hiss, biting my nail. Nick's eyes widen at this preposterous suggestion.

"She wants to talk to you NOW," Nick mimes.

"Oh, give it here," I snap. I take a deep breath, as a group of runners in colourful clothing dash past us. "Um..Hello Charlotte."

"Audrey, at last. I'm sorry to disturb you." Oh, God please help me. "I've been trying to reach you all day. I called your office. I know it's out of hours but there was someone there – Callum

Hunter?" I knew it. The bastard. "I need to see you," Charlotte insists, as Nick lights up and wanders off, hand in pocket.

"Can't it wait? I've got a lot on," I say fiddling with my left earring.

"No, I'm afraid it can't. Look, I know about the affair." I close my eyes. Oh, fucking hell. "I also know who assaulted your stepdaughter." My eyes snap open. I'm on the edge of the bench. "I will be reporting it to the police but I wanted to speak to you first. I'm a key witness. I saw it all."

"What? Bbb..bbut," I stutter. "How?" Jesus, how can she be a witness? Has she been stalking Connie? What did she do, hide in a cupboard, bug her flat? Jake said she had a jealous streak. Fuck! I wonder if she's the one who's been following me. She does fit the profile of the person at the cemetery. But how could she get into Connie's flat?

"Charlotte," I gasp, "How could you have possibly seen it? It happened in her flat."

Her long sigh crackles down the line. "Your stepdaughter Skyped Jake in the early hours of Sunday morning. We were watching a movie on Sky; he fell asleep with the computer on his lap, as usual," she laughs faintly when she says this. "When the call came through, I took it."

Charlotte goes on to say that Connie was standing in front of the screen half naked, glass in hand, bleary eyed. And in a drunken stupor told her everything – the affair, the 10k, my involvement. She even threatened to get some heavies to go round there and sort them out, before falling back onto the couch and passing out. The computer must've been on a high surface because Charlotte could still see the room. Shortly after, a figure appeared then dragged Connie off the sofa. "There was an exchange of words and a scuffle," Charlotte says, "I could just grasp bits of the conversation; then fists flying and your stepdaughter screaming."

I notice that Charlotte hasn't once used Connie's name. I suppose she can't bear the word on her lips. "Jake denied everything at first but then I got it out of him. He's a rubbish liar." Hmm...that is debatable, but now is not the time. "Anyway, he got in touch with your stepdaughter about the money, but also to have a go at her for telling me everything, I suppose. When Jake told me that your friend had been arrested for assault, I said that can't be right. It wasn't him. They've got the wrong person."

Relief tears through me like a Japanese bullet train. I can't believe this is happening. "But how do you know it's the wrong person?" I ask in a panicky voice, waving Nick over.

"Because I – "

"Charlotte?" Silence. "Charlotte, because you what? Hello? Charlotte?" I look at my phone – screensaver. Shit. I ring back immediately, hands shaking – voicemail. "SHIT, Shit" I cry.

"What is it, Foxy, what's wrong?" Nick is at my side looking worried.

"Come on." I pull him by the sleeve. "I'll tell you on the way. Where're you parked?"

We tear through the streets of London, my arms wrapped around Nick's waist on the back of his bike, weaving through the traffic. Within half an hour we're in Muswell Hill.

Nick pulls up across the road from my flat. I take off my helmet and shake my hair free. "What are you doing?" I ask.

"I'm coming in with you, of course." He puts his helmet next to mine on the leather seat. "We can talk to Connie and Daniel together – explain. Try Charlotte again and find out who really thumped her."

He goes to move but I stand in front of him. "No, no, you're not coming in. I've got this."

"But…"

"Please, Nick. I need to do this on my own." He regards me carefully. "I mean it," I say firmly. He nods, then leans forward, hesitantly. Our faces are inches apart, I can feel his warm tobaccoey-coffee breath on my cheek, so comforting, so familiar. Our noses brush, our lips almost touch and then Cat's face flashes in my mind. "Look, I'd better go." I pull away. I don't need any more complications in my life. "Go home, ring Cat, tell her the news. Open a bottle of fizz – celebrate. I'll text you when I've spoken to Charlotte."

He reluctantly picks up his helmet from the seat. "Okay, but at least let me walk you to the door."

"Don't be daft." I jab his chest playfully with my fingers. "I can cross the road on my own, you know."

I step off the pavement, smiling to myself. Halfway across, I turn, grin at him. I'm glad we're friends again. I mean, like proper friends, trusting friends, be there or each other friends. He smiles back, leaning against his bike, then lifts his hand up languidly and waves, then suddenly his eyes widen. He's darting towards me. "Audrey!"

I take a step forward, shaking my head. "What is it now?"

"WATCH OUT!"

I turn around. A black 4x4 is charging towards me. I scream but I'm not sure if any sound comes out. There's a thump and then I'm flying, flying, flying across the street. Nick is on the bonnet of the car, and then there's darkness.

CHAPTER 33

'I'm everything, yet I'm nothing
The world doesn't revolve around me
Yet I revolve around it
Usque ad mortem.'

DANIEL WAVES a pair of blue disposable shoe covers at me, other hand resting on the steering wheel, and nags me like an annoying parent, insisting that I wear them over my *Louis Vuitton* ankle boots. Ignoring his pleas, I twist in my leather seat and step onto the wet concrete, smoothing down my black sheath *Ralph Lauren* dress. I can't believe how much weight I've lost in just two weeks. It's true what they say, stress is a waist buster; the pounds have melted away since the accident.

I search for familiar faces in the small crowd ahead as Daniel hands a pair of shoe covers to Connie in the back seat, all the while whining about my boots, reminding me how expensive they are, complaining that I'm going to ruin them in the muddy trail. But I don't care. They're only things. And isn't all this his fault, anyway? I swallow back a mound of tears as I glance down at my husband. You see, some days I can see him for what he is, a sad, lost soul. But other days, like today, I can't even bear to look at him. I watch piteously while he struggles with the shoe covers in the tight footwell. Shoe covers. Only he would think of such a thing on a day like today. He's lucky I'm still here, to be honest. Anyone else would've run for the hills. He should be thankful ι

"Please ride in the car with us, Audrey," she be͵
a week ago when I called to tell her that all the a
had been made. "I can't face it without you. We'll pic.   _
protested at first, spattered out one excuse after anoth͵ put she
won me over. Connie always wins. In the end.

Car doors clank. Trees rustle in the light wind, birds chorusing
within them without a care in the world, but my heart feels like
someone has taken an axe to it. It's at times like this that I wish I'd
never given up smoking. I could really do with a fag to take the
edge off. *Come on, Audrey Fox,* I tell myself, *you can do this. Only
half an hour and it'll all be over.*

"At least it's stopped raining," Daniel says as we walk along the
path. Funny that, isn't it? How we always end up talking about the
weather, no matter what.

A painful lump forms in my throat at the sight of Louise
and Jess, just feet away from a hearse teeming with wreaths and
bouquets. I stop walking. I don't think I can do this. I want to go
home. I want Nick.

"Audrey," Daniel's voice again. "What's the matter?" I don't
answer. A fleeing of dread pumps through my veins. I feel numb.
I can't feel my legs.

Connie's walking back towards me like a lioness, faux fur coat
open, flapping around her as if in slow motion. "Aud?" she says
quietly, face full of concern. "Dad, what's wrong with her? She's
gone white."

"It's okay, Con. I've got this," Daniel says in a patriarchal tone, as
if he's my therapist. "Come on, love, people are waiting."

My eyes flit to the bare grave where Tina and Ronan stand,
heads bowed; Vicky and George behind them with Fearne, she
took the morning off to support me, bless her. How lovely is that?

Their faces are sombre, their attire dark, but not black. I told them they didn't need to wear black. Daniel's right, they're waiting for me. I can't let them down. "I'm okay," I say eventually, "I just needed a moment." Taking a deep breath, I raise my head and thread my arm through Connie's as we make our way towards the congregation.

I'm in Louise's arms, breathing in her soft, floral perfume. "I'm so sorry," she weeps, "About everything." I know she feels partly responsible for the way things have panned out because, inadvertently, she had a hand in my breakup with Nick last year over all that baby business. And although I do believe that you should think before you act, or before you speak, because your actions or words can have a huge impact on someone's life (and that goes for being kind and helpful and positive as well as negligent and selfish and vindictive), none of this is Louise's fault. It was kismet, that's all. I nod, though, because I know that's what she wants, and she squeezes my arm, wiping away a mascary tear from the corner of her eye.

Jess leans in with a bear hug, jewellery clanging. Even in mourning she looks bloody stunning. She's wearing a long, grey woollen dress and knee-high, black, suede boots. The green Parka coat was a good move, there's definitely a nip in the air. It feels more like winter than spring. It was so good of her to take a day off uni to join us, she didn't have to. I'm lucky to have so many people who care about me. I couldn't have done this without them, any of it.

"Thank you for coming," I say softly, one hand clamped on Louise's forearm, the other on Jess's. They start talking over each other – don't be so stupid, we're your friends, your family; and it's then that I feel the first hot tear slide down my face. I bat it away quickly with the back of my hand. "You're looking great, Lou," I sniff. She's looking fresh and radiant today in a navy blue dress and dark tights. And as she opens her mouth to speak, Gerry appears in the distance in a loose, crumpled, navy suit. Gerry. Louise's estranged husband. Nick's best friend. My heart could burst.

"Since when...?" I whisper to Louise.

Louise cups a hand over her mouth. "Since the night before Tina and Ronan's engagement," she murmurs. "We were out all night; got pissed and caught in the rain like a couple of teenagers. I was soaked through. Thank God the taxi driver had a blanket in his boot. Gerry paid him thirty quid for it." That's why Jess saw her wrapped in a blanket that morning. "I thought it was a one-off, but he's been calling and messaging ever since, been round for a dinner a couple of times, too, and....shhh," she hisses. "I'll tell you more later."

"Audrey," Gerry squeezes me in his arms, he smells of dust and cheap aftershave. "So lovely to see you again."

The moment Gerry releases me from his grip, I'm in Tina's arms, and then in Ronan's, swathed in a mist of his citrusy cologne. And, holding onto him tightly, I sob quietly on his shoulder. His love for Nick has really shone through, he's been a rock these last few weeks. Pulling away, I fill my lungs with the cold, fresh air, head raised stoically. Tina fishes in her bag then hands me a tissue. After blotting my tears and blowing my nose, I congratulate Ronan on his news.

"Aud, are you sitting down?" Tina had said in a breathless whisper, yesterday afternoon. "I've just weed on a stick and got a positive for a ginger." And despite my sadness, despite my aching rib from the accident, I couldn't help but give a little cry of 'yay' down the phone. Now, I spin Ronan the cliché that life is for the living, and with a little smile he nods and backs away, hands in pockets of his gunmetal grey trouser suit, gazing at the garland of flowers that George and Vicky have just placed by the grave.

"How's everything?" Tina asks, rubbing the back of her neck and throwing a glance in Daniel and Connie's direction, eyes full of contempt. They're huddled together, talking, whispering, faces full of remorse.

"I'm bearing up, Tean, thanks."

"I can't believe you're even speaking to him," she says, twisting her lips, and, because I have no answer for her, I drop my gaze to my black boots, already splashed with bits of muddy lawn. "Anyway, at least you've started divorce proceedings. It'll all be over soon and then –"

"Audrey," Daniel cuts in, "they're about to start, love."

We circle the grave. Daniel to my left, arm slung around Connie; Louise, Gerry and Jess to my right; Tina and Ronan behind them with George and Vicky and Fearne. I don't recognise the row of mourners in front of me. They must be family or old friends. I nod as Vicky squeezes my shoulder and whispers, "I'm right behind you."

And then I hear the priest's voice, "*God, we thank you for the gift of life. A journey that is full of joyful moments and love; obligation and hardships. May we ask today that you.....*"

His voice becomes a distant babble as if he's speaking through a fug of water. Connie is crying so hard, I can almost feel her pain. I look up briefly at Daniel, his face grave and creased, eyes dark and watery.

Tears of guilt.

I spent the night in hospital after the accident. NHS was brilliant, but I hated being in there, and even tried to escape in the middle of the night. They had to move me from the ward and into a private room in the end, because the nurses said I kept crying out in my sleep, disturbing all the other patients, calling for Nick, begging him to take me with him to the light.

In the morning they took me down to X-ray in a chair, as if I were an invalid, and as they wheeled me through a frayed, damaged door, mended with a piece of chipboard, all I could think about was how underfunded the NHS is, and how Nick would've taken a photo of the door and Tweeted about it in protest, tagging all the relevant MPs in, if he were with me now. I was lucky, the doctor said, getting away with minor injuries. They only really kept me in for observation, anyway, because the paramedics said I was hallucinating in the ambulance, that I insisted Nick was sitting by my side. But he wasn't there, of course. How could he have been? He was splattered on the ground on a pillow of blood the last time I'd seen him. Anxiety spreads around my stomach like hot tar.

If I'm honest, I suppose I've always known that Nick loved me, but I didn't think he'd take a bullet for me. But he did. He hurled himself in front of that racing car. He saved my life. *My hero. My knight in shining armour.*

My eyes sting and this time I can't stop the tears. These have been the worst two weeks of my life. I feel Daniel's arm around me, but he doesn't get to comfort me anymore. I shrug him off. Connie's tears are now audible, and despite it all, I feel a pang of sympathy for her.

Connie came to see me at my flat the day after I came home from hospital. We spoke about Jake and Charlotte first, and she admitted that I was right and she was wrong; she shouldn't have got involved with a married man and now felt responsible for everything, because, she explained, quite philosophically, that things are a chain of events, and all this is a result of her secret. However, she was glad that Charlotte saw what really happened to her that night. "It's such a relief," she said, "Knowing the truth, because, if I'm honest, it was all such a blur, Aud. I did think it was Nick to begin with, when I dialled 999, but once I sobered up completely, I wasn't so sure. But then, of course, Dad got involved, kept nagging me, got inside my head, saying it must've been Nick because there was no one else in the flat with me, and that kinda made sense, right? But, honestly, I couldn't remember a thing."

Nick had been telling the truth all along. *My love. My life.* How could I have doubted him, even for a second? But then, don't we even doubt ourselves sometimes? Like when someone insists that you said something, when you're sure you didn't. Doesn't a tiny voice inside your head whisper, 'Did I say it? Maybe I did and I've forgotten.'

"He could've gone to prison, Connie," I said sternly. "His name would've been mud."

Connie stared at her feet. "No, I wouldn't have let that happen," she said. And I don't think she would have.

I blink away the tears as the priest's voice booms in my ears, "*O Lord God, creator of all things. Give us understanding so that we may comprehend how short our journey on this earth is. Give us wisdom and light so that we can appreciate each day you give us –* "

Connie stretches her arm across Daniel now and reaches for me and I go to her, cradle her in my arms. Connie can be a stubborn, feisty, so and so, but her heart is in the right place, and, let's face it, if it weren't for Connie, the driver of the hit and run would never have been caught.

I close my eyes as the priest continues to chant, my mind spiralling back to the day of the accident like a spinning roulette ball. Connie was with Daniel and Lily in my front room when the black 4x4 came hurtling towards me at top speed. When Connie heard the blast of the collision, she dropped everything and came rushing to my side, screaming out my name, crying for help. I remember her face as I opened and closed my eyes, in and out of focus. Luckily, she hardly ever lets go of her mobile phone and managed to snap a photograph of the car as it sped off before calling for an ambulance. She was the only witness, and she's promised to give evidence if it goes to court. And I know she will because she's true to her word. Unless I piss her off, that is, which is unlikely as she won't be seeing much of me anymore.

The police arrested Katrina at her home and charged her. Her plea was that she lost control of the wheel but I don't believe her, and I'm sure the judge and jury won't either. She's got a history of stalking her husband's and boyfriend's exes. One of them even had to take out an injunction on her. Looks can be so deceiving, can't they? She seemed like such a lovely lady.

The black Range Rover belongs to her popstar son-in-law, Judas Keyes. He was away touring or recording most of the time, and his car was parked in his double garage in Hampstead, so she could drive it at her leisure. Katrina told the police that I was trying to take her husband off her, that I was a jealous ex-girlfriend, said she was just keeping an eye on me, that she didn't mean to hurt me. But when they told her about Charlotte Bahar's statement, she broke down and confessed all.

On the night of the engagement party, Katrina stood next to Nick and made a mental note of Connie's address as he programmed it into his SatNav. Alone in his flat later, she waited and waited and waited for him to come home, growing more and more suspicious by the second. When he didn't show up, she jumped in a cab to Connie's. The main door to the building was open, there was a party going on in one of the flats, people were outside smoking and drinking and having a laugh. Upstairs, Connie's door was ajar. Nick, in his haste to get out, had left it open. So she just slipped in, found Connie asleep on the couch half naked, put two and two together, lamped her a few, and slipped out again unnoticed – what a stroke of luck. She said that Connie was so drunk and delusional she'd never recognise her, and if she did, she'd just deny it. It would've been Connie's word against hers. She was gloved, so there were no fingerprints. Little did she know that behind her, Charlotte was watching it all on Skype. And as for CCTV, she said in her statement, they often don't work (she was right, it wasn't working) but she snuck in, head down, wearing a red headscarf and Prada bug-style sunglasses, just in case. Sounds like the irritating MacBook Woman from the café in Muswell Hill. What a clever disguise – well, Katrina was a make-up artist for 10 years. I reckon she'd been following me for weeks.

"And at the end of our lives on this earth, when we take our final breath, may you lead us home to eternal life. Amen."

There's a shuffle of footsteps, a rustle of fabric. It's over, thank God. People are starting to leave, their voices drone like a mass of bees in my ears. I wipe away my tears with a tissue and stuff it up my sleeve. I thank my family and friends for coming, for supporting me.

"I'll call you later," Louise yells as she climbs into her car while Gerry straps himself in next to her and Jess pulls out her phone in the backseat. A picture of happiness. Just like old times. Tina waves and blows kisses at me as she and Ronan scurry along the uneven path to her bright green Corsa, arm in arm, Fearne trotting behind them. They're giving her a lift home – the Fiat 500 is in for a service.

"I'll catch you later, sis," George says as Vicky squeezes me in her arms and compliments me on a beautiful service.

Then it's just me, Daniel and Connie.

"I'm glad that's all over," Connie says, "Shit. I need to get these stupid fucking blue bags off my feet. I'll see you guys in the car." I nod, but I won't be going back with them.

Daniel and I watch as she hobbles towards the car, stopping and cursing along the way.

"What time's your flight?" Daniel asks.

"Not until this evening."

"Cyprus is great at this time of year. Give your parents my best, won't you, and tell them I'm sorry for ruining their daughter's life."

I stare at my mucky *Louis Vuitton* boots, arms folded. Daniel was right. I should've worn the covers.

"I can't thank you enough for –"

"It's okay, Daniel," I cut in, unable to keep the irritation out of my voice. "It was just a memorial service."

I've known Father Joseph since I was little. He was more than happy to come along and say a prayer for Connie's mum today, especially when I told him that she didn't get a decent send off when she died. In a tearful confession, Daniel told me that he and Sarah were the only attendees at Sophie's funeral, they wanted to keep it private. Family only. Her parents just about managed to get through the church service before her mother fainted and got carted off in an ambulance. A suspected heart attack turned out to be a panic attack.

"Yes, but it meant a lot," he says. I don't answer. I did it for Connie, but a little bit of me did it for Sophie, too. "How did it get to this, eh?" He stares at his black shiny shoes peeking through the muddy blue covers, hands in pockets of his dark Armani suit. "If only I'd been honest. If only –" He looks up at me briefly then shakes his head, because we both know that it's too late for 'if onlys.'

"You can't have everything your way, Daniel, you can't control everyone," I say quietly. He doesn't answer but he looks contrite. "Anyway, I'm glad Connie got to say goodbye to her mother. Properly."

Daniel nods, sniffing away a tear. A man-tear disguised as a snuffle. "And I'm glad your friends came, it meant a lot to both of us. It was very good of them." They did it for me but I don't need to relay that, because today is about forgiveness and kindness and understanding. "Connie needed closure," he goes on, squinting at the sky. The sun has appeared, it's turning out to be a nice day. "I suppose we both did. We're going to put a new headstone up now, visit more often. Sarah insists on going halves on the cost."

"I didn't see Sarah today."

"No." He hesitates. "She and Brian are having a few – " He scratches his chin and gives me a lazy, lopsided smile. "Issues." I wonder if these 'issues' have anything to do with him. I don't probe. It's none of my business anymore. "Besides," he exhales loudly, "Ryan would've found it difficult. He doesn't like cemeteries or funerals. They set him off."

"I see," I smile. Connie and Sarah are getting on like a house on fire, by the way. Their bond was immediate. Funnily, finding out about her grandparents and being half Spanish didn't have the effect I expected. "I'll always be Greek, Audrey," she said to me. "It's more about upbringing and culture than blood. I love Auntie Sarah and Ryan, but Aliki and Yiayia Despina will always be my real family."

"And I'm sorry about Nick, about what we've put him through," Daniel goes on. "It can't have been easy." I raise an eyebrow, it can't have been easy for him to deliver that apology either. "It's okay," I say with a sad smile. "He's a big boy, he can handle it."

A car horn hoots loudly. "Anyway, I'd better get off," Daniel says. "Connie's getting impatient. Can I give you a lift?"

The roar of a motorbike drones in the distance. I look round and smile. "No, it's okay, I think my chauffeur's just arrived."

Nick was far more robust than I imagined and took the impact well, but that was largely because Katrina hit the breaks the moment he leapt in front of me. His injuries looked a lot worse than they were - cuts, bruises, and a torn ligament in his arm, which has healed nicely, thanks to my pampering – he says I've got the magic touch. Although, he does claim to have leapt out of his body when he hit the ground and passed out. Insists that he followed me into the ambulance because he didn't want me to be by myself. Daniel had necked half a bottle of Jack Daniels and was in no fit state to look after Lily, or accompany me to the hospital, so I had to go alone. Nick told me it was the force of my love that made him slip back into his body when he arrived at A&E in a separate ambulance.

Climbing onto the back of the motorbike, I slip on my helmet, and as I wrap my arms around the love of my life, I feel something smooth and cold sliding along my finger. I hold out my hand and gaze adoringly at the green plastic bubble ring, then pull the visor of my helmet down and squeeze him tight – *My Burning Love. My soul mate. Till death do us part.*

"Ready, Foxy?" Nick says in his slight Irish twang, firing up the engine.

"Abso-bloody-lutely."

HER SECRET

HER SECRET

Acknowledgements

Many, many thanks to my readers, reviewers and book bloggers for all their support; my husband Joe for being such a brilliant and helpful beta reader, my niece Valentina for her fabulous idea for the cover, my family and friends for their love and encouragement, and last but not least, big thanks to Urbane for making the magic happen.

HER SECRET

HER SECRET

Kelly Florentia was born and bred in north London, where she continues to live with her husband Joe. *HER SECRET* (2018) is her third novel and the sequel to *NO WAY BACK* (2017).

Kelly has always enjoyed writing and was a bit of a poet when she was younger. Before penning her debut, *The Magic Touch* (2016), she wrote short stories for women's magazines. To Tell a Tale or Two… is a collection of her short tales. In January 2017, her keen interest in health and fitness led to the release of *Smooth Operator* – a collection of twenty of her favourite smoothie recipes.

As well as writing, Kelly enjoys reading, running, drinking coffee, scoffing cakes, watching TV dramas, and spending way too much time on social media.

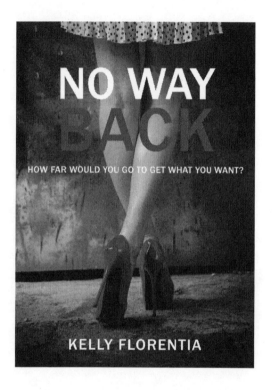

'a must-read for anyone who loves intelligent, grown-up romance.'

Louise Douglas, bestselling author of
The Secrets Between Us

'A brilliantly-woven tale of love, friendship, heartbreak and hope - I couldn't put it down.'

Jill Finlay, Fiction Editor of The Weekly News

When two eligible and attractive men are vying for your heart, it should be the perfect dilemma...

Audrey Fox has been dumped by her unreliable fiancé Nick Byrne just days before the wedding. Heartbroken and confused, the last thing she expects when she jumps on a plane to convalesce in Cyprus is romance. But a chance meeting with handsome entrepreneur and father-of-one Daniel Taylor weaves her into a dating game she's not sure she's ready for. Audrey's life is thrown into further turmoil when she discovers on her return to London that Nick has been involved in a serious motorcycle accident that's left him in intensive care. Distraught yet determined to look to the future, Audrey must make a decision - follow her heart or listen to well-meaning advice from family and friends? Because sometimes, no matter what, it's the people that we love who can hurt us the most...

URBANE

Urbane Publications is dedicated to developing new author voices, and publishing fiction and non-fiction that challenges, thrills and fascinates.

From page-turning novels to innovative reference books, our goal is to publish what YOU want to read.

Find out more at
urbanepublications.com